*We have a marvellou...
many of them give...
Christmas trees, ca...
carol singers, fireside...
feast, seeing family and friends and, best of all,
kisses under the mistletoe!*

Take a step back in time to a

Christmas
by
Candlelight

Visit Victorian England during Yuletide in
these two brand-new romantic novels

Christmas
by
Candlelight

HELEN DICKSON
MICHELLE STYLES

*M&B™ and M&B™ with the Rose Device
are trademarks of the publisher.
Harlequin Mills & Boon Limited, Eton House,
18-24 Paradise Road, Richmond, Surrey TW9 1SR*

CHRISTMAS BY CANDLELIGHT
© by Harlequin Books S.A. 2007

Wicked Pleasures © Helen Dickson 2007
A Christmas Wedding Wager © Michelle Styles 2007

ISBN: 978 0 263 86600 1

10-1207

*Harlequin Mills & Boon policy is to use papers that are
natural, renewable and recyclable products and made from
wood grown in sustainable forests. The logging and
manufacturing processes conform to the legal environmental
regulations of the country of origin.*

*Printed and bound in Spain
by Litografia Rosés S.A., Barcelona*

Wicked Pleasures

HELEN DICKSON

Helen Dickson was born and still lives in south Yorkshire, with her husband, on a busy arable farm where she combines writing with keeping a chaotic farmhouse. An incurable romantic, she writes for pleasure, owing much of her inspiration to the beauty of the surrounding countryside. She enjoys reading and music. History has always captivated her, and she likes travel and visiting ancient buildings.

Look out for a new novel from Helen Dickson in spring 2008, coming to you from Mills & Boon® Historical.

Chapter One

From where he stood, leaning gracefully against a silver birch tree, allowing his mount a moment's respite after the long ride from Sevenoaks, Grant Leighton was taken by surprise when two horse-riders—a man and a woman—came thundering past him like the Light Brigade hurtling into the Valley of Death.

Utterly transfixed, he heard the woman's joyous laughter as her horse's competitive spirit flared; it seemed determined to keep ahead of its mate. Its mane and tail flying, legs flailing, the horse, setting a cracking pace, was galloping its heart out. From what Grant could make out, the other horse was beginning to tire and didn't stand a chance.

Looking through his binoculars, he watched them, filled with admiration for the woman's ability and daring. It was clear that she was utterly fearless. It was unusual to see a woman riding astride, with her mane of hair like polished mahogany flying behind, a tangled pennant of glossy waves. He could see buff-coloured breeches and riding boots beneath the skirts of her dark brown riding habit spread out over the horse's rump.

The man was riding a chestnut mare and the woman a grey stallion—a huge beast, a thoroughbred and no mistake—which would take some handling at the best of times and would challenge even his own.

Wide and emerald-green, the field stretched before them. Giving up the chase, the man slowed to a canter, but the woman carried on, riding beautifully, her slender and supple body, arresting and vigorous, bent forward, her gloved hands almost touching the horse's flicking ears, urging him on. Leaping a gorse hedge and landing soundly, she then soared over a wide ditch like a white swan and rode on, following the field round and down the other side, her body moving with her horse like a lover's, encouraging him every step of the way. Coming to the far end of the field, she slowed him to a canter. Riding through an open gate, with a backward look and a wave of her hand to her companion, who seemed in no hurry to follow her, she disappeared from sight.

Long after he could no longer see her Grant continued to stand and stare at the spot where she had vanished, half expecting—and hoping—to see her appear once more. Never had he seen a woman ride with so much skill. By God, she was magnificent. Deeply impressed, he was curious as to who she might be. He hadn't seen her features, so he would be unable to recognise her again, but he would dearly like to meet her.

The early morning was cool and crisp—unusual weather for early August—but Adeline, riding back to the stables, favoured it over the sticky heat of midsummer. As always, she had enjoyed her ride on her beloved Monty enormously, feeling those splendid muscles flexing beneath her. Pausing to retrieve her bonnet from where she had left it hanging on a fence, and hurriedly arranging her hair into a demure bun at her nape, she secured the untidy mess and tied the ribbon under her chin. How she would love to toss the bonnet aside and feel the wind tear through her hair once more—but that would never do. Not for the demure and prim Miss Adeline Osborne.

Now she was close to the house there was the possibility that she would be seen and her father informed, and he would chastise her most severely for riding with such complete abandon.

Horace Osborne was a strict authoritarian, and expected little of his daughter except that she behave as a well-brought-up young lady should. Adeline thought about her father as she followed the path. She was an only child, her mother deceased, and one would have thought she would be his golden child— the adored centre of his life—but he was indifferent to her. It was as if she was some kind of reject, and she was convinced that the reason for this rejection was her lack of beauty—which her mother had possessed in abundance.

As soon as Adeline had come out of the schoolroom, and her governess had been dispensed with, she had taken on the business of running the household—instructing servants, entertaining neighbours and her father's business colleagues, making things comfortable for him.

To her surprise and dismay, Paul was waiting in the stable-yard when she rode in, his presence reminding her of the importance of the day ahead. Later there was to be an 'at home' at Rosehill, to celebrate their engagement.

The sight of him put a dampener on her ride. Paul Marlow, a widower, and twenty years Adeline's senior, was distinguished-looking rather than handsome—of slender build, with fair hair peppered with white. Women were generally drawn to him. He moved carefully and spoke carefully. He was impeccable, and his clothes fitted him in a way that only the best tailors on Savile Row knew how to fit them.

A friend and neighbour, and a close business associate of her father, he was pacing the stableyard impatiently, with both hands thrust deep into his trouser pockets, his stern features set in an unsmiling expression of disapproval as he regarded his future wife. She knew he didn't like the way she rode astride like a man, or the breeches she wore beneath her skirts, but until they were married there wasn't a thing he could do about it.

'Why, Paul!' she exclaimed, dismounting and handing the reins to a stable lad. 'This is a surprise. I didn't expect to see you so early. Are you here to see Father?'

'He invited me over for breakfast. Adeline, it is most unbecoming for you to be riding unattended,' he said with cold reproof. The ride had given her cheeks a delightful red glow, but Paul failed to notice. 'A groom should be with you at all times.'

Adeline felt herself flushing at his strict censure and began to walk to the house. 'He was—Jake—but I left him in the big field. He stayed to further exercise one of the horses. I really don't know why it should bother you so much. I have always ridden unattended. Besides, at this time of day the grooms are far too busy with the horses to waste time riding out with me.'

'But I insist. I cannot have my future wife behaving in a manner that is less than circumspect. It's bad enough you wearing those infernal breeches without that.'

'There is nothing wrong with my behaviour, Paul. I have ridden alone all my life, so it's a bit late in the day to start being concerned about appearances. A chaperon is quite unnecessary—and as for my breeches, I find them both comfortable and practical.'

Paul's brows drew together and he shot her a surprised look— Adeline rarely spoke sharply to anyone. 'There is something else to consider,' he continued, in a more tolerant tone. 'I am thinking of your safety, too. There is every possibility that you may take a tumble, and with no one on hand to assist you, where would you be?'

'I never fall off. I am an accomplished horsewoman, as you well know. However—' she turned and smiled at him '—I am touched by your concern, Paul.'

'When you are married to me I will be prepared to allow you a certain amount of freedom, but I shall insist you are accompanied by a groom at all times, or you wait till I am free to ride with you.'

'Very well, Paul. As you say,' she murmured, having no wish to argue. 'Now, I think we had best hurry lest we are late for breakfast. We don't want to keep Father waiting, and I have to change.'

'There is one more thing, Adeline. Lady Waverley has kindly invited us to her house party next weekend. That should leave you adequate time to prepare for it.'

'I see.'

She looked straight ahead. The general tedium and vacuity of Saturday-to-Monday country house parties held no appeal for Adeline, who often went unnoticed. Diana Waverley was everything Adeline was not. Adeline was as plain as she was beautiful. Diana was also a popular socialite, free and easy with her modern manners, and her house parties were said to be fast and furious— which Adeline was sure she would find highly disagreeable.

'It would be good manners to reply, but how can I when I have received no invitation? It really is most unusual. You have accepted for us both, I take it?'

'Of course. An invitation to spend a weekend at Westwood Hall is not to be turned down, Adeline,' Paul told her starchily. 'Lady Waverley is renowned for her hospitality, and it is a heaven-sent opportunity to have our engagement made public.'

'I would have thought the announcement in the papers and this afternoon's gathering should take care of that.'

'It will, my dear. But a little extra exposure will not go amiss. Of course there will be society people there.' His eyes did a quick sweep of her riding habit, and Adeline was sure his lips curled with distaste. 'You may want to visit the dressmaker, to avail yourself of a new habit. Some of the ladies are fanatical about the correct riding clothes, and I know how much you will want to join in.'

'Yes, I will. But there's no time to order any new outfits. What I have will be perfectly adequate.'

As Adeline climbed the stairs she thought of the day ahead and the forthcoming house party with little enthusiasm. She always dreaded parties, and usually spent the entire evening in a corner, playing whist with some of the more sedate elderly ladies. She had met Lady Waverley on a couple of occasions, but she had never been to Westwood Hall. If she could have refused to attend she would have. No doubt there would be a wearisome procession of tennis, garden and dinner parties, and boating parties. Thank goodness Lady Waverley kept a good stable and she would be able to escape to indulge her passion for riding.

Adeline wasn't in love with Paul any more than he was with her, but she respected his ability at managing his affairs. Seldom courteous, often impatient, and occasionally quite cruel, he appeared actually to dislike her much of the time—returning her smiles with scowls and greeting her conversation with a request for silence while he read his newspaper. He made no attempt to flatter or please her. He admired her stoicism, and the way she got on with things on the hunting field as deeply as he deplored her passion for it, and he was always quick to criticise her imperfections.

Fastidious in his habits—which quietly irritated her—he liked a well-ordered life, and while she often chafed at his high-handed manner towards her she was willing to honour her father's wish that they marry, despite it having been decided without any consultation with her. Horace Osborne was keen to see his only child wed to such an estimable gentleman. It would be an advantageous marriage.

Sons were bred to continue the line and enter the family business—but unfortunately Horace had not been so blessed. Daughters were bartered and married young, while still malleable, passed like possessions from father to husband. They were expected to obey and be happy with this change in guardianship, and Adeline would be. Her father's word was law. But it saddened her that he saw her more as a commodity than a daughter.

Uncommonly tall and straight, and with a whipcord strength, Grant Leighton emanated an aura of carefully restrained power. He was a man of immense wealth. A great deal of his fortune came from land, taking no account of his industrial interests—which were considerable—and the London properties he owned.

He was admired and favoured by women, who liked the dominance of his arrogant ways. For years gossip had linked him to every beautiful, unattached woman in society, but marriage had not been an offer he'd made to any of them, and he had left a trail of broken hearts in his wake.

At twenty-nine, he had a handsome and intelligent face, lean and brown like a gypsy's, and eyes that were silver-grey. His hair was a shade between brown and black—thick, with a side parting, and combed smooth from his brow. He had a strong mouth with a humorous twist and was inclined to smile—but not just then.

His anxiety about his mother was at the forefront of his mind. She was the most precious person in the world to him, and at present she was recovering from a serious bout of influenza. After he had found her message, on his return from Sevenoaks, his worry that her request to see him must be bad news had made him urge his mount up the narrow drive to Newhill Lodge. The square, stonebuilt, ivy-clad house stood sedately in its neatly enclosed gardens, with tall trees casting shadows on its frontage.

As he approached and dismounted, a groom appeared to take his horse. The door was opened by a fresh-faced young maid. She smiled, bobbing a polite curtsy as he entered the house.

'Good morning, sir.'

'Good morning, Edith. Is my mother in her room?'

'Yes, sir. She's expecting you.'

'Then I'll go straight up.'

Carrying his riding whip, he strode across the hall, smiling when his eyes lit on a vase of newly cut, beautifully arranged pink roses. His mother loved flowers, and insisted on a constant supply of fresh blooms to be picked from her garden or sent over from his own hothouses at Oaklands, just half a mile away. He proceeded up the stairs.

Light fell through the lead-paned windows in bright shafts upon the polished floor, casting a warm glow on the fine mahogany staircase and the crimson and gold carpet. On the landing he knocked gently on his mother's bedroom door. It opened and Stella, his mother's maid and her companion of many years, bade him enter.

'How is she, Stella?' he asked in a low voice, lest he disturb his mother if she was sleeping.

'Tired. She had visitors earlier, and she is quite worn out, but she's eager to see you. Can I get you some refreshment?'

He shook his head. 'No, thank you. If Mother is tired my visit will be brief.'

Stella went out and closed the door quietly behind her. Grant approached his mother where she was resting, propped against the cushions on a chaise longue. A book and her knitting lay discarded on the small table beside her. Sunlight filtered through the lightweight curtains, bathing the room in a soft, golden glow. Her eyes were closed, and she looked frail and drained by her illness. There were deep hollows in her cheeks and her face was starkly white. Bending over, he placed an affectionate kiss on her forehead.

'Grant?' Hester Leighton opened her eyes and held out her hand to him. It was thin and deeply veined. 'I'm so glad you have come.'

He sat down in a chair facing her, his eyes clouded with concern as he touched her cheek with caressing fingers. 'I got your message. What is it that is so important you had to send for me? Are you feeling worse? Is that it?'

She offered him a thin, tired smile. 'No, Grant. Don't concern yourself. I'm feeling very much the same—perhaps a little better. There is something I want you to do for me.'

'And what is that?'

'No doubt you will think I'm mad, and that I'm a selfish old woman, but I've heard Rosehill is coming onto the market. I want you to buy it back for me.'

Grant's dark brows drew together. 'It's the first I've heard of it. Where has this information come from?'

'Mrs Bennet, the vicar's wife, told me yesterday when she came to visit. It was mentioned to Reverend Bennet when he was attending a parochial meeting at Sevenoaks. Apparently Mr Osborne is considering moving to London to live.'

'But that doesn't mean to say he will sell Rosehill.'

'Mrs Bennet seems to think he will. He spends so little time there, and his only child—a daughter—is to be married shortly, and will surely move out to live with her husband.' Her lips trembled. 'I rarely speak of your dear father, Grant. I find it extremely painful. It's been five years now, but I do still miss him so very much. Contrary to what people say, I find the dulling of grief and the passing of time have very little to do with each other.'

Grant smiled with soft understanding. 'The doctors can only find cures for afflictions. We can hardly expect them to find a cure for a broken heart, can we?'

'I suppose not—which is why it is so very important for you to buy back Rosehill for me. It was my home—my family's home—for generations. I loved it so. It broke my heart when it was sold to Mr Osborne to pay off those debts, but things are so very different now. If he is to sell it, then I want it back.'

For a moment Grant regarded her steadily, and then he said, 'You've thought hard about this, I can tell.'

Tears came to her eyes. 'I have. Please go and see Mr Osborne, Grant. It is so important to me. I would like to end my days there. Afterwards—when I'm gone—you can do what you like with it. That will be up to you. But I want it so very badly.'

Unable to deny his mother anything, Grant nodded. 'I'll make some enquiries, I promise. Have you spoken about this to Lettie?'

'No, but she'll understand. I know she will.'

'Where is my dear little sister, by the way?' he asked, sitting back and crossing his long booted legs.

'In London, staying with that friend of hers—Marjorie Stanfield. I'm expecting her back sometime tomorrow.'

'Is she behaving herself?'

'I certainly hope so—but you know Lettie. She does keep me informed of most of her activities—although I have to say that perhaps I'm better off not knowing about some of them. Ignorance is certainly bliss where Lettie is concerned.' She smiled, indulgently. 'But I know she would never do anything to disgrace herself or the family.'

'Don't bet on it,' Grant said dryly. 'My sister is both spirited and fearless, and she will not rest until women are completely liberated from the tyranny of man.'

Hester laughed lightly. 'She always puts forward a passionate argument.'

'Which will get her arrested if she's not careful.'

'Not Lettie. I am always interested to hear about her activities with the Women's Movement—or Suffragists, as they like to call themselves. I offer advice where I can, and I accept her many extended absences. I am immensely grateful to Lady Stanfield for letting her stay with Marjorie—she is such a placid young woman, and I hope she has a calming influence on Lettie.'

'Be that as it may, Mother, but it's time she thought of settling down and finding herself a husband.'

'Maybe—but you are extremely fond of her, and for good or ill she is your sister. There's not a thing you can do about it. And, speaking of settling down, I have been hearing gossip about you and a certain lady of late. Grant, I know that in the past there have been rumours linking you to several young ladies—some of dubious reputation,' she pointed out with quiet censure, 'and until now I have never asked you to verify or deny them.'

'Then why now?'

'Because of *this* rumour—about you and Lady Waverley.'

Something in the soft romanticism of her words irritated and irked Grant. He did not like being the subject of gossip and speculation. 'I can see word of my recent visit to Westwood Hall has reached the ears of your visiting ladies. Really, Mother. I credited you with more sense than to listen to gossip.'

'Can you blame me?' She smiled. 'When I hear that my eligible son—a man who seems to avoid young ladies of impeccable background as if they have some kind of dreadful disease—is suddenly seen visiting a beautiful socialite? And on more than once occasion, it would appear.'

The Leighton brow quirked in sardonic amusement. 'At twenty-eight, and a widow of five years, Diana can hardly be classed as a "young lady", Mother.'

'Then at fifty-five I must seem positively ancient to you. You know nothing would please me more, Grant, than to see you settle down with someone who will make you happy.'

'I will—in time. But not with Diana. Six years ago I might have, but she chose to marry Patrick Waverley instead.' He spoke dispassionately, giving away nothing of his feelings. 'The idea of being Lady Waverley outshone that of being plain Mrs Leighton. But I am still fond of her, and enjoy her company from time to time.'

'I only met her on one occasion, and I was not in her company long enough to form an opinion. Did she hurt you?'

Grant shrugged and smiled wryly. 'I was young, and easily drawn to a pretty face. I think I was more angry and humiliated by her rejection than anything else.'

Hester studied her son intently. 'And now you're not—drawn to a pretty face?'

'Now I tend to look beyond the pretty face. It's what's on the inside that determines a person, not what's on the outside. Diana is beautiful, intelligent, well bred and well connected. But—and you said it yourself—she is a socialite. She is an appalling flirt who likes to play hard. Her husband left her well provided for, but Diana is a spendthrift and will soon have nothing left if she doesn't curb her spending. Money is important to her. She would sell her soul to have more.' He grinned. 'I soon realised she did me a favour by marrying Patrick. Believe me, Mother, you would not want Diana Waverley as a daughter-in-law.'

Hester sighed and rested her head wearily against the

cushions. 'Oh well, that's a pity. But if she is as you say, then you must avoid her. You are in a position to choose better.'

She gave him the beguiling smile that, ever since he was a boy, had been able to get him to do almost anything she wanted, but on the subject of marriage he remained unmoved. 'When I choose a woman who is most suited to be my wife in every way, there will be affection and respect. When I finally settle down I expect to be made happy by it. Marriage to Diana would ensure nothing but misery.'

'And love, Grant? Does that not come into it? It is necessary if you are to have a good marriage, you know.'

Standing up, he laughed and kissed her forehead. 'I might have known that would concern you. You always were sentimental. When I decide to settle down you will be the first to know. I promise you.'

On arriving back at Oaklands—the magnificent Leighton residence situated in a verdant valley in the heart of the Kent countryside, so large it made Newhill Lodge look like a garden shed—carelessly dismissing his mother's desire for him to settle down, Grant thought seriously about her other request. He would write to Horace Osborne and request to see him—perhaps stay overnight with Frederick.

Grant had never met Horace Osborne, but he knew him to be a shrewd, hard-headed and self-made businessman. He was a parvenu, but he had been accepted by the leading members of established society with far more favour than most of the newly rich.

The Leightons were 'old money', and because Grant seemed to have the golden touch when it came to making investments they still had plenty of it. For his mother's sake Grant would ask that Mr Osborne give the proposition he would put to him serious consideration. Not for one moment did he think Horace

Osborne would refuse his offer—and if he should prove difficult Grant didn't have the slightest doubt of his own ability to
negotiate and persuade him.

The gathering later that day at Rosehill was a quiet and digni-
fied affair, attended by elderly relatives from both sides and a few
business associates. As Paul and Adeline were congratulated on
their engagement on this day, which should have been the
happiest day of her life, Adeline felt as though she was standing
at the bottom of a high cliff, on top of which a huge boulder
teetered.

Everyone complimented her on how she looked, but she knew
they were only being polite.

'Too thin,' Paul's elderly Aunt Anne said. 'Too tall,' said
another. 'Too plain,' someone else commented.

But what did any of that really matter when her father was a
wealthy businessman and respected in the circles in which he
moved?

Adeline knew she didn't make the best of herself. Her deep
red hair was usually fashioned into a bun, and she wore dresses
in varying shades of brown, beige and grey that did nothing for
her colouring and made her look like some poor relation. Her
eyes were foreign-looking, and in her opinion her cheekbones
were too high and her mouth too wide. As a rule men took one
look at her and didn't look again.

But if anyone had been inclined to look deeper they would
have found that behind the unprepossessing appearance there
was a veritable treasure trove. Twenty years of age, and for-
midably intelligent, Adeline had a distinct and memorable per-
sonality, and could hold the most fascinating conversations on
most subjects. She had a genuinely kind heart, wasn't boastful,
and rarely offended anybody. She was also unselfish, and willing

to take on the troubles of others. She never showed her feelings, and she seemed to have the ability to put on whatever kind of face was necessary at the time.

She was also piercingly lonely. Her maid, Emma, was her only companion, her only source of love and affection since her mother had died, when Adeline had been ten years old.

A knot of people crowded the platform. Between them, Emma and Paul's valet took charge of the luggage—Paul was talking to the stationmaster. As the train to take them to Ashford pulled into the station, in a cloud of smoke and soot, Adeline stepped forward and watched as it came to a stop in a hiss of steam. The passengers began to get off. Pushed and jostled as people seemed to be going in all different directions, she dropped the book she was holding, which she had brought to read on the journey.

Suddenly one of the passengers who had got off the train stepped forward.

'Allow me.' The man, taller than Adeline, and dark, bent and retrieved the book before it was trampled on and handed it to her.

Adeline took it gratefully. Looking up, she met a pair of silver-grey eyes. There was no overlooking the sensuality in the mould of his mouth, even when it had a sardonic twist, as it did now. 'Thank you so much. That was careless of me.'

He smiled. 'These things happen.' He tipped his hat. 'Good day.'

Without a second glance, and dismissing the incident from his busy mind, Grant walked away. Frederick was to have sent his carriage to meet him. He was to stay overnight with Frederick before going on to Rosehill tomorrow—where he had arranged to see Horace Osborne.

What an attractive man, Adeline thought as she watched him walk towards the exit with long athletic strides. She wondered who he could be. There had been a cool purposefulness about him—a confident strength that emanated from every inch of his body.

Feeling a hand on her elbow, she turned to find Paul beside her.

'Come alone, Adeline,' he ordered briskly. 'We don't want the train to go without us.'

On arriving at Ashford, they found Lady Waverley had sent her carriage to the station to meet them. When they reached Westwood Hall, Emma and Paul's valet disappeared to see which rooms had been allotted to them.

Westwood Hall was a large, sprawling half-timbered Tudor structure, and so beautiful that when Adeline first set eyes on it she temporarily forgot her reluctance for this weekend party. The lawns had been mown to resemble smooth velvet, and the terraces all around were ablaze with trailing roses in various colours, and pots of flowering shrubs.

Most of the privileged, rich and well-connected guests had already arrived. Swarms of titled, wealthy and influential people invaded the house, lawns and terraces, their colourful gowns, jackets and painted parasols echoing the bright colours of the flowerbeds and the graceful sculptures.

Lady Waverley, widowed after just five years of marriage, was flitting among them like a butterfly. With her confident manner she presented an imposing figure.

On seeing Paul, she made a beeline for him, her red lips stretched over perfect teeth in a welcoming smile.

'My dear Paul. What a pleasure it is to see you. It has been altogether too long. I trust you are not too fatigued after your journey?'

Looking distinguished in an elegantly tailored tweed jacket, Paul smiled at her and stooped politely over her hand. 'Not at all. It's good to see you again, Diana.' Taking Adeline's hand, he drew her forward. 'Allow me to present Miss Adeline Osborne—my fiancée.'

Lady Waverley received Adeline with noticeable coolness. But she was also curious, and Adeline was uneasily conscious of being measured up. She decided there and then that she didn't like Diana Waverley. There was a cloying scent of musk about her, which Adeline found sickly sweet and unpleasant. Not unaware of the woman's exacting perusal, of a sudden she wished she had taken more care over her appearance. The dark brown hair of Lady Waverley was exquisitely coiffed, and she was gowned with costly good taste in a high-necked russet and gold-coloured dress, offset by ribbons and flounces.

'I appreciate your invitation, Lady Waverley,' Adeline said, determined to be polite.

'Well, now, I could hardly invite Paul without you, could I? You must call me Diana, and I shall call you Adeline. Still, I like the title, and it is one of the few good things—this house in particular—that my late husband left me. Any feelings I had for him I left at his graveside five years ago.'

Adeline's raised eyebrow betrayed some amazement, but out of good manners she didn't dare question a woman on such brief acquaintance.

Diana laughed at her expression. 'Oh, it's no secret—please don't look so shocked. Everyone knows about my marriage to Patrick Waverley. He was a gambler and a drunk, but he died before he could gamble away all his wealth, thank God. Still, I make the best of what he left me. You will find my house parties are very informal. I must congratulate you on your engagement, by the way. Do you have a date set for the wedding?'

Paul shook his head. 'Not yet—perhaps early spring.'

Adeline's eyes shot to him. This was the first she'd heard about it. But, as with everything else that concerned her, she was never consulted by either Paul or her father.

Diana nodded and looked at Adeline. 'It's a shame you have not been to one of my weekend parties before, Adeline. They are an experience to be enjoyed—is that not so, Paul?' Her full lips curved in a smile and her eyes were half closed as they settled on Adeline's fiancé. '*You* never fail to miss an invite.'

Adeline already knew that this was not the first function Paul had attended at Westwood Hall, and she did not like being reminded so blatantly of the fact.

'I've been in London for several weeks,' Diana continued, 'but with too many parties behind me I have removed my aching feet from the city's cobblestones and settled for the calmer joys of the country. However, I do make Westwood Hall quite lively when I'm here, and surround myself with company. I do so hate an empty house. Now, I will have you shown to your rooms, and afterwards I will introduce you to my guests—I insist on you enjoying yourself to the full while you are here.'

Westwood Hall was as elaborate inside as out—ornamentation, decorative scrollwork, heavy furniture, gas and lamplight on polished panelling. There were so many guests it was impossible to be introduced to all of them. Some Adeline knew, some she didn't, and she quickly lost interest in them. There was one person she *was* pleased to see, however, and that was Frances Seymore. She had been invited along with her older brother, Mark.

Frances was older than Adeline but just as plain, deemed to remain a spinster, unlike her three sisters—all sweet-faced, plump-breasted and coppery-haired—who had made splendid marriages. Frances was very dear to Adeline. The whole family was dear to her. They had befriended her when her mother died and had been very kind. She also suspected they felt sorry for her—motherless, and living with an arrogant, authoritative man who seemed to be indifferent to her.

Relieved that Adeline had found someone to talk to, Paul quickly excused himself. Adeline watched him heading Diana off in the direction of the terrace. She saw him slide his arm about the waist of their hostess, saw his head bend towards her upturned face, and with a stirring of irritation sensed that what they felt for each other was more than friendly regard. When Paul dropped his arm Diana took it, and pressed her breast against his sleeve. The contact was evidently intentional, for Paul did not draw away.

Feeling that she had witnessed something she had not been meant to see, Adeline turned away to accept a glass of spiced wine. She was embarrassingly conscious to find that some of the other guests were giving the couple a second glance, too. It seemed their closeness was too conspicuous to be ignored—and the weekend had only just begun, Adeline thought. More annoyed by the scene she had just witnessed than hurt, she turned to Frances, who was looking at her with quiet understanding.

'Diana has a penchant for handsome men, Adeline. Paul is no exception, and I suspect his maturity appeals to her gregarious nature.'

'I see.' And she did see. Quite clearly.

'In fact if you and Paul hadn't recently become engaged I would have said Diana Waverley has set her cap at him. I've been here twice before—I always seem to get invited with Mark. I only come along because I have nothing else to do—and it can be quite entertaining, I suppose. Diana goes to great pains to see that her parties are highly pleasurable to those who have a taste for sexual intrigue and illicit liaison. She is always an everwilling and resourceful collaborator.'

Adeline raised her brows, quite shocked. 'Are you saying that she *encourages* that sort of thing?'

'Oh, absolutely. When an illicit couple come to an understanding, it is usually agreed that something is left outside the lady's bedroom door to signify that she is alone and the coast is clear.' She laughed, vastly amused by the whole thing. 'When you hear the stable bell ring at six o'clock in the morning—providing a reliable alarm, you understand—there is always such a rushing about on the landings as everyone returns to their respective rooms and their own beds.'

'Goodness! If that is the case then I shall be sure to lock my door—and I hope that Paul does likewise,' she murmured as an afterthought.

Frances studied her thoughtfully. 'You know, I must say that I have misgivings about your engagement, Adeline. You deserve better than Paul—someone with a more generous nature, with passion in his veins. Someone who will care deeply for you.'

Adeline gave her a wry smile. 'You always were too sentimental, Frances. I don't require passion in a husband.'

'Of course you do—every woman does. Beware the perils of a pompous husband.'

Later, sitting under the trees where tea tables had been laid, Adeline sat drinking tea out of china cups and eating dainty cakes with Frances.

The afternoon was hot. With the sun shafting through the trees, the noises from the tennis court as background, people laughing, people talking, birds singing, it should have been perfect. But it wasn't. Adeline wished she could feel the happiness such a lovely day demanded instead of being alternately angry with Paul for neglecting her and miserable, exhausted and bored with the sheer physical effort of smiling and chatting to people she didn't know. What she really longed for was Monty, and to ride away like the wind.

Dinner was a long drawn-out affair, and everyone could not have been more gracious in their compliments. The food was sublime, the wine superb, but the choice of conversation was different from what Adeline was used to.

As the meal progressed, and more wine was consumed, cheeks grew florid and talk raucous. Few remarks were addressed directly to her, and when they were she replied with a murmur or a smile or a nod. Most of the time she was unhappy with the trend of the conversation—its content became shallow, and leaned towards the vulgar—so she kept quiet, for fear of making a fool of herself, and then began to fear that her silence was creating precisely that impression.

She was appalled when Diana suddenly looked down the table and spoke to her.

'You are very quiet, Adeline. I suppose as the proper, dutiful daughter of Mr Horace Osborne you don't find the conversation as interesting or as stimulating as it is at Rosehill—perhaps you find all this superficial social chit-chat rather boring.'

Adeline stared at her. Was she mocking her? She saw no sign, but she sensed it. Her quietness had been misinterpreted as intellectual boredom. She didn't intend to alter that impression, but nor was she about to forget that she was at Westwood Hall on Diana's invitation. She would not be rude, but she would be the butt of no one's joke—especially a woman who was making a play for her fiancé, however subtle her methods.

Adopting a pleasant smile, she said slowly, and with great restraint, 'You're quite right. It isn't easy to work oneself into a passion over who is having an affair with whom. And with so many doing so surely they must be at the point of exhaustion in their search for pleasure for much of the time?'

There was a moment of silence before the laughter came.

'Bravo, Miss Osborne!' a gentleman across from her called out. 'Your fiancé can be amusing—but you must know it is only play.'

'I know my fiancé plays as well as any man. In fact I often think it is his—playfulness—rather than his search for pleasure that so exhausts him.' She had the courage to look directly at Paul. He looked back at her, his face set in the kind of frozen disapproval he seemed to reserve just for her.

'Why, my dear,' Diana said, her eyes full of mock consolation, 'and here was I thinking you were shy.'

Adeline smiled back at her. 'If I am, then please don't mistake it for lack of backbone.'

'No, I wouldn't dream of it.'

The dinner was over and the guests settled in the large drawing room for talk and music. Green-jacketed servants passed among them with more champagne, brandy and fortified wines.

As the evening wore on, and Adeline sat engrossed in a game of whist, partnered by Frances, from the corner of her eye she watched Diana making a play for Paul across the room. Responding to her blatant attention—his chest puffed out like a stuffed peacock, his natural arrogance greater than ever—Paul raised his glass and bowed briefly to his hostess. Adeline saw the subtle, conspiratorial look that passed between them and witnessed the imperceptible inclination of Paul's head in reply.

Seeing Adeline's interest, Lady Waverley drew away—but not before her eyes had met Adeline's, with that same challenging, mocking look she had bestowed on her earlier. Adeline knew Paul was physically attracted to their hostess. She also knew when they each left the room by separate doors.

Anger surged through her. Damn him! How could he do this? Was he so insensible to her feelings—to her as a woman? Perhaps if she cared more for him it would hurt, but as it was all she could feel was anger. She thought of him with cold distaste—and a sense of wonder that she had allowed herself to be bullied into marrying him by her father.

She would have to be stupid and fairly thick-skinned not to see what was going on right under her nose. But what could she do about it? Confront him? Make a fuss? Make herself look silly and childish? For after all Paul wasn't the only one doing it. To this smart gathering of supposedly civilised beings at the party adultery, intrigue and sexual liaison were an amusing fact of life. The women, with their jealousies and quiet war-mongering, wove webs of deceit, and the men were just as bad, with their love of competition and of bettering the next man.

Adeline really should have declined her invitation to the party—not that she'd received one personally, she thought bitterly. That was how little she was thought of—how unimportant she was. She would go to bed and pretend she hadn't seen her fiancé leave the room with Diana. She told herself she could manage—that no one need ever know about her humiliation, her rejection.

When she heard the six o'clock stable bell ring the following morning she stood in the shadow of a huge jardinière that held an elaborate array of ferns and watched Paul scuttle out of Diana's bedroom.

Afterwards she had no idea how long she stood there, gazing at Diana's bedroom door, for her gaze was turned inwards, on herself. It was as if she were witnessing a different creature being born anew out of these frightening emotions. The force that was rising within her was horrifying. All she wanted to do was go into that room and vent all her fury on Diana Waverley— to strike out at her again and again.

It was several minutes before she could move and blindly make her way back to her own room. She was determined to carry on as if nothing had happened, to get through this unpleasant time until it was time to return to Rosehill and she could decide what to do about Paul's sordid affair.

One thing she was sure of: she would not be made the object of censure, gossip and ridicule. But she had one more interminable day to get through—and one more night. How was she going to stand it?

Chapter Two

When Grant went to Rosehill to meet with Horace Osborne he didn't know what to expect, never having met him. But each man knew of the other, and both were admired and respected for their business acumen.

Horace had made himself what he was, and had spared himself nothing in a mighty effort which had brought his father's business back from near bankruptcy to marvellous prosperity. So it was not to be wondered at that he looked older than his fifty years. Grey hair was swept back from his forehead, and below it his narrow face was deeply lined, his cheeks sunken.

He greeted Grant cordially, curious as to the reason for his request to see him. His eyes swept over him, seeing a man reputed to have the same ruthlessness as himself, but taller, darker, and with a lean, powerful face.

'You wanted to see me about something important?' he said,

ushering him into his study and offering him a chair before seating himself behind his richly carved desk.

'Yes. I want to buy your house,' Grant said, coming straight to the point.

Horace looked at him hard. 'Then I'm afraid you are going to be disappointed. Contrary to what you might have heard, Rosehill is not for sale.'

Not to be deterred, and with the impudence of the devil, confident that he could make him change his mind, Grant offered him a sum that would have made any other man's eyes water. But Horace Osborne would not be moved.

Horace sensed that he had met his match in Grant Leighton. The penetrating power of his eyes indicated his swift and clever mind, and Horace decided he would rather have him by his side than as his adversary. But he would not let him have Rosehill. He had more money than he knew what to do with, and, yes, he was to move to London to live, but this house was to be given as a wedding present to his daughter and her fiancé.

Grant hadn't reckoned on this, and there wasn't a thing he could do about it. He sat a moment in silence, and with shattering certainty he knew his mother was to be denied her wish. He also knew what this would do to her—what it would mean to her.

Dear God! How was he going to tell her?

Putting off the inevitable, and in need of an immediate outlet for his disappointment, instead of going home to Oaklands, Grant went to Westwood Hall—and Diana.

Adeline got through the day as best she could. After breakfast she went to church with Frances and Paul—who looked no different than he always did, which was surprising after his night spent in Diana's bed. Any other woman would have taken him to task over his behaviour, and Adeline would have—had she loved him. As things stood she was like an empty shell, senseless to pain. What tomorrow held for her she could neither fathom nor rouse a care for.

After luncheon they went for a drive, then it was tea and bridge, and after dinner more bridge.

Frances and Adeline had gone out onto the terrace, where they sat idly flicking through some fashion magazines in quiet conversation, content to watch the sun go down over the landscape.

It was his voice that first attracted Adeline's attention—deep and resonant. She could hear him all the way from the small private sitting room. She could not hear what was being said, but the voice was raised in anger.

Adeline turned and frowned, and said to Frances, 'I wonder who that can be? He sounds extremely vexed, whoever he is.'

At that moment a tall, dark, incredibly handsome figure with a face like thunder came striding out onto the terrace. Longsighted, Adeline took off her pince-nez, dangling them from a narrow ribbon around her neck, and looked at him. His head jerked in her direction, and her breath froze at the hard anger flaring in his piercing silver-grey eyes. For a brief second their eyes clashed, and then he looked away.

Adeline felt an unfamiliar twist to her heart—an addictive blend of pleasure and discomfort, and also recognition—for it was the gentleman who had come to her aid on the station platform.

With long, athletic and purposeful strides he made his way in the direction of the drive.

Frances lifted her lorgnettes and peered after him. 'I can't say I've seen him before—I'm sure I'd remember someone so terribly good-looking. But he does seem to be in a bit of a temper. I wonder why they were arguing.'

Adeline shrugged. 'Who knows?'

Their heads turned simultaneously to the doorway as their hostess appeared. She was scowling after the departing man— then her eyes lit on Adeline. She became thoughtful and then, as if something of a humorous nature had suddenly occurred to her, she smiled and went back inside.

After another couple of hours, pleading a headache and seeking the sanctuary of her room, on passing the library Adeline heard voices from inside. The door was partly open. Not wishing to eavesdrop, she was about to go on her way when she heard Rosehill mentioned. Burning to appease her inquisitiveness, she paused and glanced inside, seeing the same man who had stalked out of the house earlier. The other person was Diana.

Having discarded his jacket over a nearby chair, the man had unbuttoned his white shirt halfway to his waist. With his hair falling in disarray over his brow, his profile was hard and bitter. Adeline gazed at the recklessly dark, austere beauty of his face, at the power and virility stamped in every line of his long body, and her pulse raced with a mixture of excitement and trepidation.

Indeed, it looked as if he had been partaking rather freely of Diana's liquor for some time. A glass with some brandy left in it dangled loosely from his fingers. Lifting it up, for a moment he stared at the remaining brandy, then he tipped it up to his mouth and drained it. From the way he swayed to stay on his feet, it was obvious he was well on his way to becoming blind drunk.

'I omitted to ask you earlier if you'd got that business arrangement settled?' Diana asked, seeming unconcerned about his condition.

The man glanced at her briefly, unable to defeat the scowl that creased his brow. 'No. Osborne refused to sell.'

Diana's smile was ironic. 'Did he, now? I congratulate him. I'm glad there is someone who has the courage to say no to you when others wouldn't dare. Failure is not a word in your vocabulary. You must have met your match. What will you do now?'

A muscle moved spasmodically in his throat, but he made no effort to defend himself. He shrugged. 'Nothing. There is nothing I can do. I have to accept defeat. I have done everything that can be done, and only hope my mother will not be too disappointed.'

'Well, it was nice of you to come and tell me. I appreciate that, but there really was no need. It has nothing to do with me. Do you want to stay the night?'

'If you'll have me.' Reaching out, he caressed her cheek with the backs of his fingers. 'Don't be angry with me, Diana. You've always been a friend when I needed one. I'm sorry about earlier, and I will give your proposition some thought, I promise.'

Diana gave him a wry smile. 'Since Mr Osborne has turned your proposition down, could you not redirect the money you would have spent in bailing me out of a tight situation which has become quite desperate. The bank has refused to extend my credit.'

'I'm hardly surprised. Perhaps you should curtail your extravagances? I mean, was this weekend party absolutely necessary?'

'No, but I like parties.'

'Which has much to do with the mess you are in. So the answer is still no. However, if there's anything else you ever need, don't hesitate to call on me.'

Diana straightened her spine and did her best to smile. 'I'm afraid what I need most you can't give me—and you know I'm not referring to the business matter that got you so riled up earlier. You've made your feelings quite clear—unless you've had a change of heart.'

His face was wiped clean of emotion, and his silence was an eloquent declaration that he hadn't.

Obviously deflated, Diana sighed. 'I see. Well, now—if you'll excuse me, I must return to my guests.' She regarded the empty decanter. 'If you intend cauterising your wounds I'll have some more brandy sent in. You can't drink yourself into oblivion without it.' She walked towards the door, where she turned and looked back at him. 'Oh, and if you intend joining me in my room later, it's on the landing to the left of the stairs. Look for the door with this ribbon tied around the handle,' she said, indicating the scarlet ribbon about her waist.

'Diana, are you involved with anyone?'

'I might be. If the ribbon isn't on the door, you will have to sleep on the couch.'

In danger of being discovered eavesdropping, Adeline knew her situation was extremely precarious. Moving away from the door, she hurried up the stairs, wondering what possible business the man could have with her father.

After Adeline had prepared for the night, and Emma had left her, it was a relief when, just before midnight, she slipped between the sheets, knowing that in the morning she would be leaving for Rosehill. She had left the curtains partly open, so she could watch the moon steadily arch its way across the sky. Closing her eyes, she gradually settled her mind into the haven of sleep, and dreamed of herself as a beautiful woman in a beautiful gown, with a man holding her in a close embrace as they danced a waltz together, his eyes gleaming with warmth into hers.

Floating on the edge of sleep, she didn't know how late it was when she awoke, sensing a presence in her room. Staring into the gloom, she could make out the figure of a man, trying to stay

upright as he removed his clothes. Struggling with the buttons
of his shirt, he sounded a low curse. She recognised the voice
as being that of the man she had seen in the library—the same
man who had referred to Rosehill and her father. Gripping the
sheets beneath her chin, she stared in total horror when, totally
naked, he fell full-length upon the bed beside her. With a sigh
he lay still.

After a few moments of listening to his heavy breathing, in
desperation Adeline slowly slid out of bed, so as not to disturb
him, and crept to the door. Thankfully it opened soundlessly.
Bright moonlight streamed in through her windows, lighting the
broad landing off which were most of the bedrooms. A table had
been left with a lamp burning—no doubt for the benefit of those
with a taste for illicit liaisons, she thought bitterly.

The house was silent and there was no one about. Hopefully
no one had seen him enter her room. She was about to close the
door when, looking down, her eyes were riveted on the scarlet
ribbon tied around the handle. Recalling the conversation she
had heard between Diana and the man in her bed, she froze,
staring at the offending ribbon, knowing that for some sick and
sordid reason of her own Diana intended to humiliate not only
the man but her, too.

Anger coursed through her. Did Diana consider her so chaste
and easily shocked that she would scream and create a fuss, thus
adding to her humiliation, knowing that the ensuing furor would
be disastrous for all concerned? If so Diana Waverley did not
know her. Untying the ribbon, she closed the door and flung it
into the nearest chair, before turning and looking at the man
lying on the bed.

She shivered, but it was not from the cold. Suddenly she was
warm—far too warm. Something was happening to her. It was
as if a spark had been lit that could not now be extinguished. A

need was rising up inside her—a need to be close to this stranger, to wallow in the desire that had suddenly taken hold of her, to saturate herself in this newfound passion.

She pulled her nightdress over her head, her hair tumbling down to her waist and her heart pounding in her breast, and, completely naked and carried away by her desire, returned to the bed and lay beside him. Coming into contact with his flesh, she felt something stir within her—something she had never felt before. A flicker, a leaping, a reaching out.

Even as Adeline had closed the door, through the lingering essence of the brandy clouding his brain, Grant had been aware of the blurred shape of a woman walking across the carpet and getting into bed. His mind felt slow and listless, but he had no reason to believe the woman was anyone else but Diana. Now as she lay beside him her nakedness whetted his appetite, and he realised with a surge of desire that he wanted her—wanted to fill his mouth with the taste of her and draw those inviting hips beneath him.

When he reached for her, Adeline relaxed against him with the familiarity of the most successful courtesan, little realising the devastating effect her naked body had on him. He was so different from her—earthy, vital and strong, all rippling sinews. His mouth, hard and demanding, tasting of brandy, was on hers, kissing her lips, her shoulder, her ears and her neck.

'You are wanton, Diana—and how perfect you are. I must have you. Thank you for not shutting me out.'

'Shh,' Adeline whispered against his lips in the warmest tone, thankful for the shadows that covered them both. 'Don't talk.'

She did not care that he thought she was Diana. Her body was burning and she wanted more of him. She knew deception would be easy when the bold, insistent pressure of his body made her realise that the path she had chosen was where he wished to go.

He cupped her breast in his hand. She had never been touched like this by a man before, and the feel of his hand almost melted her bones. He crushed her to him, and her mind reeled from the intoxicating potion of his passionate kiss.

It was when her thigh brushed the scorching heat of his manhood, throbbing with life, that she was suddenly made aware of her innocence. Suddenly primeval fear mixed with the awesome pleasure of his hard body. Less sure of herself, she felt fear take over and panic set in. She couldn't do this. It was wrong—totally wrong. She felt her body tightening, and she felt cold, as though her blood had turned to ice. She wanted to cry out, to tell him to stop, but his lips were on hers and her throat was constricted.

In desperation she tore herself free and rolled away from him. But, not to be cheated out of what he desired, he laughed and shot out his hand, catching her arm with a strength she had not thought possible. Though she prised at his fingers she could not escape. He pulled her back downward and covered her with his body, growing more purposeful, his hungering lips insistent. With his mouth against her flesh his tongue teased the soft peak of her breast, his hand spreading, caressing the soft flesh of her inner thigh that began to tingle and to glow.

Her fear was gone. Incapable of reason, she felt her body respond as if she were another person. And though her mind told her this was wrong, her female body told her mind to go to the devil—for this was what she wanted. There was nothing she could do but let go of herself. What was happening to her? What was he doing to her? Every fibre, every pulse, every bone and muscle in her body came alive. A shuddering excitement swept through her, and the strength ebbed from her limbs as his lips travelled over her flat belly, and hips and thighs.

She strained beneath him. They were entwined—and a burning pain exploded in her loins.

Joined with him in the most intimate way imaginable, crushed beneath his strength, Adeline became aware of a sense of fullness as he plunged deep within her. With lips and bodies merged in a fiery fusion, she gasped. His hungering mouth searched her lips and he kissed her with a slow thoroughness, savouring each moment of pleasure before beginning to move. And then she felt something new and incredible, and it all seemed so effortless as she began to respond to his inner heat.

Never would she have believed that she could feel such fierce pleasure, nor that she could respond so brazenly as she yielded, giving all her desire and passion, as if an ancient, primitive force were controlling her, driving her on. Then his control shattered, and as though he were seeking a much-needed release for his mind and body he claimed her fully, filling her with an urgent desire until he collapsed completely, his shuddering release over.

Still in a state of intoxication, and unable to keep at bay the oncoming forces of sleep, with his rock-hard body glistening with sweat Grant drifted away into a heavy slumber, losing all contact with reality and the young woman in his arms.

Adeline was aware of nothing but an immense, incredible joy, beyond which nothing was comparable. Sated and deliciously exhausted, her body and lips tender from his caresses, she nestled against her lover's warm, hard body, closed her eyes and slept.

A hint of dawn fell on the slumbering forms. Grant emerged slowly from sleep. His eyelids, feeling like sandpaper, flickered open—and closed immediately to ease the throbbing ache that shot through his head. He groaned and tried to move. That was the moment he became aware of the warm, sweet-smelling form cradled against him, and the vibrant mahogany-coloured hair spread over his chest.

Diana! He smiled, although the remembrance of the woman who had been so warm and vibrant beneath him brought confusion. He found difficulty in equating it with Diana. Opening his eyes, he was relieved when the pain in his head began to ease a little. He frowned, feeling an uneasy disquiet. Something was wrong. Looking down, he disentangled himself from the long limbs entwined with his—limbs that were surely longer and shapelier than Diana's. Carefully pushing back the hair that covered the woman's face he stared in disbelief. It wasn't Diana. Who was it—and how the hell had this happened?

Without the warmth of his body, Adeline half opened her eyes and, remembering the night, smiled and stretched her long slender form, reaching high with her arms above her head and emitting a deep, contented sigh. Her heart skipped a beat as she gazed up at the powerful, dynamic man looking down at her. Masculine pride and granite determination were sculpted into every angle and plane of his swarthy face, and cynicism had etched lines at the corners of his eyes and mouth.

Grant looked at her naked, luscious shape in appalled silence. Her face was not beautiful in the classical sense, but it was attractively arresting and he was drawn to it. Her lips were soft, full and sensuous, her eyes—heavy with contentment, fringed by thick black lashes—were almond-shaped and clear, and a sparkling shade of green. An abundance of dark red hair framed the flawless, creamy-skinned visage. His breath caught in his throat. And, dear Lord, what legs—what a body! He must have been drunk out of his skull to have thought she was Diana.

Drawing himself up, he tightened his mouth. 'Good God! Who the hell are *you*?'

Adeline opened her eyes wider and met his gaze. 'I might ask the same of you,' she retorted, her voice quite deep and disturbingly delicious in its shadowy luxury.

Though she shrank before him, her eyes never left his—which were wide and as savagely furious as a wild, wounded animal. He was six feet three inches of splendid masculinity, wide-shouldered and narrow-hipped, his chest covered with a light furring of black hair. Without haste she sat up and pulled the sheet into place, running her fingers through her wildly disordered hair. Disconcerted, and embarrassed by the way the sight of his naked body was affecting her, she lowered her gaze. Last night, when he had been in his inebriated state, she had for a time felt confident and in control. Now she felt confused and strangely vulnerable.

'Do you mind telling me what happened here last night?'

'I think we both know that.'

'I thought you were—'

Her eyes met his. 'Diana?'

'She said she'd—'

'What? Hang a scarlet ribbon on her door so you would know where to find her?' Adeline's lips twisted wryly. 'How appropriate. A scarlet ribbon for a scarlet woman.'

Ignoring her sarcasm, Grant rubbed a hand between his brows, making an effort to recall the last few hours and failing miserably. 'How do you know that?'

'I think the ribbon tied to the handle of my door speaks for itself.'

Grant looked stunned. 'Are you saying that Diana set this up?'

'That's precisely what I'm saying. And I ask you not to give her the satisfaction of letting her know that her sordid attempt to embarrass us both has worked.' Adeline tilted her head to one side and slanted him a quizzical look. 'Now, I wonder why she did that? Perhaps you know?'

Grant scowled, beginning to dress with feverish haste. 'I have an idea.' He paused while pulling on his trousers and shot her a look. 'I must have been very drunk.'

The lean, hard planes of his cheeks looked harsh in the watery dawn light. 'You were. Blind drunk.' Adeline watched his expression harden, and at the same time his voice became chillingly polite.

'For that I apologise. It is not my habit to drink to excess. Did you have no control over what so obviously happened between us?'

'Perhaps.' A little smile played on her lips. 'You can be very persuasive,' she murmured softly.

'You could have cried rape.'

'No, I couldn't—not without waking the entire household, which would have proved embarrassing for both of us. Besides, it wasn't rape,' she confessed quietly.

He stopped and looked at her. The grey eyes seemed sheathed in ice, fury and horror, and his mouth was fixed in a stern line. 'Did you plan this?' His voice was quiet, controlled.

'Certainly not. The first I knew was when I awoke and found you getting into my bed. I can see that you're angry—'

His eyes slashed her like razors. 'How very observant of you,' he mocked scathingly. Frowning, he peered down at her, trying to read the quicksilver light in her eyes. 'Did I hurt you?'

Adeline considered his question. Her body was limp and aching, and still throbbing with a strange kind of tenderness. But she had wanted him to make love to her and he had granted her request—even if he couldn't remember any of it. 'No, you didn't hurt me.'

Grant's gaze went to the dark flecks of blood marring the stark whiteness of the sheets, which told their own story. He was incredulous. The evidence was overwhelming—damning. He couldn't deny what he had done, and the inevitable consequences of it hit home. When he spoke again the husky savagery of his voice shocked Adeline into intense awareness.

'You were a virgin. I have ruined and ravaged a virgin.'

Adeline winced at the fierce accusation in his tone. 'Yes. Does it matter?'

A muscle flexed in his jaw and the metallic grey of his eyes was dim as he buttoned up his shirt. 'Yes—and if you have any measure of self-respect it should matter to you.'

'Please don't feel any sense of guilt,' she said, tossing her hair over her shoulder.

'How do you expect me to feel? I have wronged you—dishonoured you.'

'I don't feel wronged or dishonoured. If you feel that way then that is unfortunate, and for you to deal with. Your dishonour is not mine. Whatever happened between us, I did it on my terms.'

'Because I was drunk?'

'Yes. Oh, you needn't worry. I have no intention of demanding that you do the honourable thing.'

He froze. Slowly he leaned forward, his hand reaching out and grasping her chin so that she was forced to look into eyes that blazed with white fire just inches from her own. 'Lady, let me assure you that you don't want to be my wife,' he gritted through his teeth. 'Let's not play games. I've already played them all, and you wouldn't enjoy them even if you knew how to play. Unlike other men, who enjoy bedding innocents, I prefer the women I take to my bed to be experienced and knowledgeable—women who know how to please a man, sensual and willing.'

Adeline tried turning her head, but the strength in his fingers held her chin firm. 'I believe the word for a woman like that is prostitute.'

'Aye, lady, and if you go on behaving as you did last night you are going the right way about becoming one yourself.'

The blood drained from her face. 'I am not a whore.'

'You have all the makings of one. Women like that are ten a penny. They are expendable.'

'Why—how dare you?'

'I do dare.' His eyes were two slits of hard, unyielding steel. 'It isn't the first time an innocent young woman has insinuated herself into my bed with marriage as her goal. Most of them are out of the door on their backside before they can take their hats off. I am experienced—as you clearly are not—so it is useless to try extracting money out of me, if blackmail is what you have in mind.'

Insulted to the core of her being, Adeline shot him an angry, indignant glare. 'I am no scheming opportunist. You seem to forget that this is *my* bed and it was you who insinuated yourself into it.'

Releasing his hold on her chin, he stepped back, his look one of cold contempt. 'Whatever. I will not marry you. Crude as this may be, there is only one thing I would be interested in—and it's a lot safer for me to find it in a brothel.'

'And I would not marry *you*—besides, I am hardly in a position to do so. Despite the attraction you seemed to have for me last night, you do not know me—so how can you care for me in any sense that would result in a happy union? I would appreciate it if you would refrain from mentioning what happened to anyone.'

'You can be assured I won't mention it. I'm not that much of a fool. Can you assure me I won't have an angry father challenging me to pistols at dawn?'

Adeline lifted her gaze to his. 'I don't intend to tell him or anyone else. What is done cannot be undone, but I do ask you to forget it happened.'

'Of that you can be guaranteed. I'm glad we have an understanding. Do you care nothing for your reputation? Do you hold yourself in such low esteem that you thought nothing about giving yourself to a complete stranger?'

Those words, uttered with such biting contempt, hurt her. Stunned and stricken, she looked away from him, beginning to resent his effect on her, the masculine assurance of his bearing. She would never forgive him for turning something that had been so wonderful into something quite ugly.

'You have said quite enough. Please get out of my room.'

He raised one well-defined brow, watching her. 'There is just one thing I would like to ask you before I go. Could you have stopped me?'

'Perhaps. I don't know.'

'Then why didn't you?'

'I had my reasons.'

'Do you want to tell me? I've been told I'm a good listener.'

Uncomfortable with both the question and the penetrating look in his steely grey eyes, Adeline averted her gaze, fixing it on a rather fancy ornament of a spaniel on the dressing table. In spite of her prior intimacy with this man, he was still a stranger. How could she tell him about Paul's betrayal with the woman this man had wanted to spend the night with?

'No, I don't think so. I am not obliged to share them with you.'

'And did you enjoy what I did to you?'

Despite having willingly participated in her own seduction, she flushed and found it impossible to lie. 'It was the most wonderful thing that has ever happened to me.'

Shrugging on his jacket, he gave her a long, assessing look. When he next spoke his tone was sarcastic and cruel. 'Good. I don't like to leave a woman unsatisfied. I have my pride to consider.'

'I'm sure you have,' she whispered.

His attitude to what had happened between them made her

feel worthless, so cheap and so ashamed of herself. It seemed incredible now that not only had she allowed him to make love to her, she had instigated it. Bright flags of humiliated colour stained her cheeks and tears stung her eyes.

She pointed across the room. 'There is the door. Please—just go, will you?'

He stared at her in silence and then, with nothing further to say, turned on his heel and walked out, without so much as a nod to her.

A feeling of anger, frustration and a profound sense of shame raged through her. She meant nothing to him. How could she when he didn't know her? When he had never laid eyes on her before? He had been drunk and, roused by a temporary passion, had taken his pleasure where he found it—with a willing body. Instant gratification. To be forgotten and discarded afterwards.

She thought of Diana Waverley with shame, and knew she could never equal *her* sexual experience. She could not believe the ease with which she had given herself to a stranger—a man whose name she didn't even know, who would scorn her, laugh at her. She had behaved so out of character. Now, in the cold light of day, it was so ugly—so horribly shocking. What she had done was sordid. She was corrupted and beyond forgiveness. And to humiliation and her sense of guilt was added the fear of pregnancy. Dear Lord, don't let it be so.

When Emma came in Adeline appeared composed, and put on a cheerful face, while in truth she was struggling with shame and mortification. For now she'd had time for calm reflection she greatly regretted her rash behaviour. Throwing away her virginity because of a childish desire for vengeance hadn't solved her problem with Paul; it had simply created another. As for his affair with Diana—what could she do? Besides, wasn't she guilty of the same?

Thinking how her time at Westwood Hall had changed everything, she realised that she would still have to face Paul and deal with the situation. Of course she would have to marry him—pretending that all was well, playing out a polite farce for the rest of her life—but she realised that pretending nothing had changed in their relationship would prove a severe strain.

Grant left Westwood Hall for Oaklands—no more than three miles away—before the other guests were stirring. The ride helped clear his head, but he was unable to shake off the memory of what had happened. It hadn't occured to him until he'd left Westwood Hall behind that he didn't even know her name, but he was unable to shake off the feeling that he had seen her before.

He was consumed with a bitterness that was directed not at the young woman but at himself—he was a man who could usually hold his liquor. Embarrassed and shamed by his temporary lapse, and his lack of proper decorum, a wave of guilt washed over him. Miss Whoever-she-was had told him she had known what she was doing, but he could not escape the fact that he had taken her without the slightest courtesy or endearment, with less feeling than a dog for a bitch—and what made it a thousand times worse was that he couldn't remember a damned thing about it.

A memory of the young woman flicked across his mind—a mercenary little flirt with a body that had drugged his mind. He could not rid himself of the image, or of the hot, smothering desire that coursed through his body, and it shocked him to think how much he still desired her.

He knew he could find her if he wanted to—he had only to ask Diana—but since she had engineered the whole sordid episode, in excruciatingly bad taste, he refused to give her the satisfaction of letting her know he had fallen for her ploy, hook, line and sinker. Diana was intelligent and direct, and she wanted more from him than he was prepared to give. But it was too late—six years too late—and there was no going back. But that did not stop him enjoying her company now and then.

Hopefully he would never cast eyes on the young woman again. And, dismissing her from his mind, he concentrated on how he would break the news that he had failed to buy back Rosehill to his mother.

On the train taking them back to Sevenoaks, Paul and Adeline were alone in the carriage. Paul glanced across at his fiancée. With her lips compressed in a thin line, her glasses on the end of her nose, she had her head bent over her book. He realised she had not spoken to him directly all morning, and she seemed to find it difficult meeting his eyes. And had he imagined it, or had she shrunk from his hand when he had offered to assist her onto the train?

'Have you enjoyed the weekend, Adeline?'

'It wasn't what I expected,' she answered, without raising her head.

'Why? What did you expect?'

Her face was shuttered. Paul never knew what she was thinking—and in this instance if he'd been made privy to her thoughts he would have been both shocked and appalled.

Adeline was trying to feel abused and furious about what had occurred, but the memory of the stranger making love to her stirred something more akin to warmth and passion, a feeling of wanting to sample what he had done to her more fully. It was wrong what she had done—she knew that—and she knew she had sinned far more devastatingly than she had ever done. But it had felt wonderful, too—and important. How could anything as wonderful be so sinful?

Resting her book in her lap, she looked at Paul as she would an annoying, persistent fly she wanted to swat away. This man she had pledged to marry had an odd mixture of high intelligence and an almost total incapacity for laughter. He also had a gravity that was totally without delicacy or tenderness. Now she saw him as he really was—a weak, shallow, horrid individual. This time forty-eight hours ago she would have thrust such thoughts deep down into her mind, there to stay out of respect for her fiancé. But by his own actions Paul had killed all respect in her.

'I saw little of you, Paul. You spent a lot of time with Lady Waverley.'

'Diana?'

'Yes, Diana.'

'I was being sociable—which is more than can be said of you.'

His deprecatory tone stirred Adeline's ire. 'Please explain what you mean by that.'

'You really should try to be more outgoing, Adeline—more convivial. You spent the entire weekend with Frances Seymore to the exclusion of everyone else.'

'Perhaps that was because my fiancé was too busy giving all his attention to someone else,' she responded tersely. 'I *did* notice.'

Paul was taken aback by the sharpness of her tone. 'What's come over you, Adeline? It isn't like you to criticise.'

'I'm not criticising. It's just that you were with Diana for most of the time.' She looked at him with an unusually defiant expression. 'Are you carrying on an affair with her, Paul?'

His eyebrows shot up. 'Now you are being ridiculous.'

Adeline looked at him direct, and he had the grace to look away. 'Am I? I don't think so.'

Her bosom rose and fell, and her eyes darkened with anger. Nothing was more sure to upset Paul than the discovery that he had been caught out in an indiscretion. It might be that it was merely one of those affairs that distracted men from time to time—a sudden appetite that once sated lost its hunger—and after being made love to by an experienced, incredibly handsome stranger, Adeline now knew what that hunger could do to a person.

She told herself not to torture herself about last night, and to further insulate herself against going mad decided to firmly put an end to her thoughts about him. But, feeling badly done by, she was out of sorts, and it gave her satisfaction to stand up to Paul for once.

'I may have been tucked out of the way in a corner at Westwood Hall for most of the time, but I do have eyes—and so has everyone else. Don't embarrass me, Paul—or my father.'

'Really, Adeline,' he snapped, shifting his position uneasily. 'You read too much into my friendship with Diana. It is you I am to marry, after all. I am very fond of you, you know. You accuse me of neglecting you, but you could try showing me more affection.'

She merely looked at him. Her face was inscrutable. How could she show what she didn't feel? The thought of all the days and nights of her life being so soft and impassive while he carried on one intrigue after another enraged her beyond measure.

'Now, if you don't mind, my dear,' Paul said, unfolding his newspaper and beginning to scan the columns, 'it is a subject I prefer not to discuss.'

Lowering her head, she looked at her book, but instead of the print she saw Diana as she had looked when she had come into the breakfast room earlier. So brazen, so self-assured and smug, Diana had settled her shrewd eyes on Adeline, trying to gauge the effect of her machinations—but to no avail. Having already decided to behave as if nothing untoward had happened, and keep Diana wondering, Adeline had smiled pleasantly, said good morning and hoped that she had slept well, and without giving Diana time to respond lowered her gaze and attacked her boiled egg.

She resumed her reading. Having always been conservative in her choice of authors, when others could have enlightened her more fully, she now told herself she was no longer ignorant of the ways of the world and men. Her two days at Westwood Hall had furthered her education in such a way that she would never feel the same again.

That same evening, Adeline and her father had finished their evening meal—eaten in silence for the main part—and retired to the drawing room. Adeline poured them each coffee. Her father never drank alcohol—he said it clouded the mind, loosened tongues and made fools of men, and following Adeline's encounter with the handsome stranger at Westwood Hall she now realised how much sense there was to his words. The whole episode seemed unreal to her, and she looked back on what had happened with total disbelief, but nothing could take away the memory of what it had felt like, and she was discomfited by the warm rush of feeling that accompanied the memory.

Her father seemed quieter than usual, more subdued. He had presence, and he made himself felt by his temper and sharp tongue. He was both respected and feared by every member of his household, but Adeline had lost her fear of him. His temper no longer affected her, but she always felt duty bound, and would never disobey him.

With his stern grey eyebrows drawn together, Horace looked

at his daughter. She was composed, but she looked different—older, a woman. Having been married to a beautiful, warm and giving woman, he was disappointed in Adeline. She managed his house as efficiently as a wife, but she had always been devoid of womanly attraction. He didn't imagine that marriage to Paul Marlow would improve matters in that direction, but there was a change in her.

'Have you enjoyed your weekend at Westwood Hall?' he asked now.

'Yes—it—was pleasant,' Adeline replied hesitantly.

Horace nodded, not particularly interested, and didn't ask her to enlarge on it. 'We've been invited to spend a weekend at Oaklands—which isn't far from Westwood Hall.'

'Oaklands?' Adeline put down her cup and stared at him. Not another weekend house party, surely?

'Mr Grant Leighton's place.'

'Who is he? I do not believe I've heard of him.'

'That's hardly surprising,' Horace said brusquely. 'He came to see me recently—made me an offer for Rosehill.'

Adeline stared at him. His pronouncement rang a bell in her mind, and she recalled the conversation she had overheard between Diana Waverley and the gentleman in the library at Westwood Hall—the man who had later made love to her. But she didn't put any importance on it just then.

'He did? Why? I didn't know you wanted to sell it.' Her father wouldn't have told her if he did anyway.

'I don't. I bought the house from his mother's family—they hit on hard times and were forced to sell. Rosehill was in her family for generations and she has fond memories of the place. Somehow it's leaked out that I'm moving out to live in London. She wants to buy it back. I refused Leighton's offer, of course. I intend to make it over to you and Paul as a wedding present.'

Adeline stared at him. This was the first she'd heard about it. 'Why, that's extremely generous of you, Father.'

'I want you to have it. I don't need it—I'm always happier in town—but nor do I want to part with it. Besides, Paul will be looking for somewhere to live when you're married. Can't live with your in-laws. Wouldn't be right.'

'And Mr Leighton?'

'He thinks that by inviting us to Oaklands he'll get me to change my mind.'

'And you won't?'

'Absolutely not. But it may prove to be an interesting and enjoyable weekend. I liked Grant Leighton. He's got sound business sense and mature judgement, which brings confidence. You need confidence to run a business of any kind. Reminds me of myself when I was that age.'

'Is it necessary for me to go?'

Obviously disappointed in her lack of enthusiasm, her father said irritably, 'We are all invited. It would be discourteous of you not to come along.'

Adeline sighed, resigned to spending another interminable weekend in someone else's house. Unfortunately there would be no Frances to help see her through. 'Then I suppose I'd better go.'

The Leighton family had a long and distinguished history. It had been Grant's great-grandfather who had bought the extensive Oaklands estate in Kent and settled his family there.

The original house, built in the mid-eighteenth century, had been old-fashioned and cumbersome, and he'd lost no time demolishing it and building anew. The present house was built in a restrained Italianate style, the main block long and two-storeyed. Its classical style, the simplicity of its form, the way it sat solidly in its own secluded woodlands of oak, beech, lime and yew, hiding the house from all unwanted views, and its formal gardens, drew admiration from all who visited the house.

As the coach proceeded along the winding tree-lined drive, Adeline looked out of the window at the façade of the great house. She couldn't help but be impressed. She fixed a smile on her face as servants rushed forward to assist the new arrivals, and they were shown into a memorable entrance hall—Mr Leighton's impressive collection of Italian white marble sculpture, reflecting one of his abiding interests, standing out against the different-coloured marbled walls.

Suddenly a man appeared from one of the rooms and came striding across the hall to greet them. In Adeline's mind a bell of recognition rang.

'Mr Osborne! I'm delighted you could come.'

At the sound of his voice—the deep, well-modulated tones of a gentleman—Adeline stood stock still. Thunderstruck, she stood as one paralysed. Then she lowered her head blindly, her breath coming so rapidly she feared the lacings of her corset would burst. How dreadful! What a terrible thing to happen!

Ever since she had lain with him she had remembered what it had been like to wake up to his manly, shadowy form, standing tall and silent at the side of her bed, his furred chest and broad shoulders void of shirt. She'd had dreams about him—dreams about him kissing her, making love to her—dreams that made her wake up feeling hot and confused. She had thought never to meet this man again—the man she remembered her father telling her wanted to buy Rosehill. And here he was, taller and more elegant than she remembered, and ruggedly virile. And she had to spend two days in his house!

She could only stand and stare as Grant Leighton shook her father's hand. For what seemed an eternity she waited, existing in a state of jarring tension, struggling to appear calm, clinging to her composure as if it were a barrier she could hide behind as, with dread, she waited to be introduced.

'Allow me to present my daughter, Adeline. Paul you already know.'

Adeline was thankful the brim of her bonnet kept most of her face in shadow. If he was taken aback by her rather dour appearance he was too polite to show it. He stooped courteously over her hand and then, as if she were of no importance, turned to Paul and shook his hand.

'Good to see you again, Paul. Glad you could come.' Grant found Paul Marlow irritating, and didn't particularly like him, but seeing as he was his invited guest he forced himself to be civil.

'Your invitation surprised me,' Horace commented.

Grant grinned broadly. 'I knew it would. But I don't give up easily.'

Horace gave one of his rare smiles. 'I knew that from our meeting. How is your mother—forgiven me, I hope?'

'Not a chance. She's more determined than I am.'

'Really? She strikes me as being a remarkable woman. I'd like to meet her.'

'You will. She's determined on it.'

'And I am intrigued.'

'Come—I care little for standing still. Come and sample my brandy.'

'Tea will do. I don't drink. Never touch the stuff.'

'Then I'm sure Paul will appreciate it. I've invited just a few friends to stay. You may know them—or some of them.' He turned to Adeline. 'I'm sure you would like to freshen up after your journey, Miss Osborne. Your maid has already arrived—along with your father's and Paul's valets. Mrs Hayes, my housekeeper, will show you to your room,' he said, with a gesture to indicate the hovering housekeeper.

Adeline couldn't hide her face away any longer. Taking the bull by the horns, and fully expecting the worst, she lifted her head and turned the full force of her gaze on him. Recognition was instantaneous. She saw his reaction go from surprise to abject horror and cold, ruthless fury. His jaw clenched so tightly that a muscle began to throb in his cheek. Thankfully he had his back to her father and Paul, so they couldn't see that anything was amiss.

Meeting his eyes in absolute complicity, she said quietly, 'Thank you, Mr Leighton. I would like that.' Bestowing a smile on Mrs Hayes, she moved away from him and followed her up the stairs.

Chapter Three

Adeline couldn't believe this was happening. It was like re-
living a nightmare, and trying to escape it was pointless.

As she followed Mrs Hayes her knees were shaking so violently she was afraid she'd fall. She tried desperately to keep her
emotions under control so that she could think clearly. Little had
she realised, when she had climbed back into that bed for a night
of passion with a complete stranger, the consequences of her
actions. She had been a naïve and gullible fool. Now she could
not believe she had been so reckless.

The thought of going downstairs and having to behave as if
everything was all right filled her with dread. She considered
pleading illness, but that would be no good. It would only be
putting off the moment. She had to face him sometime.

By the time she went downstairs some sanity had returned,
but panic was heavily mixed with it. When she reached the hall
she saw he was waiting for her in an open doorway, like a guard

on sentry duty, his presence potent and powerful, undermining everything honourable she had ever thought about herself.

How she wished she could sink into the ground and disappear.

Attired in Norfolk jacket and tweed trousers, he had the stamp of implacable authority on his stern features. He really was the handsomest man she had ever seen, but there was no softness in the lean, harsh planes of his cheekbones, the long, aquiline nose and the implacable line of his jaw. He was every inch the aloof, elegant gentleman—the master of all he surveyed.

'Miss Osborne—I would like a word with you in private, if you please.'

Encased in a tight ball of anguish, Adeline paused and looked at him. It was important that she remain calm. In tense silence she moved towards him. He stood aside, and when she had swept past him into the room he closed the door. She was in a library, but she took scant notice of the magnificent leather-bound tomes that lined the walls from floor to ceiling. It seemed like an eternity before he finally spoke.

'Please sit down.'

'I'll stand, if you don't mind.' That way he wouldn't seem so tall and intimidating.

'As you wish. This is unfortunate, Miss Osborne.'

She faced him fully. In place of the cold animosity she had expected his tone was polite and impersonal, his features hard and implacable. 'I agree. I had no idea who you were. If I had I would not have come.'

'And if I had known who you were I would not have invited you.'

'Well, you did. So we'll just have to make the best of things, no matter how unpleasant the situation is for both of us.'

'I agree. So if you are wise, Miss Osborne,' Grant said in a chilling voice, 'you will be careful to avoid me while you are in my house.'

'I have every intention of doing so, Mr Leighton. Believe me, there is nothing that disagrees with me more than having to spend time with you.'

'Then we understand each other perfectly.' Looking at her now—dressed with a sobriety which bordered on the austere—he couldn't believe that anything of an intimate nature had happened between them. With his hand behind his back he moved closer, his eyes like two shards of ice as they fastened on hers. 'Now, listen to me very carefully and heed me well. One way or another we will get through this weekend, and when it is over you will leave here with no one any the wiser. We will not meet again.'

'I sincerely hope not.'

'In the meantime, to allay any suspicion, we will be polite and amiable towards each other. I hope that will not be too difficult.'

'Contrary to your low opinion of me, I have no desire to see either of us disgraced. I shall try to be a good actress.'

'I am certain that among your other brilliant talents is the ability to act. In fact when I recall your past performance I'm sure you will succeed admirably, Miss Osborne,' he commented wryly.

'And how can you know that when you had drunk yourself senseless, Mr Leighton?' she countered, with biting sarcasm.

'That, to my shame, I cannot deny. I am not proud of myself. However, it will not be in either of our interests to let our sordid secret out. How do you think your fiancé would react,' he taunted lightly, 'if he were to learn of—what shall I call it?—your indiscretion?'

She was reluctant to speak of the matter in such a blatant manner, and embarrassment and anger brought a bright flush to Adeline's cheeks. 'I must confess that I really have no idea. But that is for me to worry about, not you.'

'Then let us hope for both our sakes that Paul doesn't find out. When you took it into your head to admit me into your bed instead of kicking me out—which is what I deserved—you placed us both in a difficult situation.'

Anger blazed hot and fierce in Adeline. 'You really are the most loathsome, hypocritical, conceited man I have ever had the misfortune to meet. How dare you have the gall to criticise my behaviour? The fault lies with us both, so don't you dare shift the blame onto me. I have tried to blame you, but my conscience refused to let me. If I am guilty then you are equally so,' she declared wrathfully.

Grant raised a dark brow and considered her flushed cheeks, her green eyes sparking ire with icy arrogance. 'What happened between us was unfortunate. I'm convinced you did not expect a proposal of marriage, financial gain and a life of luxury from what you did—so we will put it behind us.'

'I am not interested in luxury,' Adeline snapped.

'Of course not. I realise your father is an extremely wealthy man. Although I have always harboured the delusion that all girls yearn to snare wealthy husbands, regardless of their upbringing and background.'

'Plain and serious, and with no feminine appeal whatsoever, Mr Leighton, I am not like other girls.'

'No—I realised that when I woke up in your bed.'

Adeline heard the insult in his smoothly worded comment, and almost choked on her anger. 'What you or anyone else thinks of me does not matter. I learned to live with and accept the way I am a long time ago.'

Her admission struck Grant, and brought a strange ache to his heart. Momentarily distracted by the myriad of emotions playing in her expressive eyes, he was staring at her in utter astonishment as he recalled with vivid clarity all the womanly attributes concealed beneath her shapeless, unfashionable brown dress. He recalled seeing her stretched alongside him, as naked as a babe, and he remembered how white her high young breasts were, well-rounded, the nipples as wide and pink as rose petals. Why on earth she chose to wear her glorious wealth of hair in that unflattering, hideous bun at her nape he could not for the life of him imagine.

'You may not make the best of yourself, Miss Osborne, but when I awoke in your bed I did not see you as plain, and you certainly did not lack feminine appeal—and I am prompted to say that despite our differences I suspect we were compatible in bed.'

Adeline stared at him, unable to believe he could describe the passion they had shared with such clinical calm. She failed to notice he had just paid her a compliment, for her fury was so great it was uncontainable.

'You have no idea how hard I have castigated myself for not *"kicking you out"*, as you so aptly put it. It would have saved me all the misery I have endured since. You cannot possibly know how I have hated myself for my own lack of character and restraint for actually being tempted by you. I will never be able to forgive my stupidity.'

Grant put his hands on his lean hips and regarded her coldly. 'I had no idea you would be so hard on yourself,' he said sardonically, raising one dark brow.

'That, Mr Leighton, is putting it mildly. For one night of illicit sex I behaved no better than all the other vacuous women who were guests at Diana Waverley's party, and I cannot deny the awful truth that I sacrificed my principles, my virtue, my honour and my morals.'

'You knew what you were doing.'

'Yes—and unlike you I blame no one but myself. I made you

a gift of my body and you can't even remember. How do you think that makes me feel, Mr Leighton? I will tell you—insulted, dirty and defiled are the only words I can find to describe it. You are heartless, and I cannot believe I let you touch me. It is a shame I will have to live with for the rest of my life.'

Without further ado she turned on her heel and strode to the door, where she turned to deliver her parting salvo. 'One more thing. Just in case you are wondering—although somehow I doubt it's even entered that arrogant head of yours—I am not pregnant. So that's one concern taken care of—and I hope the last.'

Grant watched the door close behind her. My God, she did have a way of knocking a man between the eyes. Devil take it, how had he ever got himself into this situation? Try as he might, he could not completely blame or acquit her. That there might be a child as a result of his stupid, irresponsible behaviour *had* bothered him. Thank God she wasn't pregnant. He stood perfectly still, bemused and unable to shake off what had just transpired—or to believe that the beautiful creature he had made love to had quite unexpectedly turned up at his home when he'd thought he would never set eyes on her again.

Ever since that night his mind had been tortured by her. He could not forget even the smallest detail of her glorious body. Why she chose to dress the way she did, as if for some reason of her own she wanted to make herself inconspicuous, was a puzzle to him. Women with such courage and daring and fire in their veins as Miss Osborne possessed did not try to hide themselves away.

The weekend had lost its shine. Shutting out the reality of Miss Adeline Osborne's presence under his roof was going to be impossible.

Adeline paused at the other side of the door and tried to compose herself before facing the other guests. She was trapped in this house, therefore she was going to have to find some way to remain here in relative harmony for the duration. In order to survive the ordeal she would simply have to ignore Grant Leighton's inexplicable antagonism and take each moment as it came. She would be poised and polite and completely imperturbable, no matter how coldly or how rudely he behaved.

With that settled in her mind, she went to join Paul and her father.

Oaklands was made for grand occasions. By six o'clock the huge table in the dining room was laden with an impressive array of silver cutlery, Crown Derby and exquisite crystal glassware. There were few table decorations, and what there were created a light and graceful effect. Vases were filled with blooms which had been grown in Grant's own hothouses.

Well-presented delicious food would be served, along with many various wines. No guest ever left the table at Oaklands with less than complete satisfaction.

Two beautiful crystal chandeliers were suspended from the high ceiling in the large drawing room. One wall was a wide sweep of windows, with French doors thrown open to the scented breezes of the garden and a broad stone terrace ablaze with pots of flowering shrubs, affording breathtaking views of the manicured lawns, the magnificent gardens giving way to a lake and surrounding countryside.

Grant moved among his guests—twelve in all—with the confident ease of a man well assured of his masculinity and his own worth. He conversed politely, seeming to give each his full attention, but the major part of it was concentrated on the door, as he waited for Miss Adeline Osborne to make an appearance.

Adeline entered the room feeling more than a little trepidation. Directly ahead of her was the impressive figure of their host, and he was looking straight at her. With a defiant toss of her head she lifted her chin and walked forward between Paul and her father.

Grant disappeared for several minutes, and when he returned had an elderly lady in turquoise silk on his arm. They circulated, laughing and chatting to guests, and eventually crossed the room to where Horace Osborne stood with a rather stiff-looking Paul and an apprehensive Adeline. When Grant introduced the lady to Horace she eagerly extended a thin hand in greeting, giving him all her attention.

Small, trim and white-haired, Hester Leighton gave the physical impression of age, yet her twinkling blue eyes and easy, willing smile were the epitome of eternal youth.

'I am so pleased to meet you, Mr Osborne—and Mr Marlow and your charming daughter.'

Horace bowed politely over her hand. 'Likewise, Mrs Leighton.'

She smiled sympathetically at Adeline. 'How young you look, Miss Osborne. I'm afraid you're stuck with a lot of old fossils for the weekend. I don't think there's anyone here under the age of forty—excluding Grant, of course,' she said, smiling fondly at her son.

'Oh, I'm sure I'll survive, Mrs Leighton,' Adeline replied, for the most part keeping her gaze averted from their host.

'Less of the old fossils,' Grant chided mockingly. Speaking to Horace, he said, 'Mother is still youthful, despite having raised four children.'

Horace arched his brows, seemingly surprised. 'Four? And are they all present this evening?'

'No,' Hester replied. 'Just Grant—and my daughter Lettie will be along later. My youngest son Roland is in India with his regiment. I had a letter just last week, informing me he will be coming home for Christmas—as will my daughter Anna and her family, from Ireland. It's all very exciting—a Christmas to remember. It will be the first Christmas we have been together as a family for many years. Do you have other children, Mr Osborne?'

Horace shook his head. 'Sadly, no. My wife died when Adeline was a child. I never remarried.'

Hester smiled at Adeline. 'It's a pity Lettie isn't here—but she will be later on. At least I fully expect her to be. She's only just arrived home from London, so she will miss dinner, I'm afraid.' Her gaze was drawn back to Horace. 'I really am so glad you came.' She turned to Grant. 'You have seated me next to Mr Osborne at dinner, I hope, Grant?'

He smiled indulgently. 'As you requested, Mother.'

'Good. We have so much to discuss.'

Horace smiled. Her light-hearted charm was infectious. 'I hope you don't hold a grudge because of my refusal to sell Rosehill?' he questioned.

'Of course not. I'm disappointed, naturally, but I never hold grudges.'

'I'm relieved to hear it.'

Mrs Leighton was as gracious and kind as she was witty and warm. Adeline was surprise to see that her father was captivated. Her surprised deepened as his face took on a rare sparkle of humour.

At that moment the butler announced that dinner was about to be served.

Mrs Leighton turned at Horace. 'Will you be so kind as to escort me into dinner, Mr Osborne?'

He offered her his arm. 'It will be my pleasure, Mrs Leighton.'

'Oh, you must call me Hester. We are very informal at Oaklands, you know.'

Horace's eyes twinkled. 'And I would like it if you would call me Horace.'

The rest of the evening passed in a relaxed and congenial atmosphere. Adeline listened, and conversed when spoken to, and smiled when it was appropriate. Often when she looked in Grant Leighton's direction she found him watching her with a strange sort of intensity she could not define—as if he were making a study of her person.

After dinner everyone gathered in the drawing room to partake in various amusements. Grant leaned on the piano, listening to Mrs Forrester play some Chopin nocturnes—both she and her banker husband were his guests from London. She was a clever, interesting woman Adeline had conversed with at length at dinner, and she was extremely proficient on the keyboard.

Adeline surreptitiously watched Grant's tall, lounging figure. His head was bent low as he listened attentively to the music. Without warning he turned, and Adeline was caught in the act of staring at him. His gaze captured hers, and a strange, unfathomable smile tugged at the corner of his mouth. Immediately she jerked her gaze away and looked down at her book.

Unable to resist speaking to her, Grant went and perched on the arm of the sofa where she sat, looking down at her. He had noticed that her face in repose had a vulnerability to it that was startling, as if pain were familiar to her. She could not have been aware of her expression or she would have been more guarded. Now she peered up at him in surprise through her spectacle lenses.

'I think you may have lost your way, Mr Leighton. Please don't feel you have to speak to me.'

'I don't. I suppose we must play out the farce to its conclusion.'

'It looks like it. But do you have to be so disagreeable all the time?'

'I intend to continue being disagreeable while you are in my house.'

Adeline sighed and closed her book. 'It might please you to know that I am paying dearly for my lack of judgement—which is only right. And even though I am now in the most dire straits because of it, I suppose that, too, is justice.'

'Exactly what do you mean by that?' Grant asked, in spite of himself. 'Something to do with your lack of loyalty to your fiancé, perhaps?' he mocked lazily, watching tension and emotions play across her expressive face.

'Either that or his loyalty to me.' She grimaced. 'Paul doesn't know the meaning of the word.'

Her tone was scathing, and her reply left Grant puzzled. Despite his resolution not to give a damn what her problems were, he was a little disturbed by her answer—but he didn't want to enlarge on it.

Sensing he was softening a little, Adeline dinted her pride and presented her advantage. 'Mr Leighton—'

'Grant.'

'What?'

'Please feel free to call me Grant. Everyone does. It will seem odd if you don't.'

'Very well—then you must call me Adeline.'

'Please continue—Adeline. You were about to say something?'

'Yes. Surely nothing that has happened between us should make us behave badly towards each other?'

Grant lifted an arrogant sleek brow. 'No?'

'Neither of us were hurt.'

'We weren't?'

'No. So there is no reason why we can't be cordial to one another—for the time I am here.' She gave him a small beguiling smile and, removing her glasses, looked at him directly. 'Believe me, if I could I would leave. But I can't—so we are stuck with each other.'

Her smile was so disarming that Grant experienced the first crack in his defence. Her clothes may be severe—almost puritan—but her face threw out a challenge. It was a face with a capacity for merriment and cheerful cynicism, and there was impudence in the tilt of her nose. Suddenly he was surprised to find he wasn't nearly as immune to her as he wanted to be.

'It seems like it,' he replied. 'You know, you look so much better without your spectacles.'

'So do you,' she replied with a trace of sarcasm.

Grant laughed, not in the least offended. Without her spectacles to distort his view, he thought how beautiful her eyes were—green and large, and surrounded by thick black lashes. When he had first seen her earlier he had thought how unattractive she was, and had found it difficult to believe he had found anything striking about her when he had awoken in her bed. But looking at her now, bathed in a golden light, her lips—sensitive lips, full, sensuous and sweet—her expression soft and alluring, and looking very young, he was forced to revise his opinion.

'I would also like to remind you that like everyone else I am your guest, so I would appreciate being treated like one and not as an intruder. You have hardly been the soul of amiability towards me.'

Grant tilted his head to one side, studying her. He was considering whether or not there would be an advantage in putting their hostility aside. Concluding that there would, he nodded in agreement. 'Very well. I want the time that you are here to be pleasant for both of us, and for the weekend to run smoothly for all concerned. I will make every attempt to be civil.'

'Are you sure you're up to the challenge?'

'I shall prevail.' Suddenly he smiled at her, and that smile was as bright as the sun coming out from behind a cloud.

Completely caught up in the heady power of that smile, Adeline warmed to him, appreciating the considerable charm he could wield without any effort at all. 'Thank you.'

'It may interest you to know that Mrs Forrester has been singing your praises. It would appear that you have hidden talents, Adeline. She says you are an extremely knowledgeable young woman who can converse on most subjects. She was delighted to find herself in the company of another clever, intelligent woman.'

'That's nice of her.' Adeline's smile became mischievous as she gave what he'd said some thought. 'Clever and intelligent? Oh, dear—for an intelligent woman I'm not doing very well. Look at the mess I made of things at Westwood Hall. My life hasn't been the same since.'

'It's a little late in the day to start thinking about that, but you'll soon get it back in order—when you marry Paul Marlow.'

Adeline looked at him and tried to feel some enthusiasm, but failed. 'I suspect you don't like Paul.'

'You suspect right.'

'Then why did you invite him?'

'Because I was afraid your father wouldn't come otherwise.'

'So you could try to persuade him to sell Rosehill?'

Grant nodded.

'He won't, you know.'

'I know that. He was most definite about it. But it means a lot to my mother,' he said, with a teasing twinkle in his eyes, 'and I couldn't deny her the opportunity to use her persuasive charm on him.'

'Father never succumbs to charm.'

'And he's not an easy man to live with I imagine.'

'Not really. He's always worked hard, and he has become set in his ways—he always believes he's right.' She smiled, then looked away. 'He's terribly strict, but not cruel. He's the kind of father who allows me every indulgence, except the freedom to choose my own husband. Not that there's anything unusual in that. Most fathers are stiff and virtuous, and keep a very short rein on their daughters, regardless of how plain they are.'

Grant lifted an eyebrow, surprised at her outspokenness. 'And do you regard yourself as plain?'

'Oh, absolutely. Still,' she said, laughing softly, 'since Mrs Forrester says I am intelligent and clever, I don't suppose I can have everything—and if I had to choose between the two then I would choose intelligence over everything else.'

'Then I must introduce you to my sister Lettie. I think you will find you have much in common. Speaking of which—' he said, looking beyond her towards the door, where there seemed to be some kind of a disturbance. He rose to see better the cause of it.

Lettie's entry was like a whirlwind coming through the door— a fresh, airy breeze sweeping through the house. Adeline saw a slim young woman clad in rose-coloured satin. Bestowing smiles on everyone she passed. The new arrival made a beeline for her brother, and with her came a freshness and vitality that shone.

Grant smiled tolerantly as she threw her arms around his neck and hugged him tightly. 'Dear Lord, don't throttle me, Lettie,' he complained, but his firm lips were stretched in a grin as he held her at arm's length and surveyed her. 'You're looking well.'

'It's been a whole month, and I've been working very hard, I'll have you know, so I must look a sight—but bless you for the compliment. It's lovely to see you again—and Marjorie sends her regards, by the way. I've missed you. Have you missed me?'

'Like a bad headache,' he drawled, pleased to see her nevertheless.

Adeline was more than a little charmed by Lettie. She smiled a great deal, and her bodily movements were as lively as her expression. Dark-haired, with deep blue eyes, a pure complexion, a waist the requisite handspan and a dazzling smile, there was no doubt in her mind that this was Grant Leighton's sister. They were so alike.

'I'm sorry for the disturbance. I do hope you'll forgive me for being late.'

'You're always late, Lettie.'

'I only got back from London tonight, and I've had simply heaps to do. You're not cross with me, are you, Grant?'

Grant grinned at her, slipping an arm about her narrow waist and hugging her close. He was clearly very fond of his sister.

'I was none too pleased that you missed dinner, but at twenty-three years old you're a bit too old for me to take you across my knee, Lettie.'

'You always were a tyrant,' Lettie teased, laughing gaily.

The love in Lettie's voice was discernible to Adeline. It was clear to her that Grant and his sister enjoyed a warm family relationship of a kind Adeline had never known and never would.

Grant turned and looked down at Adeline. 'Lettie, this is Adeline Osborne. She is here with her father and her fiancé, Paul Marlow.'

Adeline stood up and smiled at Grant's sister, finding a pair of fearless sparkling eyes scrutinising her curiously. Then a delighted smile dawned on her pretty face and she clasped Adeline's hand in a warm gesture of greeting.

'I can't tell you how pleased I am to meet you—or how relieved I am that I will have someone nearer to my own age to talk to. Grant has a disagreeable habit of inviting people to his parties who are either too long in the tooth or have nothing of interest to talk about—although to be fair to them I have known nearly every lady and gentleman present for most of my life, and they are all extremely nice people.'

'My sister is a rebel, Adeline,' Grant provided with mild humour. 'Liberal and free-thinking, and she has strong opinions about most things. She is an independent young woman who flouts convention disgracefully. She argues passionately about rights for women and she has a habit of championing the unfortunate.'

'Really?' Adeline smiled, glancing at Lettie with something akin to admiration. 'How commendable.'

'You may think so. Mother is remarkably tolerant of her earnest convictions—me less so. Take care not to offend Adeline, Lettie,' Grant warned with mock gravity. 'She is a gently reared young lady who spends most of her time buried in the country and has probably never heard of the Women's Movement and Suffragists.'

His words were highly provocative to a sensitive Adeline. Her eyes snapped to his. 'On the contrary. Because I spend most of my time "buried in the country" it does not mean that I am stupid. I have heard of the Women's Movement and I am full of admiration for what it is trying to achieve. As for myself, I have many accomplishments. I am well read, and conversant in several languages. I am also a capable horsewoman. I swim and fish, and I excel at fencing—a talent you might like to test some time, Mr Leighton.'

He smiled broadly, his strong white teeth gleaming from between his parted lips. 'I might consider it,' he replied, open to the challenge and deliberately baiting her. 'But are you good enough, I am prompted to ask?'

She raised an eyebrow. 'As to that, I invite you to be the judge.'

'Then I shall look forward to disarming you.'

Lettie laughed good-humouredly. 'You'd better watch out for Grant, Adeline. He's quite a ladies' man.'

Grant gave his sister a dark look. 'And your only diversion is to shock and annoy me, Lettie. I'm seriously thinking of putting a muzzle on you. Your manners are atrocious. That said, I will leave you two to get acquainted. I've neglected my other guests long enough.'

Lettie placed a restraining hand on his arm. 'Grant—wait.' He paused and glanced at her. 'Will you be riding in the morning?' He nodded. 'Good. I'll see you at the stables at seven.' She laughed when he raised a dubious brow. 'I won't be late, I promise.'

'I'll believe that when I see it. You're always late.' His gaze shifted to Adeline. 'What about you, Adeline? If you ride as well as you say you fence, then perhaps you would care to join us? Most of the guests will be along, and I have several splendid mounts.'

'Thank you. I'd love to join you.'

He nodded, and after excusing himself went to circulate among his other guests.

Immediately Lettie pulled Adeline down onto the sofa and began chatting animatedly.

Adeline found the conversation extremely stimulating, and joined in with an enthusiasm that surprised her. She listened in fascination to Lettie's visionary ideas about how one day the dark days of repression would end for women and they would overcome the stigma of inferiority and become completely liberated. Adeline didn't believe it, of course, but she liked to think Lettie was right.

When Lettie accused most men of being tyrants, Adeline found herself glancing across the room at Paul. In conversation with an elderly gentleman, he looked morose. Meeting her gaze, he regarded her with the air of an inquisitor. Looking away quickly, Adeline was inclined to think Lettie was right in her assertion, which boded ill for the future.

Suddenly Paul appeared in front of her. She hadn't even seen him approach.

'Paul—I believe you are acquainted with Grant's sister?'

Paul bowed his head politely. 'I am. It's a pleasure to see you again, Miss Leighton. Adeline, have you forgotten that you promised to partner me at bridge?'

'Bridge?' Lettie remarked amusedly. 'Oh, but Adeline and I are just getting to know each other, and we have much to talk about. I'm sure you can find someone else to partner you, Paul.'

Paul was not amused, Adeline could tell. He had been cold, distant and argumentative ever since they had arrived, which she put down to the company and lack of female attention.

A hardness entered Paul's eyes, and they narrowed on her with censorious annoyance. 'Adeline, are you coming?' he persisted.

'No, Paul. Suddenly I have an aversion to the game.'

He looked most put out. 'You never have before.'

Her smile was defiant. 'I have tonight,' she replied, reflecting that she would need to be prepared for a scolding from him later.

Normally Paul would have insisted, and she would have relented—but, not wishing to make a scene, he had to accept it. He thought—quite correctly—that she had come under the influence of Miss Leticia Leighton—for it was well known that she held some ridiculously extreme radical views regarding the rights of women. Although he had also noticed of late that Adeline seemed to have developed a subdued aversion to him, which was both a mystery and a source of irritation. Because he had never had any difficulty getting on with the opposite sex, he was forced, therefore, to set the blame entirely down to her, and hope things would improve when she became his wife.

'Very well. Will you be riding in the morning?'

'Yes. I'm looking forward to it enormously. Will you?'

'Of course.' So saying, he excused himself and walked away.

'Dear me,' Lettie murmured, her eyes following Paul across the room. 'Why on earth are you marrying him?'

Normally Adeline would have been uncomfortable with such a pertinent remark, yet she was so amazed at Lettie's outspokeness that she wasn't offended by it in the least. 'You don't like Paul, do you, Lettie?'

She shrugged. 'Not much.' Lettie glanced at Adeline with concern. 'I hope you don't mind me speaking my mind. I always do. Mother says it's one of my bad points.'

'Not at all. But do you mind if I ask why you find him disagreeable?'

'Well, for a start he's absolutely convinced of his own superiority. There's also something secretive about his manner which makes me uneasy—and besides, he's much too old for you.'

Adeline sighed. Lettie was right, of course, but out of loyalty and duty—more to her father than to Paul—she made no comment. 'Father doesn't think so. He considers it a suitable match.'

'And you go along with that?'

'It's easier than arguing with him.'

'Really, Adeline! My first impression of you was that you are a fighter. You must stand up for yourself.'

Adeline was amused by this. She was completely taken with the easy friendliness of Grant Leighton's sister, and accepted the feeling as mutual. 'Are you saying I should disobey my father?'

Lettie seemed to give it some thought before saying, 'Yes—yes, in this instance I am.'

* * *

Feeling restless and despondent, and unable to sleep, and being a great reader, Adeline looked for her book. When she was unable to find it she realised she had left it on the sofa in the drawing room. The hour was late and, thinking that everyone would have retired to their rooms long since, she pulled her robe over her nightgown and left her room. The house was deathly still, and only the chimes of a distant clock tolling one o'clock broke the silence. She glanced about her, peering into shadows and dark recesses as she went down the stairs.

Grant was in the drawing room, enjoying some time alone before going to bed. The room was in semi-darkness, with only a couple of lamps left burning. Having removed his jacket, he was seated before the dying fire with his legs stretched out in front of him. Looking through the open door and into the hall, he was amazed to see Adeline move smoothly down the stairs, looking like a fantasy—flowing white in ribbons and lace.

Immediately he was on his feet and moving quietly to the door. Adeline turned and gasped when he suddenly stepped in front of her. His bold silver-grey eyes raked her quite openly.

'Ah, another night owl.'

His voice, as soft and smooth as the finest silk, stroked Adeline like a caress. She felt its impact even as she realised how intently he was studying her face. His potent virility made her feel entirely too vulnerable.

'Oh! I'm sorry. I didn't mean to disturb you.' Adeline flushed. 'I came to look for my book. I believe I left it on the couch.'

Grant stepped back and swept his arm inward in a silent invitation for her to proceed. Adeline complied, and Grant watched in fascination the play of firelight through her clothing. His breath caught in his throat as the outline of her long, lithe body was subtly betrayed through her flimsy nightdress.

His mind returned to the memory of that night, and her beautiful figure and glorious long legs. He was quickly brought back to the present when she retrieved her book from where it was in danger of disappearing behind a cushion and came back to him.

Adeline was uneasy. As he dragged his eyes upward from her body to her face his gaze was far too intent, thoughtful and serious. He was too close and too masculine. She averted her gaze, hot-faced and perplexed.

Grant knew enough about Adeline Osborne to know that she spelt trouble to him, but there was something unusual and provocative about her—something that stirred him and drew him to her. Reaching out, he ran a finger lightly down the curve of her cheek. Pausing at her mouth, with his thumb he traced the soft fullness of her lower lip.

Sensations of unexpected pleasure stirred within her. She trembled, and could almost feel the bold thrust of him between her thighs. Uncomfortable at the knowing look in his eyes, and sensing he was on the verge of kissing her, in order to retain her sanity she took a step back.

'Please don't,' she whispered.

'Why? Does my touch offend you?' He smiled knowingly. 'Spare me your maidenly protests. It didn't, as I recall, on one occasion.'

'An occasion we both agreed never to speak of.'

'There's nothing wrong with talking about it between ourselves—although you have the advantage.'

'I do?'

'You remember everything we did, whereas I…'

'You were completely foxed,' she reminded him sharply. 'That is your problem, not mine.'

'Are you not curious to find out if what you experienced is

still as good as it was then? Didn't you say that it was the most wonderful thing that had ever happened to you?'

'Perhaps it was the danger…the risk that made it so exciting,' she whispered lamely, in an attempt to find an excuse to explain why she had told him that.

'Whatever it was, I am curious to discover what I missed.'

What he was suggesting startled Grant, and made him doubt his sanity. Although, having made the suggestion, he was beginning to see no great harm in it.

To Adeline, his statement confused her. She stared at him in dazed wonder. Self-conscious, she let her gaze dwell on his finely moulded lips, watching as a faint smile, a challenging smile, lifted them at the corners.

'What do you say, Adeline? Are you afraid to find out?' he asked, his voice low and husky. Reaching out, he fastened his hands on the curve of her exceedingly trim waist and drew her close. 'Finding you floating through my house at this late hour looking as you do, you are too tempting by half.'

In her confused state of loneliness and longing it was all too much. She made no protest when he bent his head and took her lips in a feather-light kiss, warm and inviting her to respond. Paralysed, she felt all the passion he had shown her before sear through her body. She couldn't believe it was happening again. She felt that familiar burst of exquisite delight as she let him hold her in the complete lassitude of surrender.

Raising his head, Grant looked down at her upturned face. It was soft in the lamplight, her eyes large and dark. His lips lifted lazily. 'Is that how you remember it?'

Unwilling to surrender her secret memories of tenderness and stormy passion, she kept her gaze on his lips and murmured, 'Something like that.'

'Care to try it again?' Grant invited, still willing to indulge in a few more pleasurable moments—so long as there was no pretence that it was anything but that. 'Why don't you show me how you remember it?' he teased as his lips came closer. 'Show me…' His hands slipped beneath the heavy wealth of her hair and moved round her nape, sensually stroking it as his mouth felt the softness of her cheek and the disturbing lasciviousness of her lips. She was a woman of such contrasts.

Seduced by his kiss and caressing hands, Adeline clung to him, sliding slowly into a dark abyss of desire as once again she felt the wanton, primitive sensations jarring along her nerves. The feeling suddenly frightened her. She drew back, her heart beating sickeningly fast.

'I think you forget yourself,' she whispered. 'You shouldn't be doing this—not again. Do you forget that my father and my fiancé are guests in your house? What you said to me that night at Westwood Hall led me to presume you are not so fussy over where and when you accept favours from a certain type of woman. I am not like that. Despite what happened between us, my father brought me up decently. I am nothing like the women of your experience—like Diana Waverley.'

A sensual smile played about his lips. 'How quickly you become defensive. It is precisely what *did* happen between us not so very long ago that makes you not so very different. You can't change that, nor what you are, Adeline,' he said lazily, his arms still encircling her, not letting her go. 'A decently reared young woman would surely have been scandalised on finding a strange man about to get into bed with her. She would have shouted for help, alerted the rest of the household. You did not react that way, however hard you protest.'

Adeline gasped at his arrogance. 'And what am I?' she said bitterly. 'Do you see what I did as an open invitation to seduce me whenever you get the opportunity? Believe that because I gave myself to you once I'm fair sport to be ravished when the fancy takes you?' And with his expertise Adeline had no doubt that he would succeed, feeling as she did about him. She was drawn to him, and felt unwilling to resist.

'I've no intention of taking you here and now. But don't doubt my needs, Adeline,' he murmured softly, drawing her closer. 'Or my intention of repeating what we did. But not here. Not like this. When the opportunity arises it will not be a quick lift of your skirts in a dark corner—delightful though that prospect might be.'

Adeline stared at him, registering all that he implied. His handsome face was all planes and shadows and his eyes glittered sharply. 'You shouldn't be speaking to me like this,' she whispered. She knew it was wrong, and yet she could not deny that it was so wickedly exciting.

Pleasurably wanton feelings rippled through her at the memory of how she had felt when he had made love to her, her eyes glazing slightly as she conjured up the magic of his hands on her soft flesh, cupping her breasts. Instead of trying to stifle her feelings when he bent his head to cover her lips once again, she allowed them to flood through her. She received his kiss with innocent passion, and the offering of her mouth caused Grant to seize it in a kiss of melting hunger that deepened to scorching demand.

Lust roared through him, and he splayed a hand across her spine, forcing her into contact with his own hard, aroused body. Automatically his hands pressed her buttocks against his arousal, and then, suddenly aware of what he was doing, he tore his mouth from hers and stared down at her as he tried to regain control of his senses.

'Well? Was it the same as the last time I kissed you?'

She nodded. 'And some more.'

They pulled apart and stood facing each other, Adeline still clutching her book to her chest. Grant was debating whether to kiss her again, or try to pass the matter off as some light occurrence, when a male voice suddenly erupted from the doorway.

Chapter Four

'Good Lord, Adeline! What's going on?'

Adeline spun round in mindless panic, her gaze flying to Paul. Mortified to the very depths of her being by the realisation that he had almost caught her in Grant's arms, she braced herself for a tirade on the subject of what Paul would consider to be her disgraceful behaviour. She stood and looked at him, rigid with shock. Meeting his eyes, somehow she managed to calm herself. Afraid of rousing some conflict between the two men, she could not let him see the flush of passion on her cheeks, or the warm light of desire in her eyes.

Paul's alert, suspicious gaze moved from Adeline in her night attire to Grant.

'Paul—I—I was just…' She cast a nervous, pleading look at Grant and found him regarding Paul not with shame but with irritated amusement. Paul's face hardened and he threw her a reproachful glance. Dear Lord, she thought, if he were to know the truth... But, no matter what was going through his mind, the last thing he would want would be a scene—he hated the vulgarity of scenes. As long as you didn't put a thing into words, it didn't exist.

'Adeline came to retrieve a book she left in the drawing room earlier,' Grant said, in a voice that struck Adeline as amazingly calm, considering what had just transpired between them. 'She was just returning to bed.'

Paul looked sternly from Grant to Adeline. 'That is no excuse. You should not be wandering about in your night attire.'

'I was unable to sleep, and didn't think anyone would be about at this hour.'

'Then you were wrong,' Paul retorted stony-faced as he glanced at Grant. 'Excuse us, will you? I'll escort Adeline back to her room.'

Bidding Grant goodnight, Adeline left the room without a backward glance. Not until Paul had left her outside her door and she had closed it did she lean against it and close her eyes, her mind racing beneath the force of what had just occurred.

Grant stood for several moments after they had left, thinking about Adeline Osborne and the impact she had made on him. She was a young woman of many contrasts. Possessed of a bright and brittle intelligence, stunningly direct, polite but candid, she also had a provoking sensuality and was brimming with deeply felt emotions.

Despite having lost her virginity to him, there was no disguising the fact that she was still an innocent girl whose life was slowly pushing her out into the heady stream of sexual maturity—like a boat on the Thames River. She had no idea how desirable she was, how captivating—for, unlike Diana, she had not learned—nor ever would—how to use her attraction cruelly or cynically, simply for the pleasure of seeing her admiring swains dancing on a string.

Adeline rose early the following morning. It was a fine, sunny day. Wearing a tweed riding jacket over a silk shirt, and a bowler clamped to her head, her hair secured at her nape by a red ribbon, she went to the stables with a spring in her step. Apart from the grooms saddling horses, few people were about. She was pleased to see Lettie, who had ridden over from Newhill Lodge, where she lived with her mother.

'Glad you decided to join us,' Lettie said, striding across the yard, her dark blue riding habit flattering her trim figure.

'I always like to ride early when I'm at home. Have you seen Paul, Lettie? He said he would be riding.'

'About ten minutes ago. He was already mounted and ready to go. He rode off on his own towards Ashford—which isn't half as pleasant as riding through the park.'

Adeline's head jerked up. 'Ashford? Oh, I see.' To hide her suspicion and sudden anger, she turned away. To her knowledge Westwood Hall was between Oaklands and Ashford, and she strongly suspected that Paul was calling on Diana. Deliberately shoving the matter to the back of her mind to be dealt with later, she determined not to let thoughts of Paul spoil her ride, and concentrated all her attention on the next hour.

Her eyes lit on the rather splendid chestnut stallion with a black mane one of the grooms was leading out of the stalls. The horse whinnied as she approached him with her hand outstretched, and nuzzled her with affection, blowing his warm breath onto her cheek.

'What a magnificent animal,' she breathed, running her gloved hand over his coat, which rippled like satin. Eyes aglow, she turned to Lettie with unconcealed excitement. 'Please say I can ride him?'

'If you like—but I must tell you that he's highly strung and not easy to handle—he'll also bite you as soon as look at you. His name's Crispin, by the way.'

'He won't bite me—will you, boy?' Adeline whispered, rubbing his nose. 'I'm not afraid of him. I'm sure we'll get along nicely.' She turned to a groom. 'Saddle him for me, will you? And I don't ride side-saddle,' she was quick to add.

The groom gave her an appalled look before turning to Lettie for permission.

Seeing Adeline was determined, and that it was plain she was comfortable with the horse, Lettie laughed and nodded. 'Do as she says, Ted. I'm sure we don't have to worry about Miss Osborne falling off.'

When the horse was saddled, Ted linked his hands to receive a well-polished boot and give her a leg up. She was up in a flash, her feet feeling for the stirrups. Ted's eyes almost popped out of their sockets when he saw she was wearing buff-coloured breeches beneath the skirt of her riding habit. He'd never seen anything like it.

'You won't mind if I ride off by myself, will you, Lettie? I'm dying for a good gallop.' Feeling the thrill of excitement, the throbbing expectancy of the ride to come, Adeline was unaware that Grant had just entered the stableyard, and had paused in astonishment on seeing Adeline being hoisted onto the huge stallion.

With no idea where she was going, except that it was away from the house, and oblivious to the hush that had descended on the stableyard, putting her heels to the stallion's sides she was away.

'Did my eyes deceive me, Lettie?' Grant murmured, coming

to stand beside his sister, his eyes glued to the disappearing speck moving across the park.

'No. That was Miss Adeline Osborne. She insisted on riding astride—and she was wearing breeches beneath her skirt.' Lettie smiled, unable to hide her admiration. 'There's nothing commonplace about *that* young lady. She certainly doesn't conform to the usual mode of riding. She was eager to be away—as you will have seen for yourself.'

'Without a groom?'

'The way she was riding that horse, she'd leave him standing.'

'I am intrigued by our Miss Osborne, Lettie—intrigued and fascinated. I must see which way this phenomenon has taken.' Without more ado Grant shouted for his horse to be saddled immediately.

The stallion was fresh, his spirits high. Adeline set an easy pace, but she had her hands full for the first ten minutes. When he settled down, she bent to his ear. 'Now, let's see what you can really do.' And she gave him his lead.

Nostrils flared wide, Crispin swiftly exploded under her. Sure-footed, he moved like a dream, easy and fluid. Adeline laughed, the trees becoming a blur as they fairly flew over the ground. Her skirts ballooned over the horse's flanks, to reveal her long breechered legs, and her mane of deep red hair flew out behind her, her red ribbon flapping like a kite. Cresting a hill, she slowed him to a canter, exhilarated by the ride.

Hearing hooves thundering over the turf, she paused and looked back to see who it was. Recognising Grant, perched atop a great black horse which showed all the compressed power of good breeding, she waited as he approached. He looked so dapper in his tan coat, fawn breeches and waistcoat. He wasn't wearing a hat, and his hair flopped over his brow. Recalling what had passed between them the previous night—the way he had held her and kissed her, and how her body had responded just like that other time—she felt her spirits soar as she looked at his darkly handsome face.

Drawing rein beside her, Grant smiled broadly, his white teeth gleaming from between his parted lips. He'd watched her ride across the park, seen she was light in the saddle, handling the usually difficult mount with expert skill. His eyes appraised the long, lean legs encased in breeches astride the stallion. She was full of energy and emotional vigour, her cheeks poppy-red and her eyes sparkling green, and in that moment he thought she was the most striking-looking woman he had ever seen in his life. He was fascinated by this extraordinary young woman.

'Well, young lady, you are full of surprises. If my eyes do not deceive me, there is not much anyone can teach *you* about a horse. One can tell a born rider by watching the way he…' He paused and smiled. 'Or she. After watching you ride, I can see you certainly speak their language.'

Seeing the way Grant controlled his animal effortlessly, without thought, as fluidly and as softly as the horse himself moved, Adeline was thinking the same thing about him. She returned his smile, and for a moment there seemed to be only the two of them in the whole world.

'Thank you. I'll take that as a compliment—although he is a splendid horse, almost as fast as my own beloved Monty.' From beneath carefully lowered lids, Adeline slanted him a long, considering look. 'Shouldn't you be with your other guests?'

'Lettie will take care of them—although most of them won't surface until mid-morning. When I saw you riding out on Crispin I couldn't resist coming after you.'

'I love riding.'

He quirked a brow in amusement. 'Oh, I can see that. Do you hunt?'

'Absolutely.'

He grinned. 'A girl after my own heart.'

She darted him a sideways glance. 'Really? And I was sure you were wishing you'd never laid eyes on me.'

'Shall I tell you when I did first set eyes on you?'

'I already know. It was when I was boarding the train to Westwood Hall. You got off at Sevenoaks. When I dropped my book you picked it up.'

His eyes widened with surprise. 'I remember. Was that you?'

She nodded, giving him a puzzled look. 'If that wasn't the time you were referring to, then when *did* you first see me?'

'When I was staying with an old schoolfriend of mine— Frederick Baxter. I saw you out riding early one morning— dressed as you are now. I'd no idea who you were—until now. You were riding a grey stallion. I remember it was a huge beast—I thought at the time it was too big and spirited for a woman to ride, but you soon put me right. You are one of the most skilled riders I'd ever seen mounted. I can see you are no ordinary young woman. I'm impressed by your prowess.'

'I had no idea I was being watched.'

His grin was boyishly disarming. 'How could you? You were flying like the wind at the time.' A crooked smile curled his lips as he let his leisurely perusal sweep over her. 'Nice breeches, by the way.'

Grant's smiling eyes captured hers and held them prisoner until she felt a warmth suffuse her cheeks. 'I always wear them when I ride. They're so practical.'

'I'm sure they are. I also remember what you look like without them.'

Her flush deepened and she lowered her eyes, seeing the hard muscles of his thighs flex beneath his own tight-fitting breeches as he sat his horse. 'You do remember something about that night, then?'

'I never forget what a woman looks like when she is naked in my bed, Adeline.'

'My bed,' she was quick to remind him, the light of mischief dancing in her eyes.

'Very well—your bed,' he amended with a low chuckle. 'Where's your fiancé this morning, by the way? I thought he was to join us.'

'Paul rode out early—in the direction of Ashford.' Briefly their gazes met, and Adeline wondered if he knew the nature of the relationship that existed between Paul and Diana. The direct look he gave her told her he did.

'Ah—I see.'

'Yes, so do I.' She wondered if he minded, and decided not to ask.

Grant's horse was becoming restive. 'Come—I'll race you back to the stables.' His eyes twinkled roguishly and his mouth curved in a devilish grin. 'I'll beat you.'

Adeline tossed back her head and threw him a confident smile. 'I don't think so—you'll have to be content with second-best.'

'Never,' he declared with laughing certainty.

'You're very bold with your challenge, sir,' she stated, a flicker of mischief in her eyes.

'When I'm allowed to be I'm not easily dissuaded, and I usually take the initiative when I know I can win.'

'So it would seem—with a race.'

His eyes glowed and he smiled at her. 'With everything, Adeline.'

Adeline did not dare to contradict him, nor ask him to enlarge on his statement. 'When you lose I'll be magnanimous in my victory, I promise.'

'Adeline,' he threatened, in a soft, ominous tone, while his eyes danced with amusement, 'if I lose you'd better ride for your life in the opposite direction.'

'You'll never catch me.'

Grant gave a shout of laughter as he kicked his horse into action. 'If that's your game, Miss Osborne, lead on. I will welcome your attention and the challenge—and I'll make you eat your words.'

Together their horse's hooves thundered over the hard green turf in long, ground-devouring strides as each fought to take the lead. They vaulted a low hedge effortlessly, then another with flourish. At one point Adeline gained a lead on Grant, but he soon closed the gap.

They rode at a breakneck pace. Leaning forward, Adeline felt exhilaration and jubilation, at one with her mount. Her hair, losing its ribbon, became unbound, and the glorious tresses unfurled like a pennant behind her. They soared over a ditch in perfect unison, and then turned their mounts at full speed towards the open stableyard gates.

'Good God, what a ride!' Grant exclaimed with an admiring laugh, his horse having finished alongside Crispin. Swinging his leg over the horse's back, he dismounted and strode to Adeline as she landed on both feet in front of him. Her colour was gloriously high and she had a wide smile on her full lips, her eyes liquid-bright. The sight of her almost stole his breath.

'Miss Osborne, you are quite the most outrageous, outstanding rider I have ever had the privilege to ride with. A draw,' he declared.

'No, it wasn't,' she objected laughingly, determined not to let him off. 'I beat you by a head and you know it.'

'A nose?' he beseeched, looking almost humble.

Adeline's eyes gleamed with laughter. 'Very well, a nose it is—but I still beat you.'

They were both breathing hard, the exhilaration of the ride still flowing through their veins. Removing her bowler, Adeline threw back her head and her hair rippled and lifted on the breeze. A strand wisped across her face and caught in the pink moistness of her lips. Reaching up a hand, she brushed it away. She looked into Grant's face, into his bright silver-grey eyes, and felt again the heat, the rush of sweet warmth she'd felt in his arms. Embarrassed by her thoughts, she took Crispin's reins.

'I'd better go,' she said, beginning to lead him into the stable-yard, where she would hand him over to one of the grooms. 'I promised I'd have breakfast with Father, and I have to change.'

'I'll ride out and join the others. I'll be along later.' When she turned to walk away, he said, 'Adeline?'

She turned and looked back. His face, devoid of laughter, had taken on a different look, more serious.

'Thank you. It was a pleasure riding with you. We must do it again.'

'Yes—yes, we will.'

Later, when Adeline had changed and entered the breakfast room, she found her father alone.

Horace glanced at his daughter as she helped herself to bacon and mushrooms from the large silver dishes on the sideboard, kept heated by rows of little spirit lamps underneath. As well as hot food there were cold hams, tongues and galantine laid out on a separate table, along with porridge, coffee, and Indian and China tea—China indicated by yellow ribbons and Indian by red. Adeline chose the Indian, which was more to her taste.

'I didn't expect to see you—thought you'd have gone on the

ride,' Horace remarked as she came to sit down, observing her still-shining eyes and flushed cheeks.

'I did—and most enjoyable it was, too. Have you seen Paul this morning, Father?'

'No. I thought he was with you.'

'He rode off early—by himself.'

The harsh tone of her voice brought a frown to Horace's forehead. 'There's nothing wrong between the two of you, I hope?'

'No, of course not—at least nothing that can't be put right when he condescends to show his face.'

It was almost lunchtime when Paul arrived back. Partnering Lettie, Adeline was just finishing an enjoyable game of croquet when she saw him ride up the drive and disappear round the house to the stables. He found her in the conservatory ten minutes later. The building had been added to the house in recent years. With its glass walls and high dome it was filled with rare, exotic plants—an explosion of flowers, colour and fragrance. There were others sitting around in white wicker chairs, gossiping quietly and drinking tea, but Adeline sat away from them in a quiet spot, looking out over the gardens.

On Paul's approach she rose, annoyed to see there was a jaunty spring to his step. Suspicions dancing along her raw nerves, when he bent his head to peck her cheek she turned her head away. Although she was quaking inside, she rose and drew him to one side, out of sight and earshot of the few people present, who were too engrossed in their own conversations to pay them any attention anyway. She faced him with outward calm, not having realised until that moment how much she disliked him.

She had changed physically. Having tasted passion, she would want the same again—and Paul wouldn't be able to give it to her. Grant Leighton might as well have branded her. When she had been with him earlier her heart had swelled, yet she had been forced to rein in her feelings. When she married she would want a declaration of unconditional love—it was a declaration she would insist on—and she would love in return. She would settle for nothing less.

Now the moment of confrontation with Paul was at hand she was strangely relieved. His sordid affair with Diana Waverley had given her adequate reason to break off their engagement.

'Here you are. I've been looking for you.'

'Have you, Paul? Why?' She noted that he seemed more relaxed than he had been last night. Suddenly, above the scent of exotic plants, there was the smell of musk. She looked at him accusingly. 'So my suspicions were correct.'

He glanced at her sharply.

'I believe you've been well occupied at Westwood Hall, haven't you, Paul?'

He paled visibly and averted his gaze, pretending interest in a rather splendid bloom growing out of a large terracotta pot. 'Westwood Hall?' he asked, his tone guarded. 'Why do you say that?'

'You've come straight from Diana Waverley to me.' Adeline's lips curled with sarcasm. 'Her perfume is distinctive.'

Paul's face stiffened with anger. 'Adeline, do not continue with this. It is nonsense, and you are not yourself.'

'I have never been *more* myself, Paul. I am neither stupid nor a fool. I have known about it for some time. Do you deny it?'

He shrugged. 'No, but she means nothing to me. It was just a moment of weakness—nothing more than that.'

Her eyebrows rose. 'A moment of weakness? I have not the slightest doubt that it is a "moment of weakness" that has attacked you frequently for a long time past, and will continue to do so in the future.'

'When we return home we will talk about it—decide how to deal with this. But not now.'

'No, Paul,' Adeline replied unsteadily. '*I* will decide how to deal with this now. When we were at Westwood Hall I knew you and she were… Well, thinking it would blow itself out, I tried to ignore it. But I can't. I consider our engagement at an end. I will not be played false. I will not marry you.'

Paul, his face suddenly ashen, and a pulse beginning to throb in his temple, could not believe what he was hearing. 'Don't be ridiculous, Adeline. Of course we will be married. It is what your father wants. What we all want.'

'It's no longer what I want. It never was. Father has strong principles regarding moral conduct, and he will be the first to understand. I will not marry a womaniser,' she upbraided him coldly.

Paul rounded on her, his face a mask of indignation and malice. 'And you, I suppose, have no deficiencies? Look at you, for God's sake. You have a lot to learn about your own limitations, Adeline. You have hardly been inundated with admirers, have you? If it were not for me you would remain a spinster for the rest of your life, and you know it.'

Enraged by his insult, but managing to remain self-contained, without taking her eyes from his she moved closer. 'And so I should be grateful to you? Dear God, Paul, I no more want to marry you now than I did in the beginning. Better to be a spinster than married to a man who has so little respect for his future bride. I had no idea you saw me in such an unfavourable light. But I am not as pathetic as you so obviously think I am.'

'What does that mean?' Paul demanded. For the first time he saw something in those eyes of hers—a fire that promised vengeance.

'Just this. Since you require a chaste little virgin for your wife, you should know that if I did marry you, you wouldn't be getting the virgin bride you expected.'

Paul's eyes narrowed, and he looked at her hard. 'What are you saying?' he asked, in a voice that had suddenly turned ominous.

Adeline checked herself abruptly, realising that in her furious state she had said more than she ought.

Paul read into her words and her expression exactly what she meant. His face darkened.

'You slut,' he breathed. 'You damned slut.'

And before Adeline could move, losing his gentlemanly control, he raised his hand and slapped her across her cheek and jaw. The impact sent her reeling. She staggered wildly, but regaining her balance she managed to whirl around, facing him in expectation of another attack.

Paul would have struck her again but, because he hated violence in any form, Grant reacted, quickly and deadly, and the cold, biting fury of his voice checked him.

'If you strike her again, Marlow,' Grant said, his expression savage, 'I swear it will be the sorriest day of your life.'

Paul's face froze into a mask of disbelief, as did Adeline's, when they spun round and saw Horace and Grant standing just behind them. Until then neither of them had realised they were present. Horace's expression looked far more ominous than amiable, and Paul was concerned with the tangible danger emanating from Leighton.

'And I second Grant.' Horace's voice was low and horribly calm, like the eye of a hurricane.

Adeline stood mute and unmoving before her father's accusing, unwavering stare, realising that he might have heard too much. He certainly looked his fiercest. His face had turned crimson; his sideburns were almost bristling.

Feeling himself pushed beyond the bounds of reason, Adeline's outrageous outburst having humiliated and diminished him in the eyes of Grant and Horace, Paul gave a snarl of fury. 'You whore.'

'Watch your tongue, Marlow,' Grant growled. He looked at Adeline. 'Are you all right?'

She nodded. The sudden blow had caused a tenuous strand of her hair to come undone from the bun at her nape and frame her cheek. It coiled down across her bosom and curled up provocatively at the tip. Despite her haughty stance, her eyes were glittering with unshed tears.

Horace looked from his daughter to Paul. 'Is it true what I overheard? Are you having an affair with Lady Waverley?'

Clearly embarrassed at being caught out, Paul flushed and shifted guiltily beneath the older man's hard stare, his fury diminished. 'I'd hardly call it an affair.'

'It makes no difference. Good God, man—you've been carrying on a relationship while engaged to my daughter. I would not have believed it of you. I thought better of you— thought you had more sense and self-restraint—and more discretion. You have made an unforgivable public exhibition of Adeline's virtue.'

'I can see that I owe you an apology, Horace,' Paul said, the rough edge of nervousness now tingeing his voice as he tried to bring all his faculties to bear, 'but I hardly think that a meaningless dalliance can be construed as a capital crime.'

Horace was rigid. His features were grim, his mouth set into a tight hard line. 'When it involves my daughter I regard it as serious. You have shamed her. I like to think I am a forgiving man, as well as a stern one. But I am not an idiot. I have never been an idiot and I never will be—and you won't make me one, I promise you. Our families go back a long way, and we have been friends and business associates for a long time, but what you have done is unacceptable.'

With that, he turned to Grant. 'I think enough has been said for now. I think we should discuss this matter further when we have all calmed down. I apologise for this unpleasantness, and do not wish to draw you into a situation that is none of your affair.'

Paul's face darkened, and he was trembling slightly as he glanced from Adeline to Grant and then sliced back to Adeline, comprehension dawning. 'Last night when I caught you swanning around in attire designed for the bedroom, you went looking for more than your book, didn't you?'

Adeline shifted uncomfortably, careful not to look at Grant. 'No! Of course not! That was precisely what I was doing— looking for my book.'

Paul turned to his host. The look on Grant's face caused a frisson of fear to trickle through him. He had thought his host completely malleable, but now he read a hardness of purpose and a coldness of manner beyond any previous experience. Strange and explosive emotions lurked in the hard, glittering silver-grey eyes. Pent-up fury crouched, ready to leap and destroy him.

'You will say no more, if you know what's good for you,' Grant said, aware of Paul's train of thought and of his silent accusation. His words were low, barely heard, but menacing enough to stop Paul from saying more.

Horace, his sharp ears attuned to what was going on, was fully aware of what Paul was implying—which was in all probability the reason why he had struck Adeline. He was unable to believe the situation could get much worse, but it appeared it could. When he looked directly at his daughter, all she could do was look back at him mutely.

There was a moment of unexpressed emotion which Adeline would never forget. Her father stared at her with such anger that she almost believed a fork of lightning would flick from his eyes and strike her dead.

Horace turned to Grant. The two men stood without moving, staring at each other. 'I am compelled to ask you, sir. Is it true what Paul is implying?'

Grant nodded, trying not to show the self-disgust welling in him. He tried telling himself that Adeline wasn't his problem or his concern, since it had been her decision to allow him into her bed while she was engaged to Paul, but he could not escape the fact that it was his ravishment of Adeline that had precipitated this mess.

'Yes, it is.'

Horace looked at Adeline coldly. 'I am disappointed in you. It seems I do not know my own daughter. Not only have you concealed what you have done, you were prepared to enter into marriage dishonestly. I don't want to hear the details of what you've done. I haven't the stomach for it.'

Shock drained the blood from Adeline's face. Somehow she managed to find the strength to control herself. 'Father, I am sorry.'

'And so you should be. You are twenty years old, and until you are married you are answerable to me, your father. I thought you understood your duty to me—that you would cleave to it no matter what and conduct yourself properly. Can you imagine how embarrassing it is to announce my daughter's engagement one minute only to discover the next that she's been carrying on with another man? The humiliation to me and to Paul's family, after spending so much time and energy in bringing about a union between the two of you has ended by making us a laughing stock.'

'That's the trouble,' Adeline complained, her courage reasserting itself. 'It's what it means to *you*. But what about me? Why didn't you ask me if I wanted to marry Paul? You just took it for granted that I would comply—which is what I have done ever since Mother died. My marriage to Paul was like a—a merger—it was business—cold and dispassionate—and that's not what I want.'

'What are you trying to say?'

'What I should have told you at the beginning. That I do not want to marry Paul. I will not marry him. Not now—not ever.'

The outburst surprised even her. But it was said now, and she was glad.

'Whether it's true that Adeline and I have a special regard for each other hardly matters now—nor does why Marlow found her in the drawing room looking for her book after midnight—and that was the real purpose for her being there, whatever interpretation he wants put on the incident.' Turning to Adeline, his jaw set in a hard line, his grey eyes like slivers of steel, Grant took her hand and drew her to his side. He glanced down at her pale face before fixing his gaze on Horace. 'I have asked her to end her engagement to Paul and do me the honour of agreeing to become my wife.'

At that blatant falsehood Adeline stared at him in confused shock. His announcement had rendered her speechless. He had spoken calmly, and held her hand almost lovingly, but Adeline was close enough to detect the underlying currents in his tone and in his body. He was seething with anger.

At length, Horace asked, 'And what is her answer?'

'I'm still waiting.'

Grant's revelation was too much for Paul. His eyes fastened malevolently on Grant, and his voice was incongruously murderous. 'So I was not mistaken. I knew it.'

Towering over him, Grant spoke, his voice like ice. 'What's the matter, Marlow? Can't you accept the fact that Adeline doesn't want you—that she might prefer someone else? If you find the concept impossible to understand or accept, that's for you to deal with. Get over it. That's the way the world works. And it's simply too bad if you don't like it.'

Horace turned to his daughter. 'You really have decided not to marry Paul?'

She nodded. 'Yes.'

Horace stood unflinching. Every trace of emotion had drained from his face. When he spoke, his voice was devoid of feeling. 'Very well. But I would not have believed it of you.'

Adeline sighed and turned away. 'No, Father. I don't suppose you would. Please excuse me.'

'Where are you going? We have to talk about this.'

'There's nothing more to say. I'm going for a walk.'

Grant looked at Paul. 'You are no longer welcome in this house. I would like you to leave as soon as you have packed your things. A carriage will take you to the station. I don't want you here.'

'Save your breath. I'd already decided to leave.'

Grant smiled tolerantly. 'No doubt Diana will be pleased to see you at Westwood Hall—and will help you lick your wounds.'

As Adeline walked, with nowhere particular in mind, she began to feel that something momentous had happened and that her life had changed beyond recall. The sudden breeze that rose and stirred the grass, swayed the trees and went searching and whispering through the branches and leaves, was like a secret message, telling her it was time to be free.

Back at the house, Grant was facing Horace Osborne alone, forced to listen while the older man delivered an eloquently worded blistering tirade concerning his unacceptable behaviour towards Adeline.

'I cannot condone or excuse what you have done. Because of you my daughter will be made the subject of public censure, and her engagement to Paul is off.'

'I think Paul has much to do with that,' Grant pointed out firmly, angry about being taken to task over his behaviour, and yet at the same time admiring everything about the man doing it—a man with strong principles about what was acceptable and what was not. A hard man, yes, who saw his daughter as little more than a commodity, but also a man of honesty and integrity, who expected the same behaviour from those around him.

'Do you deny that you seduced Adeline?' Horace demanded.

'No,' Grant admitted, without trying to defend himself.

'And did it not concern you that she might be pregnant?'

'She isn't.'

As Horace digested this some of the hostility went out of his voice. 'Thank God for that. But you did this despite the fact that she was engaged to Paul at the time—a man from a fine and decent family, with principles.'

'Paul is no plaster saint.'

'No man is that. At least you didn't try to shirk your duty to Adeline. You say you have proposed marriage?'

Grant nodded, watching Horace warily. 'As yet she hasn't given me her answer.'

'She will. Marriage is a foregone conclusion.'

'Assuming she agrees. Adeline may have other ideas.'

'My daughter will do as she is told,' Horace said curtly. 'Under the circumstances it is the right and proper thing to do. This dreadful business will make things very unpleasant for her. It is always uncomfortable to be closely connected to a public scandal, and vulgar curiosity will set people staring and talking, if nothing worse.'

'Adeline is an intelligent young woman. She has the right to make up her own mind.'

Horace's gaze was direct. 'Her wishes count for nothing. I shall insist on it. When the time is right you will announce your engagement, and after a suitable length of time you will be married. Until that time there will be no intimacies between the two of you. If the sacrifice of physical satisfaction is too much, then—'

'It won't be,' Grant bit out.

'Fine.' Horace's countenance suddenly relaxed, and his smile was almost paternal. 'Then everything's settled.'

Surfacing from his private thoughts, Grant wondered how the hell he had managed to let himself be coerced into this situation, thinking that an hour ago something as outrageous as tying himself to Miss Adeline Osborne for life would have been absolutely out of the question. He nodded.

'I'll speak to Adeline.'

Horace nodded, too, satisfied that the matter had been settled to his satisfaction.

Chapter Five

Grant found Adeline sitting on a stout fallen log at the edge of the wood, some considerable distance from the house. She didn't turn when he approached but, seeing her back stiffen, he knew she was aware of his presence. Shoving his hands into his trouser pockets, he propped his back against a tree, his narrow gaze trained on her. Having half expected to find her in a distressed state, he was surprised to find her looking unruffled and as cool as a cucumber.

Adeline saw Grant was wearing the same grim expression she had seen when she had left the house. He looked strained with the intensity of his emotions, but slowly, little by little, he was getting a grip on himself. His shoulders were squared, his jaw set and rigid with implacable determination, and even in this pensive pose he seemed to emanate restrained power and un-yielding authority. There was no sign of the relaxed, laughing man she had ridden with earlier—no sign of the passionate man who had kissed her so ardently last night.

Where he was concerned her feelings were nebulous, cha-otic—yet one stood out clearly: her desire for this man. She hadn't known herself when she had been in his arms, and last night she hadn't wanted him to stop kissing her. He was weaving a web about her and she could do nothing to prevent it, to deny the hold he already had over her senses and her heart. She wanted him with a fierceness that took her breath, wanted to feel again the depths of passion only he was capable of rousing in her. But she was determined not to let him touch her again.

While she had been sitting there thinking, a strange calm had settled on her, banishing even her shame. She had left Grant to argue it out with her father, and whatever decision they had come to she was resolved to do things her way from now on. It was her life, to do with as she pleased, and no man would order her to do his bidding ever again.

Raising her brows, she gave him a cynical smile. 'What a strange turnabout this is,' she said, in a flat, emotionless voice, giving no evidence of how the mere sight of him set her heart pounding in her chest, how the thought of never seeing him again almost broke her heart. 'Don't you agree?'

'I have to admit they're not the most romantic of circum-stances.'

'No.' She let her eyes dwell on his face. How well he shielded his thoughts. 'I expect you are feeling a bit like a rabbit caught in a trap.'

'I wouldn't put it quite like that.' Grant lifted one hand and massaged the taut muscles at the back of his neck. His mind was locked in furious combat about what he was about to do. All the way here he had been straining against the noose of matrimony he could feel tightening about his throat. What had possessed him to announce that he'd asked Adeline to marry him? Now that he had, he was honour-bound to abide by his declaration, and there was no going back. 'Your father certainly knows how to make a man feel small.'

'I thought he only did that to women.' Adeline knew Grant would surmise that she was so weak and malleable that she would gratefully accept anything he had to suggest, but she was determined to have some control over this. 'Thank you, by the way. It was chivalrous of you to say what you did.'

'I wasn't being chivalrous.'

'Nevertheless, I didn't ask you to. In the view of conventional morality the loss of my virtue can only mark my downfall.'

He was frowning. 'I take full responsibility for all of this.'

'Why? You weren't the one I was engaged to, and nor were you having an affair with Diana Waverley—well, you might have been, but that is beside the point and has absolutely nothing to do with me.'

'Diana and I might have married once,' he told her tersely, 'but she married someone else instead.'

'And now?'

'Now we're—friends—of a peculiar kind.'

Adeline tilted her head to one side and looked at him. Not for the first time did she wonder what their bitter argument had been about when he had stormed out on Diana at Westwood Hall. 'By "peculiar" do you mean that now she is a widow she would like to be Mrs Leighton?' The look he threw her told her this was exactly as it was. 'And that is not what you want?'

'No,' he gritted. 'I don't give second chances.' Grant looked at her coolly.

'And how do you feel about her affair with Paul?'

'I don't feel anything. It won't last. Diana soon tires of her lovers. But enough of her. It's you and me we have to worry about.'

Adeline raised her eyebrows in question. 'You and me?'

'You have no need to worry about your future. It will be taken care of.'

'Really?' Adeline was quietly infuriated. It was as if she had no say in the matter. 'Grant,' she said, laughing lightly, 'you're not telling me that when you told my father you'd asked me to marry you that you actually meant it?'

'I never say anything I don't mean—and your father insists on it.'

Adeline felt an uneasy disquiet settling in. She could not believe what Grant was saying. He looked and sounded so cold, so dispassionate. 'Does he, indeed?'

'He has decided that our engagement will be announced when this unpleasantness has died down. We will be married following a decent interval of time.'

'That's a bit extreme.' She gave him a quizzical look. 'I'm sorry, but I seem to have missed something. I don't recall you asking me to marry you, Grant.'

'That's because I haven't.'

Adeline's expression dared him to attempt control of herself. 'Now, why do I feel this has happened to me before?' she retorted, her voice heavy with sarcasm.

'I apologise if that's how it seems to you. My only regret is that it was my intoxication which led to this.'

'And you are one of those men who has to do something noble in life?'

'It's not noble. We have no choice. You must see that.'

'No, as a matter of fact I don't.'

'Well, we haven't. I took that away when I announced to the world that I had asked you to be my wife.'

'And I recall you saying I had not given you my answer. I simply cannot believe that you want to marry me—a woman you hardly know, a woman you have no personal regard or respect for.'

Shoving himself away from the tree and running an impatient hand through his dark hair, Grant began pacing to and fro in frustration. 'How can you know that?'

'Because last night you accused me of being little better than a harlot,' she reminded him coldly.

He stopped and looked at her, his expression one of contrition. 'I'm sorry if I implied that. But that was last night.'

'And nothing has changed. To my mind all this talk about marriage and doing the honourable thing is wholly unnecessary. You are under no obligation to marry me.'

He stopped pacing and glared at her. 'Dear God! I appreciate the wrong I have done you, and that compounds my obligation to marry you.'

No longer able to contain her temper, Adeline shot to her feet in angry indignation, her hands clenched by her sides. 'And you assume in your arrogance that I am so pathetic, so desperate for a husband now Paul and I are no longer engaged, that I will accept you—me, plain, serious Adeline Osborne, who by all rights, as Paul so cruelly pointed out, should remain a spinster because no man unless he were blind would want me.'

'I think you undervalue yourself.'

'Perhaps you're right. But what a weak-willed idiot I must seem to you. Despite all my diligent efforts throughout my life to be the model of propriety, I let a total stranger—a handsome, inebriated stranger—make wonderful love to me—a man who wouldn't have given me a second glance had he been sober.'

'Now you insult me. I am ashamed of what I did to you. I can't blame you if you hate me for it completely, but it cannot be nearly as much as I hate myself.' This was true. Grant *did* despise himself for what he'd done to her—and the mess she was in because of it—and for the unprecedented weakness that made him want to repeat the act. 'Damnation, Adeline, can't you see that I'm trying to do the right thing by you?'

Fury flared in Adeline's eyes. 'How dare you say that to me? Don't you dare pity me, Grant Leighton.'

'I don't pity you. That's the last thing I feel. But you must realise that because of this, and what Paul might disclose, you will become the subject of gossip, your reputation in ruins.'

'And marrying you will shift the sentiment, I suppose, and find general favour?' she mocked. 'Given an interval of time I shall produce an heir for Oaklands and cause no further scandal—which will in turn bring redemption through association, all my transgressions forgotten.'

'Something like that.'

Adeline drew back her shoulders and lifted her head, the action saying quite clearly that she knew her own mind. 'Do you know, Grant, I don't care a fig about any of that? What people think of me no longer matters. I've got a broad back. I can endure the slights and slurs. Besides, I certainly don't see a husband as the solution to my problems. You're not required to marry me. If I agree to this mockery of a marriage you will hate me for ever and I will be miserable for my entire life—as I would have been if I had married Paul—and no doubt longing for release in an early grave.'

'Now you exaggerate.' His biting tone carried anger and frustration.

'I don't think so,' Adeline bit back. 'My reputation is already besmirched, I agree—but do you know I don't feel guilty or ruined? Yes, the future is an uncharted path, and will possibly be filled with censure, but for the first time in my life I feel completely at peace. When you came to my bed I knew what I wanted and I took it. If I don't marry you nothing will change—

at least not immediately. But given time any scandal will be forgotten.'

When realisation of what she was saying dawned on him, Grant stared at her in disbelief. 'Are you saying you don't want to marry me?'

'Yes. I don't want to be any man's wife.'

Placing his hands on his hips, towering over her, he glared down into her defiant face. 'You might at least show some gratitude. You are behaving as though I've suggested we commit murder. I'm offering to deliver you from a barren future—a way out—an answer to your dilemma.'

'How do you know I want one? You did a noble thing by offering, but it was spur-of-the-moment—a moment of madness— an absurd compulsion. Once said, you couldn't in all honour retract it, but I have no intention of holding you to it.'

The corner of his mouth twisted wryly in a gesture that was not quite a smile. 'No? I'm surprised.'

'Why? Because I melted in your arms like the naïve and silly woman that I am?' She smiled. 'You are persuasive, I grant you that, but I don't know you and I don't trust you.'

'But you *do* want me,' he said, with a knowing light glinting in his eyes.

'That's beside the point, and has nothing to do with marriage. Men are the cause of my troubles—my father, Paul, and now you. As far as I am concerned men make excellent dancing partners, but beyond that are no use at all to me. In fact, the more I think about them the more depressed I become.'

'Now you're beginning to sound like Lettie.'

'If I am then I consider it a compliment. Your sister talks a great deal of sense.' She moved close to him, and suddenly he seemed enormous, his powerful body emanating heat, reminding her of what could be hers if she complied to his will and that of her father. But she would not back down. Meeting his gaze directly, she said, 'Let's stop all this nonsense, shall we? Be honest about it, Grant. You don't want to marry me any more than I want to marry you.'

With his face only inches from hers, his eyes boring ruthlessly into hers, he ground out, 'You're absolutely right. I don't.'

'And you agree that the whole idea is absolutely ludicrous?'

'Right.'

'I've decided that I'd make an exceedingly poor wife, and on reaching that conclusion I consider it wise to avoid that particular state of affairs. That is my final resolve.'

Her rejection of his proposal put her beyond his tolerance, and his voice took on a deadly finality. 'That's extremely wise of you. I'd make an exceedingly bad husband.'

'Good. I am glad we are in agreement. Then it's settled. We won't marry. Your duty, obligation to me—call it what you like—is now discharged.' Stepping away from him, she raised her head haughtily. 'And now, if you will excuse me, I will go and tell my father.'

Grant stared after her, feeling bewildered, misused, furious with himself and with her, and seriously insulted—for what man who had just offered a respectable marriage proposal expected to be rejected? What was he to do? He supposed it had been rather arrogant of him to assume she would fall in with his plans—and her father's—but damn it all, he was asking her to be his wife—a position he had never offered to any other woman. So it wasn't conceited of him to expect her to accept. Was it?

In his anger he had tried to blame her for what had transpired at Westwood Hall. He shouldn't have. She was proud, courageous and innocent. He knew damned well she wasn't promiscuous, shameless or wanton, but he had implied that she was and then treated her as if she was, and she had endured it and let him kiss her again.

Furious self-disgust poured through him. Bullied by her father, taken for granted, treated as less than a second-class citizen by Paul Marlow, and then told that she would have to marry him, Grant, little wonder she'd had enough of men and wanted her independence.

But none of this lessened the fury that ran in his veins. By making their sordid night of passion common knowledge and then turning down his offer of marriage she had humiliated and shamed him voluntarily, and no one did that. He hoped that when she left Oaklands on the morrow he would never have to set eyes on her again.

With courage and determination, Adeline sought her father out in his room. When his voice barked out for her to enter, she set her teeth on edge, inwardly trembling but outwardly calm, and entered his presence. She knew that he would have plenty to say when she told him she would not marry Grant Leighton, and she was not disappointed. He broke out into such a fury of anger that Adeline thought he might actually strike her.

What had possessed her to behave so wantonly? Had she no morals, no grain of sense or the slightest feeling of gratitude for all he had done for her? And if Adeline thought she had heard the last of it, she was very much mistaken.

And so he ranted on.

Adeline merely stood and felt the fierce scolding beat her like a stick. And yet, despite her wretchedness, she could not help noticing his own suffering at knowing all he had hoped for for his only daughter had crumbled into dust. Curiously enough, Adeline felt sorry for him, and with some degree of self-control she was able to apologise. She begged him to forgive her, and to try to understand why she could not marry either Paul or Grant. She had behaved extremely foolishly, and would never again be so selfish as to forget all he had done for her.

Her sincerity was as evident as her determination to stand firm on her decision. When her father realised this and spoke to her, at last his voice had lost its anger. On a sigh, his shoulders slumped with dejection, he told her that they would leave Oaklands for Rosehill as planned the following morning, where they would discover how seriously this unfortunate incident would affect her future.

Later, when Adeline was preparing for dinner, she sat in front of the mirror and looked at the image staring back as if she were seeing herself for the first time. When she had left her father, for the first time in her life she had begun to feel alive—but when she stared at the face looking back at her now, she knew she was in danger of losing her fragile newfound courage.

Attired in a plain beige dress, which seemed to drain the colour from her face, expensive though it was, never had she felt so drab. It did absolutely nothing for her. The fashion was for pastel silks offset by contrasting ribbons, beading, fringing, tassels and lace, in a style of gown that gave more emphasis to the back of the flat-fronted skirt, with complex drapery over a bustle trimmed with pleats and flounces.

As she surveyed her reflection she was far from satisfied with what she saw. On a sigh, she turned away.

Answering a knock on the door, her maid Emma opened it to admit Lettie, who breezed in and swept across the carpet to where Adeline was sitting. She perched on the end of the dressing table.

'Ooh, why the frown, Adeline? Why so pensive? Do you not like your gown?'

'Since you ask, no, I do not. But it's one of my best.'

Lettie was wearing a forget-me-not-blue taffeta with trailing skirts, and she looked radiant. 'You, Adeline Osborne, need taking in hand very seriously.'

'I do?'

'Most definitely. A visit to the dressmaker is what I advise—and someone to arrange your hair into a more flattering style.'

Adeline had the miserable notion that Lettie was right. She cast a surreptitious glance at the fashionable woman. Did she dare ask for guidance from her? Yes, she did—and she was willing to listen to any suggestions that would improve her looks.

Reading Adeline's mind, Lettie laughed softly. There was an ease in their communication, as if their friendship were natural. 'I will look forward to accompanying you to the shops, if you like. You must come and stay with me in London. I should love it if you could. You would be such good company for me, and I could introduce you to all my friends—when we're not visiting the fashion shops.'

'And I always thought feminists dressed in practical, unadorned clothes. You certainly don't look like a Suffragette.' This was true, and it was a conflict these women faced between the desire to be feminine in appearance and decrying what this entailed.

'I always try to make the best of myself, and I see no point in denying the side of my nature which adores finery. I enjoy wearing glamorous clothes, and refuse to be ashamed of the feeling—nor to agree that wearing nice clothes is only to please men. Not for one minute would I think of donning any kind of feminist version of sackcloth and ashes just to resemble a caricature of what a feminist is supposed to look like.'

'And do people take you seriously—looking as attractive as you do?'

'Some don't—especially people in authority. I confess that to look attractive is both a weapon—which I use to excess when necessary—and a hindrance. To be feminine is to be thought frivolous and empty-headed, and in my case,' she said, her eyes dancing with mischief, 'more than possibly wicked.'

'I suppose if I wanted to make a mark at all it would not be for my beauty but my individuality.'

Lettie's expression became serious. 'There's no reason why you can't have both, Adeline. But, you know, beauty isn't everything.'

Adeline smiled ruefully. 'Beautiful women always say that.'

'But you are a very attractive woman—Grant must think so, too, considering the intimacies you've shared. If there's one thing Grant's not, it's blind.'

'But we're not—I mean…' Adeline hesitated, knowing she was blushing to the roots of her hair and wondering who could have told Lettie. She didn't know how to say this. 'We—we aren't sharing a bed,' she managed to whisper, thankful that Emma had disappeared into the dressing room.

Lettie frowned in puzzlement. 'But when I spoke to Paul as he was leaving—and he was most irate, I must say—he accused you of doing just that. And when he told me that Grant had asked you to marry him—well, I assumed you were—conducting an affair, I mean.'

'Well, we're not.'

'Adeline, I'm not trying to pry, but I know there must be more to this than meets the eye.'

'Oh, Lettie, I just don't know what's going on.' Adeline briefly described the circumstances of her involvement with Grant, omitting—for her pride's sake and Grant's—the fact that Grant had been blind drunk at the time.

At the end of the tale Lettie stared at her with a combination of mirth and wonder. 'Goodness!' she exclaimed. 'It's too delicious for words. The two of you—and under Diana Waverley's roof at that. How intriguing. And are you going to marry Grant?'

'No, I'm not going to marry him, Lettie. It was a mistake. We both agree about that. And what he said about having asked me wasn't true. He thought he was doing the honourable thing, that's all.'

'Knowing my brother, he will be filled with remorse for what he did while you were engaged to Paul.'

'He did ask me—after he said what he did in the conservatory—but I said no. I told him my future from now on is my own affair.'

'I see. Loss of respectability can be unexpectedly liberating, you know—although I'm sorry to hear you turned Grant down. I would love to have you as a sister-in-law. But if you're not in love with him then you did right to refuse him.' Glancing at her obliquely, she said, 'You're *not* in love with him, are you, Adeline?'

Adeline's flush deepened and she averted her eyes. 'No, of course I'm not.'

Lettie wasn't at all convinced by her statement. 'But you can't admit to a supreme indifference to him, can you?' she persisted. 'It's written all over your face.'

'Am I really so transparent?'

Lettie smiled with gentle understanding. 'I'm afraid you are.'

'I only hope this unpleasant business soon blows over. The last thing I wanted was to involve your brother in my break up with Paul. The gossip will be dreadful.'

Lettie gave her a mocking sideways glance. 'Grant won't care two hoots about that. What he *will* care about is having his offer of marriage turned down. As far as I am aware he has only ever proposed marriage once before, and when the lady married someone else he vowed he would never again offer marriage to any woman.'

'Was the woman Diana Waverley?'

Lettie nodded. 'Grant was deeply affected by it. Hardening his heart, he became cold and distant, killing whatever feelings he had for her. He cut her out of his life without a backward glance—until Lord Patrick Waverley, Diana's husband, died. After that Grant began seeing her again, but he'll never marry her. Diana burnt her bridges when she rejected Grant for a title. He never gives anyone a second chance.'

Adeline recalled Grant saying the same thing to her. 'She must have hurt him very badly.'

'She did—although I think his pride was hurt the most. And, knowing my brother like I do, this latest will have left him seething. Grant is quite awesome when his anger is roused.'

'Then I shall endeavour to stay out of his way until it's time for us to leave. After that I doubt we shall see each other again.'

'Men can be difficult enough without marrying them—and you must remember that no one can force you to marry Paul, Grant or any other man, come to that. Even the smallest steps in a woman's life are guided by and controlled by the men around her—father, brother and husband—who think women should be passive and inactive except in matters concerning the home.'

Adeline liked Lettie enormously, but she doubted she would ever get used to her candid way of speaking.

'I can see I shock you. I am a feminist, but I am also a realist. I like having my independence—I also like having a good time. For myself, I want everything: career, husband, or lover—' her eyes twinkled '—which is so much more exciting—and children. My husband must back everything I do, and believe my work to be as important as his.'

'And do you have a gentleman in mind?'

'I do have someone—but I will never marry him.' Sadness clouded Lettie's eyes and she turned her head away, but too late to hide it from Adeline. 'I do not see marriage as an element in a love affair. But we're madly happy, of course.' She laughed— rather forced, Adeline thought—and, getting up, went to the door. 'I'll see you downstairs.'

As she went in search of her mother, Lettie considered her conversation with Adeline. Although she had told her that her future from now on was her own affair, Lettie thought that perhaps she could make it her affair as well. She knew her brother to be a man of passionate feeling, despite his outward demeanour. Having seen the way he had looked at Adeline in the stableyard, and the unconcealed admiration in his eyes when he had watched her ride hell for leather across the park, she just knew he was attracted to her.

And Adeline had confessed she had feelings for Grant. She was also a young woman who'd had the temerity to stand up to him. That boded well for the future. How wonderful it would be if they could be brought together. She was sure they would make each other happy.

Ten minutes after Adeline had left him—in high dudgeon and frowning like thunder—knowing how concerned his mother would be by Paul's sudden departure, Grant found her in a small sitting room, away from the guests.

As soon as Grant entered she arose, her face strained with anxiety. She studied her son for a moment, noting his narrowed eyes and the grim set of his mouth. Even to her, it was a little intimidating.

'Horace has informed me of all that has transpired, Grant. You

cannot mean to go through with this? Surely not?' she said
without ceremony.

'You will be relieved to know Miss Osborne has turned me
down,' he informed her brusquely, pacing up and down in agi-
tation.

'Oh, I see.'

'But I should tell you that if she hadn't, I intended to marry
her.'

'But why?' Hester demanded. 'You hardly know the girl—
unless what Horace says is true and the two of you have been
conducting an affair.'

Grant had the grace to look contrite. 'Not an affair, exactly.'

'But the two of you were involved in a relationship of—an
intimate nature?'

'Yes.'

'While she was engaged to Paul Marlow?'

'Yes.'

'Oh, dear!' Sitting back down, she folded her hands in her lap.
'Then perhaps you ought to marry her.'

'I've told you, she won't have me.'

Hester seemed to find his dry comment amusing. Grant
sounded outraged—baffled, too—without any comprehension as
to why Adeline had turned him down. 'I can scarce believe it.'

'Believe it, Mother. It's true.'

'Why did you offer to marry her?'

'Because I felt sorry for her,' Grant replied with brutal frank-
ness. 'And, like it or not, I'm also responsible for what has
happened. It's as simple as that.'

Hester frowned. 'If what I've heard is correct, isn't Paul
Marlow equally to blame? Has he or has he not been conduct-
ing an affair with Diana Waverley? Your—mistress, I believe,
Grant?' she said, her eyebrows raised with knowing humour.

'Yes,' he said, trying to keep his voice calm, while irritated that his mother seemed to take some quiet delight in reminding him of something he preferred not to think about just then.

'How extraordinary.' Hester smiled. 'You do seem to be quite put out. Although I fail to understand why you should be if, as you say, you only asked her because you felt sorry for her. You should be relieved.'

Grant was clearly not amused. 'I am. Immensely.'

'In which case there is nothing else to be said on the matter, as I see it, so there is no point in beating yourself up about it.'

'I'm not.'

'Paul and Adeline are responsible for the break-up of their engagement, and if Adeline doesn't want to marry you then so be it. Although I have to say there is something about that young lady that I like. She seems such a serene, steady sort of person.'

'Appearances aren't always what they seem.'

'No—well, where Adeline is concerned you would know all about that, wouldn't you?' Hester said, giving him a meaning-ful glance. 'I really can't imagine why she refused you...' She paused, and her eyes narrowed on Grant. 'Did you *ask* her, Grant, or tell her? Which—however much I have come to like Horace—is what he would do. Is that how it was? No doubt that is the reason why she stuck her toes in—so to speak.' She laughed lightly. 'Good for her is what I say.'

Grant frowned. He found his mother's amusement at his expense irritating. 'I can see you're enjoying this, but you are supposed to be on my side.'

'I'm on no one's side, Grant, but I'm beginning to admire Adeline more and more. She is a young woman who deserves to be courted. You cannot expect her to obey an order to marry you—which is what she must have done when she became engaged to Paul Marlow.' Lowering her eyes, she said, 'At least Horace seems to have taken it in his stride.'

'When I left him he was reconciled to Adeline's change of husband. How he'll react when she tells him she doesn't intend marrying either of us, I have no idea.'

As if the incident in the conservatory had never happened, dinner was a relaxed, convivial affair. Grant fulfilled his role as host with careless elegance, but beneath the polite façade, as Lettie had predicted earlier, he was seething. Adeline's refusal to marry him, when he'd made the gesture against his will and to make things easy for her, had placed her beyond recall.

Later, when she was leaving the drawing room to fetch her book from her room, Adeline watched in astonishment as her father led Mrs Leighton off in the direction of the conservatory. She suddenly realised they had spent a good deal of time together, and that a singular affection was growing between them—which she suspected might have something to do with why her father had decided not to cut their visit short. She saw his hand slide about Mrs Leighton's waist, saw his head lean towards her upturned laughing face, and Adeline knew that what they felt for each other was in danger of becoming more than friendly regard.

Turning to her right, Adeline saw Grant standing not two yards away from her. He, too, was watching her father and his mother, his whole body tensed into a rigid line of wrath. When he looked at her she could almost feel the effort he was exerting to keep his rage under control.

Moving closer to her, he met her gaze coldly. 'So that's the way of things.'

'And what do you mean by that?'

'Your father and my mother appear to enjoy each other's

company. It has not escaped my notice that they spend a good
deal of time together.'

'And do you find something wrong with that? They are both
adults. If anything were to develop, would you disapprove?'

'It's not for me to approve or disapprove—but there's one
thing I do know.'

'And what is that?'

'If my mother wants something really badly, she gets it.'

'Not always. She didn't get Rosehill.'

'No?' Grant looked at her and smiled a wry, conspiratorial
smile. 'Not yet, maybe. But it's not too late.'

'We shall see. After tomorrow Father and I will be on our way
home—back to reality. You can forget all about us then.'

Grant's eyes swept contemptuously over her. 'I intend to.
When you leave in the morning we will not see each other
again,' he said scathingly. 'This unfortunate business is over.
Done with. It should never have happened. The proposal was
an insane idea, and I regret and curse ever having made it.'

'Not nearly as much as I do.'

'You have caused too much disruption to my life, and when
you leave I don't give a damn where you go or whose bed you
occupy. You, Miss Osborne, have a highly refined sense of
survival, and you'll land on your feet wherever you go.'

Adeline felt as if he'd slapped her, but her wounded pride
forced her chin up. 'Yes, I will,' she said with quiet dignity. 'That
is what I intend.'

Without bothering to excuse herself, turning from him, Adeline
went up the stairs. Oh, damn you, Grant Leighton, she thought
in helpless rage. I never want to see or think of you again. But
she knew she would not be able to stop thinking of him. She had
no power over her thoughts. She was trapped by her own nature.
Tears gathered on her thick lashes and trembled without falling.

* * *

The following morning, when they were leaving and everyone was saying their farewells, displaying a calm she didn't feel, Adeline searched Grant's hard, sardonic face for some sign that he felt something, anything for her—that he might regret her leaving. But there was nothing. The awful feeling that there was nothing she could do beat her down into a misery too hopeless for tears.

Adeline had been back at Rosehill three weeks when a letter arrived from Lettie, informing her that she was in London, staying with Lord and Lady Stanfield at Stanfield House in Upper Belgrave Street, and that they had invited Adeline to come and stay with them. Adeline was delighted—it was just what she needed at this time, when she seemed to be at an impasse in her life.

Her father was none too pleased at the prospect of her gallivanting off to London. He had always demanded respect and subservience from her as his right as her father, but now, since leaving Oaklands, although there was still respect there was no subservience. Of course she was still piqued at discovering Paul had been carrying on with Lady Waverley. It was natural, he supposed, and therefore he must make allowances, but her own behaviour hadn't been much better.

When he saw how determined she was to go to London he capitulated. Their relationship had been strained since their return to Rosehill, so perhaps it was for the best. However, he insisted that she stay at their own London home in Eaton Place, where Mrs Kelsall, the housekeeper, would be able to keep an eye on her. Horace spent a great deal of his time in London, so the house was always kept in a state of readiness.

He was acquainted with Lady Stanfield—a strong woman,

who followed an exacting campaign of work for the Women's Movement—and he was concerned that Adeline, with her new-found confidence, drive and determination, might become drawn in. He was worried that she might be led even more astray...

Determined to enjoy her new freedom, accompanied by Emma, Adeline boarded the train for London. She was looking forward to seeing Lettie. To Adeline's experience, Lettie was the most stimulating woman imaginable, and she felt a mixture of excitement and insecurity at the thought of being with her—certainly life would never be dull.

Chapter Six

The capital was enjoying the last days of summer, while leaves still clung to the trees in the parks and guardsmen sweated in their uniforms along The Mall. Lettie was delighted to see Adeline, although she was disappointed that she wasn't to stay with her—but since there was no great distance between Eaton Place and Upper Belgrave Street it wouldn't matter all that much.

As soon as Adeline entered Stanfield House she was greeted with unaffected warmth. She felt this was a house where courtesy and mutual affection ruled in perfect harmony. Lady Stanfield was happily married. She had one daughter, Marjorie, and a bright twenty-year-old son, Anthony, who had recently joined the Foreign Office. He was a keen fencer, and was looking forward to testing his skill against Adeline's.

Marjorie Stanfield was a small, rather plump twenty-two-year-old brunette, with bright blue eyes and rosy cheeks, whose quiet, unhurried ways were in agreeable contrast to the forceful whirlwind of Lettie. She was not the type to go out looking for experience, but just waited for it to happen. She was deeply in love with a young man called Nicholas Henderson, the eldest son of Lord and Lady Henderson of Woking in Surrey, and there was much excitement in the house over their forthcoming engagement party, which was to take place a month hence.

Determined that the first thing to be done was to get Adeline out of her dull, dark clothes and turn her into an elegant, fashionable young woman, Lettie adopted an air of critical superiority that neither surprised nor annoyed Adeline. She was prepared to accept Lettie as more adult and proficient in worldly matters than herself, and so Lettie and Marjorie whisked her off to the shops. The three of them could be seen almost every afternoon in and out of the fashionable shops along Regent Street, and when Lettie was too busy Adeline went with Emma.

Her father had always given her a generous allowance to spend as she wished, but, having had no interest in self-adornment until now, she had left most of the money gathering interest in the bank. Suddenly shopping became a whole new and exciting experience, and for the first time in her life—urged on by Lettie and Marjorie—she bought hats, gloves and evening purses, and had fittings for riding habits and dresses that were the very height of fashion, colourful and feminine, frivolous and completely impractical.

When she looked at herself in the mirror, adorned in one such gorgeous concoction and with her glossy hair arranged in an elegant chignon, Adeline no longer saw the plain young woman who wore reading spectacles and faded into the background.

'You look so beautiful,' Marjorie enthused breathlessly. Her eyes, dreamy and full of admiration, suddenly became rueful.

'And so tall. How I wish I were as tall and as slender as you, Adeline.'

Adeline could not believe that silks and satins in pastel shades adorned with ribbons and frothing lace could bring about such a change. Yes, she thought, with her colouring, her high cheekbones and her green eyes, she really did look quite wonderful.

Stanfield House was a veritable hive of activity, with people coming and going all the time. It was an exciting time for Adeline. She had been to London often, but now she saw it with different eyes. Suddenly it offered an active social life without the restrictions laid down by her father. The intensity of her enjoyment was no doubt due to the feeling of release which had come with her sudden emancipation from the frustrations of her life before her break-up with Paul. It was as though she had been born anew as a result of some new process of gestation.

She went to the opera or the theatre twice a week, walked in the pleasure gardens during the day, fed the pigeons in Trafalgar Square, rode side-saddle in a high silk hat between the elms along Rotten Row, and journeyed across the river to a concert at the Crystal Palace in Sydenham.

She attended parties at the homes of several people who were prominent in the Women's Movement, and even went to one of the Suffragist meetings, which she found interesting, listening to both Emily Davis and Millicent Garrett Fawcett—two extremely important women who made a deep impression on her.

She met writers, political and religious figures, and people she had read about in the society columns. They all came to drink tea in Lady Stanfield's elegant high-ceilinged drawing room with its watered silk walls. There they had the freedom to speak as openly as they wished on whatever subject they wished— from higher education for women, better employment opportunities for women, right down to the sexual persecution of women—unencumbered by most of the prevailing notions of female propriety.

Much as Adeline liked and respected the women she met, and the work they did, she had decided from the beginning not to become one of them—at least not for the time being.

It was at one such party that Lettie, sipping champagne, told her how the social world gave her pleasure.

'Indeed, I often feel guilty at my willingness to leave my work in order to enjoy dissipation,' she joked.

The remark caused Adeline to give her a frowning, suspicious look. Lettie often went out alone at night. She gave no indication of where she went, and she rarely returned until the following morning, so Marjorie had confided to her. In fact, Lettie had begun behaving rather oddly of late, she'd said, and she was often very pale.

It was clear that Marjorie was worried about her, but Adeline, not wishing to pry into her friend's private life—and presuming her outings were connected to her work—did not raise the subject. However, she sensed all was not as it should be with her friend, and that she assumed a cheerfulness she did not feel.

It wasn't until Marjorie told her that Lettie always implied to her mother that she was spending the night at Eaton Place with Adeline that Adeline, beginning to think there was more to Lettie's nocturnal activities than her work, and that the man she had told her about at Oaklands might have something to do with it, thought it was time she spoke to her.

'When are you going to introduce me to your young man, Lettie?' she asked outright.

Lettie suddenly became tense, and glanced at her sharply. 'Do you want to meet him?'

'Of course. I'm curious. You never talk about him.'

'That's because he—he's not the type of man that you're used to.'

Adeline laughed lightly in an attempt to lighten the conversation. 'Why? Has he got two heads or something?'

Lettie smiled. 'Silly—of course he hasn't. He—he…'

'He?' Adeline prompted, sensing Lettie's reluctance to discuss him but determined to find out more. 'Does he have a name?'

'Jack. His name is Jack Cunningham. He's respectable, of course,' she uttered rather forcefully—more to convince herself than Adeline, Adeline thought.

'What does he do?'

'He—he owns a nightclub in the West End.'

Adeline was surprised. It wasn't what she'd expected to hear, and she felt an uncomfortable stirring of unease. 'Oh, I see. How interesting. How did you come to meet him?'

'Diana Waverley introduced us at the Drury Lane Theatre. She was there with a large party, celebrating something or other. Jack was among them. As soon as I saw him I was attracted to him.' Lettie sighed. 'I can see you're shocked, Adeline. Mother wouldn't approve—there's nothing more certain—and Grant would definitely have a great deal to say about it. But Jack really cares for me. I know he does.'

The way Lettie emphasised those last four words made Adeline think she was trying to make herself believe this.

'I'd introduce you to him if I could,' Lettie said quickly, 'but it's rather difficult, you see. He—he's so busy. And besides, I couldn't possibly take you to a place like that.'

Adeline looked at her steadily. 'What? A nightclub?' Lettie nodded. 'But you go, don't you, Lettie?'

She shook her head. 'I've been on one occasion, that's all. Jack doesn't like me to go there. He has a house in Chelsea.'

'And you stay all night?'

Sensing Adeline's disapproval, Lettie stared right back at her, and there was defiance in the sudden lift to her chin. 'Yes. It's the only time Jack and I can be together. Adeline—I am an adult. I know perfectly well what I am doing.'

Lettie's words had shocked Adeline, but the sharpness with which they were spoken shocked her more. 'I'm sure you do, Lettie, and I'm not going to be judgemental, I promise. But— well—you do seem to be behaving out of character. I think I know you well enough by now to know it's not like you to carry on a clandestine affair.'

Lettie's eyes clouded over and she sighed. 'I suppose it must look like that to you. Love—or whatever you like to call it— physical attraction—does strange things to people. All I know is that when I'm with Jack I don't want to leave him. He makes me come alive. I feel excitement, danger and passion all wrapped into one. You must know how that feels, Adeline. Didn't you feel that way when you and Grant…?'

Adeline stiffened. She wasn't enjoying the conversation, or the turn it had taken, which threatened to resurrect all the feelings and emotions concerning Grant Leighton she had carefully locked away in her mind. 'Stop it, Lettie. Whatever happened between Grant and me is over, so there's no sense in talking about it.'

'I'm sorry. I didn't mean to upset you. Did I tell you that Grant is in London? He's on his way to France, but he has some business here to attend to first—something about some land he's interested in buying that's to be developed across the river. He's staying at the Charing Cross Hotel.'

'No, you didn't, Lettie—and in any case your brother's activities are nothing to do with me,' Adeline replied, doing her best to ignore the sudden lurch her heart gave at the mere thought of Grant being so close. Quickly she dismissed Lettie's attempt to steer the conversation away from her and Jack Cunningham. 'I—I just wish you hadn't told Lady Stanfield you were staying here with me. I don't like untruths, Lettie. They have an unpleasant habit of being found out.'

'I know, and I'm sorry about that,' she said, sounding contrite. 'I didn't want to involve you. But it's the only way I can see Jack.'

'Can I meet him?' The need to see what Jack Cunningham looked like was driving all caution from Adeline's mind.

Lettie shifted awkwardly and her expression became guarded. 'I don't know. I've told you—he's always working.'

'You can't get out of it that easily. He doesn't work all the time, surely? We can go to his club. If he's busy then we'll either wait until he's finished or go back another time.'

Lettie, knowing that Adeline wasn't going to be put off, reluctantly relented. 'I'll see what I can do.'

The following afternoon they took a cab to the heart of the West End, made up of dance halls, glittering restaurants, rough and tumble hostelries, brothels and dubious hotels of every kind. Leaving the main thoroughfare, they went down a narrow passage towards a projecting porch that threw the door into deep shadow, for it was two-thirds below ground level. A sign above advertised the Phoenix Club. They went down a flight of steps and came to a room below street level. A row of pegs and a short counter—a pay desk, Adeline assumed—were facing them. A couple of lighted gas-brackets hissed on the wall.

Pushing her way through a double swing door, Lettie urged Adeline to follow her, telling her that Jack was usually in his office at this time. Adeline stared around her in amazement. They were in a long vaulted room brightly lit by flaring gas, its floor of polished boards. There were alcoves, each with its own curtain—looped back for now—which could be released from its restraining cords to offer the inhabitants more privacy. Mirrors and pictures adorned the walls, and spittoons were plentiful. The décor was rich and subdued, the chairs plush. At the far end of the room was a raised dais with music stands and chairs, and to the side of this was a spiral staircase, rising into the dark.

A woman, unaware that she was being observed, was almost at the top, and only the lower half of her body could be seen. The train of her gown—a bold saffron-coloured silk with crimson trim—trailed behind her. Adeline watched until she'd disappeared, aware of the cloying fragrance of musk in the air—a fragrance not unfamiliar to her, which brought Diana Waverley to mind. But the woman could have been anyone. The scent was not unusual, and was favoured by many women of her acquaintance.

For the moment the Phoenix Club, flagship of Jack Cunningham's empire, remained dark and silent and private. But during its hours of activity Adeline could imagine how it would look. The cleaners had done their job, clearing away the previous night's debris, but the air was still thick with the odours of stale cigar smoke and liquor.

Suddenly a man appeared from a side room, smoking a cheroot, a glass of brandy in his hand. About thirty-five, he was swarthy, tall and well built, with tight curling black hair, side whiskers and a neatly trimmed moustache. An arrogant, smiling mouth dominated a square jaw.

On seeing Lettie, Adeline observed how his pale blue eyes had narrowed—with annoyance, she thought—but it was quickly gone, and his mouth stretched into a wide, unconvincing smile.

'Hello, Princess. This is a surprise—you know how I dislike you coming here,' he remarked, placing his glass on a table.

Taking Lettie in his arms, he planted a firm kiss on her lips. Over Lettie's head his eyes slid to Adeline, standing a few steps behind, watching her gaze about with evident uncertainty. 'I didn't realise we had a visitor.'

Adeline met his eyes, and he looked back at her mockingly. She noticed how he worked his way from her face to the outline of her breasts. Unappreciative of his somewhat brazen interest, she stepped back. A hungry look came into his eyes and she shuddered—violently.

'And a lovely one at that.'

'I—I hope you don't mind, Jack. I know how busy you are, but we were shopping close by and I didn't think you'd mind if I brought Adeline in to see the club—and to meet you, of course.'

'I'm delighted you did. I'm never too busy to see you, Princess, you know that. I've heard all about you from Lettie, Adeline.' His smile was open and beguiling as he held out his hand and his voice came over to Adeline silken-smooth.

She extended her hand in a businesslike manner and quickly withdrew it after a slight shake, glad she was wearing gloves. Leaning against him, Lettie looked relaxed and happy, with Jack smiling down into her eyes, plainly trying to make a good impression on Adeline. But Adeline could see below the surface.

The moment Adeline had set eyes on Jack Cunningham she'd known she didn't like him, and she'd withdrawn, backing away from his company. It was a mental trick of hers, seldom used, and only when her mind was troubled. When she looked at him she was aware of her own mixed feelings—and something else that she felt. Something not quite nice. The man exuded cockiness. His expression had a certain arrogance that repelled her completely.

No doubt women found him attractive—Lettie certainly did.

His demeanour was correct. He moved and spoke carefully. Yet for all his gentility Jack had an untamed air about him. Adeline was afraid. She didn't like the feeling. What did he want with Lettie? When he looked at her the look was intimate, triumphant—one of ownership—the look of a man incapable of love.

'Now you've braved the doors of the Phoenix,' Jack said, his eyes fixed intently of Adeline, 'you can't leave without taking refreshment. You must join me in a drink.'

'Yes,' Lettie said, somewhat breathlessly. 'We'd love to, Jack.'

'Good—something suited to a lady's taste. A glass of champagne, I think.'

'Thank you,' Adeline said composedly, 'but I don't drink anything stronger than tea in the afternoon.'

Jack lifted his glass in a wry salute. 'Very wise. And are you a member of Lettie's ladies' movement—emancipation and equality and all that nonsense?'

'No. Up to now I have not been drawn in.'

'You have different opinions?'

'Not at all. I agree with everything I hear. I admire the work they do enormously, and all they strive to achieve.'

'You're not one of those damned temperance fanatics, I hope, who won't be happy until they've closed down every club and tavern in London?'

'No, I'm not one of those, either.'

The atmosphere was uncomfortable. Lettie was aware of it, and also of the tension inside Adeline. She gave a nervous laugh. 'Look, Jack, do you mind if we forgo the drink? We have heaps to do, and the shops don't remain open all day. I'll probably see you later.'

He shrugged. 'That's a shame. You must arrange to bring Adeline out to Chelsea some time, Lettie—then we can become better acquainted.'

Adeline met his direct gaze without blinking. 'Thank you. I would like that,' she lied. 'Goodbye, Mr Cunningham.'

'The pleasure's entirely mine.'

When they emerged from the club the narrow, dimly lit passage seemed a mite chillier, and the thought of seeing Jack Cunningham again even less appealing. Suddenly a woman stepped out of the shadows, barring their way. In the gloom her age could have been anything from twenty-five to forty. A shawl that had seen better days was wrapped protectively about her thin body.

'Are you Miss Leighton?' she said, her voice low as she addressed Lettie.

Adeline could tell by the way her eyes kept darting to the doorway of the Phoenix Club that she was nervous.

'I am,' Lettie replied.

'I want a word with you—it's about Jack.' She glanced at Adeline. 'Private, like.'

Lettie turned to her friend. 'Would you mind, Adeline? I'll only be a moment.'

'Of course not. I'll wait for you at the end of the passage.'

Looking back, Adeline saw the woman had drawn Lettie back into the shadows and that she was speaking animatedly. After five minutes Lettie joined her, her expression grave.

'What did she want? And how did she know who you were?'

'She—she's seen me with Jack,' Lettie told her with a sudden wariness. 'She knows the work I'm involved with, and has come to me for help. She—she's ill—probably bronchitis—I can't be sure—and she can't afford to pay a doctor. I gave her the address of a charity clinic I know of run by volunteers, where street women who are ill or injured can go. They'll help her.'

'I see. And that's all she wanted?'

'Of course.'

When Lettie moved away to look for a cab, Adeline turned over what she had said, her sixth sense telling her that Lettie was not revealing the whole of it, and for some reason was unwilling to say more.

'You don't like Jack, do you?' Lettie remarked when they were in the cab taking them back to Eaton Place, the woman forgotten for the moment. 'Don't deny it, Adeline. It won't be any use, because I know you don't.' She didn't speak aggressively. She sounded calm and unemotional.

'No,' Adeline replied. 'Since you ask me so directly, I don't especially.'

'I knew you wouldn't.'

'He's not the sort of person who appeals to me—but I'm not the one he's seeing. I don't know him, of course—you obviously know him very well.'

'I'm not sure that I do,' Lettie murmured, averting her eyes.

'Then you should. You should know the man you're—'

Lettie turned and fixed her eyes on her candidly. 'What? Sleeping with?'

'I was going to say having a relationship with, but I suppose sleeping with is the same thing.'

'Do you think I'm wicked?'

'No, of course I don't, Lettie. Please don't think that. To me you are a dear friend, and the kindest, nicest person I have ever known, but I cannot like Jack Cunningham. If you must know, I thought he was absolutely dreadful. He has an air of danger about him—something that's not quite nice—sinister, even— and I do urge you to be careful. Do you intend to go on seeing him?'

Lettie nodded and looked away. 'Yes. I must. I like him. He's fun to be with and he excites me—at least for now.'

'You are of age—I can't stop you doing this foolish thing.'

For the first time Adeline saw a mutinous twist in the set of Lettie's lips.

'No, no one can.' After a moment's silence she looked back at Adeline and took her hand firmly in her own. 'Please don't tell Lady Stanfield, will you, Adeline? Promise me you won't.'

'But you must see this is wrong, Lettie,' Adeline said, as calmly as she could.

'Promise me,' Lettie demanded, a fierce, hard light in her eyes. 'This is no one's business but mine, Adeline, and I shall resent interference from anyone. Do you understand?'

Adeline nodded. 'Very well. I promise not to mention it to Lady Stanfield.'

That night Adeline lay awake most of the night, worrying miserably and imagining problems each more fantastic than the last. Her mind was in too much of a turmoil to work coherently. The serious implications of what Lettie was doing gave her no rest. She pictured Lettie—quick, clever and vivacious Lettie— brought low at the hands of Jack Cunningham. He was dangerous, and Adeline was afraid he would love Lettie lightly and discard her—his depth of commitment shallow. What would that do to her?

One thing she knew was that she could not remain detached. But she was out of her depth. She wasn't the kind of person to fall apart in a crisis, but this was something she had never had to cope with. Oh, dear God, what to do for the best? She couldn't go to Lady Stanfield because she had promised Lettie she wouldn't. But who else was there?

Grant! Lettie had told her that he was here in London, staying at the Charing Cross Hotel. Immediately she sat upright in bed. The idea that had just occurred to her was so simple she wondered why she hadn't thought of it before—but she *did*

know why. It was because Grant had told her he never wanted
to set eyes on her again. But this matter was too important for
her to be deterred by the furious rantings of a spurned suitor.

Grant would know what to do. Grant would make Lettie stop
seeing Jack Cunningham. Oh, brilliant, wonderful hope. He
would put it right. Yes, she thought, Grant. There was no one
else.

Her mind made up, suddenly she felt as if a weight had been
lifted from her shoulders, and her relief was so great she felt
weak. The thought did occur to her that Grant might not want
to see her but when he knew how important it was, and that it
concerned Lettie, he would have to.

And so the following morning found her ordering the
brougham to take her to the Charing Cross Hotel.

The hotel was every bit as grand and opulent as Adeline had
expected, with deep carpets and a plethora of flowers. As she
passed through the foyer she couldn't stop herself from indulging in a tormentingly sweet fantasy—a frail hope that made her
heart accelerate—that when Grant saw her he would be glad to
see her. She looked at the well-to-do people milling about. Her
face was flushed as she realised she had never felt so unsure of
herself in her life. The qualms she had kept firmly at bay rushed
at her. Until now the need for haste and a determination not to
anticipate trouble had sustained her, but she felt far from heroic,
alone and clutching her reticule.

To her relief she saw Grant almost at once. He was immaculately dressed in a dark frock coat and narrow pin-striped
trousers. His chiselled features, his glossy dark hair and his
wide shoulders were emblazoned on her brain. He was standing
by the main desk, talking to the concierge.

As if sensing her gaze, he turned and looked at her directly—

and she saw his face, ruthless and dominating, that rebellious lock of hair dipping over his forehead. Their eyes locked—and those hard silver-grey eyes struck her to her heart—eyes that had not so long ago melted her. She clutched at her memories as recognition flashed between them at the speed of light. Without taking his eyes off her, he strode across the distance that separated them.

Grant stared at her. 'My God!' The words came out unbidden. 'My God, Adeline…' Was this really her? Plain, rather serious Adeline? This tall, stylish goddess of a creature, as rakishly elegant as a fashion picture, with her gleaming dark red hair swept back and up in a perfect chignon beneath an adorable little hat. The arched wings of her eyebrows and the thick rows of dark lashes emphasised her brilliant green almond-shaped eyes. This was a different Adeline Osborne from the one he had known before. He hardly recognised her. She looked stunning.

Then he recollected himself. The mere thought of Adeline Osborne, the reminder of his stupid gullibility where she was concerned, made him want to drown himself in liquor—which was ironic, really, when he remembered it was liquor that had brought them together in the first place. When she had left Oaklands he had told himself that it was over and done with. But it was not as simple as that. She might have disappeared from his sight after flinging his proposal of marriage into his face, but he had been unable to banish her from his heart and mind, and he resented her for having the power and the ability to do that. And seeing her now, looking as she did, was crucifying him, since he had told himself—and believed—that she was nothing to him.

His expression changed, and Adeline actually flinched at the coldness that entered his narrowed eyes—like slits of frosted glass. Her indulgent fantasy that he would be pleased to see her died an immediate death and withered into nothing. It was incredible to her that those firm lips had kissed her, that those hands had caressed and fondled her naked flesh and given her such delight.

'Hello, Grant. How are you?' she said, amazed that her voice sounded calm when she was trembling inside. His grim expression as he met her gaze boded ill.

'I was doing nicely until a moment ago,' he replied curtly. One brow lifted in arrogant enquiry. 'What the hell are you doing here?'

Adeline's heart sank at his uncompromising antagonism. 'I have not come here to aggravate you, if that's what you think. I know you do not want to be involved with anything that has to do with me—'

'Right. At least we agree on that.' His face tightened, but his voice was ominously soft. 'How did you know where to find me?'

'Lettie told me you were staying here. I had to come—though I nearly didn't.' Somewhere in her whirling thoughts Adeline registered that Grant was treating this meeting with a cold nonchalance that was not at all appropriate. 'Do you think we could go somewhere more private?'

'I was on my way out,' he pointed out evasively.

'This really can't wait. I would like to speak to you on a rather serious matter. A few minutes of your time is all I need.'

With an impatient sigh and a brief look at his watch, he said, 'Then since you're determined to enact a Cheltenham tragedy I suppose I'd better listen to what you have to say.'

Momentary shock gave way to a sudden, almost uncontrollable burst of wrath. 'If you think for one minute I *wanted* to come here and see you again, then nothing could be further from the truth,' Adeline retorted frostily. 'I find your company both offensive and repugnant, and I cannot wait to be out of here. You seem to enjoy humiliating me, and you will continue trying

to humiliate me as long as we stand here. Are you going to listen
to what I have to say or not?'

Grant's jaw tightened, and a muscle began to twitch dangerously in the side of his neck, but he nodded. 'My room. It's on
the third floor, so we'll take the lift.'

'Thank you. It won't take long.'

'Fine,' he snapped.

Neither of them spoke until they entered Grant's richly or-
namented, opulent suite of rooms. Through an open door
Adeline could see a huge, comfortable bed which she did her
best not to look at.

'Would you like to sit down?' he asked, casually gesturing
towards a velvet chair by the window.

'No, thank you. I'll come straight to the point. What I have to
say is that I am deeply concerned about Lettie—and so is Marjorie.'

'You are?' Grant repeated with insolent amusement, perching
his hip on the edge of a table and crossing his arms over his
chest. The startling silver-grey eyes rested on her ironically. 'I
can't think why. Lettie is old enough, and quite capable of
standing on her own feet. She has done very much as she pleases
for a long time. Mother has accepted the work she does that
keeps her away from home and so have I.'

'It has nothing to do with her work. I wish it had. But it's more
serious than that. She—she's seeing someone…'

Grant shook his head in baffled disbelief. 'Lettie—seeing
someone? What's so very wrong with that? I'm happy to know
my sister has the same urges and emotions as every one else.
She's been so wrapped up in that damned Women's Movement
I was beginning to doubt it.'

Adeline stared at him and began to wonder what had induced
her to seek out this cold and uncaring man. Spinning on her heel,
she turned to the door. 'Even for a man who believes he has jus-

tification for being hostile towards me, that was a nasty remark to make about Lettie. I can see this was a mistake,' she uttered acidly. 'If you cannot bring yourself to listen to why I am so concerned about your sister, then I'll go. I'm sorry to have taken up so much of your time and inconvenienced myself. Please excuse me.'

In six long strides Grant was at the door as she opened it, shoving it closed with a force that sent it crashing into its frame.

'Since you are here, and I'm already late for my appointment, you'd better say what you have to say.'

Adeline spun round and faced him. His black brows were up and his eyes gleamed. Anger leaped in her breast so sharply that it stabbed at her heart like a knife-thrust. 'You really are the most appallingly rude man I have ever met. Do you *really* think I would be here if it weren't important? I am extremely concerned about Lettie—and so will you be if you would have the courtesy to listen.'

Shoving his hands into his trouser pockets, he nodded. Deep inside him he knew it must be a matter of some considerable importance to have brought Adeline to see him, feeling as she did about him. Despite everything he knew her to be, when he looked at her he saw spirit and youthful courage—and also fear in her eyes. Fear for Lettie?

Going to the window, he stood looking out, his shoulders tense. 'Tell me.'

Steeling herself against his reaction, drawing a deep breath, Adeline quickly gave Grant the facts. White and stony-faced, he listened to her, appalled by her disclosure. Scarcely able to grasp the reality of it, he turned and stood looking at her, his composure held tightly to him, his drawn face as blank as still water. Adeline had seen him angry, and she had seen him irritable, but now he was white with a quiet, controlled fury.

'You are telling me that my sister is involved with a night-club owner?' He began pacing the floor in restless fury.

'Yes.'

Fire sprang to his eyes. 'Dear God in heaven! Is that what she's doing when she's not putting the world to rights? Has she taken leave of her senses? What's he like—this Jack Cunningham?'

'Quite the gentleman—but no more than that. I did not like him at all. There's an air of danger about him. He's a taker, a man of terrible force. Lettie will be like putty in his hands.'

'How did you meet him?'

'I was curious about him. I asked Lettie to introduce us.'

Grant's eyes flashed unexpectedly. 'A brave action, and not to be commended. I know about men like Jack Cunningham. You are right to think he's dangerous. Is Lettie determined to carry on seeing him?'

'Yes. She is strongly attracted to him. She resented me warning her against him, and she is annoyed at what she considers to be my interference.'

Grant considered this for a moment. 'Annoyed, is she?' he muttered slowly. 'It seems a poor return for all your kindness and consideration.'

'I suspect she sees more of him secretly than she admits to. She is answerable only to herself.'

'She might think she is—for now. Lettie has always been a bit wild, and appears perfectly independent and careless of her own welfare. Mother and I have let her be too free. We shouldn't have allowed it all this time.'

'Lettie is the victim of a casual affair, and I fear that any day she will be cast aside and hurt by it—deeply so. You have to speak to her. For without your intervention she is doomed.'

'I intend to.' Becoming thoughtful, all at once he ceased his restless pacing. He turned then, and looked at her for a long time, his face quite expressionless, his eyes hidden by the shadows of his brows. The respite had given him back his outward composure, but his face was still marked with anger. Knowing his sister as he did, he felt dread, persistent as a thorn in his foot. 'What's the name of Cunningham's nightclub?'

'The Phoenix Club. Will you go there?'

Grant studied her for a moment, eyes narrowed, and then shook his head. 'No, not immediately. I'll speak to Lettie first. If she agrees to stop seeing him then the affair will die a natural death. But, just in case I intend to find out all I can about Jack Cunningham.'

Adeline bent her head and lowered her eyes for a moment, to shut out the sight of the man who stood before her. He was so stern and oppressive, and yet so very attractive. He took her breath away. Why was she so strongly attracted to him? He had treated her with little more than grudging tolerance since he had known her. His eyes were filled with concern now—but not for her; she knew that. But for Lettie.

'You cannot imagine how difficult it was for me to come here. I feel like a traitor, yet I know that Lettie is prey to her emotions and needs someone to speak some sound common sense to her. I have tried, but she won't listen. She made me promise not to disclose any of this to Lady Stanfield, which is why I have come to you. Have I done the right thing—telling you? Have I helped her or merely betrayed a confidence?'

'You did right to come to me. Anything that concerns Lettie concerns me. It is not for me to admit or deny her right to independence, but anything she does that will hurt my mother or our good name I will not tolerate. You have done all that could be reasonably expected of you, and I am sorry you have been burdened with this.'

'It's no burden. Lettie is my friend.'

'Nevertheless, I suspect it is the most difficult thing you have ever done—and the bravest. You obviously care about Lettie.'

Adeline felt warmth begin to seep through her entire body at his stirring words, and she took heart as his sternly carved features softened. 'Yes, I do.'

'Are you staying with Lady Stanfield?'

'No—at our London house in Eaton Place. I became concerned when Marjorie told me Lettie was staying out all night and implying to Lady Stanfield that she was at Eaton Place with me.'

'And she wasn't?'

'No.'

'Then Lettie ought to have thought more of your having to account for her absence. I am sorry.'

'There's no need to be. Lettie spends a great deal of her time organising committees, or doing the detailed work that goes into mounting campaigns, but according to Marjorie she has lately continually failed to turn up for some of her usual meetings, and is often missing from the house. It's only a matter of time before Lady Stanfield takes note and starts asking awkward questions.'

'Then I must speak to Lettie soon. I apologise for my callousness earlier. I appreciate what you are doing for Lettie.'

'I can only hope she does—but somehow I don't think so. She will take exception to me coming here, so I beg of you not to tell her.'

For a moment Grant looked at her in silence. His well-tailored coat emphasised the breadth of his shoulders. There was a warm glint in his eyes. 'I won't tell her you came to see me. I promise.'

'Thank you.'

A flicker of amusement lit his grey eyes. 'Don't thank me yet. This could get worse. When I tell Lettie to stop seeing Jack

Cunningham she'll be like a pit bull with a headache. It could even result in war.'

Adeline laughed. 'Then I shall be completely neutral, and let the two of you get on with it.'

'I may have thought you to be many things, Miss Osborne,' Grant teased lightly, 'but cowardly is not one of them.'

'Oh, I can be the world's biggest coward when it comes to violence.'

'Then we must see that it doesn't. Tell me, has my sister managed to lure you into the Women's Movement yet?'

'I find the work that she does interesting—although she isn't nearly as fiercely fanatical about it as some of the women she's introduced me to—but I prefer not to become involved at this time.'

'But you might?'

'I don't know.'

'Why? Because you think your destiny in life is to marry, make a home and have children?'

'I do want that—eventually—and I shall expect love, consideration and respect. But I will not marry a man who will expect me to be subordinate to my husband, who will wrap me in luxury and see that my every desire is satisfied except for independence and a will of my own.'

'Now you're beginning to sound like Lettie.'

'Perhaps that's because we've spent a lot of time together since I came to London. But we do also seem to spend a great deal of time shopping. As soon as I appeared in town she insisted on changing my appearance, and has almost drained my allowance dry.'

An amused quirk appeared at the corner of Grant's mouth as he regarded her attire, cut with ostentatious flattery. 'I've noticed. What you are wearing is certainly of a more eye-catching colour than I suspect is your natural choice. However, the change flatters you. But I am surprised.'

'You are?'

He looked at her from beneath raised brows. 'I would have thought it uncharacteristic of you to conform—to wear clothes to please society and to be noticed.'

'You are wrong. I now wear fashionable clothes like this to please myself, not society, and I am grateful to Lettie for showing me how to. Do you find something wrong with that?'

'Nothing at all. It's just that I thought the prim and proper Miss Adeline Osborne was immune to the magic of pretty clothes.'

She smiled slightly. 'Then you were wrong about that, too, for it would seem I am just as weak as all the rest.'

'So it would. You look—extremely elegant—and very lovely,' he murmured, thinking that she also looked so young—in fact he had never seen her looking so young. It was as if in discarding her plain clothes and unflattering hairstyle she had thrown off surplus years with them. When he'd first seen her he had imagined her to be anything up to twenty-five. Now she looked a vulnerable girl of eighteen or nineteen.

His compliment brought an attractive flush to Adeline's cheeks. There was something in what he'd said, or perhaps in the slight tremor she'd heard in his voice as he'd said it, that made her want to believe he meant more by it than he really did. But she did not delude herself to think so. Grant Leighton really was the most unpredictable man. One minute he was making love to her, the next asking her to marry him and then rejecting her completely. He'd told her he never wanted to set eyes on her again, and yet now he was telling her she looked elegant and very lovely. What was she to think?

'Flattery indeed, coming from you.'

'I never flatter anyone, Adeline. My opinions are always given honestly.' His eyes did a leisurely sweep of her fashionable high-necked, svelte-waisted cobalt blue jacket. Her straight-fronted skirt was making him think of the long, glorious legs beneath. A scent of warm violets filled his nostrils and made him want to lower his lips to the curve of her neck. It was all he could do to keep his hands from sliding around her waist and pulling her into his arms. 'A woman can be as beautiful as she feels herself to be.'

'I must confess to never having thought about it.' Adeline looked at him almost candidly, almost shyly. 'Do you mind if I ask you something—and will you promise not to be angry?'

'Ask away. I am all ears.'

'That night—when we were together—when you awoke—did you really think I was the kind of girl who would give herself to anyone?' She looked up into his eyes, trying to read his expression.

There was a moment's silence. Grant watched her face with a slightly cynical lift of his brows, then he shrugged slightly and turned away.

'I must confess to never having thought about it. I thought you were beautiful—but then when a man wakes and finds a naked woman in his arms he thinks all kinds of things—a woman's face can be deceptive.'

Adeline gave a hard, contemptuous laugh. 'I see—and you must have thought it had been so easy to get me into bed.'

Grant swung round and came to her. Adeline could discern in his features no trace of his earlier anger. He was grave, but calm.

'When I awoke I was in so much agony I was convinced a full orchestra was tuning up inside my head. When I saw you lying there I didn't know what the hell to think. I have never been so confused in my life. And when I realised what I'd done I was shocked, appalled and disgusted with myself.'

Despite herself Adeline smiled almost shyly. 'Me, too—at myself, I mean.'

Looking down at her, Grant felt his conscience choose that moment to reassert itself for the first time in weeks, by reminding him that he hadn't been able to keep his hands off her that night at Westwood Hall. How it had come about no longer mattered. He'd subjected her to public embarrassment and censure. Compounding all of that by robbing her of her virginity was inexcusable, but the weak protest of his conscience hadn't been enough to deter him.

Looking at her now—different in her new finery and elegantly styled hair, yet still the same Adeline Osborne underneath it all, despite everything—he thought she was the most alluring woman he had ever met.

'You—will help Lettie, won't you?'

Grant looked down into those beseeching green eyes. Slowly he nodded. Adeline smiled at him. His brain captured the moment in a flash. He wanted her, and neither his conscience nor anything else was going to deprive him of having her again. Only the next time he would make sure he was in full control of all his faculties.

Drawn by the depths of her eyes looking into his, by the soft fullness of the lips slightly parted to reveal moist, shining teeth, and unaware of the passage of time, he made a move towards her. But Adeline turned away from the threatened kiss. The spell was broken.

'I fear I have kept you from your appointment for far too long. I think I'd better go.'

'Yes, I think you better had. I'll come down with you.'

'No, you needn't. I can find my own way.'

'I insist. Besides, I have an appointment to keep.'

'You'll be late. I'm sorry.'

'Better late than never.'

They had just stepped out of the lift when Adeline's attention was drawn by a slight disturbance in the foyer. A woman had entered. In a shimmering gown of saffron-coloured silk with crimson trim, her dark hair pinned and curled beneath a fashionable, elaborately feathered headdress, she was stunning. Like everyone else, Adeline could not tear her eyes off her. When the woman's gaze searched the crowd and came to rest on Grant, Adeline frowned, disquieted.

It was Diana Waverley—the woman she was now certain had been at the Phoenix Club.

Chapter Seven

Pinning a brilliant smile on her face, Diana crossed towards them.

When Grant saw her he stiffened and stood absolutely still, aware and wary. His face was blank, all emotion withheld by an iron control, and then, conscious that Adeline was by his side, watching him, with a lazy, sardonic smile he stepped forward and lifted Diana's hand to his lips for a brief kiss.

Diana looked up at him with a questioning frown. 'Why, Grant. I did not think I would have to come looking for you. You cannot have forgotten our appointment.'

'Diana! I apologise. No, I did not forget. I had an unexpected matter of considerable importance to take care of.'

Diana gave Adeline no more than a brief glance—as if she were of no consequence—before settling her gaze once more on Grant. 'Yes, so I see.' Immediately her attention flew back to Adeline and she gasped. 'Why—goodness me! If it isn't Miss Adeline Osborne! How nice to see you again,' she said, the tone of her voice and the cold look in her eyes belying her words. 'I do apologise. I hardly recognised you. How changed you look.' She was angry. This was not what she had planned. Not at all. Expelling her breath in a rush of frustrated impatience, she looked up at Grant with a questioning frown.

'Your apology is unnecessary,' Adeline said. 'In fact it is I who should apologise to you for keeping Grant so long.'

'Really?' Diana smiled as her gaze passed over Adeline. It was not a pleasant smile, it was a malicious smile, and instinctively, with the feminine intuition that recognises what is in another woman's mind, Adeline knew that Diana considered Grant her property, and was telling Adeline to keep off.

'Grant and I were—'

'Stop it, Adeline,' Grant was quick to retort. 'There's absolutely no need to explain to Diana.'

'Well, since I have just observed the two of you coming out of the lift, I can only assume that Grant has been entertaining you in his room.' When she looked at Adeline her feelings were transparent—the emotions of jealousy and dislike were hard to mask when they lay so near the surface. 'I am sure it is none of my business, but perhaps it's not something you should choose to bandy about in public.'

Adeline took exception to the slur. Diana's tone, lightly contemptuous and at the same time more than a little suspicious, made Adeline's hackles rise. However, although she was still seething inside from Diana's machinations at Westwood Hall, she faced her with well-feigned assurance.

'You're right, Diana, it is none of your affair. So kindly watch your tongue,' Grant admonished sharply. 'Now you are here we will have luncheon. Adeline is just leaving. I will see her out to her carriage and then I'll be with you.'

At that moment the concierge approached Grant and drew

him aside to speak to him on a trivial matter, but it meant he left Adeline alone with Diana.

'Well, I certainly didn't expect to see *you* at the Charing Cross Hotel, Adeline.'

Absently Adeline noted that rubies like droplets of blood dripped from Diana's ears and neck. Adeline's flesh turned to ice when she met her stare. That Diana Waverley hated her was plain.

'I came to see Grant on a family matter. Make of that what you will, Diana. I have apologised for keeping him from his appointment with you, but it really was important and could not wait.'

'So was his appointment with me. Still, it's not too late. We can take care of our business just as well here as at my house. Unlike you, I ceased to consider my reputation a long time ago. I have known Grant for a long time, and I know him about as well as any woman can.'

Adeline met her eyes. 'Then we are not so very different. I may not have known him as long as you have, but I have known him just as well.' Her smile was meaningful, and they both knew she was referring to the night Diana had tied the scarlet ribbon to her door.

White-lipped, Diana glared at her, knowing she had been caught out. She was reminded that instead of acting like the prim and proper miss she had assumed Adeline Osborne to be, and alerting the whole household to the embarrassing fact that Grant had entered her bedchamber uninvited, she had quietly taken full advantage of the situation—and enjoyed every minute of it, too, no doubt.

Adeline added coolly. 'How is Paul, by the way? I believe you know *him* just about as well as any woman can, too. You know, Diana, I have much to be grateful to you for. I am well rid of

him. You may have missed your chance for snaring Grant, but
I am sure you will find Paul amenable. I wish you well of each
other. Good day. Please tell Grant I can find my own way out.'

Diana felt her cheeks grow hot with the sting of defeat. The
reality of what Adeline had said hit her with all the force of a
hammer-blow. Her dream of Grant asking her to be his wife had
faded to leave a bitter taste in her mouth. She watched Adeline's
trim figure leave the hotel. How that little bitch must be laughing
at her fate.

After Adeline had left Diana with Grant at the hotel her imagination ran riot. Her emotions were so confused that she felt they
were choking her—protests, recriminations, accusations, all
were tumbling about in her mind. They were to have luncheon,
Grant had said—where, she wondered? In the hotel restaurant
or in Grant's room? An image of the bed she had seen—big and
comfortable, a veritable erotic pleasure ground for lovers—
entered her mind. Thinking of them in it, and what they would
do, made her blood run cold. The shock of it all triggered off
some sleeping thing inside her, bringing to life and revealing to
her the true state of her heart.

So much for Grant's declaration that he never gave second
chances, and that what there had been between him and Diana
was over, for it was as plain as the nose on her face that he was
undoubtedly sharing the favours of that woman with Paul.
Perhaps Grant found such a situation entertaining—a bit of fun
with no hearts broken—but what he was doing was highly
immoral in her opinion. He was just like everyone else—
enjoying his little dalliances and flirtations—but she would not
be one of them.

However, because she had approached him about Lettie it was
inevitable they would meet again. Whatever happened, she

vowed she would never again lose her composure as she had in the past, when he had confused her to such a degree that she scarcely knew right from wrong. From this moment on things would be different. She would be completely imperturbable and polite. She was no longer the innocent young girl he could hurt and seduce for his own amusement.

Adeline spent the rest of the day at home, glad to have some time to herself. The London house was large and imposing, and reflected her father's taste to as great a degree as Rosehill did.

The following morning she was debating on whether to go to Stanfield House, in the hope of seeing Lettie, or take a quiet stroll in the park, when Anthony Stanfield arrived to take her up on her offer of a fencing bout. At first Adeline stared at him in confusion, and then recalled she had indeed invited him over.

'I'll go away if it's inconvenient, or you're not up to it,' Anthony offered, his expression telling her that he hoped she was.

Adeline laughed and led him to the salon, glad of any respite from the quiet atmosphere of the house. 'I wouldn't dream of it. Fencing is just what I need right now, to draw me out of the doldrums. I'll show you where the rapiers are kept and then I'll go and change.'

Shortly before eleven o'clock, Grant arrived at the house to see Adeline. When Mrs Kelsall opened the door and he asked to see Miss Osborne, the housekeeper raised her brows in astonishment. Few visitors came to Eaton Place when Mr Leighton was not in town, and suddenly two gentlemen had turned up within the same hour to see Miss Adeline. She didn't approve of young gentlemen calling uninvited when she was alone, but since Miss Adeline had come to London there had been a change in her, an open confidence and self-assurance Mrs Kelsall had never seen before.

'Is Miss Osborne at home?' Grant enquired.

'She is, sir, in the salon—fencing.' Though Mrs Kelsall was fond of Miss Adeline, she never ceased to voice her disapproval of young ladies indulging in gentlemanly activities, and for them to wear trousers—which Miss Adeline insisted on doing— was quite shocking and unthinkable.

'Then if you will be so kind as to direct me, I will introduce myself.'

Grant opened the door to the salon, where the carpet had been rolled back. He entered quietly, unnoticed by the pair of duellists, their identities hidden by facial masks. One was evidently female. Her lithesome figure was clad in revealing dove-grey trousers and a white silk shirt, and she was fighting with the skill and address of an experienced duellist, moving with an extraordinary grace, as if movement were a pleasure to her. The other, a young gentleman, was not so skilled.

Propping his shoulder against the wall, Grant watched with interest as they parried and thrust, moving ceaselessly about the highly polished parquet floor.

After Adeline had left the hotel yesterday, Grant had sat through luncheon paying no more attention to Diana across from him than he had to the business proposition she had put to him. This had been completely out of character, for he always gave matters of business his whole attention, considering them with unfailing instinct and dispassionate logic and calculating the odds for success before he acted. The only rash act he'd performed in recent years was his behaviour with Adeline at Westwood Hall, and when she'd left the hotel he had set his mind to seeing her again just as soon as he could manage it.

Folding his arms, with a slight smile on his lips, his unswerving gaze now watched her every move, feasting on the graceful lines of her slim hips and incredibly long legs, her whole form outlined with anatomical precision. Adeline was, Grant realised, a brilliant swordswoman, with faultless timing and stunningly executed moves. There was an aura of confidence and daring about her that drew all his attention.

Still unaware of his presence, Adeline suddenly cried enough and whipped off her mask to reveal her laughing, shining face. 'Very good, Anthony. You're improving tremendously. We'll fence some more tomorrow, if you like.'

She was breathless and her cheeks were flushed, her eyes a brilliant dancing green. Her abundance of hair was tied loosely on top of her head, with riotous locks tumbling about all over the place. To Grant at that moment she looked like a bandit princess, vibrant with health and life. His eyes soaked up the sight of her, for which he was more thirsty than water by far.

Anthony was the first to become aware of Grant's presence. His face broke into a welcoming smile as he recognised Lettie's brother. Taking off his breastplate and wiping his damp forehead with his sleeve, he crossed the room towards him and shook his hand. 'Mr Leighton. I didn't realise we had company. It's good to see you.'

'I was enjoying watching you. I didn't want to interrupt such fine swordplay.'

'As you will have seen,' he said, turning towards his attractive partner, his adoring gaze and unselfconscious absorption not going unnoticed by Grant, 'Adeline is more than a match. She has much to teach me.'

Across the room, on hearing Grant's voice, Adeline spun round, her heart giving a sudden lurch. 'I'm sorry. I didn't know you were there.'

He smiled. 'I'm glad. You are an excellent swordswoman,

Adeline. Had you been aware of my presence you would perhaps not have performed so well.'

Her sudden smile had a warmth to contend with the glowing
sun slanting through the windows. 'You are mistaken. I fence
the same regardless of whether I have an audience or not. What
has brought you to Eaton Place?'

'I have a matter of some importance to discuss with you. I
didn't think you'd mind me arriving uninvited.'

'I'll leave you, Adeline,' Anthony said, shrugging himself
into his jacket. 'I have to get back.'

'That's all right, Anthony. I'm glad you came for a practice
bout. If Lettie's at home, tell her I'll be along later.'

When she was alone with Grant, she looked at him askance.
'Why do you smile?'

'That young man's in love with you—or if he isn't now he
very soon will be.'

Adeline gasped and laughed awkwardly, embarrassed that
such a thing could happen. 'Really, Grant, your imagination runs
away with you. Anthony and I are friends—good friends—and
nothing more, so please don't read more into our fencing bouts
than there is.'

His eyes crinkled with amusement. 'There is none so blind
as will not see, Adeline. Time will tell.'

'You are being ridiculous. He's only a young man.'

'Exactly! He's a man—and you, Miss Osborne, are an attractive young woman. He couldn't keep his eyes off you.'

Adeline suddenly became embarrassingly self-conscious of the
way she was dressed. 'If you don't mind I'll just go and change.
I'll have Mrs Kelsall prepare refreshments and then we can talk.'

'Not so fast.' Grant quickly divested himself of his coat and
waistcoat, rolling back his shirtsleeves over powerful forearms.
Removing his cravat and shirt stud to allow more freedom, he

began fastening himself into the breastplate discarded by Anthony. 'I have a desire to test your fencing skills for myself. That's if you're up to it?'

'I'm tougher than I look.'

'So am I.'

He was looking at her with just a gleam of mischief at the back of his impassive handsome face. 'So you court danger, do you, Mr Leighton?'

'All the time, Miss Osborne.'

'Do you fence often?' she asked, curious as to how skilled an adversary he would make.

Grant was already crossing the room to help himself to one of the many fine weapons on display in a glass-fronted cabinet. 'Not as often as I would like.'

'In which case I imagine you'll be a bit rusty,' she taunted, with an innocent smile curving her lips.

His grin was roguish and the gleam in his eyes more so as his hand closed over the hilt of a weapon with a strong, slender blade. 'Imagine anything you like, Miss Osborne,' he retorted, flexing the supple blade between his hands before swishing the air in a practised arc, 'but my infrequency at practice does not mean that I shall be complacent or clumsy, or in need of lessons in self-defence.'

'Maybe not, but I don't think this will take long.'

'Planning to thrash me, are you?' he drawled, one brow arrogantly raised.

'Soundly,' Adeline told him.

Donning a face mask, he advanced towards her. 'As a matter of interest can you see properly? Without your spectacles, I mean,' he goaded.

'My vision is only impaired when I try to read. Otherwise I can see perfectly well.'

'I'm glad to hear it. But don't ever complain that I didn't warn you,' he said with tolerant amusement. 'Replace your mask and prepare to defend yourself, Miss Osborne, or I swear I'll pin you to the wall.'

The challenge to participate in a sport that was as enjoyable to her as riding a horse was much too tempting for Adeline to resist. With a vivacious laugh she replaced her mask and picked up her rapier. In one swift movement she was in the centre of the room, and Grant found himself engaged. Hidden from his view, a feverish flush was on her cheeks and a wild, determined light in her eyes. She moved skilfully, confident she could best him, but careful not to underestimate his ability.

Grant was an excellent sportsman, and accounted an excellent blade, but he soon realised he had his work cut out as his slender, darting opponent left no opening in her unwavering guard. The bright blade seemed to be everywhere at once, multiplied a hundred times by Adeline's supple wrists.

After the initial thrusts Adeline accepted that beating Grant was not going to be easy. He fought with skill, continually circling his opponent, changing his guard a dozen times, but Adeline never failed to parry adroitly in her own defence.

Grant could imagine the face behind the mask—the excitement of the fight would have put colour into her cheeks, a gleam in her eyes and a rosiness on her full lips. The image sent desire surging through him as foils rang together, meeting faster and faster as he forced her to a killing pace. Sweat now soaked her fine silk shirt so that it clung alluringly to her body, outlining the tender swell of her breasts.

Adeline was beginning to weaken, finding herself held at bay by a superior strength. Grant knew this, and with a low chuckle doubled his agility. With a triumphant cry and a snake-like movement he slipped under her blade and decisively thrust home.

Accepting that she was beaten, fair and square, Adeline

whipped her mask from her laughing face. 'So, Mr Leighton, you have made good your threat. No doubt you regret wasting your time on such a weak opponent?'

'Nonsense. You were already considerably weakened by your earlier bout with Anthony,' Grant remarked, removing his mask, thinking how truly adorable she looked in complete disarray.

'You are too kind. There are no excuses for my defeat. I was beaten by a superior strength. I accept that.'

'A master?' he pressed, with a broad, arrogant smile.

'You conceited beast. I refuse to flatter your vanity further.'

Grant's grin was wicked. 'And you are magnanimous in defeat. I look forward to repeating the exercise.'

'Next time you won't be so lucky,' she quipped, with a jaunty impudence Grant found utterly exhilarating.

'I'm looking forward to it already. Who taught you to fence?'

'Uncle Max—my mother's brother. He was a military man and fought in the Crimean War. Sadly he died last year.' She placed the rapiers in the cabinet and turned back to him, feeling extremely self-conscious in her trousers. 'I must look a sight. I'll go and change.'

Lifting his gaze from the feminine curves of her breasts, slowly Grant let his eyes seek hers, and Adeline basked in the unconcealed admiration lighting his face. His amusement had vanished. An aura of anticipation surrounded them. It was blatantly sensual and keenly felt by Adeline. It widened her eyes and lingered in the curve of her lips.

Grant's own firm mouth curved in a sensuous smile. 'Believe me, there's nothing wrong with the way you look, Adeline,' he murmured.

Her senses heightened by his closeness, Adeline flushed and smiled tremulously, thinking how incredibly handsome he looked with his hair dipping over his forehead. 'Not to you, maybe, but I cannot possibly sit down to lunch like this. Mrs Kelsall has objections enough to what she considers to be my unladylike attire, and will refuse to feed us unless I change.'

He cocked a sleek black brow. 'Us? Are you inviting me to luncheon, Adeline?'

With an effort, Adeline tore her gaze from Grant's amused grey eyes and looked in the direction of the door. 'Yes—that is, if you like. It's almost lunchtime anyway, and I'm sure you must be hungry after your exertions.'

After showing him to the drawing room, Adeline escaped to her room to swill her burning face in cold water.

Mrs Kelsall had laid a light lunch for them in the dining room. They took their seats opposite each other.

'Please help yourself,' Adeline said, indicating the various cold dishes. 'I must try not to over-indulge, since I am going on a picnic this afternoon.'

'A picnic?'

'Yes.' She laughed. 'I enjoy idling away my days in frivolous pursuits. It's such a lovely day I thought Emma and I would go for a drive along the Embankment and go on to the gardens at Chelsea.'

They applied themselves to the food with unfeigned appreciation, and after commenting on the culinary delights they conversed little until the end of the meal.

Adeline, used to dining in silence with her father, did not babble on, as other women were wont to do, and Grant found this a pleasurable change. There was nothing awkward about the silence, which was comfortable and agreeable. However, he was of the opinion that while women prattled on, they weren't thinking, and when he glanced across at Adeline's serene countenance he was curious as to her thoughts.

Wearing a gown of ruby-coloured taffeta, unadorned and

simple, with a well-fitted bodice, she had drawn her hair back from her face. Her almond-shaped eyes and high cheekbones gave her a rich, vivid and almost oriental beauty.

When they had finished eating they retired to the drawing room, sitting across from each other in two large wing-backed chairs. Grant stared at Adeline's profile as she turned her head slightly, tracing with his gaze the lines of her face, the brush of her thick eyelashes, the delicate hollow at the nape of her neck, where a stray strand of hair had come to rest, nestling against her pale skin like a dark red spiral.

'Have you spoken to Lettie?' Adeline asked, looking to where Grant was sitting silently watching her, holding her with his gaze.

He shook his head. 'Unfortunately I haven't had the opportunity. I called on Lord and Lady Stanfield before coming here, but Lettie was out at one of her meetings, somewhere in Kensington. And you?'

'No. Maybe later. What is it you wanted to see me about?'

'I've made enquiries about Jack Cunningham.'

'Oh? Have you found out much about him?'

Grant nodded slowly, his expression grave. 'It wasn't difficult. He's extremely well known, is Mr Cunningham—notorious, in fact—and steeped in vice. One thing I've learned is that he isn't working for good causes—and you are right, he's a dangerous individual. Apparently he isn't one to meddle with, and no one crosses him twice.' A grim smile twisted his lips. 'I suppose if he is to succeed in the hard and dangerous trade he's chosen then he needs to appear a man no one would dare cross.'

'Where is he from?'

'He was born in Whitechapel—one of nine children, father worked on the docks. He's self-made, shrewd, aggressive, determined and unscrupulous, and he has power over a lot of people. He has friends—of a sort. Mostly there are those who hate him and those who are frightened of him—and those who are both. Women seem to like him, but he treats them badly. I suspect he wants Lettie because she stands for something he's never had.'

'And what is that?'

'Class. He's a powerful figure in the underworld, where he reigns over an empire of corruption and debauchery. Nothing is too scandalous to be tolerated. The Phoenix is a gambling and drinking den, and a house of assignation—prostitution. He derives handsome profits from its exploitation. In fact he's made a lot of money out of his seedy nightclubs and brothels scattered all over the West End.'

There was a good deal more that Grant could have told Adeline about Jack Cunningham—his involvement in the sex-trafficking of both women and children he purchased through a network of agents to install in his brothels. Grant considered this widespread victimisation of children an abomination, but he would not embarrass or distress Adeline by divulging this part of Cunningham's sordid empire.

'After visiting the place, somehow it doesn't surprise me to hear that.' Adeline shuddered at the memory.

'Cunningham never soils his own hands with violence. Others do it for him—he has plenty of henchmen. He carries people in his head and moves them about like chess pieces. He also lends money at high interest rates—expending very little risk since for his investment he is careful to command property of a much higher value or favours as security. He's used to getting what he wants, and if anyone opposes him he shows no mercy.'

Adeline paled visibly, appalled by what she was hearing. 'I can't believe Lettie has got involved with somebody like that.'

Grant looked at her sharply. 'How did she meet him? Do you know?'

'Yes. It was at the Drury Lane Theatre—Diana Waverly introduced them.'

Grant stared at her, dumbfounded. For some reason this bothered him. 'Diana knows Cunningham?'

'Yes. As a matter of fact I believe she was at the Phoenix Club at the same time that I was there with Lettie. I saw a woman disappearing up a spiral staircase. I was too late to see her face, but she was wearing the same dress yesterday at the hotel.' Adeline was looking at Grant steadily, trying to measure the emotion lying behind the façade. 'You—didn't know Diana was associated with Cunningham?'

'No.' Grant felt oddly betrayed that Diana had never spoken to him of Cunningham—but then she had no reason to. Until Adeline had brought him to his attention he had never heard of him.

'Well, if she is that is her affair. But he sounds a thoroughly bad lot.'

'He is, Adeline, believe me. Lettie may be independent and twenty-three, but she is still innocent, trusting and unworldly to a man of his calibre. I intend to do everything in my power to put an end to his association with my sister—preferably without coming into contact with Jack Cunningham.'

'That's sensible. If he's as obnoxious as you say he is then it could only lead to trouble. Best to let Lettie finish it quietly— although I hope she doesn't love him so much she will stand against you in defence of him. Is Lettie anything like your other sister who lives in Ireland?' Adeline asked, suddenly curious about Grant's other siblings.

'Anna?' His expression lightened and his lips curved in a smile. 'No. Not at all. Anna is mild-mannered, unselfish, genuinely kind-hearted and willing to take on everyone's troubles. Mother hasn't seen Anna and her family for eighteen months—since she went over for a visit—and naturally she's excited about them coming for Christmas and an extended stay.'

'I'm sure she is. I seem to recall her saying that your brother is also coming home for Christmas?'

'That's right. He's coming home on leave for a few weeks. All his life Roland has wanted to be a soldier. He loves India, and no doubt he will go back there to his regiment when his leave is up.' Grant stood up. 'I've kept you long enough. You'll be wanting to go on your picnic. I'll call at Upper Belgrave Street and see if Lettie has returned.'

Adeline went out into the hall with him, where they paused. 'I do wish you every success with Lettie. Truly. I wish no harm to come to her at the hands of Jack Cunningham.'

Grant looked at her earnest, upturned face. He felt humbled by her generosity of spirit and her compassion for Lettie. Her full mouth was soft and provocative, her shining eyes mesmerising in their lack of guile, and her smooth cheekbones were flushed a becoming pink. Courageous, unpretentious and unaffected, she sparkled from within and shone on the surface. She was, he decided, the most interesting female he had ever met. She was also becoming embarrassed by his scrutiny. Her long ebony lashes had flickered down to hide her eyes.

Grant smiled, his grey eyes glinting with admiration. 'Nor do I.'

'I—enjoyed fencing with you,' Adeline said, suddenly nervous, self-conscious, trying desperately to sound normal. 'The exercise was good, and I can't tell you how good it was to fence with such an expert as yourself. I rarely get the opportunity. I—don't know how to thank you.'

His heavy-lidded gaze fixed meaningfully on her lips. 'We'll have to think of a way,' he murmured softly.

At that moment Mrs Kelsall bustled into the hall, her face in subdued lines. 'What is it, Mrs Kelsall? Has something happened?'

'No, Miss Adeline. Your picnic basket is all prepared, but Emma isn't feeling too well and doesn't think she's up to going out.'

'Oh, I'm sorry to hear that. She was complaining of a headache earlier. I'll go to her.' Adeline was clearly concerned about her maid. She turned to Grant and smiled weakly. 'It looks as though my picnic will have to keep for another day.'

A sudden gleam entered his eyes. 'It needn't. Perhaps you would allow me to accompany you?'

Silver-grey eyes met hers, and she felt her cheeks warm. 'Oh—I couldn't possibly. I couldn't impose on your time.'

His smile broadened into a grin. 'It's no imposition. I have a totally free day.'

'But you don't enjoy picnics.'

He arched one dark brow. 'I don't?'

'Well—I wouldn't have thought you were the type that did.'

'I happen to love picnics.'

'You do?'

'Absolutely. Just make sure there's a bottle of wine in the basket.'

'I'll go and put one in this minute.' Mrs Kelsall was quick to oblige, happy that all the work she'd put into the basket wouldn't be wasted after all.

'You really don't have to do this,' Adeline said to Grant, protesting even while unable to quell the stirring of pleasure his offer aroused.

'I want to. I promise I shall be a capable and attentive escort—and besides…'

'Besides, what?'

'It would be a shame to waste the food.'

'But I thought you were going to see Lettie?'

'I shall call on her later—there will be more chance of catching her then.'

Adeline searched his bold, swarthy visage, unsurprised by his nerve. 'Your persistence amazes me. I shouldn't be going anywhere with you on my own.'

He chuckled, smiling a wicked smile. 'Why not? We might both enjoy the outing. I favour your company, Adeline, and I shall endeavour to be on my best behaviour and as charming as my nature will allow.'

Adeline looked at him with doubt. 'We shall see. It should prove to be an interesting afternoon.'

'It will be what we make it. Now, go and get ready.'

Seated across from Grant in the Osborne landau, with its grey upholstery and the hood down, Adeline experienced a strange exhilaration. She felt wonderfully, gloriously alive for the first time in years as she instructed the driver to take them to the Embankment. There was something undeniably engaging about her handsome escort. He made her feel alert and curiously stimulated.

'You look exceptional, Adeline,' he told her. 'Radiant, in fact. I am honoured by this privilege.'

Adeline smoothed her dark green woollen skirt, knowing it became her extraordinarily well. She wore a fitted three-quarter-length matching coat and hat, which was adorned with small brown feathers. The ensemble combined rich, stylish flair and good taste.

'I am often in London, and I really can't name a sight that I haven't seen. Is there anywhere else you would rather go than the Embankment?' she asked Grant.

'I am at your disposal entirely. The Embankment suits me perfectly well.'

On reaching the Embankment they left the landau, and with a slight breeze in their faces strolled along. The early autumn day was overcast, but it was warm. People strolled along, like themselves, and open carriages passed by, with women showing off the latest fashions. Street peddlers were selling various kinds of food, from drinks and pies to sweets, and further along a brass band competed with a hurdy-gurdy playing a popular dance tune.

The dancing silvered river was busy with shipping of every kind—ferries, lighter men and a string of barges—making their way steadily upstream, the movement keeping the waters constantly on the swell. There were sounds of laughter from the pleasure boats crowded with people enjoying themselves. A woman's hat blew off into the river, causing much hilarity. Some waved to the people watching from the Embankment, and with laughter on her lips Adeline waved back.

Grant looked at her, thinking how adorable she was with her pink cheeks and shining eyes. She put him in mind of a child opening its presents at Christmas. 'Enjoying yourself?'

'I am. I love the Embankment, and today is just like London should be.' She turned towards the river. 'Can you smell it?'

'Smell what?'

'The salt on the incoming tide.'

Breathing deep, Grant could detect a tang in the air—the smell of salt and what he thought might be tar.

For a while they were both engrossed with the scene before them, then they walked back to the landau to continue on their way to Chelsea. Reaching their destination, they told the driver to return to Eaton Place. They would take a cab when it was time to return.

Carrying the picnic basket, and a rug over one arm, Grant gallantly presented his other arm to Adeline, at the same time catching her hand and pulling it through the crook of his elbow, not giving her a chance to deny him. Adeline was tempted to withdraw from his contact, but a small, naughty part of her knew she liked touching him. Very much.

The gardens overlooking the river were mostly for summer strolls and musical entertainments, and the quietness of the autumn day could not be denied. The wind was fresh, but reasonably warm, rustling the dying leaves in the trees and dappling the shade, and Adeline was content to let her escort lead her along the tree-lined lanes and past beds of the last of the summer's flowers. As promised, Grant lent himself to a most gentlemanly comportment and treated her with polite consideration, making her feel as if she were the only woman in the world.

Finding a secluded spot beneath the giant trees, Adeline spread out the rug while Grant removed his jacket, opened the basket and poured the wine. Totally relaxed, they talked about little things—oddities of fact that made simple things interesting. They told stories and joked and laughed at each other, and all the while Adeline was aware of Grant's appreciative gaze on her animated face. In all it proved to be a most enchanting afternoon, and Adeline experienced a twinge of regret that it would have to end.

Stretching out on his side, Grant leaned on a forearm and studied her profile from beneath hooded lids, wondering for the hundredth time what went on behind her placid exterior. 'You are a strange young woman, Adeline,' he murmured, focusing his eyes on a wisp of hair against her cheek.

Without thinking, he reached out and tucked it behind her ear, feeling the velvety softness of her skin against his fingers. She sat still as he ran the tip of his finger down the column of her throat, along the line of her chin to her collar and the cameo brooch at her throat.

'Suddenly I find myself wanting to know everything there is to know about you—what you are thinking, what you are feeling. You are still a mystery to me.'

'In the short time we have known each other, haven't you learned anything about me?'

'I have learned some things. I have learned that you are not the prim and proper miss you purport to be, and that you like making love to inebriated gentlemen when you are the one who can dictate the action, and that—'

'Grant, please!' Resting back on her heels, Adeline was aghast. 'Stop it now,' she retorted, her face heating. 'It wasn't like that, and you know it.'

'No? Are you saying that you *didn't* enjoy making love to me?' He reached into the basket for a sandwich and slowly began to eat.

'No—yes... Oh, behave yourself. You promised me you would.'

Grant was by no means done with her yet. 'Have you done anything like that with anyone else?'

Adeline's cheeks flamed with indignation. 'No—and I have told you so.'

He grinned. 'You have? Forgive me if I don't recall.'

'Will you please stop tormenting me about my—slip of propriety?'

His grin widened at her embarrassment, and then he gave a shout of laughter. 'I like reminding you. I like seeing you get all flushed and flustered and hot under the collar.'

She glowered down at him. 'Now you're making fun of me.'

'I know.'

Unable to stay cross with him—knowing he was teasing anyway—Adeline laughed.

Grant lay back beside her, linking his hands behind his head and staring up at the trees. 'You should laugh more often. You have a beautiful laugh.'

Hearing the sensuous huskiness that deepened his voice, Adeline shivered inwardly. 'Thank you—but you are only saying that to placate me.'

'Do you need placating?'

She sighed, tucking her legs beneath her. 'No. I'm having too nice a time to be cross.'

'Good.'

When he closed his eyes, Adeline let her gaze wander over the smooth, thick lock of hair that dipped over his brow, and the authority and arrogance of every line of his darkly handsome face. She let her gaze travel down the full length of the superbly fit, muscled body stretched out beside her. How well she remembered him lying beside her like this once before when, even sleeping, he had exuded a raw, potent virility that had held her in thrall.

As if he could feel her eyes studying him, without opening his eyes, he quirked the mobile line of his mouth in a half-smile. 'I hope you like what you see.' He sighed. 'You can kiss me if you want to, Adeline.'

Adeline's eyes opened wide in astonishment, and then she laughed. Why, the sheer arrogance of the man. 'I most certainly will not,' she objected, slapping him playfully on the chest with her napkin.

Like lightning, he reared up. His hands shot out and gripped her upper arms, and he pulled her down onto her back, leaning over her. 'If you won't kiss me, do you mind if I kiss you?' His voice was low-pitched and sensual. 'Are you not curious to find out if it will be as good as when I kissed you at Oaklands? When I found you wandering about my house like a beautiful ghost in your nightdress.' A slight smile touched his mouth, but his heavy-lidded gaze dropped to the inviting fullness of her lips, lingering there.

Hypnotised by that velvet voice and those mesmerising silver eyes, Adeline gazed up at him with a combination of fear and excitement. She tried to relax, but in the charged silence between them it was impossible. And then, as quick as he had been to pull her down onto the rug, so she rolled away from him and got to her knees.

Startled, Grant stared at her, annoyed that he was to be deprived of his kiss. 'Now what?'

'I think it's time to go.'

'If there's anything I can't abide it's an obstinate woman.'

'I'm sure you have most women jumping up to do your bidding.'

'As a matter of fact, some of them do. My fatal charm doesn't seem to work with you. I've no idea why.'

'I'm immune.'

His eyes narrowed. 'No, you're not. Do you really think you will escape me so easily?'

'Escape? What a strange term to use, Mr Leighton. Am I your prisoner?'

'No,' he said. 'It is I who am yours.'

She laughed, beginning to put things into the basket. 'How I wish.'

'You are a cruel woman, Miss Osborne,' Grant accused, getting to his feet and brushing down his trousers.

'I am beginning to understand you and your motives.'

'Which are?'

'You are wasting your time if you are looking for an easy conquest. There must be any number of easier prospects.'

'There must?'

'Mmm. I can think of one in particular who is always most willing. Diana Waverley has a habit of collecting men like other people might collect butterflies.'

'She does?'

'You must have noticed. You seem to spend a great deal of time together.'

'I'm sorry if I gave you that impression. We don't. I think you misunderstand me.'

'Oh, no.' She laughed. 'I understand you very well. I have enjoyed our picnic, but I don't attach any significance to it.'

Grant sighed with mock gravity. 'I can see how difficult it will be to convince you that I am attracted to you.'

'Not difficult at all. I told you—I understand perfectly. Now, fold up that rug and we'll get back before it comes on to rain.'

'We can always wait it out under this tree.'

'No.'

He shrugged, reaching for the rug. 'You win.'

'I always do.'

He slanted her a dubious glance. 'This time.'

When they reached Eaton Place, Grant got out of the cab to carry the picnic basket up the steps. He was about to take his leave when a sudden thought occurred to him. 'Do you ride when you're in town?'

'Yes. Often.'

'Early in the morning?'

'It's the best time.'

'I couldn't agree more. I shall be in Hyde Park at six.' Raising a superior brow he met her gaze. 'Will you meet me?'

Despite knowing there would be whispers and raised brows aplenty if she were seen riding alone with him at such an early hour, she nodded, her gaze open and direct. 'Where?'

'At the corner of Park Lane.' He grinned. 'I'll look forward to it.'

When he'd gone Adeline was so confused by what was happening to her that she scarcely noticed she was going into the drawing room. The whole day had been one of shared pleasures—but she told herself that her attraction to Grant Leighton was dangerous, that because of all that had happened between them, and his close association with Diana Waverley, nothing could come of it. It would have to stop. But when she thought of the way he had looked at her with his mesmerising silver-grey eyes, and her traitorous heart reminded her of how it had felt when he had made love to her, she forgot the danger. She told herself it was nothing—that they had been brought together by their mutual concern over Lettie's liaison with Jack Cunningham, and that he probably didn't realise what he was doing.

Chapter Eight

Grant knew exactly what he was doing—and he was already thinking of doing much more. In fact if Jack Cunningham weren't such a swine, he would bless Lettie's liaison with him, since it provided him with an excuse to see Adeline.

After reaching Stanfield House and being informed that Lettie wasn't expected back until much later, he returned to the hotel to change, then went to Boodles to meet with friends and relax and converse over drinks. Two hours later he got up to leave. In the foyer one of the stewards stepped forward with his topper, brushing its brim before handing it to him.

'Thank you, George.'

'You're leaving early tonight, Mr Leighton.'

'I have an appointment.' Grant intended calling at Stanfield House once more, in the hope that Lettie was home.

A man who had just entered paused and looked at him. He had recognised the name immediately. 'Leighton?'

Grant looked at him coolly. 'That's correct. And you are?'

'Cunningham. Jack Cunningham,' he said, puffing on an expensive cigar and sending smoke swirling into the air. 'We have a mutual acquaintance, I believe. Lady Diana Waverley.'

'Yes,' Grant replied without feeling, as if he were addressing a much lesser man. Taller than the other man, Grant neither smiled nor offered his hand. 'Lady Waverley and I are acquainted. I believe you are also acquainted with my sister, Lettie?'

'I do have that pleasure. Lettie and I have become—close.'

Grant's face hardened into an expressionless mask. 'So I gather.'

'Look, I don't know how much Lettie's told you,' Jack said with amazing calm, 'but my intentions towards her are perfectly honourable.'

'I'd like to believe that.' His tone expressed doubt.

The eyes Grant Leighton fixed on Jack with barely concealed dislike were steady, clever, unreflecting, stirring Jack's resentment and an acute discomfort. Holding his cigar in the corner of his mouth, he tapped his cane against the palm of his hand.

His eyes flicked over Lettie's brother. Attired in princely manner—claret tail coat with velvet collar, crisp white shirt, stock and dove-grey trousers—his was an elegance that could neither be bought nor cut into shape by a tailor. Grant Leighton was one of those individuals whose breeding was so obvious it would show itself even if he were clothed in rags.

Jack was overpoweringly aware of the difference between them. He lived by his wits and, in the eyes of the law, on immoral earnings. Whereas Leighton owned land and property on a massive scale, fine carriages, and a house in the country where he would have servants and ride on his land on one of the splendid mounts from the Leighton stable. In fact he had as certain a future as was possible in life.

'In case you have not heard, we are to be neighbours,' Jack said, undaunted by the other man's reserved manner and slightly veiled contempt.

Grant raised an uninterested brow. 'We are?'

'Yes. I am in the process of buying a house very close to Oaklands—Westwood Hall.'

Now Grant was all attention, but he remained guarded. 'Diana is selling Westwood Hall?'

Cunningham nodded, unable to conceal the triumphant gleam from his eyes behind half-lowered lids. When Diana had approached him for a loan he had seen the extent of her debts, and that she would be unable to pay back the money. With Westwood Hall within his sights he had generously given her what she asked for, intending to turn that generosity to his advantage. It was time to call in the debt.

Ever since he had dragged himself out of the East End he had hungered for great wealth and prestige, and he was determined to achieve them by whatever means necessary. A large country house was part of his agenda, along with a compatible lifestyle, and with Lettie—a refined and respected young woman—as his wife, and however many children came their way, his position in society would be established.

'Between you and me, Leighton, Diana's affairs have reached the point of crisis. The bank has foreclosed on her loans—along with an army of money-lenders. With no means of clearing her debts she has no choice but to let the house go. I'm looking forward to living in the country. When I am in residence you must visit.'

'It's finalised?'

'Not quite—but almost. The necessary papers are drawn up. She will sign in the next few days.'

'I see. If you will excuse me, I have an appointment—but

there is just one thing you must understand, Cunningham,' Grant said, meeting his gaze directly. 'Your association with my sister is over. You will not attempt to see her again.'

'Or?'

'You will regret it.'

'Me? Oh, no, Leighton. It is you who will regret interfering.' He smiled ruefully. 'Anyone who crosses me is either very brave or very stupid.'

'I have friends in high places and a great deal of power—enough not to be afraid of anything you can do to me.' There was a rough, dangerous edge to Grant's voice, and his eyes were cold.

'Really? I know a great deal more about you than you know about me,' Jack said, smiling with a touch of arrogance.

Grant smiled back, his look hard, as if he also had secret knowledge that amused him.

Jack saw something, and there was a subtle change in his eyes. Leighton was staring at him, and his eyes read far too much. Suddenly he was uncertain. 'I'm curious. *What* do you know about me?'

'Enough. Your association with Lettie has prompted me to find out all about you, and I don't like who you are or what you are. As to your intentions—or should I say pretensions—if it is your intention to offer marriage to my sister, forget it. It won't happen.'

On those words Grant left the club. He was deeply troubled. He'd disliked Jack Cunningham on sight—the man was as appalling as he'd imagined he would be—and the sooner he saw Lettie and told her to end the affair the better he would feel. But first he must see Diana, and find out what the hell she was playing at.

'I want your advice about something,' Lettie said, when she called on Adeline that same evening.

When Adeline had met Lettie in the hall she'd seemed agitated and troubled in spirit, and this was confirmed now Adeline saw her in the gaslight of the drawing room. She looked wan and tired, and all manner of forebodings began to trouble Adeline. Perhaps Lettie needed someone to talk to? The thought expelled her practicality and provoked her at once to force the issue.

'Lettie,' she said, drawing her down beside her on the sofa and facing her, 'you want more than advice. You want help. Please tell me what I can do. Anything. I cannot bear to see you like this.'

Lettie was distraught as well as feeling wretched. She was also annoyed with herself that her feelings were so clear, and yet she wanted to share them with Adeline. There was a need in her not to be alone in her distress. When she spoke her voice was low, but steady. 'I want to tell you something that I know will shock you. Something has happened, Adeline, and I need your particular brand of common sense to tell me what to do. Even if it's to throw myself into the River Thames.'

'That's unlikely to solve anything, Lettie,' Adeline said, trying to keep her manner calm and casual. 'Tell me what it is.'

Lettie swallowed hard, and was obviously close to tears. 'It's quite dreadful. I warn you it may be the last time you will ever want to speak to me.'

Adeline knew, even before Lettie told her, that it had something to do with Jack Cunningham. Lines of dread creased her forehead and she felt wretched. 'Don't be silly, Lettie. You do exaggerate. Of course I will. Please tell me what is the matter and let me help you.'

White-lipped, Lettie reached out and gripped Adeline's hands tight. 'Oh, Adeline,' she whispered. 'I—I am pregnant. I am going to have Jack's baby.'

Adeline stared at her in blank astonishment. Continuing to hold Lettie's hands, she sat for a moment, trying to bring order out of the chaos of speculation and shock that choked her mind. She thought for a hysterical instant that she was making some silly joke. Then she saw the truth in her eyes and knew that she meant it.

'Oh, I see.' Realising that she must handle this terrible situation with the greatest delicacy, she said, 'How long have you known?'

'I—I've suspected I might be for several weeks,' Lettie whispered, the expression of anguish on her face beginning to fade a little now it was out in the open.

'And you are certain of this?'

She nodded. Tears like fat raindrops began to slide down her cheeks. 'A—a doctor has confirmed it—this morning. I had to come to you, Adeline. There is no one else I can talk to about this—no one but you.'

Adeline's heart melted with pity at the sight of Lettie's desolation. 'Oh, Lettie, thank goodness you did come to me. But why have you kept this to yourself? If you have known about your condition for some time, then you must have known when we went to the Phoenix.'

'I did—but things have changed since then.'

'How?'

'I can't tell you that—not now, Adeline.'

'What—what about Jack? Have you told him?'

Lettie nodded. 'He—he's delighted.'

These words were spoken with so much bitterness it bemused Adeline. 'What man wouldn't be on being told he's to become a father? But there's more to this, isn't there, Lettie? If there weren't you wouldn't be so upset. Has—has Jack hurt you in some way— said something? Has—has he not asked you to marry him?'

Lettie glared at her fiercely. 'Marry him? Of course he wants to marry me—the bastard,' she hissed. 'I wouldn't marry him, Adeline—not ever. Oh, at first what we had was fun—but I didn't know him then, what he was really like. Now I do know— I know everything—and I want nothing more to do with him. Now he wants to control me, to bend me to his will—to own me.'

'But what on earth has he done that has brought about this change in you?'

Lettie gulped on her tears. 'Enough. His crimes—his appetite for money and his methods of achieving it—I can't be part of that. But there's more—much more—and it's got nothing to do with any of that. It's far more horrible.'

Suddenly a suspicion occurred to Adeline. 'Has it anything to do with that woman you spoke to outside the Phoenix Club?'

She nodded. 'Yes,' she whispered, her voice barely audible. 'That woman was Jack's sister. I've seen her again since. She— she's told me things—things I can't bring myself to speak about. It's—it's too awful—brutal and cruel. I want no part of him. I don't want Jack Cunningham's baby.' She put her hands to her face. Any reserve she had left disappeared, and she began to cry dementedly. 'Oh, Adeline, I must get rid of it—I have to. I can't bear the thought of bringing a child of his into the world. I will kill myself first.'

Adeline stared at her in appalled silence. What Lettie said was more shocking than her sheltered mind could imagine. Fiercely she took the wretched woman's shivering body in her arms and held her until she was all cried out.

Pulling herself away from Adeline, as though she must finish her tale of horror, Lettie put her face into her hands with shame. 'I—I know someone who knows a doctor who will do it. He— he's fully qualified—in open practice—so it will be quite safe.

I have been assured it will be no brutal kitchen surgery of a back street abortionist.'

What Lettie was saying was impossible—too hideous for Adeline's mind to grasp. Absolutely horrified, she reached out and gripped Lettie's arms, forcing her to look at her, unaware that her own cheeks were wet with tears of pity and compassion for her friend. 'Lettie. Lettie, my dear, dear friend, listen to me.' Lettie looked at her, and the pain in her eyes was frightening. 'You must promise me that you will not do that. It is wrong—so very, very wrong—and you could die. I will help you, I swear I will, but you must not abort your child. Oh, dear God, Lettie, I cannot bear the thought of it.'

'But I am desperate, Adeline—and in these matters I find myself as ignorant as the most wretched servant girl. The option of an abortion is more acceptable than an unwanted pregnancy—than bearing his child.'

Adeline regarded everything that Lettie said with particular horror. 'Lettie, this is a baby you are talking about. A *baby*.'

'It isn't,' she said fiercely. 'I can't think of it as that. It's a monster, and I want to tear it out of me with my bare hands.' In desperation she looked around the room. She made a vague gesture. 'If only there was some medicine—quinine, or mercury, or some such thing—something I could take.'

'No, Lettie. There isn't—and anyway I won't let you.'

Lettie bowed her head. 'How can I tell my mother? Have you any idea what this will do to her? Can you tell me that—and Grant? He'll kill me. I'm not proud of myself. I—could kill myself,' she said quietly to herself.

'Lettie Leighton! Don't you dare talk like that. Please. You terrify me. You will find a way to get through this. I'll help you. Now it's happened you must brave it out.'

'I don't know how I can do that.'

'You will, Lettie. Don't be afraid. Now,' she said, standing up, 'I think the sensible thing for you to do is to stay here tonight. I'll have Mrs Kelsall prepare a room, and I'll send word to Lady Stanfield so that she doesn't worry.'

Lettie stood up quickly. 'No, I must go back. The carriage is outside.' She gave Adeline a wobbly smile. 'Don't worry about me. Now that I've told you I do feel a bit better. I'll plead a headache and have an early night.' Lettie looked into Adeline's eyes and wondered for a moment how they could be so warm and loving after she had listened to the shocking and unbelievable things she had just heard. 'I'm sorry to burden you with this. Do you hate me, Adeline?'

'Hate you?' Adeline placed a comforting hand against Lettie's tear-drenched cheek. 'You must never think that, Lettie. Ever. Our friendship is as steadfast now as it has ever been—undiminished by the knowledge of what Jack Cunningham has done to you. We have to work out what is to be done—and we will do that together.'

Taking Lettie's hand, Adeline accompanied her out into the empty hall, where she put her arms about her and hugged her, then kissed her on the cheek. 'Come and see me in the morning, Lettie—and promise me you won't do anything rash.'

'I promise,' she said huskily. 'I know I can trust you not to speak of this to anyone, Adeline.'

Adeline opened the door to find a light mist had settled over the street. It smelled of soot. Streetlights along the pavement made small pools of ragged light. She watched Lettie walk steadily towards the carriage, her back straight, her head held high, and was suddenly struck by the clamped expression of determination on her face. She looked as though walking across the pavement to the carriage was a goal of such enormity and distance it would take all her strength to reach it.

As Adeline brooded over Lettie's sickening plight—for sickening it was to anyone who knew Lettie—she felt more and more depressed, and so concerned for her friend that she was unable to sleep or concentrate on anything else. It had been bad enough when Lettie had told her she was seeing Jack Cunningham, but this was a situation of such magnitude she didn't know how to deal with it.

Lettie had come to her in an act of trust, so one thing she did decide on was not to confide in Grant. She would support and help Lettie in any way she could, but it was up to Lettie to tell her family, when she felt ready and strong enough to do that. But what on earth could have happened to turn Lettie against Jack Cunningham in the space of forty-eight hours?

She remembered she had promised Grant she would ride with him at six in the morning, and as much as she wanted to see him she wished she hadn't. It would be awkward being in his company, knowing what she did about Lettie.

Daylight had broken when Adeline trotted towards Hyde Park. The sky was dull and overcast, threatening rain later, but it didn't dampen her spirits for the ride. On reaching the corner of Park Lane she felt a thrill of delight to find Grant already waiting for her, mounted on a tall bay gelding, his muscular thighs clamped to the horse's sides.

She was attired in a green velvet riding habit the same colour as her eyes, which fitted her slender form like a glove, with the heavy mass of her hair anchored beneath a jaunty matching hat. Grant watched her ride towards him, feeling a familiar quickening in his veins. He wasn't surprised to see she was riding side-saddle, with no sign of breeches beneath her habit. No doubt when she was in town she felt she had to bow to protocol rather than risk a scandal by riding astride and wearing men's breeches. The bay shifted restlessly and he tightened his hands on the reins.

Telling her accompanying groom to wait for her, Adeline joined Grant. He was hatless, and wearing a conventional frock coat, light trousers and tan riding boots. His gaze was unnervingly acute.

'Good morning,' he greeted her. Noting how pale and strained her face was, and the purple smudges beneath her eyes, he frowned. Narrowing his eyes, he locked them on hers. 'Is everything all right?'

'Yes, everything's fine,' she replied, forcing a smile to her lips and looking away to avoid his searching gaze. 'I'm just a bit tired, that's all. I didn't sleep very well.'

'Then perhaps a ride to clear your head is just what you need.'

'I hope so.' In no mood for conversation, she gestured towards the park, eager to get on. 'Shall we go?'

'We'll head for the Row. The track will have been prepared for galloping.'

The park was deserted as they rode over the soft green turf.

'Does your father ride when he's in town,' Grant asked, for something to say to break the silence between them.

'No. Riding is not one of his interests.'

'Unlike his daughter. I'm surprised he's allowing you to spend so much time in town alone.'

'So am I. He's not usually so amiable. When Lettie wrote asking me to come to London I was amazed at how easy it was for me to persuade him.'

'Maybe it was because he has invited my mother to spend a few days at Rosehill.'

Adeline looked at him in amazement. 'He has?'

Grant nodded.

'When?'

'About now.'

'Goodness! I had no idea. And I do find it rather odd. Whenever he's expecting guests he always needs me to take care of everything.'

'I'm sure you have a perfectly capable housekeeper to do that. And besides, maybe he wanted to have my mother to himself.'

Adeline looked at him sharply. 'And are you happy with that? At Oaklands you gave me the impression that you did not approve of them becoming *too* friendly.'

'I've changed my mind. If my mother is happy, then I shall be happy for her.'

Having reached the track, both horses tossed their heads, tugging at the reins, eager for a run. They let them go. With the heavy pounding of horses' hooves beneath them they rode neck and neck, flying past St George's hospital and the statue of the Duke of Wellington behind the trees. The sky was peppered with waking birds, but the two riders were too preoccupied with their ride even to notice them. Adeline was exhilarated. The blood flowed fast in her veins, her heart pounded and her skin tingled, and for a while the burden of Lettie's situation was lifted. Grant was right. The ride was just what she needed.

Grant gave his horse a flick with his crop, urging him to a faster pace and pulling away from Adeline by a couple of lengths. Looking back, his hair dishevelled, his coat flapping behind him and his bent arms moving up and down like birds' wings, he grinned back at her and she laughed at him, her teeth gleaming white in her rosy face.

'I'll catch you,' she shouted. 'I swear I will.'

'How much would you like to bet? A kiss?'

The redness in her cheeks deepened, but, goaded by the mocking amusement in his voice, she snatched up the gauntlet of the challenge. 'Done.'

But it was no good. With the promise of a kiss at the end of the race, Grant showed no sign of slowing down—not until they neared the end of the track and he eased his horse to a canter, beating Adeline by a length. Knowing she was beaten, and would have to suffer the consequences, Adeline dropped her horse to a walk and went towards where he was waiting.

Waiting in anticipation for her to offer him her lips, Grant couldn't take his eyes off her. The ride had tinted her face a delicate pink, and he knew that when he touched her mouth he would feel the warmth of her blood coursing beneath her flesh.

'I won,' he declared.

'That's hardly fair. You were already well ahead when you issued the challenge.'

'And that's a feeble excuse if ever I heard one, Miss Osborne. Are you reneging on our wager?'

'No,' she replied, eyeing him warily.

'I'm glad to hear it.' Turning his head, he looked towards a group of trees, smiled wickedly, and then looked back at her with narrowed eyes.

'Prepare to pay your forfeit, Miss Osborne. Pray follow me. When I claim my reward I have no wish to have the whole of London gawping at me.'

On reaching the seclusion of the trees, knowing there was no escape, with a pounding heart Adeline nudged her horse close to his, intending to give him nothing more than a peck on the cheek. But she should have known that Grant Leighton would be satisfied with nothing less than a full-blown kiss.

He leaned across to her, and instead of drawing away she shyly met him halfway. With his face just two inches from hers, for a moment his eyes held hers, and then, taking her chin gently in his fingers, he let his gaze drop to her lips. Gradually his head moved closer and his lips brushed hers, undemanding, caressing tenderly, as if testing her resilience. Then with the confidence of a sure welcome they settled over hers, becoming firm as he turned his considerable talents to savouring their luscious softness.

The contact was like an exquisite explosion somewhere deep inside Adeline. The kiss deepened, and her lips were moulded and sensually shaped to his. She felt that kiss in every inch of her body. In response, warm heat ignited and radiated through her flesh. Jolt after jolt of wild, familiar sensation pulsated through her. He parted her lips, his tongue teasing and tormenting, sinking into the haven of sweetness and claiming it for his own.

The kiss ended when Grant's horse shifted slightly and they were forced to draw apart. Adeline gazed at his face, at the harsh set lines, seeing the evidence of desire ruthlessly controlled. She wasn't ignorant of his state—had she not seen it once before? Almost kissed into insensibility, she watched his smouldering gaze lift from her lips to her eyes, and then his firm lips curved in a smile and he drew back.

'If we don't stop now I swear I will dismount, drag you from your horse and into those bushes and make love to you—which I have wanted to do ever since our first encounter—to discover what I missed, you understand. So, while I would like to experience more, I will press you no further. The time is not right. Others will soon be arriving in the park and I fear we will be caught out. I live in hope that there will be other times when I will hold you closer and for much longer, Adeline. But now we'll ride at a leisurely pace back down the track, and I shall hand you over to your groom.'

'When will you see Lettie?' Adeline dared to ask, not looking at him lest he saw the guilty secret in her eyes.

'I shall return to the hotel and have breakfast, and then I intend calling on her before she disappears to one of her meetings.'

Not until she had left him and was riding back to Eaton Place did what he had said hit Adeline—he intended further intimacies in the future to satiate his desire. Her face burned. How could she have forgotten that only the day before last she had vowed not to become one of his flirtations? How could she have forgotten how utterly amoral he was, and how supremely conceited?

But his kiss, the feel of his lips on hers, the way her body had reacted, the sensations she had felt, made her want, yearn, for what she knew he could give her.

When Lettie didn't call at Eaton Place that same morning, Adeline, deeply concerned about her, and wondering how her meeting had gone with Grant, went to Upper Belgrave Street— only to be told by Lady Stanfield that Lettie was visiting a sick friend and wasn't expected back until evening. When Adeline asked if Grant had called to see his sister earlier in the day, she was disappointed and angry to be told he hadn't.

After spending some time with Marjorie, talking about her impending engagement party, for which preparations were going on in earnest, still feeling tense and upset because she hadn't seen Lettie, Adeline returned home. She felt as though she were sitting on a volcano, and in awful suspense as she waited for something to happen.

It was shortly after nine o'clock when a cab arrived at the house with Lettie. Mrs Kelsall opened the door to her, and Adeline met her in the hall.

Lettie just stood and stared at Adeline. She looked ghastly— like death. Her face was as white as parchment, her eyes leaden and as colourless as the sea on a dull day. After a moment, as if she couldn't bear to look at Adeline any longer, she hung her head as though in the deepest shame.

That was the moment Adeline knew what she had done. Something inside her lurched in terror. Why, she didn't know, for surely the worst had happened? Nausea rose in her throat. Oh, dear, sweet Jesus, her mind whispered, what had they done to her? Concern for her friend came to the fore and propelled her across the floor.

'Lettie,' she whispered, taking her cold, trembling hand and placing her arm about her shoulders.

Mrs Kelsall hovered and stared, not knowing what to do. Adeline looked at her. 'As you can see, Mrs Kelsall, Miss Leighton isn't well. Prepare a room for her, will you? And have someone go to Lady Stanfield and inform her that she is staying here with me tonight. Tell her she is not to worry. Some tea would be welcome. We'll be in the drawing room.' She turned her attention to Lettie. 'Come, Lettie. Come and sit by the fire, and when Mrs Kelsall has prepared a room I'll take you upstairs.'

Lettie's movements were wooden as she let Adeline lead her into the drawing room and sit her in a chair close to the fire, where she began to tremble uncontrollably. One of the maids brought in a tray of tea things. Adeline poured, and held a cup to Lettie's frozen lips. But she shook her head and turned it away. Kneeling beside her, Adeline took her hand where it lay in her lap.

'Lettie, please speak to me. I know what you've done—and, oh, my dear, I am not angry, but I *am* concerned. Are you in pain?'

Swallowing hard, Lettie nodded, her eyes swimming with tears. Her lips moved in reply, but Adeline could not catch what she said.

'What is it, Lettie?' she asked, leaning closer. 'What did you say?'

This time she did hear the words.

'The baby…' Lettie's throat was so tight the words were forced out.

Trying to keep her voice from shattering with the sorrow she felt, Adeline drew a long breath and said, 'I'm really sorry you had to resort to this, Lettie. I really am.' Her eyes, too, filled with tears, and all she could do was hold Lettie's hand tighter.

'Please forgive me, Adeline,' she whispered.

'It is not for me to forgive,' Adeline answered quietly. 'Everything's going to be all right. Don't worry any more. But you look most ill, Lettie. I must send for a doctor to take a look at you.'

Lettie's look was frantic, and she gripped Adeline's hand with remarkable strength. 'No—please—please no,' she whispered raggedly. 'It's a doctor who did this to me. No more, Adeline. No more. I can't take it. It's done—over—and I thank God for the release.'

The door opened and Mrs Kelsall appeared. 'The room is ready, Miss Adeline. The fire is lit.'

'Thank you, Mrs Kelsall. I'll take Lettie up.'

'Can I—be of help?'

'Thank you, but I think we can manage.'

Somehow Adeline managed to get Lettie up the stairs and into the bedroom where, like a child, she let Adeline and Emma undress her and put her in one of Adeline's nightgowns of fine embroidered cambric. After unpinning Lettie's hair and sponging her face, Adeline laid her in the bed. Immediately Lettie lay on her side, with her back to Adeline. Closing her eyes, she drew her knees up to her chest and began to whimper.

Telling Emma she could manage, and sending her to bed, Adeline sat beside the bed and began a silent vigil, hoping and praying that Lettie was going to be all right. She was breathing heavily, and sweat stood out on her skin.

The pain got worse during the night, and she began complaining of the heat and throwing off the covers. Becoming more and more concerned, Adeline touched Lettie's head, then wrung out a cloth in a dish of water and placed it on her brow. After another couple of hours Lettie began shivering and moaning, almost senseless, tossing her head from side to side, her fingers plucking at the bedcovers.

That was when Adeline, in desperation, wrote a note to Grant. She sent one of the servants with it in the carriage, to the Charing Cross Hotel, asking him to come immediately and—even though she knew Lettie would reproach her for it—to bring a doctor.

Accompanied by another man carrying a leather bag, Grant came quickly, and saw the anguish full on the white oval of Adeline's face. She stared at him. Tension weighed heavily on his spirit.

'Adeline,' Grant said when the drawing room door had closed. 'Are you all right?' Placing a gentle finger under her chin, he compelled her to meet his gaze, having to restrain himself from taking her in his arms. Her lovely colour had gone and her eyes were haunted. 'What is it? Tell me.'

'Oh, Grant—it's Lettie.'

There was no way to tell him except with the simple truth. And in the next few minutes she told him what Lettie had done. The one thing she failed to tell him was that the decision to abort her child had been Lettie's alone.

In disbelief Grant listened in stunned silence to every word she uttered. In all his life he had never been immobilised by any emotion or any event. The worse the pressure the more energised he became. Now, however, he stared at Adeline as if unable to absorb what she had told him. His lips tightened to a thin line, then he grimaced with suppressed anger.

When she had finished speaking, drawing a long, steadying breath, Adeline looked at him and waited for him to speak.

Pain and anger blazed through Grant's brain like hot brands as he envisaged Lettie facing her ordeal alone. 'Ever since you told me Lettie was seeing Cunningham I thought that with one word from me she would stop. I never imagined I would have to deal with anything like this.' He turned to the man hovering behind him—a middle-aged man, his face creased in lines of grave concern.

'Adeline, this is a friend of mine—Howard Lennox. He is a doctor and will examine Lettie. I know we can be assured of his absolute discretion.'

Howard stepped forward. 'As you know, Grant,' he said in a brusque, businesslike manner, 'I am reluctant to make common gossip of my patients' private health matters. Not even among friends. Miss Osborne, I am happy to be of assistance in any way I can. Will you take me to Miss Leighton? In cases such as this I doubt there is much I can do, but we shall see.' He looked at Grant. 'Wait here, Grant, until I've examined her.'

Left alone, Grant stood for a second to try and calm himself—for the thought of Lettie at the hands of Jack Cunningham and the doctor he had employed to perform an illegal, life-threatening abortion on her was almost more than he could bear. He was certain that Lettie would never have done anything like this without being forced into it. Unable to control all his confused emotions—anger, hatred, bitterness, love for Lettie and the soul-destroying feeling that he had failed her—he knew his rage was so red he wanted to shout, to snarl, to hit someone, to kill someone. Peferably Jack Cunningham. But he must pull himself together before he saw Lettie.

Having woken Emma and left her to sit with Lettie, who was now quiet and seemed to be sleeping, Adeline returned to the drawing room with Dr Lennox and poured both men a good measure of much-needed brandy.

'How is she?' Grant asked, feeling he was holding onto reality by the merest thread.

Howard shook his head, then tipped his glass and swallowed the brandy in one gulp, shaking his head when Adeline offered him another. 'I have to say she is very ill.'

'She must not die,' Adeline whispered.

'Do not upset yourself, Miss Osborne. While there's life there is hope.' He looked at Grant. 'Some infection has set in, and her temperature is high. She is also in deep shock. But she is your sister, Grant. She's strong, and I believe she will pull through this.'

'Dear God, let us pray that she does.' His set features relaxed, his relief evident.

'I've examined her as best I can. There is some comfort in the fact that the operation was performed by a doctor,' Howard said. 'Some doctors can be found who *will* perform abortions—although they extract a high price.'

'That wouldn't be a problem for Cunningham,' Grant growled. 'But I am of the opinion that the doctor who did this to Lettie owed Cunningham. This doctor would have had no option but to submit to illegal practice.'

'That is a matter of opinion, Grant. Abortion is legal if performed by a doctor. You have made enquiries into Cunningham's background?'

Grant nodded. 'Cunningham controls a hierarchy of individuals who owe him—ranging from beggars at the bottom to specialised lawyers at the top. A quiet word and almost anything can be accomplished. What do you advise we do with Lettie?'

'Well, for the time being she shouldn't be moved.'

'That's not a problem,' Adeline was quick to say, dismayed

that Grant had jumped to the wrong conclusion and was blaming Jack Cunningham for Lettie's condition. But she would wait until Dr Lennox had left before she told him he was mistaken. 'She can stay here for as long as necessary. I'll look after her.'

Grant looked at her gratefully. 'Thank you, Adeline. Hopefully it won't be for too long.'

'Lettie must have been desperate—she must have seen her future as precarious to have done what she did,' Howard remarked. 'Her recovery will take time, and she will require patience and understanding as she comes to terms with what she has done and tries to rebuild her life.' Carrying his bag, he crossed to the door, where he turned and looked back at Grant. 'I understand you're leaving London for the continent shortly, Grant?'

'I am—in a few days, as a matter of fact.'

'Business?'

He shrugged somewhat wearily. 'What else? I expect to be away for several weeks.'

'I'll return in the morning to take another look at Lettie. But if you need me in the meantime you know where to find me.'

Chapter Nine

When Dr Lennox had taken his leave of them Adeline moved to stand close to Grant. His dark head was slightly bent as he contemplated the glowing embers in the hearth, his foot upon the fender. Beneath his coat his muscles flexed as he withdrew his right hand from his pocket and shoved his fingers through his hair—which, as Adeline had discovered, had an inclination to curl when he combed his fingers through its brushed smoothness.

'Would you like to go up and see Lettie now?' she asked softly.

Grant turned and looked at her, fear tightening his eyes. He nodded. 'Yes, I would.'

When Adeline opened the door to Lettie's room Emma rose from her seat beside the bed and quietly went out. Along with every other servant in the house she knew something dreadful had happened to Miss Adeline's friend—how could she not when her arrival, followed so quickly by her brother with a doctor, had caused such a commotion? They were all agog with curiosity, although so far Miss Adeline was saying nothing. But Emma, more worldly than her mistress, was no fool, and, having undressed Miss Leighton and seen the state she was in, had already reached her own conclusions.

Grant moved towards the bed. The tightly huddled woman, impervious to everything that was going on around her, did not resemble his sister. He would have said so, but the hair draped over the pillow, the familiar curve of her cheek, brought back memories of the vital, laughing face. Her eyes were tightly closed, the lashes forming shadowed crescents on her cheeks. She lay in a stupor partly induced by the heavy draught of laudanum Howard had administered.

Bending over, he gently touched her cheek. 'How did she come to this?' he murmured. 'I blame myself. I should have made more of an effort to see her.'

'It's too late to worry about that now,' Adeline whispered, silently wishing he had. If so this wretched catastrophe might have been averted. 'What's done is done.'

Standing upright, Grant moved away from the bed and turned his gaze to Adeline's face. If he hadn't been so anxious about Lettie he would have smiled as he wondered how Adeline had come by her prim and practical streak. Although there was nothing prim about those full, soft, generous lips and the compassionate, caring look in her green eyes, looking darker than usual in the dimmed gaslight.

'Dr Lennox gave Lettie some laudanum to rest her, and some other medication,' Adeline told him. 'She should sleep for a while. I'll ask Emma to sit with her, and when she goes to bed I'll stay with Lettie. I cannot rest while she is so ill.' She looked at Grant. 'Will you stay?'

'I'd very much like to.'

'Then I'll have a room prepared.'

'That won't be necessary. Sleep is the last thing on my mind right now.'

'Then we'll watch over her together.'

Leaving Emma to sit with Lettie a while longer, they returned to the drawing room. Without saying a word, with his hands shoved into his trouser pockets and his eyes hardened into slits of concentration, Grant stood staring into the hearth, listening to the sharp tick of the ormolu clock on the mantelpiece and watching the flames of the rejuvenated fire licking and dancing. He wasn't aware of Adeline standing close until he felt the pressure of her hand on his arm. Turning, he saw her eyes were anxious and suffering.

'When Lettie arrived here tonight, did she say much to you?'

'No. She was in no fit state. What will you do?' she asked quietly.

'I am a shrewd man, Adeline. All my business life I have looked men straight in the eye as they tried to convince me that black is white and vice versa. And though Cunningham is a clever and devious black-hearted villain, it will take a better man than him to hurt any of mine.'

'Are you saying you are looking for vengeance?'

'You're damn right I am. If that bastard thinks he can get away with near murder he's damn well mistaken.'

'You can't,' Adeline whispered. 'One thing Lettie did tell me is that what she did was her decision alone. He wanted the baby—and I suspect he has no idea what she has done.'

Grant was incredulous. 'Dear God, Adeline—are you saying that Lettie aborted her own child?'

'Yes. I—I don't know what Jack Cunningham has done to Lettie—it must be something quite dreadful to have made her want to do what she did—but all of a sudden she hates him with an intensity I was shocked to see.'

'If he's laid one finger on my sister in violence I swear I'll kill him. I might do that anyway.'

'Don't you see, Grant? Vengeance is a private sin to repair damaged pride. Try not to reduce this to a question of marksmanship. Lettie wouldn't want you to do that. Aside from the fact that the crime has been committed by the doctor who—who—did what he did, and Jack Cunningham for getting her pregnant, there is only one other person who is responsible for Lettie being in the situation she is.'

His shoulders tensed, Grant turned his head slowly and looked at her for a long time. 'Who?'

'Lettie herself.' Adeline stopped short, seeing those silver-grey eyes flare. Then she went on firmly. 'She went with Jack Cunningham of her own free will. She found him terribly exciting and fun to be with, and she was attracted to him from the start—she admitted as much to me. It's just one of the realities of human nature, I suppose.'

'You and Lettie must have had some interesting conversations,' Grant retorted, unable to calm his anger.

'We have. Plenty. That particular snare—sexual attraction—has kept the human race alive since time immemorial, so Lettie cannot be condemned for that. She probably loved Jack Cunningham in her own way—misplaced as that love was. She told me he had proposed marriage and she'd refused. The decision to abort her baby was hers.'

Grant's eyes glittered like glass. 'Are you telling me I should simply let that low-down bastard off scot-free?'

Adeline swallowed hard as she courageously faced him, seeing the rage and the steel inside him. 'Yes. I think you should consider long and hard before you tear open issues of which you do not know the nature or the extent.'

'I do not think you appreciate the gravity of the situation,

Adeline. This is not some Society parlour game. Lettie's well-being is at stake. Cunningham deserves no such consideration.'

'It doesn't matter. What does matter is that you don't create a scandal over this that will sink Lettie for ever.' The way Grant was looking at her sent a chill of fear through her. But she went on bravely. 'Dr Lennox doesn't think Lettie is going to die, Grant.' She looked up at him. 'It is to her mind and heart that the damage lies. You said it would take a better man than Jack Cunningham to hurt any of your family. You would be a bigger and better man if you could put this behind you. As far as Lettie is concerned the whole sorry business is over.'

'I will not let it pass. I would not be Lettie's brother if I did that.'

'What you will tell your mother and everyone else is up to you. But for now Lettie is going to need you. She is going to need both of us over the coming days.'

He nodded, accepting the sense of this. 'I shall do nothing at all—at least until we know Lettie is out of danger. The less everyone knows about this unsavoury mess the better. But one thing is certain. Cunningham needn't come looking for her after this.'

'He will. He still thinks she is with child—his child, don't forget—in which case he will think he has some claim on her.'

Grant's eyes narrowed as he looked at her curiously. 'How can you know so much? I thought you said Lettie was in no fit state to—' Grant began, and then the enormity of what she had said sank in. He felt the blood draining from his face, and his eyes, full of accusation, slid towards Adeline, trapping her in their burning gaze. 'You also said the decision to go through with this was hers, so some conversation must have taken place between the two of you when she arrived—a great deal, in fact.'

His gaze raked Adeline's guilt-stricken face, and she watched

in agony as his eyes registered first disbelief and then anger—
an anger so deep that all the muscles in his face tightened into
a mask of fury.

Adeline stared at him and seemed confused, which further
heightened his anger. 'Grant, let me explain—'

'You already knew, didn't you?' he demanded. 'You already
knew Lettie was pregnant.' Anger began to gather like a hard ball
somewhere in the vicinity of Grant's stomach. 'When Lettie
recovers I'll find out the truth from her—but that does not excuse
you from not telling me.'

'It—it was what Lettie wanted. I thought it was for the best
at the time—'

'*You* thought it was for the best? Since when were *you* an authority on what is best for Lettie?' he said, cutting her off,
passion making his voice shake. 'You *knew*. You knew when we
met this morning. We were together a whole hour and you said
nothing. You had no right to keep a matter as important as this
from me.'

'I knew, yes—but Lettie had promised me she wouldn't do
anything,' Adeline said, coming to her own defence. Forcing
herself to keep calm, she spoke in a controlled voice. 'The last
forty-eight hours since Lettie told me of her affair with Jack
Cunningham haven't been easy. In fact they have been very difficult indeed. Lettie promised me she would do nothing drastic,
Grant, and I believed her.'

'But she did mention getting rid of it, didn't she?'

'Yes—but—'

'Adeline, don't you see?' he flared accusingly, his emotions
storming inside him, his composure in shreds. 'Had I known
about any of this I could have stopped her. She wouldn't be in
the state she's in now.'

'I don't believe that. Looking back, I realise that when she

came to see me she had already made up her mind to go ahead
with it.'

'And you really believe that, do you? Well, I don't. Lettie
would never have done this appalling thing had she not been
forced into it by what Cunningham did to her.'

Adeline had to summon all her patience to stop herself
bursting out in a fury. Grant's inquisitorial, aggressive manner
angered her beyond belief. He was playing the part of the injured
party a little too well—demanding explanations without the
slightest trace of consideration.

'At least she is safe, and Dr Lennox says she should recover.
We must be thankful for that.'

'Safe, yes—no thanks to you,' he snapped unfairly.

It was as if he had thrown a bucket of icy water over her.
'That's a dreadful thing to say to me, Grant. It isn't due to me.'

'The facts speak for themselves, Adeline.'

The injustice of his accusation brought an angry flush to her
face and she looked as maddened as him. 'When Lettie came to
me she wanted to confide in someone she could trust. I broke
that trust when I sought you out at your hotel after the first time
she came to speak to me in confidence. I wasn't prepared to do
that again,' she told him, throwing back her head indignantly. 'I
did the best I could to prevent Lettie going ahead with aborting
her child, and now you storm at me for not telling you. When I
left you after our ride, I truly thought you would go and see her—
as you said you would—and that she might tell you herself.
Clearly you had other matters to attend to that were more important.'

'That was my intention. But when I returned to the hotel, D—'
He stopped himself from mentioning Diana's name, knowing
how it never failed to kindle Adeline's ire, but it was too late.

Drawing herself up, Adeline looked at him sharply, know-

ingly, and nodded. 'But Diana Waverley turned up?' she uttered
scornfully. 'Don't bother to explain, Grant. I'm not interested.
If your affair with Diana took precedence over Lettie's troubles
it has got nothing whatsoever to do with me.'

'God in heaven—there *is* no affair between Diana and me,'
he gritted coldly.

'No? You certainly behave as if there is—and anyway, I don't
believe you. Still, how you spend your time is up to you. However, that woman has done enough damage to my life, so kindly
refrain from speaking of her again in my presence. Perhaps now
you will realise how serious I considered Lettie's situation to
be. I truly thought you would go out of your way to do something about it. I was relying on you—fool that I was.'

'You still had no right to keep it from me.'

Slowly Adeline moved closer, and her eyes met Grant's
proudly, with a look as cutting as steel. 'How dare you? How
dare you put me in the wrong? How dare you transfer the blame
to me to ease your own conscience? That seems a nice, easy way
out of a difficult situation—a coward's way out. I would not have
believed it of you, Grant.'

Grant's tone was haughty, his eyes like shards of ice. He
seemed bent on regaining the advantage. 'I think you've said
enough. Who do you think you are, to meddle in my family's
affairs?'

'Lettie's friend,' Adeline stated coldly. 'But since you think
I am interfering, then I must admit I am not entertained by your
family disputes.'

'In which case I shall have Lettie removed from this house
first thing in the morning.'

'You are right,' she flared, her eyes blazing. 'What happens to
Lettie concerns you alone. I shall leave you to decide what to do
with her. Do whatever you feel must be done, but remember that

it will be against Dr Lennox's advice. Meanwhile, while she is in this house, I shall tend her. Do you have any objections to that?'

They faced one another, not speaking, their fury bouncing off each other. Adeline thought bitterly that she had never imagined the night would end like this. Her defiance had struck him to the quick of his being. Now they would simply set about destroying each other as ferociously as mortal enemies. Was it for *this* that she had befriended Lettie when she'd needed her most?

'I would be grateful,' he said curtly.

'Thank you,' Adeline said, with all the dignity she could muster. 'And now, since you can do nothing but insult me, and will clearly have no need of my assistance in nursing Lettie after tomorrow, I think you had better leave,' she said icily. 'If she should wake and find you like this it will only upset her.'

'You are right. I have changed my mind about staying the night. I can see Lettie will be in capable hands.' He crossed to the door, where he turned and looked back at her. There was a deep anger inside him. 'No matter what it costs, I cannot ignore what Cunningham has done. I do not underestimate his intelligence or his will for a moment, but they are irrelevant. It does not make me reconsider anything—only makes me more resolute. Now, if you will excuse me, I shall be at my hotel if I am needed.'

Adeline watched him go. There was no word of affection, just a cold nod as he closed the door. She stood staring at it for a long time, deeply hurt by what had just occurred. The man was a monster. It was not her fault, what had happened to Lettie, but Grant would never be convinced of this, and the tender feelings that had grown between them when they had fenced and ridden together died as a sudden frost withered a young plant.

Perhaps the kiss he had given her, having won the race, had

meant nothing at all—had been nothing more than a pleasure satisfied? Anger stirred once more in Adeline—anger at herself for so readily succumbing to the embrace of this hard, cold man who had invited her love after the aggressive nature of their past encounters.

Drawing herself up proudly, she went to relieve Emma. She, too, could be hard and cold. Grant would never know how much he had hurt her. I won't let him treat me like that again, she vowed, staring down at his sleeping sister and settling herself into the chair beside the bed. Adeline the vulnerable fool, ready to give her heart to the first man to hold her in his arms and whisper sweet nonsense, had hopefully learned more sense, she told herself, resolutely ignoring the treacherous small voice at the back of her brain that mourned her passing.

Grant didn't remove Lettie from the house in Eaton Place. When he called the following morning, Adeline sensed that he wanted to get back on the easy footing they had been on before last night, but she was determined not to risk a second rebuff.

Having left Lettie with one of the maids watching over her, tired and not in the best of moods, Adeline had been in the garden, taking a breath of air, when Grant appeared, looking devastatingly handsome in a tweed suit.

Standing on the terrace, he had paused and looked around, searching for her. When he'd seen her, standing against some tall trellising over which pink and white roses clambered in profusion, he strode towards her with that easy, natural elegance already so familiar to her.

Perfectly still, with her hands folded at her waist, she had waited for him to reach her. Ever since she had known this man she had told herself that she was drawn to him because of his compelling good-looks and his powerful masculine magnetism—the strange hold he had over her was merely an ability to awaken those intense sexual hungers within her.

But she realised it was more than that—that was just the tip of an iceberg whose true menace lay in its unfathomable depths. While she had vainly set herself against the carnal forces he inspired in her, something deeper and dangerously enduring was binding them inexorably together. How could she possibly resist him? But resist him she must if she was to have peace of mind.

'At last I've found you,' he said, taking her arm and drawing her down onto a wooden bench, where they sat facing each other. His eyes complimented her warmly on her appearance—for despite the purple smudges beneath her eyes, in her sky blue dress with a high-necked bodice, she looked fresh and immaculate.

Adeline caught the clean, masculine smell of him. The onslaught on her senses was immediate, and she longed to respond to the pressure of his hand on her arm, to feel his mouth on hers, setting her skin tingling and her blood on fire. But this was the man whom she had decided she would never allow to breach her self-control. The memory of Diana Waverley, with her sly, insolent smile, and the cruel things Grant had said to her last night stood between them.

Her lips curved in a slight smile. 'So you have, Grant. Have you been up to see Lettie?'

He nodded. 'Mrs Kelsall kindly let me go up. She's sleeping, but she does seem a little better.'

'I think so. Dr Lennox should be along soon. If you still wish to remove her from the house then I think you had better wait until he's seen her, don't you?'

'Adeline, if it's in Lettie's best interests that she remains here then I would like her to stay. She couldn't be in better hands. I know that.'

'I told you last night, Grant. Lettie can stay here as long as it is necessary.'

'Thank you. All night I've been cursing myself for a fool. I want to apologise for my boorish behaviour, for which I am ashamed. I was cruel and thoughtless and I deserve to be horse-whipped, for I realise I must have left you feeling deeply hurt. I assure you that wounding your feelings was never my intent. I am here not only to see Lettie, but to make amends.'

'Ashamed, Grant?' Adeline said brightly, giving him no help. 'I am certain there is nothing for *you* to be ashamed of. And isn't it a little late to withdraw anything you may have said to me last night?'

'Adeline, please,' said Grant in a low, rapid tone. 'I spoke hastily, and you have every right to be angry. I was knocked sideways by what Lettie had done—and when I think that I could have prevented it, had I known—'

'If I had betrayed Lettie's confidence and told you? I think that is what you mean, Grant.'

'I don't want to argue about that now, Adeline. Last night, when I received your note asking me to come at once and to bring a doctor, I imagined the worst, and my later anger was caused partly by relief yet also by a feeling of having let Lettie down in some way.'

And part sorrow, guilt and rage for having given his time to Diana when he might have been with Lettie, Adeline could have added. She would not give in to the old attraction that was making her heart race and her legs feel drained of strength.

'I don't suppose Lettie will see it like that,' she said, standing up and walking back towards the house.

Looking at her stiff back, and the proud way she held her head, Grant wanted to go after her and shake her. He knew she was playing a part. He believed that behind that bright expression and glib speech the real warm, passionate Adeline was still to be found—only he had lost the key to her. Temporarily, he hoped. Those ill-considered accusations and insults he had thrown at her when he had vented his fury on her had driven the young woman he had come to feel so deeply for underground, had replaced her with this proper, guarded person who carefully kept him at arm's length.

Getting up and striding after her, he took her arm and jerked her round to face him. 'Adeline, I am truly sorry. I shall not be happy until you tell me you forgive me.' He smiled crookedly at her, willing her to respond as she had in the park.

But there was no answering spark in her eyes as she answered abstractedly, 'Set your mind at rest, Grant,' she said with a brittle laugh. 'For my memory of last night is extremely hazy, and I really cannot recall all that you said to me. There is not the least need to apologise, so please, let us not speak of it again. Now, let us go in and await Dr Lennox.'

It took another twenty-four hours for Lettie's temperature to subside, and then she emerged from her nightmare world.

Dr Lennox visited her twice daily and said she was making swift improvement. Grant visited every day. Lettie was tearful when she saw him, and deeply ashamed that he should know of the terrible thing she had done. She expected him to be furious, to verbally chastise her, but to his credit he issued no recriminations, merely took his sister in his arms and held her, and gave her no word of censure. Adeline was relieved.

Grant called on Lord and Lady Stanfield to explain that Lettie had taken a severe chill and would remain at Eaton Place with Adeline. When asked if they could visit, he politely told them he would let them know when she was feeling up to receiving visitors.

Once the tide had turned, Lettie made rapid strides towards recovery. Luckily she was blessed with a remarkably vigorous constitution. After three days she was able to leave her bed and sit in a chair by the window, and on the fourth day she was able to go downstairs and sit out in the garden. But her face looked drawn and thinner, and there was a haunted look in her eyes. Still she had not spoken of what had turned her against Jack Cunningham, and Adeline had not tried to draw it out of her, believing she would speak of it when she felt ready.

Later she was in the drawing room, her face transparently pale, her shoulders draped in an ermine wrap. Sitting beside her, Adeline took her hand and held it. For the time being they were alone, but they were expecting Lady Stanfield and Marjorie at any minute, and Grant had said he would look in.

'I hope you are feeling up to visitors, Lettie.'

Lettie stared at her, her eyes bleak with the kind of self-knowledge she could neither accept nor pardon. 'Yes, I am looking forward to seeing them. But I do not feel brave enough in my afflicted state to return to Stanfield House and endure the inquisitive glances and questions of the many people I will come into contact with. In a few days' time I have decided to go home to Newhill Lodge—and Mother. I have to get away from London—from Jack.'

'I think that's a good idea, Lettie. I know Grant is to go to France in three days' time, so he will be unable to go with you. But Emma will accompany you.'

Lettie looked at her with eyes that were opaque, awash with tears. Her suffering was real, and a familiar look of distress crossed her face. 'That's very kind of you, Adeline. If you can spare her I would be most grateful. Besides, she knows what I've done, and she has not judged me as others would.'

'Emma can be trusted, Lettie. You can rely on her discretion.'

'You've been so good.to me. I don't deserve it. I—I think I will tell my mother what I have done. I don't know how, but I will. I cannot keep such a secret from her. I just hope she will understand. It is my vanity, my wilfulness and my immorality that has brought about this mess. I'm not proud of myself, Adeline,' she whispered. 'What I did was wrong—some may call it wicked. I thought I was doing the right thing—but I feel mutilated.'

'And Jack Cunningham?'

Lettie's eyes clouded with pain and she looked away. 'I never want to see him again. I hate him, Adeline. People say time heals all wounds. I can only hope they're right.'

Grant was the first to arrive. He strode in and gave his sister an affectionate hug before turning his attention to Adeline, who greeted him with a cool nod. He frowned. There was a quietness in her now, a restraint when they were together, and he was acutely aware of it. Adeline Osborne had become in his sight a woman as alluring and desirable as any he had ever known, and even though she rebuffed him at every turn he wanted her. She had become a challenge—a beautiful, vibrant, adorable challenge—a passion.

Lady Stanfield and Marjorie entered the house like a summer breeze, their presence creating an atmosphere of freshness and vitality that was badly needed. They were concerned that Lettie had been so ill, and glad she was beginning to feel better.

Marjorie, full of excitement over her engagement party two days hence, was disappointed when Lettie told her she did not feel well enough to attend. The truth was that she couldn't face it and, knowing this, Adeline did not join Marjorie in trying to persuade her.

Defeated, Marjorie sighed and looked at Adeline. 'You'll still come, won't you, Adeline? You have to. I must have at least *one* of my friends there.'

'Of course Adeline will come,' Lettie was quick to reassure her. 'I don't see why she should forgo your party because of me.'

Suddenly a scheming gleam entered her eyes, making her look more like her old self as her gaze slid to her brother, leaning idly against the window with his arms crossed over his chest. She smiled inwardly, not having forgotten her intention to try and bring Grant and Adeline together.

'In fact, I think Grant should escort her. After all, it's important that at least one member of the Leighton family be there to represent us—and as you know, Mother is unable to get to town just now, so that leaves Grant.' Her look became one of pure, unadulterated innocence as she fixed her eyes on her brother. 'You have no other engagement that night, have you, Grant?'

Her suggestion brought startled glances from both Adeline and Grant. Adeline was not at all in agreement, but one look at Grant and she sensed his absolute and unquestioning co-operation. A lazy smile curved his lips and his eyes gleamed wickedly.

'Nothing that can't be put off, Lettie. I shall be delighted to escort Adeline to the party.'

Grant's ready acceptance brought everyone's instant attention. Adeline stared at him blankly. There was something subtle in the way his smile had changed that made her uneasy. Her mouth opened and closed again.

'Ooh, that would be lovely,' Marjorie enthused happily.

'Absolutely,' Lady Stanfield agreed.

'It's very good of you, Grant, but I don't need an escort,' Adeline remarked, tossing him a vengeful glance.

'Yes, you do,' Grant countered smoothly, enjoying every minute of her discomfort.

'Of course you do,' Lettie agreed.

'And I would so like Grant to be there,' Marjorie said.

Adeline looked from one to the other, unable to believe she had been so easily manoeuvred into a situation she would rather have avoided. Grant was looking at her in tranquil, amused silence, but she noticed there was an infuriating arrogance about the man's smile, and even in the way he was lounging against the wall.

Grant saw her features tighten, and he recognised the ominous glitter in those narrowed green eyes. 'Am I to take your silence for acceptance?' he asked, knowing perfectly well that she couldn't object to him being her escort when everyone else was in favour.

'Don't you think it will raise speculation about us if we arrive together?'

A slow grin came with his answer. 'You seem to forget that the party is being thrown by Lord and Lady Stanfield in a very unconventional household where that sort of thing doesn't count. Besides, I never thought I would see the day when you were conscious of propriety. I think both of us have laid waste to all the usual conventions—especially among certain elements of society where they count for so much.'

Knowing that to argue further would draw everyone's curious attention, she merely glowered at him. He really was the most provoking man she had ever met. She knew what he was about, and that he would go to any lengths to make another conquest, but, as his prey, she was just as determined to make it difficult for him. He intended to seduce her, and nothing was going to deter him from trying.

For her sake, the sooner he was across the Channel in France the better.

It was late afternoon when the door bell rang. Mrs Kelsall answered it, and a moment later came upstairs to tell Adeline that a Mr Cunningham wished to speak to Miss Leighton.

Adeline rose from her dressing table, straightened her skirt, reached up automatically to make sure her hair was tidy, and walked towards Mrs Kelsall.

'Show him into the drawing room, Mrs Kelsall. I'll see what he wants. Please don't tell Miss Leighton he's here.'

Jack Cunningham was standing in the middle of the drawing room, looking totally at ease. Immaculately dressed, he had the sleek, polished patina of great affluence—every inch the gentleman, in fact. But gentleman he was not. Keeping her distance, Adeline felt a rush of distaste. Resenting his intrusion into her home, and hoping his visit would be of short duration, she didn't do him the courtesy of asking him to sit down.

Looking at him with a cool composure she was far from feeling, she said, 'Mr Cunningham! What brings you to Eaton Place?'

'Thank you for seeing me. I am here to see Lettie. I know she is staying with you and I would like to speak to her.'

'I'm afraid Lettie doesn't want to speak to you, Mr Cunningham. I find your presence in my home offensive and I would like you to leave.'

He looked surprised by her coolness, and wondered at the reason for it. His features tightened. 'Leave? Not until I have seen Lettie. Please don't fear me.'

'I don't.'

'Good. I rarely harm anyone—unless provoked.'

'Mr Cunningham, I think you had better leave,' Adeline repeated coldly.

'Really, Miss Osborne, I did not expect to be received with so much hostility, and I cannot imagine why. You speak as if I have done Lettie harm—which is not the case, I can assure you.'

'No? As a result of her association with you Lettie has been— poorly,' she told him. It was not for her to tell him what Lettie had done. She must do that herself. All she wanted was for him to be gone from her home. 'I would like you to leave at once,' she insisted, her utter contempt for him manifested in her narrowed eyes and the disdain that curled her lip. 'You are not welcome in this house.'

Jack's eyes narrowed curiously. 'Lettie has been ill?' he prevaricated. 'Why was I not informed?'

'Why should you be, Mr Cunningham?'

'I am sure you know by now that Lettie is carrying my child. I have every right to be informed if she is not well. I insist on seeing her,' he demanded impatiently. 'I will not leave this house until I have done so. Kindly go and fetch her.'

'You have no rights.' A deep voice spoke from the doorway, causing Jack to spin round and face Grant Leighton, who was striding towards him. 'You crawling bastard,' Grant hissed, his fists clenched at his sides. 'Do you think that by coming into Miss Osborne's house and raising your voice you can terrorise her into submission? You will not see my sister. I will not allow it.' His voice was implacable, his manner implying that it would give him a great deal of pleasure to throw him out.

Jack appeared not to mind. He smiled smugly. 'I am here on perfectly legitimate business, and I would be pleased if someone could tell Lettie I am here,' he persisted.

'By God, Cunningham, I'll see you dead and in hell before I let you get your filthy hands on her again.'

'Even if I say that I will do the decent thing by her?'

'Decent!' Grant's voice was pure venom. 'You are even more of a lecherous swine than I thought you were—not to mention liable to legal sanctions for all your corrupt dealings. But no matter. Decency requires sufficient imagination to see beyond one's acts to their consequences.'

'What the hell are you talking about, Leighton?'

'Please stop it, Grant. I fight my own battles.'

The quiet voice cut off Grant's angry tirade. They all turned as one to see Lettie standing in the doorway. At once Jack Cunningham was the smooth charmer, bowing his head and smiling a slow, charismatic smile which was meant to tell everyone present that he wouldn't harm a fly.

Lettie was dressed with her usual elegance in a soft lemon-coloured gown, her hair brushed back smoothly into a meshed net. As she moved farther into the room she looked at Cunningham directly. Her face was white and so were her lips, and her glittering eyes were ice-cold.

'How dare you come here? You had no right. How did you know where to find me?'

'It wasn't difficult. Do I need an invitation to see you, Lettie? Will you not spare me a few minutes so that we can talk in private?'

'She's going nowhere with you, Cunningham,' Grant growled. 'You have violated my sister, and you expect her to continue being your whore.'

Adeline flinched at Grant's choice of word, which she knew would hurt Lettie. But he could be as hard and exacting as any man, and Jack Cunningham's offensive intrusion was making him increasingly furious.

Lettie drew herself up, her face set, her eyes flashing. 'My brother is right. We have nothing to say to each other, Jack. Please go.'

'Lettie,' he wheedled, holding out his hands to her. 'Come back to me. What we have is good—'

'No, Jack. It's over. I never want to see you again. Ever.'

'Come now, Lettie. My intentions are entirely honourable. I want you to marry me—to be my wife.'

'Wife!' Lettie's indignation and fury rose, choking and hot.

'You have a warped sense of honour, Jack. What do you intend doing with the wife you already have?'

Adeline and Grant stood there, looking at Lettie for the one awful, drawn-out moment it took them to recover from her shocking revelation. It was enough time for Lettie to draw enough breath back into her lungs, to look at Jack and say with appalled breathlessness, 'Or don't you remember, Jack?'

Caught off-guard, Jack looked at her a long time without bothering to open his mouth. Lettie saw the truth in his eyes. His face changed. His smooth, masculine good-looks departed as everything in his countenance pinched and tightened, and for the first time she realised how mean he looked, how hard.

'Yes, he has a wife. Her name is Molly,' Lettie heatedly told Grant and Adeline. 'She is in the asylum, where she has been incarcerated for the past ten years, after being delivered of a still-born child—her third, I believe. Unable to forgive her inability to give you a living child, you put her there—didn't you, Jack?— letting everyone believe she was dead. The loss of her children and her freedom drove her insane. Do you dare to deny it?'

Jack looked at Lettie and his face was like stone, as were his eyes. A blue vein twitched on his temple, and a creeping chill slithered down his spine when he thought of his wife. 'How did you find out?'

'I have ears, Jack. I listen. I went to see her—in a place that must surely be as close to hell on earth as is possible to get. In the course of my work I have seen all kinds of things, but this is different—the terror, the inescapable certainty of death, helpless and without dignity. How could you do that to your *wife*?'

The eyes Jack fixed on his accuser were filled with loathing for the woman he had locked away from the world. 'No, not a wife—a madwoman who should have died when she bore another dead child and rid me of her burden. She ceased to be my wife when the asylum door closed on her. As far as I am concerned she is as dead as her stillborn children.'

'You have a wife—a living wife—which the law recognises even if you do not,' Lettie whispered, truly appalled. 'You are despicable. And you would have entered into a bigamous marriage with me—knowing your wife still lives. How could you, Jack? How could you? Have you no compassion for her at all? She is *ill*.' Lettie was unable to believe how uncaring this man could be.

'Aye—an illness that grew into insanity and violence with each day.'

'If she became insane then you drove her to it—you and that place you put her in.'

Grant saw an instant of pity in Lettie's eyes when she looked at her lover. Because she recognised his horror of the disease that had consumed his wife. He also saw that Cunningham had lost Lettie not solely by his deceit, but in her contempt—that awakening of disgust which was the end of love between a man and a woman.

'I find your obsession with having a child strange,' Lettie remarked coldly, 'when I think of the small victims who pass through your hands to satisfy the appetites of the customers in your brothels. You disgust me.'

'Enough,' Jack hissed, his eyes blazing. 'Shut your mouth.' Her unflinching stare seemed to increase his fury two-fold.

Grant stepped forward. 'Why should she, Cunningham? Lettie has every right to speak freely in this house—although I had no idea she was as aware of the extent of your sordid dealings as myself. The very nature of your *other* business, which brings about its own secrecy, makes you unfit to associate with decent, respectable society.'

Suddenly chilled by what she was hearing, and the realisation of what it implied, Adeline felt twin sensations of horror and disgust rise like bile in her throat, forming a painful obstruction as she stared at this evil that had entered her home. Too stunned to act, too sickened even to comment upon what she was hearing, she remained motionless.

'How I choose to make my money is my affair, Leighton—and so is Lettie and the child she is carrying. It is mine, and as its father I have rights.'

'There no longer is a child, Jack. So you can forget any claim you might have had,' Lettie threw at him, almost triumphantly. 'I didn't want it. I don't want anything of yours.'

He frowned. 'No child?' Suddenly comprehension dawned. It hurt him, and he could not conceal it. His body went rigid, his right hand flexed and unflexed, and the muscles of his jaw twitched in reaction. 'I understand you have been ill. Have you miscarried?'

'No, Jack. When I found out just how vile you are, I realised I could not bear the child of a monster.'

Shock and grief registered in Jack's eyes, and for the first time there was an emotion in him quite different from anger. But it lasted only an instant. 'Good God! You got rid of it.'

There was utter silence for a second, then Jack's face went white as he truly understood what he had heard. 'To satisfy your own whim, you deliberately killed our child.'

Lettie wrapped her arms around her waist and nodded. 'Yes—yes, I did. I'm not proud—but, yes. I made a choice—the right choice for me. I couldn't bear the thought of giving birth to a child of yours.'

'You bitch.'

Lettie's face was tense, and pale also. She raised her brows very slightly. 'Really?' She shrugged. 'Think what you like. Now, please go—get out. You sicken me. I don't want to see you again, and that is my final word.'

Jack looked frightening. His lips were drawn back from his

teeth in a snarl, but his body was trembling. There was hate in his eyes. He glared at Grant. 'I congratulate you, Leighton. Your digging into my private life has given you what you wanted. But if you imagine you can do that and get away with it you are mistaken.'

When it looked as if he would argue further, Grant strode towards the door and opened it. 'You heard what my sister said. Get out. If I have the least suspicion of you attempting to see Lettie, even indirectly, I shall know how to set the story of your squalid affairs circulating round town which will bring the full investigation of the law down upon you. Since both moralists and police alike have been clamouring for a London clean-up since the beginning of the decade that's bound to happen sooner rather than later anyway. I'm only surprised you've got away with it for so long, and that your establishments have remained free from searches by the police.'

'Not every policeman is honest, Leighton.'

'It takes more than a nod and a wink, Cunningham. On the whole the police are virtually incorruptible, and proud of the work they do. I know there are those who can be bribed, but I promise you I will do everything I can to bring you down.'

'By God, Leighton,' Jack breathed, his voice intense, 'you'll pay for this.' His gaze flashed to Lettie. 'Both of you.'

Never had Adeline seen such hatred. The pure, naked, terrifying hatred of Grant. And why? Because he had got the better of Jack Cunningham.

'There will be no recriminations if you know what's good for you—if you don't want to spend the rest of your days behind bars. You, Cunningham, are scum.'

He had spoken quietly, too quietly for Cunningham to muster up words to reply. Grant held his eyes with a steady, unflinching stare. There was no pretence between them.

'And one more thing. If marrying Lettie and buying Westwood Hall was your way of insinuating yourself into respectability you can forget it. Diana's luck has turned and she has repaid her debts. Westwood Hall is no longer for you. Now, get out.'

Without saying another word Jack Cunningham left the house.

Grant hoped it would be the last they saw of him, but somehow he didn't think so. Cunningham wasn't the sort of man who would simply walk away without trying to wreak some kind of vengeance. There remained the threat that he might reveal what Lettie had done, and in so doing bring her down with the scandal.

When the door had closed, Grant went to his sister, who looked shaken by the whole unpleasant episode. Adeline rang for tea. She was troubled by everything she had just heard, and Jack Cunningham's shock at the loss of his child had had a ring of sincerity she had not expected.

'Lettie, did you go to the asylum by yourself?' Adeline asked curiously.

'No. Alice was with me.'

'Alice?'

'Jack's sister—the woman you saw outside the Phoenix Club. She's fond of Molly, and does what she can.'

'So—all that talk about a charity clinic wasn't true?'

'No. I'm sorry, Adeline. I couldn't tell you what she wanted then because I didn't know myself—only that it was of a serious, secretive nature. I met her afterwards and she told me how Jack had cast his wife off as he did his family when he began to prosper. To protect her from his wrath, I didn't tell Jack it was Alice who told me. The poor woman has approached him several times for money to make Molly's life easier, but he refuses to support any member of his family.'

'Then he truly is a monster, and you are well rid of him.'

'I know that now. Imagine what it must have been like for Molly—the man she trusted, maybe even loved, threw her aside like so much rubbish when she most needed him. Sadly she remains imprisoned—not only in that place, but in her mind—beyond all human help.'

The situation was so tragic there was nothing Adeline could say. Grant seemed to be preoccupied. She watched him pour himself a large brandy, then look at it a long moment, seeing the light burn through its amber depths.

What was he thinking of? she wondered. Or who? She recalled Frances telling her that Diana was in trouble financially, but she had had no idea she was in so much debt that she was forced to sell Westwood Hall. And Jack Cunningham had been hoping to buy it. Grant must have found out about the transaction and, loath to have Jack Cunningham as his neighbour, bought it himself—which testified in Adeline's mind to the close relationship between Grant and Diana Waverley.

Chapter Ten

When Grant arrived at Eaton Place on the evening of the party, he looked up automatically and saw Adeline coming down the staircase in a gown of gold-spangled satin, which hugged her slender curves and left her arms and shoulders bare. With a rope of white diamonds around her throat, and her hair curled up and secured with diamond and emerald combs which flashed as she turned her head, she looked glamorous and bewitching and captivating—and also lovely, soft, and eternally female.

Grant stared in stunned admiration, an appreciative smile working across his face. 'My God! You are beautiful. You look like a golden goddess.'

Caught up in the anticipation and excitement of Marjorie's engagement party, in the spell of his compelling silver gaze and his proud, smiling black and white elegance, Adeline found herself laughing softly. 'I'm glad you like it. Lettie chose it. I wanted to wear something more subtle, more subdued, but Lettie wouldn't hear of it.'

In fact, for the first time in days Lettie had seemed more like her old self as she had taken a delighted enthusiasm for the event and for making her look glamorous. Grant's arrival had increased Lettie's enthusiasm dramatically—which had aroused Adeline's suspicions. Not for the first time had it entered her mind that Lettie had some romantic notion of bringing her and Grant together.

'I never credited my sister with having such excellent taste,' Grant murmured, his gaze settling on the swelling globes of Adeline's breasts above the scooped bodice. 'The gown is both elegant and daring—and perfect.'

Seeing where his heavy-lidded gaze dwelt, and almost feeling his eyes disrobing her, Adeline flushed scarlet. 'Have you had an edifying look?'

His grin was roguish. 'Not nearly enough—but I have all night to gaze. How is my dear sister, by the way?'

'Well, but resting. Would you like to go up and see her before we leave?'

'If she's resting I won't disturb her.'

Adeline reached for her satin cape, but Grant took it from Mrs Kelsall.

'Allow me,' he offered.

Scarcely breathing, Adeline waited as those strong, lean hands draped the cape over her shoulders.

'Mmm,' he breathed from behind her, his mouth close to her ear. 'You smell nice, too.' He smiled, sublimely confident and pleased. He was going to enjoy tonight.

Adeline turned her head and looked at him. The amusement in his eyes was slowly replaced by a slumbering intensity. 'I think we'd better go, don't you?'

'Your carriage awaits, my lady,' he teased, then with solicitous care escorted her out to the waiting coach.

Once inside, Adeline cast an apprehensive eye at Grant as he settled himself beside her. How handsome he looks, she thought, as she stole a glance at his disciplined, classical profile. Just being with him made her heartbeat quicken. Reminding herself that, desirable and charming as he might be, he was still seeing Diana, and that if she wasn't careful she was in danger of forgetting her vow to keep him at arm's length, she knew it was imperative that she keep her head tonight.

It was only a short distance to Stanfield House, which was ablaze with light. The street was crowded with vehicles, each depositing its resplendent occupants at the front of the house. Adeline could hardly breathe for admiration as they climbed the steps and entered a hallway as large and echoing as a church. A curving staircase swept down from the landing to the marble floor.

They were met by Lord and Lady Stanfield and the engaged couple, their faces wreathed in smiles.

'Adeline, Grant—I'm delighted to see you!' Lord Stanfield said, his florid face between bushy mutton chop whiskers alight with geniality. 'How is dear Lettie? I'm sorry her illness has prevented her attending the party. Allow me to present Lord and Lady Henderson.'

When greetings had been made, and they were moving on, Grant bent his head close to Adeline's.

'The engaged couple look well matched.'

Adeline glanced back at Marjorie and Nicholas and laughed lightly. There was no denying the melting look in their eyes when they looked at each other, and Nicholas had his arm about Marjorie's waist, hugging her to his side as if she were a flower he wished to preserve. 'They are. Perfectly. It's a match made in heaven and Lady Stanfield is very happy about it. But then who wouldn't be? Marjorie is marrying a title, and noble titles are neither to be ignored nor laughed at.'

Not impervious to the stir they were creating—for when they had entered together a whispered murmuring had descended on the guests in the hall, and every eye had turned in their direction—Grant took her hand and, tucking it possessively in the crook of his arm, proudly led her towards the principal reception room. It was a singularly possessive gesture that somehow added to Adeline's well-being.

'This has all the makings of being an enjoyable evening,' Grant commented, nodding pleasantly to those he knew.

Gliding beside him, Adeline gave him a sudden enchanting smile, determined to be friendliness personified where he was concerned for this one night. To be otherwise would spoil the party, and she did so want to have a good time. She could only hope that his restraint would continue and her resistance would not be tested. Just the memory of his kiss could sap the strength from her.

'I do hope so. I can't help thinking of my own engagement party when I thought I would marry Paul. It was nothing like this.' Her eyes sparkled with excitement and delight. 'Since coming to London I've done many varied and interesting things—but this is my first party, and I am wearing my first party gown, and I am determined to enjoy myself.'

Grant laughed, a throaty, contagious laugh, and his eyes suddenly seemed to regard her with a bold, speculative gleam. 'Then we must make it a night to remember.'

Entering the large salon, they saw that it had been converted into a ballroom for the evening. Crystal chandeliers were suspended from an ornate ceiling, and gilt-framed mirrors reflected the dazzling kaleidoscope of jewellery and gowns. The older women were attired in rich colours, the younger ones in whites and creams and palest pinks. Everywhere there was the clink of glasses, the hum of conversation and the trill of laughter, and music rose and fell. It was an interesting gathering of society people, and others involved with Lady Stanfield's work. Large doors opened out onto a spacious terrace hung with fairy lights, and in a room next door a buffet table groaned under the weight of delicious food.

Every gaze seemed to swivel their way, and Adeline had the disconcerting feeling that every person in that room was either looking at them or talking about them.

'Is it my imagination, or is everyone staring at us?' she whispered to her escort.

'It isn't your imagination.' Turning slightly away from her, his expression pleased and confident, Grant scanned the crowded room. 'Do you know anyone here?'

'Yes, several. And you?'

'A few.'

'Then let's circulate and relieve their curiosity.' Taking a couple of glasses of sparkling champagne from a salver being carried by a passing footman, he handed one to her.

Taking a sip of the wine, and fortified by its potency, Adeline looked at him as he escorted her to the nearest group, feeling a glow of warmth infuse her whole being. He really did look breathtakingly handsome in his elegant black evening attire. It fitted his broad-shouldered figure to perfection. Women seemed to gravitate towards him—and little wonder, Adeline thought, seeing many women cast flirtatious glances his way. She sensed a jealous malevolence in their attitude to her. Seeing him like this, among the glittering members of society, admired and courted for his friendship and business acumen, she could hardly believe that this was the same man who had made love to her at

Westwood Hall, and had played havoc with her senses and emotions ever since.

After exchanging greetings with those they knew, being introduced to others of note and drinking two more glasses of champagne, they found themselves alone.

Adeline sighed. 'I'm sorry Lettie didn't come. I know she was so looking forward to it before…well, before. I feel rather guilty being here enjoying myself, while Lettie is feeling so distressed.'

'You may relax. Lettie wanted you to come, and she will hardly protest if you enjoy yourself, so there's no reason to feel guilty. And the music is most entrancing.' Seeing Anthony Stanfield and two other young gentlemen bearing down on them, with the obvious intention of asking Adeline to dance, Grant looked down at her. His gaze was slow and pointedly bold as he perused her soft and exquisite radiance. 'Dance with me, Adeline,' he said, taking her hand.

Her piquant denial was prepared, but the flowing, seductive strains of the music made Adeline want to move to its rhythm. For a breathless moment she envisaged herself in his arms, dancing with him. A thrill went through her, bringing a flush of colour to her cheeks, and she could no more deny the moment than ignore the hand of this man she held close to her heart.

Placing her hand in his, she smiled up at him. 'I'd love to.'

His mouth tilted upward in a roguish grin, and the warm, glowing light in his eyes made her blood run warm. In fact, as she stepped onto the dance floor and he drew her into his arms, whirling her about in a wide sweep of the floor, she felt positively wicked. She was a woman who felt as if she were reborn, and here she was being envied by everyone here tonight for being with this man.

'You dance divinely,' Grant observed as she moved with that natural, fluid motion of hers. 'You must have had a good instructor.'

She laughed lightly. 'I did. That's one thing my father insisted on. Apparently my mother was a good dancer.'

'I see. And do you look like her?'

'No. She was smaller than me, fair and very beautiful—whereas I am something of a curiosity in the family.'

He gave her a wicked smile. 'I'm somewhat partial to curiosities.'

Adeline's laughter bubbled to the surface like a subtle flowing stream through Grant's mind, and its effect was devastating. The fact that he wanted her was becoming hard-pressing reality.

When the dance ended Lady Stanfield appeared beside them. 'I'm glad to see the two of you enjoying yourselves—but you will dance with Marjorie, won't you, Grant? She's so glad you came, and she would like to talk to you about dear Lettie. Marjorie is going to miss her terribly, but I dare say she'll be back in London before too long.'

'I would think so. Lettie soon tires of the country, and as you know she is never happy unless she's busy. It would be my pleasure to dance with Marjorie. I shall ask her to dance the next with me—another waltz, I believe—before the music starts.' Excusing himself to Adeline, he disappeared into the throng.

Suddenly finding herself alone, Adeline was glad when Anthony appeared by her side. The celebration of his sister's engagement had made him more inebriated than he had ever been in his life, and, emboldened by this, he had turned his eyes on the fair Adeline Osborne, whose outstanding skill with the sword had made him her adoring slave.

'My God!' he exclaimed with unconcealed admiration when he was standing directly in front of her. 'You look ravishing, Adeline—although,' he said, bending close and speaking in a teasing conspiratorial whisper, 'I much prefer to see you in trousers. You have the most incredibly long legs—has anyone ever told you that?'

'I know perfectly well how long my legs are, thank you, Anthony,' she said jokingly. 'I do see them every day, you know.'

Anthony burst out laughing. Taking her hand, he drew her into the buffet room. 'I'm sorry, Adeline. I'm a bit tiddly, I'm afraid. But never mind. Come and meet my friends and have some more champagne, and we'll be tiddly together.'

Adeline's usually level head deserted her as she allowed him to lead her into the heart of a crowd of boisterous young people, all larking about, reclining on velvet-cushioned ottomans and having tremendous fun. Anthony handed her an over-large glass of the sparkling wine, which she drank faster than she ought, and for the next half an hour she joined in their high-spirits, making a spectacle of themselves.

She drank more champagne—far more than she was used to, and she would feel the effects later—laughed a good deal—causing heads to turn and look at her—and when Anthony pulled her onto the dance floor for a waltz it was anything but, because they polkaed about the floor.

When the music ended he danced her onto the terrace, and before Adeline had the faintest conception of what he would do, he had spun her round like a top, sending her reeling, then covered the distance he had opened between them. Catching her round the waist, he pressed his eager mouth passionately to hers.

Adeline was so astonished that for a moment she could not move. She had treated Anthony as a friend and had been having so much fun that she had scarcely noticed the adoring looks he gave her, but this was no boyish peck. It was a full blown man's kiss, hot with desire, and when they finally drew apart he whispered, 'I have wanted to do that from the moment I saw you,' and kissed her again.

Adeline pushed him away, although her sensitivities were not offended. 'Anthony, you must be mad. Please don't do this. Stop it now.'

But she was unable to resist his arms, which seemed to be all over the place, and Anthony pulled her back, uttering a torrent of lover's words against her cheek, his voice squashy with drink.

Again she shoved him away—as a voice spoke behind them.

'Well, here's a pretty spectacle.'

The voice was hard, the eyes, when Adeline turned to look, murderous and as hard as flint.

Grant stood rigid. His eyes were colder than ice and there was a thin white line about his mouth. How dared this youth kiss this lovely girl with her rosy cheeks and stars in her eyes—put his hands on what was…what should be Grant Leighton's? Did he not think of her day in and day out? Did she not fill his head and his dreams? Did he not know what it was like to hold her in his arms and recognise in Anthony Stanfield what he himself felt? And could he blame him?

Dear Lord, what was wrong with him? How could he let a woman affect him as this one did? He wanted to reach out and punch young Stanfield in the mouth, fling him away from Adeline—which was so out of character. It was with a great effort of will that he managed to keep his emotions in check, his expression one of calm composure as he looked from one to the other.

Anthony, past all caution, and seeing nothing wrong with the situation, laughed—and instinct told Adeline she, too, had to make light of it. However, when she looked at Grant she squinted her eyes, seeing double. He was all a blur. She also felt giddy and rather strange.

'Why, Grant, how stern you look. I can't think why you should. Anthony and I weren't doing anything wrong—in fact, Anthony feels he must kiss all the ladies present? Is that not so, Anthony?' She giggled and hiccupped, and clutched at Anthony's arm for support.

'That's right,' Anthony mumbled, struggling to stand straight and beginning to look a bit green around the gills. His teeth felt as if they were afloat at the back of his mouth…he really must find somewhere to be sick. 'Would you excuse me?' he said, his voice straining with the effort. 'I think I need to go somewhere.'

Adeline and Grant didn't say a word as he weaved himself down the steps of the terrace and disappeared into the darkness of the garden, but Grant watched his departing figure with a mixture of pity, amusement and disgust. Despite the absurdity of it, he felt the first sharp twinge of jealousy in his adult life.

'There goes a young man who will have one hell of a hangover in the morning.'

'Poor Anthony. He really has drunk a lot of champagne—enough to sink a ship.' Adeline looked at Grant and tried desperately to focus on his face. He was a dark, invincible figure, forbidding, intimidating, and yet strangely compelling. 'Why did you come looking for me, Grant? Must you watch me so closely?'

Grant raised one black devil's eyebrow. 'I am your escort. I'm merely safeguarding your honour.'

Adeline giggled. 'It's a bit late in the day to defend my honour, Grant. You of all people should know that.'

'You seem to be enjoying yourself,' he commented, ignoring her statement for the time being.

'I'm having a truly wonderful time. Really, Grant, do you have to look so—pompous, so aloof?'

Her reproof brought a scowl to his face. 'Come inside and have something to eat.'

'I'm not hungry, but I'd love some more champagne.'

'Don't you think you've had enough?'

Adeline looked at his face, which was a hard, angry mask. She frowned her annoyance. 'Grant, there is one thing you should realise. My whole life has been one of compliance. I have never been able to please myself. And suddenly I feel like a bird that has been set free from its gilded cage,' she said laughingly, throwing her arms wide to demonstrate the fact, and doing a rather wobbly twirl. 'I am enjoying myself as I have never enjoyed anything in my life. Please don't spoil it.' She smiled up at him serenely, clutching his arm to maintain her fragile balance. 'Have you come to ask me to dance?'

'I would, if I didn't think you would fall over,' he remarked. The anger he had felt at seeing her kissing young Stanfield was abating, for in her weakened state she really did look both vulnerable and adorable and incredibly lovely—a loveliness not just of face and form, but in her heart and soul. It shone from her, and she was completely unaware of it, and that was what was so special about her.

'Yes, you're right. I do feel a bit wobbly,' she said, relinquishing her hold on his arm and flopping down onto the low terrace wall. 'I'm feeling a trifle dizzy from all that dancing.'

Grant cocked a dubious brow and, propping one shoulder negligently against the trellising, regarded her attractively flushed face and shining eyes with a twisted smile. 'Dancing? Are you sure it's not the effects of the champagne?'

Looking up at him, she smiled, thinking how incredibly handsome he looked in the soft glow of the fairy lights. 'It could be, I suppose.'

'That was quite a show you put on on the dance floor. Do you normally dance a polka to a waltz?' he said quietly, his lips twitching in ill-suppressed amusement.

Adeline blinked up at him. 'Did we?' She scowled, seeing a

glint of censure in his eyes despite his smile. 'Grant, are you cross with me?'

'No—although you did make something of a spectacle of yourself. Perhaps you should rest awhile?'

'I'm having too good a time to rest.'

'Adeline, have you eaten anything at all?' he chided.

She chuckled at his dark scowl. 'No, not yet. I don't seem to have had the time.'

'Perhaps if you'd spent less time drinking champagne and kissing Anthony Stanfield you might have found the time.'

'Grant? You cannot be angry at a young man's tipsy kiss— or…' she murmured, tilting her head to one side and looking up at him askance. 'Or is it the green eye of jealousy, perhaps?'

He looked down at her. 'Should I be jealous?'

'Of course you should. Anthony kisses very well.'

'Like hell he does. I marked well how little you resisted—no doubt these kisses are a frequent occurrence when Anthony visits you at Eaton Place on the pretence of fencing lessons.'

Adeline threw him an indignant look. 'Now you are being silly—and you are beginning to sound just like my father. But you were right, you know. I think Anthony *does* have feelings for me—or it might be the champagne, I suppose,' she murmured airily. 'We are both a bit tipsy.'

'Tipsy? That is obvious. Drink makes a window for the truth, Adeline.'

'And you would know all about that, wouldn't you?' she accused, standing up and jabbing a tapered fingernail into his chest. 'The first time we met you were disgustingly drunk.' An unconsciously provocative smile curved her lips and she moved closer to him, her narrowed eyes warm and meaningful on his. 'Pity you can't remember the incident as well as I can.'

He grinned impenitently. 'Care to try it again? You can show me what I missed.' He raised a brow as he waited for her answer—and his eyes clearly expressed his wants.

Adeline felt herself falling under the spell of that rich, deep voice, and the bold stare touched a quickness in her that made her feel as if she were on fire. 'You—you're jesting.'

'No, I'm not. You told me how wonderful it was for you. Wouldn't you like to experience that again?'

'And become your mistress? Do you know that to almost everyone here tonight the general consensus is that I am already your mistress?'

Grant smiled. By escorting her to the party he was making certain everyone thought she was. 'And does that concern you?' he asked, watching her intently.

'Of course it does—because I'm not,' she retorted, in a voice of offended dignity. 'If I was it wouldn't matter. But you'd be quite worn out trying to keep two mistresses happy and content.'

Grant's amused laughter took the sting out of her words. 'When I have expended so much energy on you, Adeline, can you believe I have any interest in another woman? Is it my association with Diana that raises your ire?'

'My ire, as you call it, is justified and you know it. Carrying on with Paul and not even bothering to hide it. Her behaviour was quite disgraceful.' She paused, thoughtfully. 'Although if she hadn't I suppose I'd have had to marry him, so if for nothing else I must be grateful to her for that. You have seen a good deal of Diana of late, so why shouldn't I think the two of you are having an affair?'

'And why should you care if I am seeing Diana?'

Her eyes snapped. 'How conceited you are, Grant Leighton. I don't.'

'Yes, you do.'

Those glowing eyes burned into hers, suffusing her with an

aura of warmth. How could she claim uninterest in this man when his presence could so effectively stir her senses?

Grant's gaze dipped and lightly caressed her breasts before moving back to her face. 'I am single-minded in my pursuits, Adeline.'

'Really? What are you saying?'

'That I want you.'

Adeline took a step back, resisting all on the strength of her fear. Grant saw her fear and played on it gently, lest her fear destroy the moment, but it took extreme exercise of will.

Taking her hand he drew her back to him. 'I would like to see what your determination to stand against me can bear, Adeline.'

His nearness sapped Adeline's strength and weakened her will, drawing out her every resolve until she didn't know what to think any more—what to do. She knew with certainty that she would never be free of Grant Leighton, and with each day he grew bolder. She saw the hard flint of passion strike sparks in the silver-grey eyes as they moved upon her face.

Grant realised that beneath her fine clothes she was what every man dreamed of—a vision of incomparable beauty—and he wanted to see for himself, to possess it. His long-starved passion flared. She had got under his skin, into his blood, and her mere touch, the scent of her, sent desire running through his veins. She was sensual, unaffected and yet sophisticated, and as he looked at her his mind drifted back to when he had robbed her of her virtue.

It gave him satisfaction to know he had been the one to take it, and he was impatient for the time when he could repeat the act—only this time he would be the most tender of lovers, and have her moaning with rapture. His eyes revelled in their freedom as they feasted hungrily on her face—her lips.

Adeline felt it, felt devoured by it, and it took an effort of will to remain pliant beneath his probing eyes. 'What—what is it you want?' she asked. Her voice didn't sound her own to her ears.

'You,' he answered.

'Oh, I see.'

'Yes—and I think you want me. Let's get this clear. You don't want to eat. You don't want to dance. So—why are we still here?'

Adeline kept her eyes carefully on his face. 'Where should we be?'

'Somewhere else.'

'Where do you suggest? Your—hotel room, perhaps?' she whispered, her eyes on his lips.

'Yes, but not tonight. Not when your head is clouded with champagne. When you come to my bed—'

'When?' Her eyes snapped. 'You are certain of that, are you? Not if?'

'It's inevitable, Adeline, and only a matter of time—perhaps tomorrow, when we have taken Lettie to the station.' His smile was salacious. 'That will give you something to think about from now until then. When you come to my bed—of your own accord—it will be an intoxication of a different kind that brings us together. We shall both be fully aware of what is happening between us, I promise you,' he said, on a note of tender finality. 'But I warn you—you may find something more eternal, more binding than a simple act of love.'

In her fuddled mind, Adeline had no idea what he meant by that. Earlier she had made a conscious decision to keep him at arm's length—now she was about to renege on her decision. Nervous, she turned her gaze away and gnawed on her bottom lip.

Grant watched her warily, and her eyes wavered beneath his direct gaze. Lifting a finger, he slowly traced the soft fullness of her bottom lip, then murmured, 'You're trembling.'

'Am I?' She watched his gaze turn warm and sensual.

Gently taking her chin between his thumb and forefinger, he nodded. 'I'll forgive you for kissing that young reprobate if you kiss me now.'

Adeline's whole body stilled as his finely chiselled lips began to descend to hers, and she sought to forestall what her heart told her was the inevitable by saying, 'What if someone should come out onto the terrace and see us?'

A flame appeared in his eyes and kindled brighter, and his warm lips trailed a hot path over her cheek to her ear. 'Let them. It doesn't matter,' he murmured huskily.

His tongue lightly touched the lobe of her ear, delicately probing the crevices, until Adeline shivered with the waves of tension shooting through her. The instant he felt her trembling response his arms went round her, drawing her into his protective embrace. His hand curved around her nape, sensually stroking, and his warm breath caressed her cheek as his mouth began tracing a path to her lips.

Imprisoned by his embrace, seduced by his mouth and caressing hands, Adeline pressed herself close to his hard body, moving her hands up his broad chest, her fingers sliding into the soft hair at his nape, her body arching to his, fitting his powerful frame. Slowly she slipped into a dark abyss of desire as she fully received his kiss, first with hesitancy, then with welcome, then with passion, feeling a wild, incredible sweetness.

The tender offering of her mouth wrung a half-laugh, half-groan from Grant, and, tightening his arms, he seized her lips with his in a kiss of scorching demand, crushing down on them, parting them, his tongue driving into her mouth with a hungry urgency. Adeline's world careened dizzily. His mouth was insistent, demanding, relentless, snatching her breath as well as her poise as primitive sensations went jarring through her entire body. The fierceness of his kiss changed to softness, to the velvet touch of intoxication, and the breath that sighed through her lips was the sigh that came when a woman was deep in the pleasures of the flesh.

When Grant finally released her lips an eternity later—which took more effort than he'd expected, leaving him feeling almost bereft—Adeline surfaced gradually from the sensual place where he had sent her, still feeling the thrill of the invasion of his tongue, and all the sensations that had followed. Forcing her eyes open so that she could look at his face—hard with passion, eyes smouldering—with trembling effort she collected herself, and as he looked down at her she drew a deep, ragged breath.

Until now she had tried to convince herself that her memory of the passion that had erupted between them at Westwood Hall was exaggerated, but his kiss had surpassed her imaginings. A breeze riffled through the trellising, teasing the trailing roses and caressing her bare shoulders. His hands stroked soothingly up and down her arms and his eyes held hers. Suddenly the sounds of music and laughter began to penetrate Adeline's drugged senses, and a noisy group of young people burst onto the terrace.

Grant's sensual lips curved in a half-smile and, reaching out, he tucked a stray strand of hair behind her ear. 'It's getting late. Would you like me to take you home?'

'Yes. I promised I'd call in and see Lettie before going to bed. I'm going to miss her when she goes home.'

Grant's grin was tigerish. 'Not immediately, I hope.' As much as he didn't want to send Lettie back to their mother, he was impatient for the short time he would have alone with Adeline before he had to leave for the boat train to the continent. 'I shall try and restrain myself until tomorrow, when we will settle this matter between us—you will be mine before the day is done.'

Adeline stared at him, realising he meant every word he said.

Her mind reeled beneath the impact of the last few minutes. Grant meant what he said and she was absolutely certain that she would be unable to withstand his persuasive, unrelenting assault—and now she wasn't at all certain that she wanted to.

The next morning it was a pale and troubled Lettie that Grant and Adeline put on the train for Ashford. Emma was to go with her. Weak as she was, Lettie was going home to Newhill Lodge and her mother. She felt she would stifle if she stayed in London any longer, with her mind going round and round in distressing circles of—what? Sorrow, aching loss, regret, guilt? What she did acknowledge was that the physical pain had diminished, and so had the mental pain, if she would admit it to herself.

Adeline and Grant watched the train until it was out of sight, and then they left the station and returned to where the carriage was waiting. Assuming they could carry on where they'd left off last night, and refusing to relinquish control, acting on his words and intending to have things his way, Grant instantly told the driver to take them to the Charing Cross Hotel.

Seated at his side, Adeline looked at him. Before Marjorie's party she had told herself she would refuse any attempt he made at seduction. Then at the first possible moment she had practically thrown herself at him. Grant turned his head and caught her watching him, and a shock of lightning seemed to shoot from his body straight into hers. Without moving a muscle or saying a word he was emanating an aura of predatory male that was tangible enough to cut with a knife.

Adeline wondered what she was letting herself in for. Last night her head had been so fuddled with champagne that she'd have agreed to anything he suggested—but that had been last night, and now her stomach cramped with nervous uncertainty. But Grant was hardly a stranger, an unknown entity. There was no denying that she was wildly attracted to him. She thought of him a thousand times a day, and every thought was sweeter than the last. And there was no denying that the idea of repeating what she had experienced before made her knees weak.

'What time do you have to leave for your train?' she asked, for something to say—anything to break the silence between them.

'Why?' His brows drew together and a gleam of intent entered his eyes. 'Are you afraid I'll be rushing off?'

'No,' she said, looking away. 'I—I just wondered, that was all.'

Placing his finger beneath her chin, he turned her head back to his. In silence he studied her face, as if he were searching for an answer, then he leant forward and captured her mouth, kissing her long and deep. When he finally lifted his head he gazed down into her eyes, unconsciously memorising the way she looked, all flushed and alluring.

'Four o'clock,' he murmured in answer to her question. 'So that leaves us plenty of time to—' his eyes fastened greedily on her lips once more '—get to know one another.'

Adeline's senses were beginning to reel with the shock of her decision and his closeness, and her treacherous heart began to beat a trifle faster. She suffered what remained of the journey in a state of tension, anticipating what would happen when they reached his rooms.

The hotel was busy with people coming and going. They took the lift to the third floor. On opening the door to his suite of rooms, Adeline was surprised and more than a little embarrassed to see a well-groomed, middle-aged man standing at a desk, carefully putting papers and files into a large leather case. He looked up and smiled.

'Ah, Vickers,' Grant said. 'Allow me to present Miss Osborne.

Adeline, this is John Vickers—my secretary, valet. Call him
what you like, but I could not do without him.'

'I'm pleased to make your acquaintance, Miss Osborne,' Mr
Vickers said courteously, closing the case and carrying it to the
door. 'Now, you must excuse me. I have things to do before we
leave.' He looked at Grant. 'I'll see you in the foyer at three-
thirty, Mr Leighton.'

Grant followed him, giving the stalwart secretary a set of instructions before closing the door on him. 'Vickers is to accompany me to France,' Grant explained, walking back to Adeline.
'He's been with me a long time. He's highly competent, discreet
and indispensable.' Suddenly he became aware of Adeline's
stillness and he frowned questioningly at the look of apprehension on her face. 'Adeline? Is there something wrong?'

Clutching her reticule with both hands, Adeline looked at
him, her faltering courage beginning to collapse. 'I can't do this,'
she whispered. She'd spent the time while he was talking to Mr
Vickers trying desperately to decide whether her misgivings
were based on good judgement or panic.

Wordlessly, Grant took her reticule and placed it on the desk,
then he took her gloved hands and drew her towards him. 'What
do you mean, you can't?' he demanded gently.

'I can't, Grant. Not now.' Her voice trembled and she looked
towards the door in her desperation to escape. 'I—I think I need
time.'

Drawing her hands from his grasp, she moved away from him.
But the urgency and regret in his deep voice checked her in
midstep and made her fear of him absurd. 'I am to leave for the
continent at four o'clock, Adeline. Time is the one thing we
don't have.'

That there'd be time enough for loneliness when she returned
to Rosehill made her realise how foolish she was being to turn

down an opportunity that was heaven-sent. All her defences began to crumble. She could not deny herself the memories he'd make for her if she stayed.

When she looked at his handsome features an ache swelled in her chest. 'Grant,' she whispered a little shakily, and watched his expression soften at the sound of her voice. 'I'm sorry.' She held out her hand in a gesture of conciliation. 'For a moment I—I panicked.'

Grant saw the yielding softness in her eyes, and somewhere deep inside him he felt the stirrings of an emotion that made him reach out and draw her into his arms. He wanted her so much he couldn't bear to think she would deny him now. When she melted against him, the hot, sweet smell of her whipped up the blood in his veins. Releasing her without a word, and with his eyes holding hers like a magnet, he took her hand and drew her into the bedroom, closing the door firmly behind them.

Taking off his outer garments, he then removed Adeline's hat and with infinite care unpinned her hair. When the last pin was out she gave her head a hard shake, and her hair tumbled down her back in a shining mass. Grant marvelled at its luxuriant, thick, rich texture and colour, running it through his fingers, pausing now and then to kiss her lips, her cheek, her neck.

Her eyes drifted closed and her breath came out in a sigh as she kissed him softly and felt his lips answer, moving on hers, while his arms tightened around her. Breaking the kiss, she half opened her eyes and saw that the silver-grey eyes were beginning to smoulder.

With his lips against hers, Grant murmured, 'Let's go to bed,' his long fingers beginning to unfasten the buttons down the front of her three-quarter-length coat.

Grant obviously had no inhibitions about undressing in front of her, but Adeline was self-conscious enough for them both.

When she turned away, Grant realised that she was embarrassed and shy about revealing her naked body. With an understanding smile he went to her and turned her round. Placing his finger beneath her chin, he tilted her head to his.

'Do you forget, Adeline, that I have seen you naked before now? You have a beautiful body—so why the reticence? Come. Since there is no lady's maid to assist, allow me to oblige.'

The sight of Adeline's naked body—a miracle of ripe curves and glowing flesh—made Grant's heart slam against his ribs. Her breasts were perfect, her legs just as long and shapely as he remembered. In fact, she was stunning. Whoever had thought Adeline Osborne plain and uninteresting did not know her—and nor would they, he vowed, swearing that no other man but himself would ever see her like this.

'You take my breath away,' he whispered, drawing her against him.

When she wound her arms around his neck and placed soft, feather-light kisses on his neck, the solid wall of his chest and his sinewed shoulders, his heart constricted with an emotion so intense, so profound, that it made him ache. Her breath was sweet against his throat. Dear God, she was so warm, so womanly, long and slender, but curving against his body, doing what she could to get even closer. His male body rejoiced in it, for it told him he held a warm and willing woman in his arms.

To Adeline, the moment was one of poignant discovery. His skin felt like warm silk over steel as her fingers slid through the short, dark matting of hair on his chest. His jaw was set, his cheekbones angular, his mouth firm yet sensual, his eyes hard and dark with passion—and for now he was hers.

When he pulled her down onto the bed their restraint broke, and together they were caressing, seeking hands and eager mouths. They were both aflame, both burning with the same need. He was kissing her with a raw, urgent hunger, his hands claiming her body, sliding over her breasts, her waist and back to her face, shoving his fingers into her silken hair, holding her a willing prisoner. She moaned with joy as his mouth touched her breasts, and so lost was she in the desire he was so skilfully building inside her that she scarcely noticed when he eased her body beneath his own.

As he entered her she expelled a breath at the exquisite sensation of her body opening to him like a flower. No holding back, she strained towards him with trembling need, each instinctive, demanding thrust pushing her closer to the edge and bringing exquisite pleasure. Grant, unlike Adeline, did hold back, for he wanted her to experience as much as his body would allow before he lost control.

Afterwards, when their passion had finally exploded in a burst of extravagant pleasure, in languid exhaustion and bone-deep satisfaction they lay close together, facing each other, breathless from exertion, clinging to the fading euphoria. Contentment stole over them both, lapping gently. They trembled with the rapture of their union, the passion which Grant had known with no other woman. Sliding his fingers over her spine, he watched her open her eyes. Smiling, she nestled closer. Grant placed a kiss on the top of her head.

'You are exquisite. How do you feel?'

'Wonderful,' she breathed, and she did.

As sanity returned it became obvious to her that the man who had just made love to her was indeed the same man who had made love to her before—but this time his technique had been perfect, unimpaired by alcohol. He had taken her not just sexually, but with a deeper, infinitely more alluring need—something profound.

'What we did was very, very special to me.' She raised her

head and gave him a slumberous smile, sated and happy, the smile of a woman fulfilled. 'Thank you.'

He shoved the hair from her smooth cheek, his eyes warm and serious and very tender. 'My pleasure, Miss Osborne. Now I know what I missed, I am impatient to make up for lost time.'

Nestling closer to him, Adeline closed her eyes, letting the warmth deepen inside her, driving out everything else. At length she whispered, 'I'm going to miss you. Will you think of me in France?'

His arm tightened round her. In that moment he realised that leaving her was going to be the hardest thing he had ever had to do. 'All the time. I wish I didn't have to go.'

She sighed against him. 'So do I. Why are you going?'

'Like your father, I am a businessman, Adeline, and a number of speculative ventures have come to my attention. I am interested in investing in several companies in France, and arrangements have been made for me to meet some prominent businessmen over there.'

'But why go there? If the companies are limited why not simply buy shares in them?'

'Because, my darling girl, I wish to know the real position of the companies I am to sink my money into, to be sure in my own mind that they will not fail to meet their liabilities. If they do, and my investments collapse, then I will only have myself to blame.'

Adeline sighed against him. 'You are very astute, Mr Leighton.'

'I have to be.'

'Must you go?'

He nodded his head, and even though his voice was still soft, it was steadier and more resolute. 'Yes. Don't make it harder than it already is.'

Adeline wondered desolately how it could possibly be any harder, but she swallowed down that futile protest. 'I won't. I suppose if it's business then you have to go.'

'Do you intend staying in London?'

'For a little while. I've never been away from Rosehill for so long—or from my father—and I'm rather enjoying my freedom.'

'I'd like to see the look on his face when his daughter returns as a stylish, independent young woman.'

'He probably won't notice.'

'Yes, he will. You'll see.'

'Will—will you write to me?' she asked hopefully.

'Only if you promise to write back.'

She nodded. 'You know I will.'

They fell silent, each content to hold reality at bay for the time they had left together. After a prolonged moment of silence, Adeline whispered, 'What are you thinking about?'

Grant tipped his chin down, the better to see her, wiping shining strands of hair from her forehead. 'I was thinking how lucky I am to have you here with me now. I knew within minutes of seeing you that you were quite unique.'

'Yet you knew nothing about me, about my character, which is what makes a person.'

'I knew by the way you rode your horse. It was obvious you didn't give a damn what people thought about a woman riding astride—and wearing breeches to boot. I was full of admiration. I also thought you were the most vital, energetic young woman I had ever seen—quite magnificent, in fact. And now I have come to know you I realise I was not mistaken in my opinion.'

Rolling onto her stomach and leaning on her elbows, Adeline looked into his fathomless eyes. 'Truly?'

'Truly.'

'And were you not disappointed when you realised who I was—plain, shortsighted Miss Adeline Osborne from Rosehill? People have always had the most odd reaction to my looks.'

'I can't imagine why,' he said, his mouth quirking in a half-smile as he pulled her down onto his chest. 'I have never considered you plain—interesting, yes, and discerning, certainly not dull, and never plain.'

In Grant's opinion he spoke the truth, because as she sprawled across his chest, her deep mahogany-coloured hair shrouding them both, she looked like a bewitching, beautiful, innocent goddess.

'But I have odd eyes, don't you think?'

'Take it from me, Adeline,' he murmured, his senses alive to every inch of the form so languorously stretched across him, 'there is absolutely nothing wrong with your eyes, or your nose—which is adorable, by the way—and your mouth is perfect and extremely kissable. So you see, along with all your other feminine assets, you have all the requisite features in all the right places.' His gaze settled on her mouth. 'And, speaking of your mouth,' he said, watching her tongue pass over her full bottom lip in a most seductive manner that made him acutely aware that his body was stirring to life with alarming intensity, 'I think it's time you kissed me. We haven't much time left, and I don't want to waste a minute of it.'

Happy to do as he asked, Adeline lowered her head and lightly placed a kiss on the corner of his mouth. Her eyes darkened with a love she wasn't trying to conceal from him any more. 'What is it I have to do to please you?'

Rolling her onto her back, he smiled down at her. 'I'm open to suggestions. Show me.'

Chapter Eleven

Loving Grant from the bottom of her heart, Adeline tried to block out the painful moment when they would have to part. When it was time for him to leave, Adeline accompanied him to the ground floor of the hotel. It wasn't until they reached the foyer that she realised she had left her reticule in his rooms.

'I'll go back and get it,' Grant offered.

'No, I'll go. You go and find a cab. I won't be long.'

Having retrieved her reticule, Adeline stepped out of the lift and looked around her, searching the people milling about for the face she loved. And there he was. She was about to cross to him when she saw him bend his head to the woman who seemed to be clinging to his side. His arm was half about her waist and her hand was placed possessively on his arm.

It was Diana.

It was the expression on Diana's face that caught Adeline's attention and held her momentarily transfixed. Her eyes were direct, intensely earnest, and she was looking at Grant as if she were telling him something profoundly important. Grant, standing with his profile to Adeline, was speaking softly, closer to Diana than was customary for mere friends, and he seemed— at least for the moment—oblivious to anyone else.

Numb with shock, she felt a silence seem to fall around her— a silence in which every sound was muted, a silence in which she seemed embalmed for a moment. And then she spun on her heel and walked out of the hotel. She got inside a cab and told the driver to go to Eaton Place, and to hurry. The man obeyed instantly, snaking his long carriage whip over the horse's back and urging it forward, ignoring delivery carts, drays and other hansoms which swerved out of their way.

Inside the cab, Adeline felt as if she were existing in some kind of remote space, isolated from everything. The only thing she could think of was Grant and the pleasure he had given her—the intense, undreamed of, unimaginable pleasure—and now Diana had appeared once again to spoil everything. She felt desperately wretched and unhappy. How could he? she thought angrily. But anger did not help her. She felt lost and bewildered.

As soon as she entered the house, Mrs Kelsall handed her a letter that had arrived earlier. It was from Rosehill.

When Adeline didn't meet him in the foyer, Grant returned to his room to find she wasn't there either. Puzzled as to where she could be, he waited a while in case she turned up before going to Eaton Place—only to be told by Mrs Kelsall that Adeline had received an urgent message from Rosehill. Her father had been taken ill and she had left for the station almost immediately.

For the second time that day Grant rushed to Victoria Station, in the hope of seeing her. But he was too late. He was to leave himself to catch the boat train shortly, so he was unable to go after her, but he was curious as to why she had left the hotel without saying goodbye. Then the reason why she had gone hit him like a hammer-blow.

Diana! She must have seen him with Diana—and, based on her reaction, she had imagined the worst. She was torturing them both this way because she was angry and hurt. 'You little fool!' he murmured, staring at the empty railtrack. She had done it again, without giving him an opportunity to explain. And now it was too late.

He could imagine the wrenching look on her face when she had seen him with Diana—and the image haunted him. It tore at him, along with his other worries about her. There were so many things he needed desperately to say to her—and he would. He would write to her the moment he reached his hotel in Paris.

All the way to Rosehill, Adeline was filled with a mixture of emotions: in particular, worry about her father, and second to that a growing fury—a furious disbelief—that she had allowed a man to treat her as Grant Leighton had done. She felt rage that he had had the audacity to do so. She had the desire to shout her rage out loud. What sort of a woman did he think she was? How *dared* he? How *dared* he lure her to his hotel room and do what he had when all the time Diana Waverley had been waiting downstairs? No matter how hard he denied they were having an affair, she did not believe him and never would. How could she when she had seen the evidence with her own eyes?

Well, she could do nothing about Grant Leighton just now. Her father was ill and he needed her—but, dear Lord, she'd have something to say to him when the time came.

On reaching Rosehill, Adeline knew her face was set in lines of anxiety.

'How is Father?' were the first words she asked Mrs Pearce, who had been the housekeeper at Rosehill for as long as Adeline could remember.

'Dr Terry's with him now, Miss Adeline.'

'What's wrong with him?' Adeline asked, removing her hat and gloves and handing them to a hovering maid.

'It's his heart, Dr Terry says. He collapsed last night at dinner. We managed to get him to bed. It was fortunate Dr Terry was at home and able to come at once.'

'Is he conscious?'

Mrs Pearce nodded her grey head. 'He's very poorly, but the doctor will tell you more.'

When Dr Terry faced Adeline he was as reassuring as he could be.

'He's had a minor heart attack, which I believe was brought on by stress. I've advised him time and again not to work so hard—but you know what he's like. His condition is stabilised, and I don't believe there is any danger—providing you can get him to take things easy.'

'I'll certainly do my best.'

'I've given him a draught that seems to have relaxed him, and he'll be relieved to see you, my dear. Your presence will hasten his recovery, I am sure.'

Knowing full well that her presence was unlikely to make any difference whatsoever, Adeline let her lips curve in a wry smile. 'Let us hope so, Dr Terry.'

'I've taken the liberty of employing a nurse—a Mrs Newbold—who is extremely competent. She arrived this morning and has already settled in to her duties.'

'Thank you. I do appreciate that.'

'There's nothing more I can do for now. I'll call tomorrow. Just make sure he stays quiet.'

As soon as Dr Terry had left, Adeline went up to her father. He was propped up against the pillows, his face grey and drawn with the hint of tiredness and pain. The signs of fleshiness were beginning to fight against the hardness of it, showing his advancing age, but his intelligent eyes were keen as he watched her approach the bed with quiet assurance.

'Adeline,' he said throatily.

She bent over and lightly kissed his cheek. 'Hello, Father,' she said, searching his face. He had always seemed so indestructible. Nothing had seemed beyond the reach and scope of his energy and intelligence. 'I came just as soon as I could. How are you?' she ventured. 'Dr Terry seems pleased with your progress.' She smiled. 'You always did confound predictions.'

He nodded, his gaze on her face. 'I'm glad you're home, Adeline. All this fuss.' He glowered at Mrs Newbold, hovering across the room. 'I can't stand it.'

'It won't be for long. I'm sure you'll soon be up and about—but you're going to have to take it easy for some time.'

'So everyone keeps telling me—and I fear they're right.'

A sad smile rested briefly on his lips, and when he looked away Adeline knew his very attitude was an admission of weakness. He who had always had determination, stamina, will—who had demanded and been paid the homage of lord and master for so long—had in the last moments been toppled from his pedestal, and the recognition of his fall was mutual.

He looked at Adeline and a softening entered Horace's eyes. 'I've missed you, you know.'

'Have you?' Adeline could say no more in her amazement. Her father, who had always seemed so remote—uncaring—had missed her, and he was looking at her in the most extraordinary way. She marvelled at it, and something inside her softened and shattered. Her quick, observant eyes saw the varied emotions flickering in his own. He had changed. Never before allowing her to come too close, now he seemed to welcome her.

Smiling softly, a warmth in her eyes, and taking his hand, she sat on the edge of the bed facing him. 'I've missed you, too. When I left for London there was so much constraint between us—of my doing entirely. I accept that, and I am so sorry, Father. I never meant to hurt you. Truly.'

'It doesn't matter now,' he said hoarsely, gently squeezing her hand. 'I'm just glad to have you back. You look—different, somehow—quite fetching, in fact. Your hair…'

Adeline laughed brightly. 'It's supposed to be the new me, but I'm still the same underneath. I—I saw Grant Leighton in London. I—understand his mother has been a guest at Rosehill whilst I've been away?' Did she imagine it or did a twinkle enter his eyes?

'She has, and most delightful she is, too. We have much in common, Hester and me. In fact I would like you to write to her—tell her what's happened and that she must feel free to visit any time. I—would like to see her.'

'I'll do that.'

'So, you've seen Grant Leighton, have you?'

'Yes, on—on several occasions,' she said, lowering her eyes.

Horace settled into the pillows, observing his daughter with careful scrutiny. He didn't need a crystal ball to tell him that all was not as it should be with her. 'Do you regret not accepting his proposal of marriage, Adeline?'

She shook her head. 'It's in the past, Father. At the time there was so much unpleasantness. I—prefer not to speak of it.'

Horace did not question her on the subject of Grant Leighton any further. There were areas of the heart into which one did not intrude.

* * *

Adeline greeted Hester Leighton in the hall, relieved that she had come at last. Her features were as soft and feminine as she remembered, but there were shadows under and around her eyes that had not been present before.

'It's very good of you to come, Mrs Leighton. Father is so looking forward to seeing you.'

'I would have come sooner, but I didn't want to appear intrusive,' Hester said, smiling softly.

'You knew my father was ill?'

Hester raised her brows delicately. 'I had a letter from Grant. He mentioned that he'd seen you in London, and the reason why you had been summoned back to Rosehill.'

'I see.' And Adeline did see. What Mrs Leighton had said told her that Grant must have followed her to Eaton Place when he had found she had left the hotel. Had he been surprised? Had he realised why? 'The hall is chilly. Come into the drawing room. It's warmer and faces on to the garden...' She smiled suddenly. 'But you will know all about that, since Rosehill was your home for many years.'

'I do, and you are right.' Hester accompanied Adeline across the hall and into the warmer, far more agreeable room. 'I always loved it in here. It gets the sun for most of the day, and the garden is as delightful as I remember.' Her eyes misted as she looked out of the long windows. 'I have so many memories wrapped up in this house—happy and sad. When I heard your father might sell it I sent Grant to see him, to try and buy it back. Did you know?'

Adeline nodded. 'Father intended giving it to me as a wedding present when I married Paul—but that's in the past. But what am I thinking of? You must have some refreshment after your journey. Then I'll take you up to see Father.'

'Thank you,' Hester accepted. 'I would like that.'

When they were seated, Hester asked, 'How is Horace?'

'You will be pleased to know he is a little better. The doctor is pleased with his progress and thinks he will make a full recovery.'

Hester's relief was evident. 'I am so glad.' She paused before continuing, as if considering her next words carefully. 'Adeline, I do so hope you don't mind, but on your father's invitation I stayed at Rosehill while you were in London.'

'Mrs Leighton, this is my father's house. I think he is old enough to invite who he wants to stay. I certainly have no objections.'

Hester smiled with relief and sudden genuine pleasure. 'So you don't mind?'

'Not one bit. Between you and me, Father spends far too much time working—which, in Dr Terry's opinion, may well have something to do with his heart attack. Some female company is what he needs.'

It was after dinner, after Hester had spent some considerable time with Horace, talking and reading to him, when, stirring her coffee, she tilted her head to one side and studied Adeline. She said with a smile, 'You know, you do look different.'

Adeline laughed. 'I know. It's all down to Lettie. She thought I needed taking in hand.' Adeline saw a shadow cross Mrs Leighton's face. She waited. To ask its cause would be an intrusion, but instinctively she knew it concerned Lettie. 'How is Lettie?' she asked, speaking calmly.

Hester sighed. 'She is well, considering all she has been through—although I do worry about her. I wanted her to come to Rosehill with me but—well… I know what happened to her in London,' she said quietly. 'She told me everything, Adeline. I was appalled and extremely shocked—angry, too—to think my darling daughter endured what she did alone. I have you to thank for everything you did for her. Thank you so much for taking care of her.'

Adeline looked at Mrs Leighton and saw her exquisite high-boned face was drawn, her eyes far away, sad and angry. 'I am glad she felt that she could confide in me.'

'Poor Lettie. I feel an intense sadness for her. She had the passion, the intelligence and the courage to dare anything. Now she sits brooding and just looking at nothing for most of the day. I cannot condone her affair with that—that nightclub owner, or what she did.'

She looked dejectedly down at her hands, folded in her lap. 'I cannot even bring myself to speak his name. I wish she'd never set eyes on him, and I cannot forgive the hurt he has caused her. Lettie espoused the Women's Movement because she cares about injustice. Where's the justice in what that man has done to her? However, I will not allow my anger to make me forget myself. Yes, Lettie told me many things—things best kept silent, if we are to live in any kind of peace. I am sure if you will consider it you will agree with me.'

Adeline understood that Mrs Leighton was asking her to keep what she knew to herself—not to tell her father. 'I agree with you. Sometimes to forget is the only sane thing to do—otherwise one becomes imprisoned by the past. Console yourself with the fact that the affair is over. Lettie is strong and will put this behind her. She has the support of her family and some stalwart friends.'

'Yes, I know. But there will always be a part of her that is damaged, and when I think of what that man is guilty of—that he has simply walked away unpunished... At least as far as Lettie is concerned.' She shook her head. 'Grant says he is being investigated by the police for crimes which I know very little about—nor do I wish to.'

'I am glad he's under investigation. But if the truth were to come out about Lettie it would bring shame on her, and Lord knows she has already paid a high enough price for her foolishness.'

Reaching out, Hester squeezed Adeline's hand in gratitude. 'That I do know. The injustice of it pains me greatly, but you are right. Lettie must move on—we must all move on and look to our good name. Scandal can be so damaging, so destructive. We mustn't let it.'

'I couldn't agree more.'

Suddenly Hester brightened. 'Adeline, how would you and your father like to spend Christmas with us at Oaklands?' She saw doubt cloud Adeline's eyes, and, afraid that she was about to refuse, went on quickly, 'I will not take no for an answer— and I know I can speak for Grant. I take Christmas very seriously—even when the family isn't complete. I make it an event every year, and savour the ritual. I would so like you to be there.'

Adeline had grave doubts about returning to Oaklands, but not so her father. He was delighted at the prospect of spending some time with Hester. The time she had visited him at Rosehill, when Adeline had been in London, seemed a long way in the past, and since his heart attack he had been realising more and more every day how he missed her.

He continued to get better, and when the time came for them to leave for Oaklands he was back to his old self.

Adeline's time had been taken up with writing and sending out Christmas cards to friends and family, and buying presents. She had chosen two rather beautiful silk scarves—one for Lettie and one for Mrs Leighton. Because she wasn't sure how many children would be there, she had also bought a selection of novelties and chocolates.

Grant was more difficult. After a great deal of deliberation she had chosen a gold cravat pin—plain, yet tasteful—hoping it would be an appropriate gift for their host and that he would like it. She had tried to keep herself focused on preparing for the visit, but her fragile control had begun to crumble the closer the time came for them to leave for Oaklands.

Grant had promised to write to her and he hadn't. She could only assume that what had happened between them hadn't meant as much to him as it did to her. She tried to imagine their meeting. Would he be angry because his mother had invited them? Would he be glad to see her or want to show her the door?

With firm determination she pulled her mind away from this nonsensical preoccupation and concentrated on what she would take with her. A terrible premonition of Christmas being a disaster quivered through her—and yet she felt she had been serious too long, and should be none the worse for a little light entertainment, which she intended her Christmas at Oaklands to be.

Since they had left Rosehill the day had become colder, with a knife-edge to it, and the sky was lower and heavy, with more snow in the air. There had been a fall during the night, with slight drifting in places, disrupting both road and rail travel. As the Leighton carriage, which had met them at the station, approached Oaklands, Adeline was as impressed by the house in its colour-bleached surroundings as she had been on her first visit.

Seated across from Adeline and Emma, her father was tucked beneath a thick rug, his chin sunk deep in the collar of his coat, his fur-trimmed hat pulled well down over his ears. Beside him, attentive and concerned for his master's well-being at all times, sat Benjamin, his manservant of many years.

They climbed out just as the door opened, and Hester came to welcome them. Horace strode the couple of paces over to her and took her in his arms. Normally Adeline would have been slightly shocked by this show of familiarity, but at that moment she could think of nothing other than seeing Grant again.

Hester stood back and gave Horace a close look. 'I'm so glad you're feeling better, Horace. Indeed, you do look much improved since I saw you last, thank goodness. Do come inside,' she said, after greeting Adeline warmly and ushering them into the hall. 'We were beginning to think you might not make it with all this snow—and more on the way by the look of the sky. Still, the children are loving it, and it keeps them occupied so we mustn't complain.'

Leaving Emma and Benjamin to follow on with the cases, Adeline entered Oaklands. The hall, which was lavishly decked with holly, mistletoe and red-veined tree ivy, was warm and inviting, with happy-faced servants flitting to and fro, and delicious Christmassy smells drifting on the air from the kitchen.

Removing her bonnet and warm coat and handing them to a servant while her father was conversing with Hester, she felt Grant's presence. Adeline's gaze was drawn towards him. He stood in the doorway to the drawing room, the daylight shining in from the windows behind him. There was a moment frozen in time when they looked at one another across the days that had gone by since they had parted in London, and then he was striding forward.

Dressed casually, in an open-necked shirt, tweed jacket and cord trousers, he was just as she remembered—his dark hair outlining his darkly handsome face, the same magnetism in his silver-grey eyes, the same firm yet sensual mouth. The hall seemed to jump to life about him as his presence filled it, infusing it with his own energy and vigour.

His eyes having taken their fill of her, Grant let his mouth curl slightly at the corners, suddenly alive with interest as he strode towards her. Adeline could feel the heat of embarrassment creep from her neck up her face. She was conscious of his nearness, of every detail about him once more, and the energy that radiated from him. Unable to drag her eyes away from his, she felt the black wave of apprehension lifting a little.

'Welcome back to Oaklands,' he said, shaking hands with Horace before letting his silver-grey gaze sweep over Adeline's face once more. 'It's good to see you both.'

Adeline could do nothing but stare at him. The rush of familiar excitement had caused her to become tongue-tied, strongly affected by the force of his presence.

Emotions swept over her as she remembered the intense passion they had shared. Sometimes at night she imagined him in her bed, and her heart would beat faster—to both her disgust and her rising passion—her thoughts would be in disarray, desire and reason conflicting. Then she would reproach herself. The presence of Diana Waverley in his arms still haunted her, but the eyes looking at her now dared her to fall into the same dangerous trap in which she had allowed herself to be ensnared in London, causing her to lose her self-respect and her sanity.

Pulling herself together, she chose directness. 'Thank you for inviting us to share the Christmas celebrations with you. We had intended spending it quietly at Rosehill—Father's illness, you understand—but when Mrs Leighton invited us to Oaklands, Father was easily persuaded.'

He raised a questioning brow. 'And you, Adeline? Were you easily persuaded?'

'No,' she answered truthfully. 'But I was outnumbered.'

He nodded slightly, knowing just how difficult it must have been for her to come here with matters unresolved between them. 'I'm glad you were,' he said quietly, and then went on to say, in a more conversational manner, 'You will find a large complement of family staying. As you know, my sister Anna and her husband David have travelled over from Ireland with their children. They have brought David's sister Kathleen and her two children with them. Her husband's a sailor and somewhere on the high seas. And Roland arrived from India just last week, so it promises to be a lively affair.'

'I'm looking forward to meeting them—and I'm longing to see Lettie again. Is—is she well?' she ventured to ask.

'Subdued, but on the whole she is quite well, and looking forward to being reunited with her good friend.'

A woman came to stand behind him. She was fresh-complexioned, and sufficiently like Grant to tell Adeline that this was Anna, his sister. She smiled warmly.

'You must be Adeline,' she remarked. 'I am Anna, and I'm so glad to meet you at last. I've heard so much about you from Lettie that I feel I already know you. You must come and meet David, my husband, and our boisterous brood of three.'

Adeline followed her into the drawing room, where a log fire blazed in the enormous fireplace. Immediately David, a charming, easy-mannered man, handed her a glass of punch. She was overawed by the large gathering, and seemed to be surrounded by an onslaught of people—not only immediate family, but aunts and uncles, and she was sure she was introduced to a major and a lord whose names she couldn't possibly remember just then. They were all from different parts of the country, and all of them were welcoming, promising a Christmas unlike any other.

Roland's pale blue eyes appraised Adeline. Friendliness and charm he possessed in good measure, and there was a similarity of features between the two brothers. Like Grant, Roland was dark-haired and tall, but he seemed to lack the power and authority of his older brother. As Grant introduced them she warmed to him as he took her hand and kissed it, bowing with an essence of grace and charm.

'I am delighted to make your acquaintance, Miss Osborne.'

'Please—you must call me Adeline.' She gave him the warmest of smiles.

His answering grin was roguish, his even teeth very white against the tan of his skin. 'Thank you. I shall. I'm glad you were able to come, Adeline. Lettie's been singing your praises ever since I arrived—and I can see why. Are you aware that apart from Lettie you are the only unattached female here?'

Laughter crept into Adeline's voice when she replied. 'No, I am not. But I don't think I've ever been made to feel so welcome.'

'The Leightons are famous for their hospitality—is that not so, Grant?' he said, slanting a look at his brother, who returned his sideways glance with an identical one of his own, hiding his irritation behind a mask of genteel imperturbability. He knew his brother was trying to bait him. 'I don't think anyone would blame me if I took it upon myself to get to know you better before you disappear back to Rosehill.'

Adeline was unable to suppress her laughter. She looked at him directly and smiled enchantingly. 'Then I would advise you to be careful. You're liable to turn my head,' she teased—something the old Adeline would never have dreamt of doing with a complete stranger. 'Are you always so impetuous with the ladies, Roland?'

'As far as I am aware a young lady has yet to catch Roland's eye,' his mother remarked jokingly as she passed them in a rustle of bronze taffeta to sit beside a rather stout Aunt Maud, who was looking decidedly flushed from imbibing too many glasses of punch. 'At least one of my sons is still heart and fancy-free—as the saying goes.' She exchanged a penetrating look with Grant before saying, 'Is that not so, Grant?'

Grant's lips twitched in a smile and he merely nodded.

Mrs Leighton's casual remark went straight to Adeline's heart, and for a moment she was bewildered. What had she meant by it? Who was the woman that held Grant's heart?

While Adeline's attention was diverted elsewhere, Grant moved closer to his brother. 'Roland,' he drawled, in a steely voice that was in vivid contrast to the expression of bland courtesy he was wearing for the sake of his guests, 'while you are at Oaklands, brother mine, feel free to lavish your attentions on any one of the available females from round about, but I am already committed to that particular young lady—as you well know.' The grooves beside his mouth deepened into a full smile that was complacent and smug. 'I have no desire to be free of the obligation. Is that clear?'

'As crystal,' Roland replied with a low chuckle. Giving his brother a conspiratorial wink, he murmured, 'Far be it from me to spoil the surprise you have in store for Miss Adeline Osborne,' before sauntering away.

Trying hard not to look at Grant, Adeline was glad of the distraction when she felt a tug on her dress. She looked down into the shining face of a little boy no more than six, beaming up at her.

'Hello. I'm Gerald.'

'And I'm Mary,' said a little girl with rosy cheeks, huge blue eyes and black curls, perhaps four years old. 'Would you like to come and see the Christmas tree? I can show you.'

'Not now, darling,' Anna said, scooping the child up into her arms. 'Miss Osborne has only just arrived. There will be plenty of time to show her the tree later.'

'Oh, but I'd love to see it,' Adeline said, smiling at Mary. 'Will you show me, Mary—you, too, Gerald?'

'Yes,' they cried in unison, and Mary wriggled out of her mother's arms and grasped Adeline's hand.

'You'll be sorry,' Anna warned her laughingly. 'They'll never leave you alone now.'

'I hope not. I think they're charming.'

'Off you go, darlings,' Anna said, shooing them away as another boy and girl of similar ages—Kathleen's offspring—joined them. 'Nanny will be down shortly, to whisk you off to the nursery for tea, so be quick.'

'Uncle Grant must come, too,' Gerald enthused, jumping up and down with excitement.

Playfully ruffling his nephew's curls, Grant looked at Adeline and gave her a long-suffering smile. 'Woe betide me if I refuse.'

Altogether, amidst a great deal of chattering and laughter, the children made a wild dash along the passage to the big library—Adeline and Grant following at a more sedate pace. The door stood open to allow all those who passed a glimpse within and an invitation to step inside.

The children piled in. Holding hands, they advanced towards the light until they stood in the very centre of it. It was a glorious moment of realisation. They stood in a line, as still as statues, gazing with something like awe at the sight that confronted them. There was something magical in the air, and the delicious fragrance of singed fir branches permeated the room.

The Christmas tree, an import from Germany and popularised by Prince Albert, was the centrepiece of the decoration. Surrounded by a multitude of gifts, this particular tree was planted in a brightly decorated tub in the corner of the room and towered high above their heads. Secured at its pinnacle was a beautiful fairy with golden hair, a flowing sequin-spangled white dress and a wand. The tree was brilliantly lit by a multitude of little tapers, and everywhere sparkled and glittered with bright objects, reflecting warmly on the leatherbound gold-lettered books which stocked the shelves that lined the walls.

'Why, it's beautiful!' Adeline exclaimed, as awestruck as the children.

'And essentially for the children,' Grant laughed, pointing to a rosy-cheeked doll hiding behind a branch. 'It's also dangerous, and Mother makes sure there is always one of the servants with a wet sponge on tree patrol to guard against fire.' He looked at her. 'No doubt you celebrate the festive season at Rosehill in similar style?'

'Yes, and often several elderly relatives come to stay. Sadly we lack children. We always have a tree—but not nearly as large as this.'

Adeline knelt on the floor with the children in front of a nativity scene that had been set up, gazing with wonder at the wooden image of the baby Jesus in the crib, surrounded by figures of people and animals. She laughed when the children enthusiastically began telling her who the figures were supposed to represent, all talking at once, some louder than others, to make themselves heard.

She was rescued by the sudden appearance of Nanny. Wearing a starched white apron, she came bustling in and ushered her young charges out and up to the nursery for tea.

Left alone with Grant, Adeline moved closer to the tree. To be within close proximity to him was agonisingly difficult, and she couldn't help thinking what a strange situation this was. When she had last seen him she had been furious with him, fully intending to give him a piece of her mind when she saw him again, but here she was, unable to utter a cross word and thoroughly nonplussed by his manner.

Grant perched his hip on the edge of the desk, and a slow, lazy smile swept across his handsome face as his eyes passed over her shapely figure with warm admiration. He watched her tuck a stray wisp of hair behind her ear before reaching forward and lightly touching a decoration on the tree. For a moment the bodice of her gown stretched tight across the slim back.

The firelight and tree lights had turned her glossy reddish-brown hair a darker shade, touched her lips to a deeper red. Her face was in repose—vulnerable, thoughtful, like the children dreaming of Christmas, dreaming of something wonderful to happen. He had missed her. When he had found her gone from the hotel it had been like an arrow to his heart. How well he remembered the enchanting sexuality that she had brought to his bed, the wanton loveliness.

In his experience with women—and his experience could not be truthfully termed lacking—he had been most selective of those he had chosen to sample. Yet it was difficult to call to mind one as delectable as the one he now scrutinised so carefully. Even now, having known her as well as a man could know a woman, there was a graceful naiveté about Adeline Osborne that totally intrigued him.

'What are you thinking about?' he asked quietly.

Adeline turned her head and found him studying her. 'Nothing too profound,' she hedged. 'Just—things in general.'

'Care to tell me about them?'

Trying to avoid both his searching gaze and the entire discussion, she looked away at the Christmas tree. 'They really aren't worth discussing.'

'Why don't you let me decide that?'

She looked back at him, thinking of the short time they had spent together in his hotel rooms, how he had made love to her with that mixture of exquisite tenderness and demanding urgency. Unfortunately, with the passing of time she was finding it more difficult to cling to the illusion that he was her devoted lover. Now she was unhappily aware that the man who had made love to her with such wonderful passion, who had made her feel that she was the only woman he had ever made love to, had also made love to countless others—including Diana Waverley. She had been reduced to the status of an old friend—a passing acquaintance.

Grant had never intended falling in love with her. He had simply needed her then, that was all. She had never loved Paul, so he had never had the power to hurt her. But she did love Grant—with all of her heart—and he did.

'Have you always been so persistent?' she said, in answer to his question.

'Mother always did tell me it was one of my most unattractive qualities.'

Aware that someone had entered the room, Adeline looked beyond him to the doorway. It was Lettie. Adeline's eyes became riveted on the lovely brunette clad in an emerald-green gown. The two of them looked at each other and slow smiles dawned across their faces. Lettie's voice was a whisper filled with pure delight.

'Adeline! I'm so glad you're here at last.'

As Lettie approached with her arms outstretched, Adeline noted the dramatic changes in her and wondered a little apprehensively if the changes went too deep to be put right. But the ties of friendship pulled them together, and suddenly they were flinging their arms around one another in fierce hugs, laughing joyously.

'Oh, Adeline, you look wonderful. I've missed you so much.' Lettie laughingly hugged her again.

'I've missed you, too.'

'How long are you staying?'

'Until the day after Boxing Day.'

'Then I shall do my best to try and persuade you to stay longer. Oh, I'm so glad Grant invited you.'

Adeline stiffened. 'Grant?' She looked to where he had moved, to lounge gracefully against the window. His hands were thrust deep into his trouser pockets, his jacket open and pushed back to reveal the pristine whiteness of his shirt. He was looking at her with that half mocking expression which she knew so well. '*You* invited us?'

'Of course he did.' Lettie was quick to answer for her brother. 'Didn't you, Grant?'

'But I—I thought your mother…'

'Mother asked you on Grant's behalf. Is that not so, Grant?'

He nodded, not in the least embarrassed at being found out. 'I was in France, remember? I wrote to Mother, asking her to invite you and your father.'

'Oh! I—I didn't know.' Suddenly Adeline's heart almost burst with happiness. Grant *did* care for her after all. He had wanted her here.

'While you were in London, as you know, Mother and Horace saw a good deal of each other and became close. When I heard of his sudden illness it got me thinking. I thought that perhaps they would like to spend Christmas together—providing your father had recovered and was fit enough to travel.'

'Oh—I see,' Adeline managed, in a relatively normal voice, her heart sinking. And she did see. And the knowing took away the pleasure she had in seeing him again.

She felt as if he had slapped her. He was treating her as if there had been nothing between them—as if they had never shared the intense passion between a man and a woman. It was incredible to her that those arms had held her, that those hands had caressed her, that those firm lips had kissed her. Feeling abso-

lutely wretched, deeply hurt and disappointed, she hoped she
did not show her feelings. She should have guessed, of course.
He hadn't been thinking of her at all.

Sensing the distress Adeline was doing her best to conceal,
Lettie glowered at her brother, wondering how he could be so
insensitive. 'Grant, stop being obnoxious.' Slipping an arm
through Adeline's, she smiled at her reassuringly. 'Ignore him,
Adeline. He's teasing you. You don't mind if I steal her away,
do you, Grant? It's ages since we saw each other, and I'm so
looking forward to catching up.'

'Go ahead. Adeline hasn't been shown her room. You can do
the honours, Lettie.'

With a blizzard raging outside, dinner was a merry meal. The
children were in bed, and everyone was chatting away amicably,
with no awkward silences. The topic of conversation varied
from the agricultural depression and Captain Webb's swimming
of the channel in August, to the state of the nation. The Major—
Grant's paternal uncle—sat across from them. He was a tall,
elderly man with a shock of iron-grey hair, who had never
married and had fought in the Crimea. Always one to appreciate
an audience, he regaled them with tales of his travels throughout Europe and beyond, and told them humorous stories about
his time in the army.

Seated beside Lettie, who looked relaxed and was more like
her old self, Adeline felt a lightening of her spirits—but she was
hurt by Grant's seeming uninterest.

She would have been surprised to know that she rarely left
his sights as he watched her covertly from beneath his lashes.

For the remainder of the evening Grant was the perfect host.
Every time Adeline glanced his way he was conversing with
another aunt or uncle, her father or his mother, and all the time

her heart cried out for him to look at her, for him to come and speak to her, to see the same look in his eyes as when he had made love to her.

Chapter Twelve

The following morning, which was two days before Christmas Eve, the blizzard had passed, and after breakfast the men, equipped with spades, began shovelling snow from the drive.

Holly bushes, bright with red berries, and trees, their branches heavy with snow, stood sharp against the azure blue sky, and the sun shone on the glittering white unblemished landscape. A fox had made his way across the garden, leaving his paw marks in the snow. The air was sharp and crystal-clear, and everything was still. Beyond the gardens, men, women and children from the village and round about whooped and whirled in exhilaration on skates on the frozen lake.

Wearing colourful scarves and gloves, and hats pulled well down over their ears to combat the elements, adults and children with happy voices dragged toboggans and floundered comically in the deep snow, stepping out of the house into the magical wonderland and making their way to a hill beyond the gardens.

Roland and Grant were to supervise the sledging, while Lettie and Adeline, serviceably attired in warm coats, woollen skirts and stout leather boots, preferred to stay closer to the house to build a snowman.

With much hilarity, and enjoying themselves enormously, together they began to roll the bottom half of the body. The larger it got the heavier it was to push and, panting with the effort, they turned round and braced their backs against it, laughing helplessly as they pushed it along. Suddenly Roland appeared, and immediately engaged Lettie in a snowball fight, shrieking and dashing about like children. He playfully shoved some snow down Lettie's neck, and when she was thoroughly wet they disappeared into the house to change.

Grant watched the antics from his vantage point on the hill, never having imagined he would see Adeline doing such a mundane thing as building a snowman and playing in the snow. When he saw Lettie and Roland disappear, unable to resist the temptation to go and help her finish the snowman, he went to join her, leaving Anna and David with the children.

When she saw him a smile appeared, lighting up her whole face, and Grant melted beneath the heat of that smile.

With hands on hips he inspected the ball of snow gravely, looking the picture of vastly amused male superiority. 'It looks like a man's job to me,' he said.

Adeline gasped, her expression one of mock offence. 'Don't you dare let Lettie hear you say that. She'd make you retract every word.'

'I don't doubt that for one second. But I still say you need a man to roll that thing. Permit me.' And without further ado he rolled the ball of snow a bit farther.

Laughing as she watched him flounder beneath the strain, plunking her hands on her hips, Adeline gave him a look of comic disapproval. 'There you are, you see—it's not as easy as you think.'

Determined to roll it a bit farther, tensing his muscles, Grant rolled it until Adeline shouted that it was quite large enough, thank you. Standing back and slapping the snow off his leather gloves with a triumphant grin, he looked admiringly at the huge ball of snow and said, 'There you are. It's much improved, don't you agree?'

When Adeline replied her voice was soft and extremely sweet. 'Yes, Grant, I'm sure you're right,' she said with uncharacteristic meekness—and the next thing Grant knew her hands had hit him squarely on the chest, catching him completely by surprise, sending him flying backwards to land spread-eagled in a snowdrift.

'Why, you little hellion,' he cried with a bark of laughter as he struggled to get out of the drift.

'That,' she told him, joining in his laughter, 'was for arrogantly assuming I am incapable of building my own snowman. Pride comes before a fall, don't forget. Come on, Grant—get up.'

'My pride is in ruins,' he laughed. Getting to his feet and brushing the snow off his caped coat and hair, he knew he wasn't immune to the absolute exhilaration that came from being out of doors surrounded by snow—which he'd always hated before—while Adeline, her hair tucked beneath a multicoloured tam-o'-shanter, cheeks the colour of her bright red scarf, was a breathtaking marvel, with her huge jewel-bright green eyes and wide, laughing mouth.

'It's dangerous to be within my range,' she shouted, moulding a snowball. 'I have an excellent aim.'

'That does it. You'll pay for that,' Grant shouted as the snowball hit him on the side of his head. Reaching down with both hands and scooping up some snow of his own, he squeezed it into a ball, grinning broadly, and with a dangerous gleam in his eyes purposefully advanced on her.

'Oh, no—no, you don't,' she cried, beginning to back away, choking on her laughter. 'Stop it, Grant—you mustn't. Let's be sensible about this. I don't like snowballs—I'm warning you…'

Suddenly Grant lunged and landed a direct hit on her shoulder. With a shriek, bent on revenge, she made another snowball.

'You devil. You're mad. I'll get you back. I promise to snowball you senseless if you don't stop.' And, so saying, she flung it at him before whirling and making a dash for it.

'And I'll teach you the folly of daring to provoke me,' Grant shouted after her, scooping up more snow and giving chase.

Encumbered by her skirts and the deep snow, when Grant tackled her Adeline pitched forward with a screech, landing face down in the snow with Grant on top of her.

'Help!' she cried. 'Help me up.'

Grant shifted his weight and got up. Rolling onto her back and laughing helplessly as Grant bore down on her once more, wiping the snow from her face, she scrambled to her feet, begging for mercy and holding her hands in front of her to defend herself from the threatening snowball. But he showed no mercy as he began pelting her with more snow, which only made her laugh harder. It was impossible not to respond to this man as his masculine magnetism dominated the scene. A curious sharp thrill ran through her as the force between them seemed to explode.

Determined to get her own back, and not to go down without a fight, her face shining, convulsed with glee and excitement, she impetuously joined in. They became like a couple of children, cavorting about and shattering the quiet with their laughter, until they were thoroughly spent and covered in snow.

Reluctant to return to the house and end this pleasant interlude, they turned their attention to the more serious business of finishing the snowman. It was a poor effort, but the lump of snow with its funny hat, Adeline's scarf tied around its neck and a bent carrot for its nose made the children laugh hilariously.

A quiet but happy band of children and adults slowly made their way back to the house to partake of hot mince pies and toasted crumpets deep in hot butter before a log fire roaring in the grate.

Later there was a progressive round of children's games which required a great deal of frolicking, popping in and out of rooms and hiding behind curtains and chairs, then hunting the thimble and Blind Man's Buff, in which both children and young adults participated—the adults leaving off to chastise a child that was becoming too boisterous, or to pick up one that had fallen, becoming tearful and needing comfort. They finished off with something quieter—conjuring tricks, performed by a remarkably talented David.

After breakfast the following morning, Lettie and Adeline, carrying skates and with linked arms, headed for the lake which, unlike the previous day, was deserted. It was surrounded by beech and oak, and the berries on the rowan glowed a deep orange-red. It was still cold, but the temperature had risen significantly overnight and already snow was dripping off the trees. The lake where the Leighton children had spent many a happy hour larking about in boats was large and teeming with fish. It was shallow around the edge, but shelved quickly towards the centre, where there were deep and dangerous undercurrents.

Adeline and Lettie spent a pleasant half-hour skating on the ice—keeping to the edge since they were unsure as to how thick it was in the middle now the thaw had set in. Adeline was not as accomplished a skater as Lettie, who laughed at her nervousness, but it was great fun—even though Adeline spent most of her time either hanging onto Lettie or down on her behind. At such times she was grateful to her wad of petticoats, which lessened the pain but did little for her humiliation.

It was when they stepped off the ice to recover their breath that they were approached by a man. They had been so wrapped up in their fun and frolics they hadn't seen him approach.

'You seem to be enjoying yourself, Lettie.'

Something of the voice penetrated the two young women's initial fear and turned it to ice-cold horror. The voice was that of Jack Cunningham. Together they spun round to stare into two glacial pale blue eyes. Adeline looked at him and froze, feeling a chill colder than the air that came off the lake.

Lettie was stunned by Jack's sudden appearance, and the way he looked—and, hardened as she felt towards him, she could not repress a gasp of horror. He was barely recognisable. His usual elegance had vanished, and with his shapeless trousers and an overcoat which had seen better days he looked more like a man who had fallen on hard times and sunk to the very edge of the criminal world.

But it was his face that shocked both girls the most and held their attention. His skin was pasty beneath the dark stubble of his chin, his cheeks sunken and his eyes hollow. His sudden harsh laugh made them jump.

'What's the matter, Lettie? Are you having trouble recognising me? I have no difficulty knowing you. You are still the same murdering bitch.'

His mocking tone reawakened all Lettie's anger against him. 'Don't worry, Jack, I recognise you. Though I must confess you are somewhat altered. Who would guess that the rich and arrogant Jack Cunningham would ever be brought so low? The police have you under investigation, I believe, on the grounds that your premises are used for immoral purposes—and not before time.'

'A complaint has been lodged against me, and as you damned well know the complainant was your brother,' he growled.

'And this time the police couldn't be bribed,' Lettie retorted scornfully. 'I know Grant went above their heads and used such powerful influence that the Home Office insisted on a strict investigation. I thought you had been arrested.'

'They couldn't catch me.'

'So you are on the run from the law.'

'Exactly.' As his words came pouring out his features grew ugly, contorted with anger and a wild hatred. 'You have made a fool of me—you and your brother. I won't go down before I've paid back the bastard who informed on me and the bitch who got rid of my child. I've been here for days, watching and waiting for this moment. I intend to savour every second of it.'

Lettie's voice was cold and disdainful. 'Come to your senses, Jack. You are out of your mind. Have you thought what the consequences of such action might be?'

'What does that matter to me now? I've lost everything else—everything I've worked for has been stripped from me—and it's you—you I blame.'

'And Grant? Are you going to hurt him too?'

Jack's eyes glittered like ice. The minute the police had entered the Phoenix Club he had known with absolute certainty that his comfortable life was at an end, destroyed by the power of Grant Leighton, stripped of everything that was of value. Nothing remained of the prestige and pleasure-seeking that had marked his existence since he had left the ranks of the working classes.

Raw emotion had robbed him of any kind of reason, any kind

of judgement. He wanted to make them suffer physically with his own hands, until they were too helpless to ask for mercy. His eyes narrowed and gleamed with a murderous light. 'I'm not going to hurt him. I'm going to kill him. As for you, I could break your neck.'

His eyes were intent on Lettie's, and she could see it was no idle threat.

Adeline felt tension coiling in the air around them, invisible but potent. The shock of Jack's appearance had worn off, and she appraised their situation. They were on the opposite side of the lake from the house, and there was no hope of raising attention. She had to believe that Jack would bluster and threaten and let them go, but the merciless way he was looking at Lettie and his tightly clenched fists told her he intended to harm her.

'Lettie, go—get away,' she urged frantically, with no thought to her own safety. 'Can't you see why he's come here?'

When Jack reached out to grab Lettie's arm she backed away and, spinning round, took to the ice. She began skating for all she was worth in the direction of the house, not thinking he would follow, or that instead of keeping to the outer limits of the lake, hoping to cut her off, he would head straight across the middle, with a roar of furious frustration.

Not having moved, with her heart in her mouth, Adeline watched in horror as the scene began to unfold before her eyes. Seeing Lettie disappear round a curve in the lake, she wasn't aware of the moment when Jack vanished. One minute he was there and then he wasn't. Horrorstruck, she stared at the empty lake stretching out before her, knowing full well what had happened. The ice had broken and Jack had gone through. In desperation she stared around for help. All she saw was a frozen white winter land—no movement, no help.

* * *

Alone in the conservatory, Grant stood looking out over the gardens, feeling strangely content and pleased with himself. The sun shone on breathtaking beauty, melting the snowman, which had given him so much pleasure in building it with Adeline. Trees stood sharp against an azure sky, the snow on their branches glittering like scattered diamonds.

Letting his gaze travel beyond the gardens to the lake, with some amusement he had watched Adeline's and Lettie's antics on the ice, which seemed to have involved a great deal of laughter. Although Adeline had had difficulty keeping her balance, they'd been having such fun. He thought of Adeline as she had been yesterday, when they had built the snowman. She had been full of fun and life, incredulous and amazingly natural. She had taken his breath away. Her cheeks had been as red as poppies, her eyes jewel-bright. And as he'd watched her from a distance, he'd felt the melting of something warm and sweet run through his veins like warm honey.

She really was quite magnificent, he thought, with a catch in his heart.

Trees and bends obliterated parts of the lake, and the girls weren't always visible. When they stepped off the ice he watched a man approach them. Too far away to see who it was, he had no reason to be alarmed—but when he saw Lettie turn and begin skating frantically away, with the man in pursuit, he looked to where Adeline stood, a forlorn, still figure against the stark white backdrop. As if he could feel her distress, he threw open the door and with long strides ran towards the lake.

On reaching the edge he stopped and looked around. The man had disappeared. Where had he gone? Then he saw Adeline. Having removed her skates, she was running towards him, pointing to the centre of the lake, where there was nothing but a black hole. Lettie had stopped and was staring at where Adeline pointed.

Absolutely distraught, Adeline could feel her heart beating heavily. When she reached Grant she was gulping her words out while she blinked up into his face. 'The ice—his weight must have been too much for the thin ice. He—he's gone through, Grant. He's in the water. What can we do? If we attempt to get him out there's a danger we'll fall in, too.'

Gathering her in his arms, he drew her close, and all the while he held her he was aware of her body near his, of her breath sweet and warm against his throat. 'There now. Don't distress yourself. Who is it? Do you know?'

'Jack—Jack Cunningham. I believe he wanted to harm Lettie— you, too, Grant—he was so full of hate. But—oh, this is all so awful.'

They were joined by Lettie and Roland who, like Grant, had seen what had happened from the house. Grooms and servants began to appear—summoned by Roland on his way to the lake—one of them carrying ropes, another planks of wood.

Acting swiftly, Grant thrust Adeline away from him. After removing his jacket, grim faced, he took one of the ropes and fastened it around his upper body.

Cold and shaken, Adeline stared at him in horror and disbelief. 'Grant, what are you doing? You can't go in there. Jack must be dead by now. No one could survive this long in freezing water.'

'I have to do this, Adeline. I have to see if I can find him, otherwise I couldn't live with myself. If he's dead, then so be it. But at least I will have tried.'

'Adeline's right, Grant,' Roland said, concerned by his brother's decision to go under the ice, where the water swirled restlessly. 'It would be impossible to withstand the cold beneath this ice for long.'

'I have to, Roland. Just keep hold of the rope and haul me out if I'm down there too long.' His face was closed when he stared at Adeline for a moment, then he turned and stepped onto the ice, making his way to where Jack had gone through.

When he plunged into the icy water, rooted to the spot Adeline fastened her eyes on the point where he'd disappeared, unaware that she was holding her breath, or that a stricken Lettie had come to stand beside her and had taken her hand in a firm grip. She couldn't bear it, standing there, safe in the sunshine, while Grant was in dreadful danger under the ice. He had been down there a long time. Why didn't he come back up? And then the sight of his dark head surfacing revived her fading hopes.

Shaking the water from his hair and gulping in air, Grant disappeared once more. The longer he remained under water, the more Adeline felt as if she were dying, and she had to fight against the creeping, growing weakness which froze the blood in her veins. Her soul, her very life itself, was concentrated in her eyes, fixed unmoving on the spot where he'd gone under. Tearing her gaze away, she looked at Lettie anxiously.

'He's been down there too long, Lettie. He'll have to come up soon or he'll freeze to death.'

'He will—look…'

Grant had located Jack's body, several yards from the spot where he'd fallen in. Dragging it to the surface, he tied the rope beneath Jack's armpits.

'Pull me out first,' he shouted to the men. 'Before you have two corpses on your hands.'

With great effort, and much slipping and sliding, this they did. A blanket was thrown over Grant's shoulders, and he stood and watched as Jack's body was hauled out before going to where Adeline and Lettie stood huddled together. His face was drawn and ashen, and water dripped from his wet hair. He smiled at them with difficulty, to try and allay their fears.

Adeline's relief was immense, but she could not control her trembling.

Grant touched her cheek, looking at her tenderly. 'I'm all right. Don't worry.'

'What will happen to Jack?' Lettie asked, looking across the ice at Jack's lifeless body.

'The police will take him away. There will be questions asked, which I will deal with. Come, let's go back to the house. We'll leave them to it. There's nothing we can do here, and I must get out of these wet clothes. We have to inform Mother what has happened, but we'll tell everyone else that there has been an accident and that some unfortunate skater has gone through the ice.'

Hester received the terrible news in complete silence, before looking at Lettie who gazed straight ahead, dry-eyed. She stood passively, showing no emotion, her mind seemingly elsewhere. Secretly she was filled with a relief so profound she truly believed she might expire from it. Jack Cunningham was dead. Now she could get on with the rest of her life.

The following day everyone was relieved to find Grant no worse after his ice ordeal.

It was Christmas Eve, and with the dark came the carol singers, lighting their way with lanterns. As all the well-loved carols were sung all those who had known Jack Cunningham were determined not to let his death intrude and spoil the Christmas festivities. Afterwards there was much jollity as mulled wine and hot mince pies were handed round. And then it was time for the children to go to bed, each one excited about the imminent arrival of Santa Claus.

Where there had been chaos now there was calm, as exhausted adults revived their spirits, roasting chestnuts and drinking port wine, and when the church bells rang out the midnight hour Adeline, along with several others, went to celebrate Midnight Mass at the village church—the oldest custom of the Christmas festival.

On Christmas morning it was church again, after which Grant handed out gifts to the staff, and at midday there was the traditional Christmas dinner in the dining room, with the mahogany table extended to its full length. Evergreens adorned the walls and candles guttered in candelabrum along the centre of the table, along with baskets of nuts tied with red and gold ribbons. Turkey was served with all the trimmings, followed by Christmas pudding, brought into the room ablaze.

When everyone was replete, Grant rose to his feet to propose a toast, and Adeline was more than happy to see he was wearing the gift she had given him earlier. As if he'd picked up on her thoughts he fingered it, and his grey eyes locked onto hers in silent warm communication. The ghost of a smile flickered across his features.

After the meal guests retired to their rooms, to loosen tight clothing and take a nap in readiness for later, when neighbours and local dignitaries had been invited to a quiet, cold buffet supper.

Having no desire to rest, Adeline went in search of Lettie, finding her in a small sitting room with her mother and Anna. Conversation ceased and gazes swivelled to her. Adeline frowned, wondering bemusedly why she sometimes caught the three of them looking at her oddly.

'I do hope I'm not intruding. Is anything the matter?'

The three of them exchanged awkward glances.

'The matter? No—no, we were just discussing the party tomorrow night—is that not so, Mother?' Lettie was quick to say.

Looking rather startled, Mrs Leighton looked from Adeline

to Lettie and back to Adeline. 'Yes—yes, that's right. Every Boxing Day night there's a traditional ball for the servants. As you will know, Adeline, they all work so hard at Christmas time. They are an integral part of the household—and it's their home, too, one mustn't forget. Since they are unable to be with their families they are given special treatment.'

'It sounds like fun,' Adeline said.

'It will be,' Lettie enthused. 'Grant has to lead the dancing with Cook, and Mother with the house steward. On the whole everyone has a good time. I hope you've brought your best party dress, Adeline.'

'My very best—which you helped me choose in London.'

'What's this about a party dress?'

They all turned as one to Grant, who had just come in.

'We were just telling Adeline about tomorrow, Grant,' Lettie answered.

He looked in alarm from his mother to Lettie. 'Tomorrow? You were?'

'Tomorrow night. You know—*the dance*.'

As Adeline looked at Grant she heard the emphasis Lettie placed on the words, and she also heard Grant expel his breath in a rush of relief.

Lettie got up and linked her arm through Adeline's. 'Let's take a stroll around the house, Adeline. I ate far too much plum pudding and feel the need to walk it off.'

'Don't feel you have to leave on my account.'

Lettie smiled sweetly at her brother. 'We're not. I just want to talk to Adeline, that's all.'

They sauntered to the conservatory, sitting in wicker chairs and looking out over the snow-covered landscape. Tall, exotic plants reached the glass roof. There was the sound of falling water, and the smell of flowers and damp earth filled the air.

Lettie told Adeline that when Anna and David returned to Ireland she had decided to go with them for a short stay.

'I feel I have to get away for a while, Adeline, to try and rebuild my life into the best I can salvage—without Jack. You know, I feel enormously relieved now he can no longer threaten me. It was rather tragic—the way he died—but when Grant told me the police had found a firearm in his pocket, I realised he did mean to kill me—and Grant. He really hated me.'

'You must put it behind you, Lettie, and try not to feel too bad about what you did.'

'I know—and I will. When I get back I intend to throw myself into my work again. It's a man's world, Adeline, with a woman's part in it defined as very little. My affair with Jack taught me that if nothing else.'

'I'm going to miss you.'

Leaning back in her chair and folding her hands in of front her, Lettie looked at her, a small, secretive smile playing on her lips. 'Oh, I don't know. I think you might have other things on your mind and will have no time to miss me.'

'What on earth are you talking about?'

'You and Grant.'

'What about me and Grant?'

'Well, it's just that you seem to be getting on well.' She smiled knowingly. 'I was watching you the other day.' She raised her brows. 'The snowman?'

Adeline felt her face go red. 'Oh, that. We were enjoying ourselves.'

'Very much, by the look of things. Are you still in love with him?'

The direct question took Adeline by surprise. 'I—like him, of course.'

'I think it's more than that,' Lettie said quietly.

'Lettie, apart from our antics in the snow, he's hardly spoken two words to me,' Adeline retorted, unable to conceal the frustration she felt at Grant's indifference. 'He treats me just like all his other guests. I don't think he sees me half the time.'

'Grant is as aware of you as you are of him. He can't tear his eyes off you when he thinks you aren't looking.'

Adeline's heart soared precariously. 'He can't?'

'He certainly knows you're here,' Lettie said, laughing. 'He's got something very special as a Christmas present for you,' she went on. 'I know you'll like it.'

'He has?' Her interest and her heart quickened. 'What is it?'

Lettie's eyes twinkled mischievously. 'Ah, that would be telling—and it's for Grant to reveal it. I hope you'll be pleased.'

Adeline was becoming more intrigued by the minute. Everyone was behaving most strangely.

Adeline stood in the hall as the evening's guests began to arrive. She was watching the door when Diana Waverley, wrapped in sables and with exquisitely coiffed hair, swept in, her manner one of haughty arrogance. The sight of her here at Oaklands momentarily scattered Adeline's defences, and she felt her heart sink in dismay. As she handed her furs to the house steward, Diana looked striking in a sweeping plum-coloured gown of costly good taste, the low-cut rounded neckline of her bodice exposing a generous glimpse of full, creamy breasts.

Adeline wholly understood Grant's infatuation, and it hurt her more than she had imagined anything could—more so as she watched Grant receive her and introduce her to his mother. Why hadn't he told her he'd invited Diana? If so she could have prepared herself. And why had he invited her anyway?

Diana's gaze passed idly over those present. When she saw

Adeline surprise registered briefly in her eyes, and then with a smug, superior curve to her lips she turned her full attention on Grant.

A while later, as Adeline surreptitiously watched Grant's tall figure moving among his guests, she saw him accosted by Diana once more. He bent his head low as he listened attentively to what she had to say, smiling at him all the while. He laughed, and Adeline flushed as she recalled the way he had laughed and frolicked with *her* in the snow. Without warning he turned, and Adeline was caught in the act of staring at him. His gaze captured hers, and a strange, unfathomable smile tugged at the corner of his mouth. Slowly he inclined his head towards her.

Stiffening her neck, she turned away from him to speak to Lettie. She couldn't trust herself to look at him again.

'What is that woman doing here?' Lettie whispered, her irate eyes shooting darts at Diana's back.

'I suppose, like everyone else, she must have been invited,' Adeline replied tightly.

'I don't think so. Grant wouldn't be so cruel as to do that to you, Adeline. Diana's been stalking him ever since her husband died.'

'He certainly looks interested enough. He's hardly left her side since she arrived.'

'If you watch carefully you will see it's Diana who is monopolising Grant. If he was interested he'd have offered for her years ago. I can't imagine how she has the effrontery to come here. I am certain she wasn't asked—but then she's brazen enough for anything.'

Adeline agreed, but her disappointment and frustration stayed with her. Having spent some time conversing with Anna, she was about to join Lettie once more when she was suddenly confronted by Diana herself.

Diana hadn't expected to see Adeline at Oaklands, and she

strongly resented her presence. Suddenly she felt her hopes of reviving an affair with Grant shrivel, and a flare of jealousy reared its miserable head.

'I didn't expect to see you here at Oaklands, Adeline. I'm surprised.'

'Really?' Adeline exclaimed, trying hard to hold onto her composure. 'My father and Mrs Leighton are close friends. Following his recent illness she thought it would be nice for them to spend Christmas together.'

'I see. Then that explains it.'

'Explains what?'

'Why you are here.'

'And I had no idea *you* had been invited.'

'No? How very remiss of Grant not to tell you. When I last saw him he was very insistent on my knowing he was to spend Christmas at Oaklands, and that there would be the traditional supper party tonight. So I knew what he meant, and that he was expecting me. I came with Sir John and Lady Pilkington—they live between Oaklands and Westwood Hall.'

Taking a glass of wine from the table Diana looked around the company milling about, eating and drinking and conversing with friends. 'Well, isn't this cosy? And such congenial company. Of course I know most of them—neighbours, you understand.' Her eyes came to rest on Grant, and she smiled. 'And Grant is the perfect host—don't you agree?'

'Absolutely.' And how handsome he looks, Adeline thought as she stole a glance at Grant's disciplined, classical profile as he circulated among his guests.

After a moment, and seeming reluctant to move on, observing Lettie laughing delightedly at something her male companion was saying, Diana said, 'Lettie seems to be in good spirits—considering.'

Alarmed by her comment, Adeline looked at her sharply. 'I'm sorry? Considering what?'

Diana's eyes were hard as they met Adeline's. 'Jack Cunningham was an acquaintance of mine, too, don't forget.'

Adeline's expression remained unchanged. Clearly Diana didn't know that Jack was dead, and she had no intention of informing her. No doubt Grant would tell her.

'Fancy asking Lettie to marry him with a wife still living— a lunatic,' Diana went on with incredulity. 'Well, who would have thought it? And when Lettie found herself to be in a— certain condition, it didn't go unmentioned by Jack.'

'If you feel any gratitude at all to Grant for coming to your aid when you found yourself to be financially embarrassed,' Adeline said harshly, having no real proof that he had, but chancing it anyway, 'I must ask for your complete discretion. Apart from Mrs Leighton no one in the family has any idea what happened, and that is what Lettie clings to.'

Diana's chin tilted upward and her eyes directed towards Adeline, their slanted gaze cold and without merriment. Her voice quivering with anger, she demanded, 'How do *you* know about my business arrangement with Grant? Has he said anything?'

Their gazes held, each reading the other's expression. 'No— he wouldn't. But I have ears, Diana, and I'm not stupid. However, that's not my concern. Lettie is. Despite her outward appearance she is still extremely fragile. I think any kind of confrontation would be a grave mistake. Please respect my wishes on this.'

Diana's eyes narrowed. 'I may be many things, Adeline, but I am no tittle-tattle. I've had dealings of my own with Jack Cunningham, so I know exactly what he is capable of. I can assure you that should Lettie's sordid little secret surface, I will not be the one responsible.'

'Thank you.'

'Please excuse me.'

Adeline was glad to.

The evening was drawing to a close when she saw Grant approach Diana and take her arm. The two left the room together. It was as if a dagger had been thrust into her heart. Christmas had changed. Diana had spoilt it.

She got through the next hour as best she could, but it was hard to keep smiling. Deeply wounded, she thought she would never believe her own instincts again. She had been so sure that Grant was beginning to love her.

Following her angry confrontation with Grant, after he had taken her to his study to speak to her, Diana left, realising she had underestimated Adeline Osborne. She had resolved herself to the fact that there was no hope for anything where Grant was concerned.

Feeling the need to get out of the house, to be by herself, Adeline went to her room to don coat and boots and slipped out of the front door, unaware that Grant was watching her. The night was bitterly cold. It penetrated her clothes. Yet she was thankful for its sharpness, for it cleared her mind of the fog caused by the day's over-indulgence.

Wistfully she gazed towards the sickle moon and starlit sky as quietness invaded her mood. Pulling the collar of her coat over her ears, and leaving the house behind, she walked to a wooded area beyond the gardens. She took the opposite direction to the lake, since she did not want to be reminded of the tragic events. Unafraid of the silence and the eerie trunks of oak, beech and lime, she was glad to be alone.

Somewhere an owl screeched, but apart from that silence

gathered around her in that white winter world. She allowed her captivated senses to propel her further into the trees. Suddenly, seeing a slight movement ahead, she paused, her senses alert. Her eyes widened with surprise and pleasure on seeing a vixen, lithe and velvet-footed, totally unaware of her presence. Her lips parted in a smile of delight on seeing two cubs rolling around close to their mother, yelping and snapping in play. Not wishing to frighten them away, without moving she watched, entranced. The sight held her enthralled, and she was bound in the spell of the moment.

A moment later instinct told her that she was not alone. Someone had come to stand behind her. Her heart began to race, urging her to run away, but she couldn't move. That was when the subtle scent of sandalwood assailed her nostrils and a powerful pair of arms slipped around her waist, drawing her back against a tall, long-limbed individual.

Lowering his head, he whispered, 'Be still. Do not make a sound unless you wish to frighten them away.'

Adeline froze for an instant of time as the familiar voice scattered her thoughts. She had no need to see the man's face to know who stood behind her. In that moment, when all her senses seemed to be heightened nearly beyond all endurance, she felt a frisson of recognition as deep and primeval as life itself. Hot breath smelling of brandy touched her skin as the warning was whispered against her ear, and she could feel a powerful heartbeat behind the hard muscle. Unable to struggle, unable to utter even the smallest sound, she was unaware that she was holding her breath. Her eyes were still locked on the fox and its cubs when the voice came again.

'A rare, enchanting sight, is it not?'

'It is indeed,' she whispered.

Adeline found herself wanting to turn and look at him, to sur-

ender to the masculine strength of him and the hypnotic sound
f his voice. The feel of his arms was electric. It flashed along
er nerves like a powerful current. Her skin tingled and grew
warm, and some dark and secret thing stirred inside her. It was
s if the very essence of herself had been altered in the space of
 heartbeat. Unable to struggle, unable to utter the smallest
ound, all she could do was remain pressed against that powerful
ody.

The anxious vixen watched her cubs, nudging them with
er nose, and to the cubs her protection was pleasing. Then
er instincts came to the fore. She stiffened and looked in
heir direction with bristling hair, her face distorted and ma-
ignant with menace. Sensing the threat of humans, her lips
vrithed back and her little fangs were bared. Passing her
nease to the cubs, she drew them back, discomfited, and slid
nto the shadows.

For all its intensity the moment had been brief. Grant released
er and took a step back. Feeling weak, as if all the strength had
een sucked from her body, Adeline turned slowly and faced
im, her breasts measuring the steady rise and fall of her chest
s she breathed. The moon was behind him so that its pale light
ell upon her face, leaving his in dark silhouette.

'Why have you followed me?'

'Because I wanted to. Do you mind?'

She shook her head. 'No.'

'I hope you are enjoying Christmas.'

'Very much—although the events at the lake have cast a cloud
over the festivities. What did you tell the police?'

'The truth—that Cunningham came here to kill me because I
had informed on him. Naturally I made no mention of Lettie. They
will liaise with the police in London, which will confirm what I
old them.' His expression softened. 'I'm glad you came, Adeline.'

'And I'm happy to have been asked. I am grateful that you
have welcomed us so generously at what was intended as a
family reunion. It has gone so quickly.'

'It isn't over yet.'

'Almost,' she said.

'No, it isn't. You have Boxing Day to get through.'

Was she imagining it or was there a hidden meaning to his
words? Moving away from him, Adeline looked back to where
she had seen the vixen, wishing she could see it once more. But
she knew it would not return. With a rueful sigh she lowered her
head. 'It's cold. We should go back.'

Placing his hands on her arms, Grant turned her to face him.
'Adeline, wait. There is something I must ask you. You have
been here for days, and yet we have had little chance to speak
privately. Why did you run away from me in London?'

She took a deep breath. At last he had raised the subject that
had been on their minds since she had come to Oaklands. 'Why
didn't you write?'

'Because what I had to say to you I wanted to say in person.
So, why did you leave without saying goodbye?'

'You know why, Grant.'

'You deserted me.'

'I didn't.'

'That's how it felt to me. Why did you let me make love to you?'

'I suppose when emotions are running high people do mad
things.'

'And are your emotions running high now?'

'When I'm with you my emotions are always running high—
in fact they're all over the place, even though I firmly try to
suppress them. You ask why I let you make love to me.' Her lips
curved in a slow smile. 'I ignored all my instincts. I went with
you to your hotel without reservation. And then I saw you with

Diana. It almost destroyed me. I'm not going to put myself through anything like that again.'

'But you want me. You can't deny that.'

Even in the gloom Adeline could see his eyes sparkle. 'I'm human. You've proved that. Why didn't you tell me Diana was coming tonight?'

'It was a surprise to me. She was not invited, Adeline. I would not be so insensitive as to do that to you. After the initial shock of seeing her I tried to play the perfect host. She clearly misunderstood something I said when I saw her briefly in London on my return from France—I had to see her to discuss the Waverley estate, and she interpreted it as an invitation.' He grinned. 'Mother was none too pleased to see her, but she coped wonderfully. Nothing ruffles her.'

Adeline understood then just how madly possessive Diana was over Grant, and that he did not love her in return. 'Did you tell her about Jack?'

He nodded. 'I saw no reason not to. She would have found out some time.' For a long moment Grant's gaze lingered on the elegant perfection of Adeline's glowing face, then settled on her entrancing dark eyes. As he had watched her earlier, mingling with his guests, he had wanted more than anything to thrust everyone out through the front door and snatch her into his arms to kiss that full, soft mouth until she was clinging to him, melting with desire.

'Adeline, there is no Diana and me. There hasn't been for over two years. She wanted commitment. I didn't. Six years ago I might have married her, but she chose to marry a title instead.'

'But both times I was at your hotel she was there. You were— familiar together. What was I to think?' She saw the twinkle in his eye, the twist of humour about his mouth.

'I think you suffer from an over-active imagination, and because of it you have suffered a lot of unnecessary heartache.

The first time you saw her she had arranged the meeting to ask
me for a loan. I refused. The second time she came to thank me
for digging her out of her financial hole—and I only agreed to
do so because of Jack Cunningham.'

'You bought Westwood Hall, didn't you?'

He nodded.

'I thought so. What will you do with it?'

'When Diana has officially moved out I'll put the estate on
the market. Cunningham gave Diana a hard time when he
realised what she'd done—turning her back on his offer and
selling to me instead. She's now decided to marry Paul.'

Adeline was astounded. 'She has? But earlier I thought she
hoped...'

'That I would marry her? Never. I had a private word with her
before she left and made her realise there can never be anything
between us. She put off giving Paul his answer until she knew
there was no hope for us.'

'Paul's a wealthy man, so she will not be disappointed in that,
but I doubt they will be happy together.'

'So do I.' Lifting his hands and pulling her collar up over her
ears, Grant looked down into her face. 'Not as happy as you and
me. I love you, Adeline Osborne, and I am going to marry you.
I have loved you from the morning I awoke and found you next
to me. You were naked and beautiful, and your hair was spread
about us both. We have been lovers ever since—we must look
on that night as a gift from fate. When you left me so suddenly
in London it tortured me. When I was in France I thought of you
all the time. I couldn't work. I couldn't sleep. My mind was so
full of you and you were so deep in my heart it hurt. I'd like this
to be our new beginning. You *will* marry me?'

He spoke in that low, husky voice that was half-whisper, half-
seductive caress. Adeline remained silent, too afraid to speak at

first. She could scarcely believe this was happening. Tilting her head, she looked deep into those sober silver-grey eyes, so gentle, so full of love. His expression was serious. She could feel the power he exuded, but she sensed his ruthlessness, too—a man would have to be ruthless to achieve what he had achieved through life.

'Yes,' she whispered. 'Oh, yes, Grant. I will marry you. I shall be proud to marry you.'

'Thank God for that. I didn't want a repeat of my first proposal of marriage, when you gave a definite no. And thank you for your gift,' he murmured. 'It's perfect. I have a gift for you—a surprise, which I shall give you tomorrow. But for now…' He took something out of his pocket.

'What is it?'

'Mistletoe.' His lips curved in a provocative smile. 'You know what that means.'

'I have a very good idea.' She glanced at the sprig he was holding just above her head and smiled teasingly. 'I see there are plenty of berries on it.'

'Naturally. When I came after you I had an ulterior motive, so I made quite sure of that. Mistletoe is a licence for intimacy—and in pagan times it was connected to fertility.'

'Really?' she whispered, arching her brows, pretending ignorance.

He nodded. 'And did you know that each mistletoe berry represents a kiss?'

'It does?' She saw a purposeful gleam in those heavy-lidded eyes.

'Every time a visitor to the house is kissed, one of the white berries should be removed. When all the berries have gone, the kissing has to stop—which is why I chose a sprig with plenty of berries on it.'

'Well, it looks as though we've a lot of kissing to get through. So we'd best get on with it before we both freeze to death.'

'My thoughts exactly.'

Before taking her in his arms, Grant pushed the stem of mistletoe into her thick hair. Despite the cold his lips were warm when they covered hers, touching her mouth with an exquisite gentleness that stunned her into stillness. They caressed, lazily coaxing, hungry and searching, fitting her lips to his own, and then his kiss deepened and he kissed her endlessly, as if he had all the time in the world.

Of their own volition Adeline's fingers curved around his neck, sliding into the soft, thick hair at his nape, feeling a pleasure and an astonished joy that was almost past bearing. She pressed herself against him, answering his passion with the same wild, exquisitely provocative ardour that had haunted her dreams since she had left him in London. The arms around her tightened, moulding her body to his, and she clung to him as ivy clings to a tree, and the strength in that hard, lean body gave her strength, gave promise of more pleasure.

Dragging his lips from hers, Grant looked at her upturned face. His eyes glowed. 'Well, I suppose that's one berry gone.'

'No—leave it. I don't want the kissing to stop. Not ever.'

Touching her cheek with his fingertips, and then wrapping his long fingers around her chin, he tilted her head back, his eyes smiling into hers. 'Anything to oblige.'

Again his mouth covered hers. And so it went on. And the sprig of mistletoe kept its berries.

Chapter Thirteen

The following morning at eight o'clock they met at the stables, as arranged the night before. The weather had turned warmer overnight. A thaw had set in and the snow was melting fast.

Grant watched Adeline walk towards him, a look of unconcealed appreciation on his handsome face as he surveyed her, warmly clad in a dark green velvet habit.

'How can anyone look so lovely at this time in a morning?' he commented warmly.

With grooms going about their chores, Adeline suppressed the urge to fling herself into the arms of her handsome lover and gave him a brilliant smile instead. But she slanted a scowl of disapproval at the horse she was to ride when she saw the groom about to place a side-saddle on its back. 'Oh, no. Not that.'

Grant quirked a brow. 'No?'

'No.' The reason was plain enough when she raised her skirt to reveal her breeches.

Grant gave a shout of laughter. 'Adeline Osborne, you are out-rageous.'

Tossing her head, she gave him an impish smile. 'I like being outrageous. In which direction shall we ride?' she asked when they were mounted, having got her way with the saddle.

'Through the park in the direction of the village, I think.'

Curious, she asked, 'Why the village?'

For some reason that question seemed to amuse him as he gathered his reins and they rode out of the stableyard. Seeing her worried look, he said casually, 'I have an appointment with the vicar at nine o'clock. Our meeting won't take long. It will give the horses a chance to rest awhile before riding back.'

Urging their horses into a lunging gallop, they crouched low over their necks, thundering over the snow-covered turf with ground-devouring strides. They rode at full speed, side by side, effortlessly leaping hedges in graceful unison. Approaching the village, they slowed their horses to a canter and rode in the di-rection of the church.

Adeline was surprised to see several people standing in the porch. The closer they got, the more she recognised them all—her father and Mrs Leighton, Lettie and Roland. Drawing her delicate brows together, she cast Grant a bemused look.

'How strange. What are they doing here? Who are they waiting for?'

'Us.'

Stopping outside the gate, Grant dismounted and asked her to do the same. Sliding from the saddle and into his arms, she looked at him.

'Us? Is there something going on that I don't know about, Grant?' Her heart was beginning to beat with nervous anticipa-tion. She looked towards the small group of people, all waiting expectantly—for what?

'I promised you a surprise and this is it. Last night I asked you to be my wife. You said yes, so I thought there was no time like the present to get married.'

'Oh!' The gasp escaped her lips as she was roused from her shock. Her eyes flew to Grant, who could only smile lamely as he stared at her. 'But how could you…? I mean—there hasn't been time…'

'I arranged it as soon as I got back to Oaklands.'

She was incredulous. 'But—that was ages ago.'

'Three weeks, to be exact.'

'You were so certain I would say yes? You assume too much, Grant!' she declared, but softened and brushed a kiss on his lips as a thrill of excitement sped through her veins.

A smile twisted his lips. 'One way or another I was determined you would be my wife.'

'Weren't you afraid that I would leave?'

'I would have followed you. You have my heart, Adeline. I love you more than I can ever love anyone again.'

She placed her gloved hand tenderly against his cheek, and her look was one of adoration. 'And I love you, Grant Leighton. More than you will ever know. But I cannot believe you have done this. And your mother—and Lettie—were they in on the deception, too?'

'I'm afraid so.'

'And Father?'

'Was let in on the secret when he arrived. He has no objections—have you?'

'What possible objections could I have? Although I am surprised Father didn't tell me. He doesn't normally tolerate deceit in anyone.'

Grant was standing close, looking at her with grave eyes, his cheekbones taut, his firm lips parted. 'Will you marry me now, Adeline—here, in this church? The vicar is waiting inside.'

Something caught at Adeline's heart—a warming hope that all would be well between them and they would enjoy each other without restrictions. Tilting her head to one side, she slanted him an adoring look. 'Well—I have nothing better to do today, so we might as well.'

'In your riding habit?'

'I would marry you in rags, Grant Leighton.'

One corner of his mouth quirked into something that was suspiciously like a grin. 'I don't think we need go quite that far.'

Taking her hand, he linked it through the crook of his arm and together they walked towards those who were patiently waiting, worried frowns on their faces, wondering what Adeline would do, what she would say, hoping Grant had managed to persuade her. It wasn't until Adeline smiled, a smile of such radiance, that they knew he'd succeeded.

'So,' she said, laughing, 'this is why there have been so many whisperings and sudden silences when I entered a room. Shame on all of you.'

'Grant planned all this very carefully,' Lettie explained. 'But it was never intended to embarrass you.' Her eyes misted with tears. 'I'm so glad you're going to be my sister-in-law.' She was holding a little posy, which she handed to Adeline. 'This is for you.'

Adeline gazed down at it in wonder. 'Snowdrops? In December?'

'From Grant's hothouses.'.

'Oh, but they're beautiful.'

'Like you, my darling,' Grant murmured.

'I would like a word with my daughter before she enters the church.' Taking Adeline's arm, Horace drew her aside.

Adeline searched for some hint of displeasure or contempt in her father's shadowed face, but only a gentle smile met her enquiring eyes. 'Father, I hope you will be happy for me?'

His reply was slow, but then he asked, 'Are you happy, Adeline? Will marriage to Grant please you after all?'

'Yes, it will please me very well. I love him—I have loved him for a long time.' Her whisper was soft and happy.

'Then that is all I ask. I shall be glad to see you properly wed.'

'But what of you? Rosehill will be a lonely place. Perhaps you should sell it and live in London as you intended before—before Paul and I separated.'

'I have no intention of selling Rosehill—especially now.'

Adeline followed his gaze, which had fallen on Mrs Leighton, who was smiling back at him with her ever-tolerant knowing gaze. 'Oh—I see.' And she did see. She smiled delightedly. 'So *that's* the way of things.'

Horace's grin was almost boyish. 'So it is. Now, I believe Grant is waiting for you inside the church.' He offered her his arm, looking at her as he had never looked at her before. 'This is a proud moment for me. Come—you don't want to keep him waiting. Are you ready?'

Taking his arm, and holding the snowdrops to her waist, Adeline looked at the church, her heart thundering with dread, hope, uncertainty—and love. 'Yes,' she murmured. 'I'm ready.'

The day was one of immense celebration, culminating in the staff ball. But before that Grant and Adeline had found time to be alone, to seal their union in the best way possible.

Entering the ballroom with Adeline on his arm, his eyes glowed warmly into hers. Fresh from their lovemaking, ecstatic bliss glowed inside her like golden ashes, long after the explosion was over. Turning to all those present, he introduced her,

immensely proud to say in a loud, clear voice, 'Ladies and gentlemen—my wife, Adeline.'

Immediately all those who had just arrived pressed eagerly
forward, bestowing good wishes on the newly wedded couple.
Grant's arm remained about Adeline's waist, claiming her as his
possession, as he light-heartedly conversed with friends.

In a break with tradition, Cook was happy to let the newly-
weds open the dancing. Grant brought Adeline into his embrace
and they took to the floor, surrounded by family, friends and
staff, Adeline resplendent in a gown of cream satin that bared
her shoulders sublimely, and Grant darkly handsome. A thunder
of applause broke and shook the rafters.

Grant looked down into the eyes of his wife of eight hours,
unable to imagine a future without her by his side. She was smiling up at him, a smile that brightened the room and warmed his
heart, and the closeness and sweet scent of her heated his blood.

'Happy?'

'Ecstatic.' She ached with the happiness she felt.

'Your cheeks are pink. You look radiant.'

'Because of you.'

He lifted a brow. 'I love you, Mrs Leighton, and if we were
alone I would quickly prove the ardour you have stirred in me.'
The heat of his stare lent the weight of truth to his words.

'The feeling is mutual, Mr Leighton. You are a wonderful
man.'

'A very lucky man.' Grant looked at her for a long moment,
caught up by emotions he could no longer conceal. 'I will love
you until I die—and even after that, God willing.'

A Christmas Wedding Wager

MICHELLE STYLES

Dear Reader,

Christmas is my favourite time of the year. I loved discovering how the modern-day British Christmas tradition has altered and grown from the one celebrated during the first half of the nineteenth century.

The early Victorian period in the North East of England is absolutely fascinating. It was a time when Britain led the world in civil engineering and design. The mind boggles at what these men accomplished and how their actions changed the course of history.

The High Level Bridge in the story does exist, and is a Grade 1 listed building. Robert Stephenson was the chief engineer, and Thomas Elliot Harrison, the assistant. Built for the Newcastle Berwick Railway, work was started on the bridge in October 1846, and completed in August 1849. Although Queen Victoria offered Robert Stephenson a knighthood when she opened the bridge, he refused. The bridge is currently closed to road traffic, but trains still trundle across it on their way into the Central Station from London. I trust you will forgive the few alterations I made to the actual history. I am a novelist writing historical romance, rather than a historian writing non-fiction.

Hopefully, you will enjoy reading my tale of Christmas in the industrial North as much as I enjoyed writing it.

Wishing you all the best for the holiday season,

Michelle

Although born and raised near San Francisco, California, **Michelle Styles** currently lives a few miles south of Hadrian's Wall, with her husband, three children, two dogs, cats, assorted ducks, hens and beehives. An avid reader, she has always been interested in history, and a historical romance is her idea of the perfect way to relax. She has a love of Rome, which stems from the year of Latin she took in sixth grade. She is particularly interested in how ordinary people lived during ancient times, and in the course of her research she has learnt how to cook Roman food as well as how to use a drop spindle. When she is not writing, reading or doing research, Michelle tends her rather over-grown garden or does needlework, in particular counted cross-stitch. Michelle maintains a website, www.michellestyles.co.uk, and a blog, www.michellestyles.blogspot.com, and would be delighted to hear from you.

Look out for a new novel from Michelle Styles in mid-2008 from Mills & Boon® Historical.

'*Ms Styles is an exciting new writer of historical romance who has written an extremely well-researched historical novel teeming with fascinating characters which linger in the mind long after the last page is turned, fiery passion, nail-biting action sequences and breathtaking storytelling prowess.*'
—*Cataromance* on *The Gladiator's Honour*

For my husband, whose support,
encouragement and belief in me and my writing
has been without measure

Chapter One

November 1846, Newcastle Upon Tyne, England

'It is no good getting your hopes up, Miss Emma, the first survey was clear, like. The Gaffer, your father, would agree with me if he were here,' Mudge the foreman pronounced with a solemn face, his words echoing off the walls of the small office.

Emma Harrison forced air into her lungs and struggled to hang on to her temper despite the overwhelming desire to scream. The last thing she needed was a lecture from Mudge about why the line of the bridge had to remain where it was. She could read a survey as well as any man. Better than most.

'My father agrees with me. I told you this. How many times must I repeat it?' She focused her attention on the plan of the site that hung on the wall.

'Your father ain't been himself lately. Begging your pardon, Miss. Everyone on site knows it.'

Emma forced a smile, ignored the growing pain behind he
eyes. Today had started badly, and showed every sign of declin
ing further. Her mind kept circling back to one question—how
was she going to ensure that the bridge would be built on time'

A few of the navvies and workmen moved through the site
overlooking the Tyne in a dispirited fashion, a full three-quarter
less than Saturday. The lantern tower of St Nicholas's Churcl
had been barely visible in the heavy fog on the way in from
Jesmond this morning. The works bore little resemblance to the
sunlit bustling place of last Saturday, when Jack Stanton had
been expected.

Emma drew in her breath with a sudden whoosh. And wha
if Jack Stanton should appear today? How would he react to the
deserted site? She swallowed hard and refused to contemplate
the horror that would unfold.

'Be reasonable, like, Miss Emma.'

'I am, Mudge.' Emma tucked a stray strand of hair behind he
ear. 'I know the excuses by heart. But it is the Monday after payday
A Saint Monday. The men will return when their pay packets, run
out and the publican's pockets are full. I grew up around railway
and wagonway projects. It is always like this, always has been.'

Mudge shuffled his feet and muttered another expletive.

She rose and glanced out of the narrow window, wrapping he
arms about her waist. The fog had lowered further, making the
brazier near the first foundation site glow orange.

'What do you want, miss? What should I tell the men?'

*To have this bridge built before my father dies. It is his life'
ambition to build the first railway bridge to cross the Tyne. A
simple request*, but one she didn't dare voice. She had to kee
the true extent of her father's illness a secret.

Emma gave a small shrug of her shoulders, and fastened the
plaid shawl more securely about her.

'A good run of weather until Christmas, maybe into the New Year. That the new survey of the riverbed proves true and we are able to get the piers erected in double-quick time.'

'You don't want much, miss.' Mudge scratched his head. 'Shall I add peace and prosperity for all while I'm at it?'

Emma ignored the remark. She refused to allow the foreman to intimidate her. She was no longer eighteen, with only thoughts about her next pair of dancing slippers in her head. She knew how bridges were built. She had learnt.

'Oh, and I forgot—the castle. The keep and the royal apartments are to be retained if possible.'

'Only a woman would be concerned about a pile of old stones. It would be far better if it was knocked down and the stone reused. It was what the first survey said.'

'Nevertheless it is to be retained. The first survey was wrong.'

'Ah, but what about the investors—Robert Stephenson and his new partner…that J.T. Stanton? They're right canny, they are.' Mudge crossed his arms. 'Your father ain't thinking straight if he agrees with you, if you don't mind me saying so. If it were up to me, I'd sell the company. Get out while he still can. Bridge-building is a young man's game.'

Emma bit her lip. She needed Mudge and his ability with the men if she was to have any hope of achieving her father's dream. She was under no illusions about the attitude towards women engineers and women directing important engineering projects. But, equally, she refused to let her father's dream and with it his company vanish simply because he had become too ill to be on site every day.

'If that is all,' Emma said through gritted teeth. 'I will take your report back to my father and return tomorrow with my father's further orders.'

'As you wish, miss. But think on what I say. I never steered you wrong before. There is none that can say that Albert Mudge ain't loyal.'

Emma scooped up the various papers, giving vent to her anger by stuffing them into her satchel. She would prevail. The keep was important.

'Miss, give your father my good wishes. There is nowt—'

'Is anyone here? Or is this shack as deserted as the site outside?' A deep, masculine voice sounded from the front counter.

Emma froze, allowing the papers to drop from her hands and cover the desk in a snowstorm. Seven years, and she knew the voice. It no longer held any warmth or intimacy, but she knew it. Jack Stanton. Fate's little joke. To make the day even worse.

'Allow me. Let me handle this.' Mudge tapped the side of his nose and moved towards the counter.

Emma forced a breath, and resisted the temptation to pat her hair or straighten her gown. She had to trust Mudge on this. Jack Stanton would not come in here. There was no need to encounter him. All she had to do was sit still, safe in her father's room. Unworthy of her, but a necessity.

'I'm expected.' The low, insistent tone echoed through the small study. 'There can be no mistake. You will allow me to pass.'

'Mr Harrison is out, sir. Perhaps if you would care to call again at some mutually convenient time?' Mudge's voice held the right amount of fawning.

Emma gave a short nod. She willed Jack to accept the invitation, to come back at an agreed time when she could be certain of getting her father here.

She eased back in the chair, heard a squeak and winced.

'Mr Harrison will see me. Tell him J.T. Stanton requires an interview. I can hear him moving in the back room.'

'Mr Harrison is unavailable.' Mudge moved to block the

loorway with his considerable bulk, shielding her from Jack's sight. 'You will have to call at another time, Mr Stanton, if you wish to speak to him. But I am happy to help you with any enquiries you might have.'

Emma squared her shoulders. She refused to hide in the back room like some frightened rabbit while Mudge showed the site and no doubt put his case to retain the current line of the bridge. She would not be defeated so easily.

Jack Stanton held no terror for her. If she allowed Mudge to continue, her father's secret would be out and the company lost. She knew Jack Stanton's reputation. Almost against her will she had followed his progress as he had risen from her father's very junior civil engineer to one of the most respected and wealthiest railwaymen in the entire Empire. But no one rose that fast and far without being utterly ruthless. She had heard the rumours about how he had fired most of the men building a bridge in Manchester, forcing the remaining to work overtime to get the bridge completed and ensure his railway opened on time.

'Mudge, send Mr Stanton in. I will speak with him.' Emma forced her voice to sound strong. She was no longer eighteen, but twenty-five, a confirmed spinster if ever there was one. Railway millionaire or not, Jack Stanton remained a known quantity. She had ended everything between them. It had been the correct thing to do then. It remained the correct thing. She'd had to put the needs of her family before a fair-weather flirtation, as her mother had called it. If Jack had truly loved her, he would have understood. He hadn't. He had left without a word.

Mudge stared at her, open-mouthed.

'Mr Stanton speaks the truth. His presence is expected, even if it has been delayed.'

'As you wish, Miss Emma.' Mudge removed his bulk from the doorway and made an over-elaborate gesture of welcome. But

she could tell from his voice that Mudge was singularly unhapp
about the situation. 'Miss Harrison wishes to see you, sir.'

Emma forced her back straight, willing Jack Stanton to hav
become a bloated man with annoying facial hair and prematurel
bald.

The black frock-coated figure stalked in, moving with th
grace of an untamed predator. The cut of his coat emphasise
his slim waist and broad shoulders. The very picture of the suc
cessful businessman, but with none of the flash one might expec
from someone as newly wealthy as he.

Emma pressed her lips together. His jet-black hair and eye
were more suited to a hero in a Minerva Press novel or one o
the penny-bloods found on railway stalls than to real life.

As with so many other things lately, God had turned a dea
ear to her prayer.

She forced her gaze away from his form and concentrated o
the cold gleam in his eye and the faint smile on his full mouth
Arrogant. Self-opinionated. Dangerous.

She extended her hand, forced her heart to forget what h
had been like seven years ago. The pain he had caused was
distant memory.

'Mr Stanton. It has been a long time.'

'Miss Harrison.'

He gave a nod but ignored her hand. Emma allowed her han
to drop to her side, wishing she had worn something more fash
ionable than last year's second best grey, but the grey offere
easier movement in the sleeves, and the skirt did not require a
many petticoats.

'May I ask what brings you here today?'

'My business is with your father.'

'Your business is with Harrison and Lowe.' She smoothed a
errant fold in her skirt. 'We expected you two days ago.'

'I was unavoidably detained. Word was sent, informing your father of my intention to arrive today.'

'Obviously the letter was misplaced.' She waved a hand at the letters that dotted the desk. She would allow him the fiction of a letter, but she knew there had been none. No doubt he wished to catch them unawares. It was exactly the sort of trick she'd expect from such a man. 'My father is unavailable. Perhaps if you could enlighten me as to why you are here?'

'It was your father who requested the meeting,' he said, with the barest hint of a smile. 'I was hoping you might be able to enlighten me.'

'I hardly think he would. Ground was broken a little over a month ago. My father and Mr Stephenson had several long meetings at that time. Everything was arranged to their satisfaction.'

'I regret I was out of the country then. My boat from Rio was delayed.' His eyes raked her form before coming to rest on her mouth. Emma resisted the urge to straighten her gown. She didn't care what he thought about her. 'By the time I returned, the ground had been broken and the project begun. I trust everything is on time? The Newcastle to Berwick line is open in March and we cannot afford delays.'

Emma gave a slight nod. His inference was quite clear. Had Jack Stanton been here he would never have chosen Harrison and Lowe for the project, despite their long association with the Stephensons. And, given what the papers had said about his recent rise in fortune, she had little doubt that Robert Stephenson would have listened to his newest partner.

She refused to worry about that. She had to make him see that not only would Harrison and Lowe complete the project, as promised, but also that the keep should be saved.

'Then you must be given a tour of the site, and I shall be sure to

point out the progress.' Emma forced a smile on her lips. She had
not endured the rigours of high society without learning the fine
art of dissimulation. 'There is a slight question of how the bridge
will go through the castle grounds. My father commissioned a new
survey, and it would appear that we can retain the keep, the very
symbol of Newcastle, even if the outer walls have to be destroyed.'

'Now, miss…' Mudge cleared his throat.

'Mudge, I believe you have other duties. I am quite capable
of showing Mr Stanton around the site and answering any questions he might have. We are old…friends.'

'*You* show me around, Miss Harrison?' One eyebrow tilted
upwards as a half-smile appeared on his lips. 'As delightful as
the prospect might be, I hardly wish to trespass.'

'Miss Emma.' Mudge made a small bow, but continued to
stand in the centre of the room. 'It is right cold out there. The
sleet has started coming down fast, like.'

'I do wish, Mudge.' Emma forced her voice to be calm. She
refused to have another screaming match with Mudge. The ob-
stinacy of the man! 'I believe I am the best person to guide Mr
Stanton around the site. We have already discussed your jobs
for the morning.'

'Very good, Miss Emma.' Mudge continued to stand there.

She looked pointedly at the door and the foreman left, grum-
bling. Emma hoped that he would force several of the men to
make a show of working despite the weather. Jack Stanton had
to see that progress, although slow, was being made. He had to.
With deft fingers she fastened her bonnet, tying the bow neatly
under her chin.

'And now, Mr Stanton—what do you wish to inspect first?
The foundations, or the ruins of the castle?'

'I look forward to the tour with anticipation, Miss Harrison.

Your dulcet tones will make a change from my usual guides.'
Jack held out his arm, which Emma studiously ignored.

Emma heard the slight emphasis on *Miss* and winced. Knew
what he must be thinking—Emma Harrison, the woman
expected to make a brilliant match, living the life of a spinster.
She had made the correct choice. Her mother had needed a
nurse in her final days, and now her father needed a companion. She did not need to explain her decisions to anyone, least
of all to a man to whom she had only been a passing fancy.

'The foundations it will be. This way, if you please, Mr
Stanton.' She tightened the shawl about her body and straightened the folds of her skirt, bracing herself against the sting of
the sleet. 'I have no doubt we both wish to spend as short a time
as possible on this tour.'

'I am at your disposal, ma'am.' He inclined his head, but the
smile did not reach his eyes. 'Can you inform me where your
father is?'

'Unavailable.' She pointed towards where a solitary man dug
in the mist. 'The sooner we begin this inspection, the sooner it will
be over. Harrison and Lowe are the best bridge-builders in the
area.'

'So your father always led me to believe.'

Emma attempted to ignore the growing pain behind her eyes.
By the end of the tour Jack Stanton would be convinced that
Harrison and Lowe could do the job. He had to be.

Jack Stanton followed Emma's slightly swaying hips out of
the hut. He had not expected to find her here. As far as he was
concerned, Emma Harrison and all she had once stood for
belonged to a former life. One he had hoped to blot out for ever.
He no longer had need of that dream.

He could well remember the number of beaux she'd had

buzzing about her. Margaret Harrison had made that clear. She'd expected her daughter to marry and marry well. Impetuously he had followed his heart and made an offer, counting on her affection for him and his future prospects. She'd refused him, never answered his letter, and he had left. He'd expected, if he heard of her at all, to discover she had married.

Only it would appear she had not. Time had been less than kind to Emma. He tried to reconcile the Emma he remembered with the woman who moved before him, her grey clothes mingling with the mist. Her hair was scraped back from her face into a tight crown of braids and topped by one of the most unflattering bonnets he had ever seen. Her skirt moved through the mud as if it were weighed down with chains. It was not his concern. The past was behind him. He looked forward to a glorious future—building bridges and railways, consolidating his companies and enjoying the fruits of his labour.

First he wanted to discover the mystery of why Edward Harrison had written to him, summoning him here. He had intended on leaving the bridge to Stephenson, simply providing the necessary financing. But Stephenson had agreed with the letter. He needed to go up to Newcastle and determine if all was well.

An icy blast of sleet hit as he exited the meagrely heated hut. Winter in Newcastle instead of the oppressive heat of Brazil. Instinctively he braced himself for the next blast, pulled his top hat down more firmly on his head. Emma had moved on ahead, gesturing, pointing out various spots where the foundations would be laid or where the stone had already been cleared.

The wind whipped her skirts around her ankles but she paid no attention. A sudden gust sent her hurtling forward towards the precipice.

Jack reached out his hands, grabbed her arm, and hauled her

back to safety. A stone gave way and tumbled down to the bottom of the castle walls. Up close, he could see her blue-grey eyes were as bright as ever, and her lashes just as long. They stared at each other for a long moment. Then he let her arm go, stepped away.

'You are safe now,' he said. 'You should be more careful. You would not have landed as lightly as that stone.'

'I know what I am doing.' Her chin had a defiant tilt to it.

'The wind is strong, and in those skirts you are a danger.'

'You can see that this is the best site for the bridge, despite its obvious difficulties, but there is still a question of the exact line.' Emma pointed out across the remains of the castle, moved away from him, ignoring his well-meaning advice. Jack glared at her. 'If the bridge is moved slightly to the left, the keep will be saved.'

She finished with a bright smile, as if she was at a dinner party and had said something witty. God preserve him from interfering women. She obviously had no idea of the time and effort that had gone into the planning of the bridge. And he did not intend to embark on some quixotic crusade simply to satisfy her. 'Both Stephenson and I are of one mind. The early surveys show the current path has much to recommend it.'

'A more recent survey—' Her jaw became set and her lower lip stuck out slightly.

He held up a hand. This farce had gone along enough. Edward Harrison had never allowed his daughters on building sites. The Edward Harrison he remembered had strict notions of propriety. Exactly when had he relaxed them for his younger daughter?

'The early surveys are accurate.' He touched his finger to his hat. 'I could explain, Miss Harrison, but I have no desire to bore you senseless with technical considerations. No doubt you would rather be having a conversation about the weather. Or the latest fashions in London. I fear I am out of step with the social niceties, having recently returned from several months in Brazil.'

'On the contrary, Mr Stanton.' She crossed her arms in front of her, dragging the shawl tighter around her body. 'One of the advantages of becoming a plain, acid-tongued spinster is that one might have interesting conversation rather than simply relating the latest bit of tittle-tattle. We must take our pleasures where we can. I would welcome the discussion.'

'An acid-tongued spinster?' Jack repeated. Spinsterhood was a fate he had never envisaged for Emma Harrison. He well remembered the number of men who had circled around her. She had been the centre of attention at the Assembly Rooms, a bright, vivacious girl with a full dance card. What had happened in the intervening years? How had she come to this? 'They are not words I would associate with you.'

'After my mother's demise, it was a choice between eccentricity or a pale but brave invalid. I believe I chose the more preferable option.' A strange smile played on her lips. 'You fail to disagree with my assertion.'

Jack started, and rearranged his features. He had not realised his thought on the ugliness of her dress and her bonnet was plainly visible on his face. He made a slight bow and sought to redeem the situation. 'I had not realised that being a spinster had much to recommend it.'

'Then you realise very little indeed.' The wind had stained her cheeks and nose a bright pink, a tiny bit of colour in an otherwise dull world. 'I find the building of bridges infinitively preferable to discussions about the latest way to trim a hat, make netting or prick a pincushion.'

'It seems a bit extreme—avoiding matrimony because you harbour a dislike of frivolous conversation.' Jack tightened his grip on his cane. 'I understood matrimony was the goal of every young lady.'

'The reasons for my spinsterhood are not up for discussion, Mr Stanton. Please know I am content with my decisions.' Her eyes blazed. 'I regret nothing.'

'A wise policy. Would that everyone adopted it.' Jack chose a non-committal response. Where exactly was this conversation leading? What did *Miss* Harrison want? Her words had a different purpose.

'And you? Have you married? Is your house full of frivolous conversation and pricked pincushions?' She gave him a level glance, with a steadiness that he had found entrancing in those long-ago days before he'd learnt about women and their fickle nature.

'Thankfully I have been able to escape the machinations of mothers and their daughters.' Jack pressed his lips together. Her remarks had made it obvious where her hopes lay. He would not have her presuming on the past simply because whatever brilliant hopes she'd had hadn't worked out.

Which was it? A duke or an earl that had not come up to scratch? He had forgotten the name of the man her mother had had such hopes for. And the proud Emma Harrison could not bear to admit she had misjudged the situation.

'But do you not long for domestic bliss, Mr Stanton? Warm carpet slippers by the fire?' That steady pair of blue-grey eyes looked up at him again.

Jack thinned his lips. Was this the reason for Harrison's letter? That he sought to make a match for his younger daughter? If so, he was sadly mistaken. He had no wish to renew his suit. The humiliation had been bad enough the first time.

'At present, my life is such that I enjoy my freedom. No wife would put up with me. I am constantly on the move, going from one project to the next—England, South America and Europe are all one to me.'

Her laugh resembled breaking crystal. 'You see, I was right. We would have never suited. I have rarely been out of the North East these past seven years.'

'I had forgotten that our names were once bandied together.' He made sure his face betrayed no emotion, but he derived a small amount of pleasure in reminding her of what she had casually thrown away. 'I would hate to think I had anything to do with your unmarried state.'

'Pray do not flatter yourself, Mr Stanton.' Emma drew herself up to her full height. Her hands ached from the cold and the sleet dripped off her bonnet, freezing the tip of her nose.

How dared he imply such a thing?

He made it seem as if she was desperately attempting to discover his marital status and had been pining for him the past seven years. She had refused him and his ungallant offer of marriage. He had not cared for her, only for her fortune and the status such a marriage would bring. Her mother had been right. If he'd cared for her, he would have waited and heard her out. He would have understood what she was trying to explain instead of becoming all correct and formal.

'My decision to remain unwed had nothing to do with you. Why is it whenever anyone sees an unmarried lady they immediately assume she is discontent with her life?'

Jack lifted an eyebrow. 'I must protest. You are putting words into my mouth.'

'You implied. As an old *friend*, I was naturally curious as to what had happened in your life.' Emma crossed her arms. He thought her a desperate hag. What did he expect her to do? Fall down on her knees and beg him to marry her simply because he possessed a fortune and good-looks in abundance? The man was insupportable. If she married at all it would be for love, because a man wanted to share his life with her, not keep her in some little box, surrounded by children and amusements suitable for a lady. 'There is nothing wrong with that. A light enquiry to pass the time.'

'I wished to be certain, that is all. I find it best in these circumstances.'

'You flatter your younger self, sir. I refused proposals before yours and after.' Emma tilted her chin in the air, wishing they were having this conversation when she was dressed in her new blue poplin rather than the grey sack that seemed to be becoming more dowdy by the second.

Jack inclined his head. His lips had become a thin white line. 'Forgive me, Miss Harrison, but what was I to think? You were the one enquiring about my marital status. I have learnt to be cautious about such things. I intended no dishonour.'

'It would serve us all better if you did not jump to conclusions but confined yourself to the facts.' She forced her lips to smile her best social smile and batted her lashes, longing for a fan to flutter.

Jack reached out and caught her by the arm as a white-hot anger surged through him.

How dared she bring up old memories? What had once been between them was in the past. He had made no apologies for how he had behaved. He had made an honourable offer of marriage seven years ago. She had refused. He had not needed telling twice. His nostrils flared.

'You forget yourself, Mr Stanton.'

She gave a brief tug and he let her go. Her hand went immediately to the spot where his fingers had gripped, held it. He pressed his lips together, hating himself, hating his sudden loss of control. It had not happened for years. He took pleasure in looking at things dispassionately. Yet within a few minutes of Emma Harrison's company he had reverted to his gauche youth, when his clothes had been bought ready-made and a ball at Newcastle's Assembly Rooms had appeared an excitingly attractive prospect.

'There is no need to go further. I have seen enough, Miss Harrison,' he said.

He turned his back and rested his hands against the cane, seeking to restore his equilibrium. It had been a mistake to come here.

'You must forgive me, Mr Stanton,' her voice called. She came up by him. An entreating face peeped out from under her ugly bonnet. 'I did warn you that my tongue was razor-sharp and that I have become accustomed to speaking my mind. You were correct. My earlier remarks trespassed on our acquaintance. I did not mean to pry. Nor did I mean to imply anything. Pray forgive me.'

'The fault is entirely mine.' Jack made a bow. 'The journey north appears to have made me ill-tempered and out-of-sorts. I should have recognised it for what it was—a light-hearted remark.'

'Shall we quarrel about that now as well?' She tilted her head and her eyes shone with a hidden mischief.

A brief pang rose in Jack's throat for what could have been. He forced himself to swallow and it was gone. He should not have returned here. On a day like today, too many old memories lapped at his mind, drawing him back to a place he'd been certain he had left far behind.

'I have no wish to quarrel with you, Miss Harrison.'

'Nor I with you, Mr Stanton.' She gave a brief nod. 'I do wish, however, to show you what progress has been made so your journey will not have been in vain. I am sure if my father had known you would be here then he'd have made every effort. As it is, today being the Monday after payday, he followed his normal routine.'

'It has been a most enlightening experience.'

They stood awkwardly. Emma pointed out where the piers should be built. Jack made a few polite comments as the sleet started to drive harder. But he could not rid himself of the feeling that there was mystery here. All was not as Emma Harrison would have it seem.

'Have you seen all that you need to?' The number of men standing forlornly by the brazier had diminished slightly. One or two had started to half-heartedly work.

'I do hope you will keep in mind what I said about the castle. At this stage plans are easily changed, but once we begin to lay the foundations in the river…'

'A building site is much like any other on a Saint Monday. Newcastle does not change.'

'It is good that you are aware of the difficulties we face.'

Jack permitted a smile to touch his lips. He disliked mysteries, but this one appeared easily solved. Her tour, although exact, showed she was hiding something.

Seven years ago Emma and her elder sister had appeared every so often, a tantalising glimpse, but her father had never allowed them to remain on site for long. The mother had seen to that.

This time Emma's words and manner seemed to indicate she knew where every last piece of stone was. Jack's eyes narrowed. At present she appeared to be in charge of the bridge-building. That foreman had deferred to her. The navvies appeared more intent on moving the stone when she was about.

She wielded power here.

An idea so preposterous he nearly laughed. Emma Harrison was a woman.

How would she cope when the foundations needed to be laid in the river? Or when the first iron rails were attached?

He could not see any female up on the scaffolding, making sure everything went according to plan. Would not *want* to see any woman put herself in that sort of danger.

Such a situation would be disastrous for the bridge and the future of Newcastle as an industrial power. The high-level scheme had to be completed on time. Already Brunel had nearly completed the rail link to Scotland on the western side of Britain. He could not allow it to happen. Newcastle could not fall behind.

'Everything seems to be in good order except for one small detail…your father.'

'My father is absent from the site today, but it has no bearing on the progress.' Her knuckles were white against the tartan of her shawl. 'It is a problem, but there is little to be done. I am hopeful of getting the foundations for all the piers laid before spring. The main construction of the nine piers can then begin in the summer, as scheduled.'

'It is what my company desires as well,' he returned smoothly.

He waited, watching Emma's eyelashes blink rapidly. A snowflake landed on her cheek and hung there sparkling for an instant before melting. Impatient fingers brushed it away but she said nothing.

Jack counted to ten twice. He had given her enough time and opportunity. He was through with her games. During the last seven years he had learnt how to play as well. This time they played according to his rules.

'Precisely how ill is your father, Miss Harrison?'

Chapter Two

Emma blinked as her mind reached for a plausible answer. Something that would explain about her father's illness without telling the whole truth about his condition. She took an involuntary step backwards from the tall figure and mumbled a few polite words about a chill.

'You fail to reply, Miss Harrison.' Jack Stanton pressed remorselessly onwards. His dark eyes ice-cold, boring into her soul. 'Your father has not been here for a while, has he?'

'He was here on Saturday,' Emma said, too quickly and too brightly. She had to remain calm. She took a breath and forced the words to tumble more slowly from her mouth. 'If you had arrived when you were expected, you would have seen him hard at work.'

'And before that?' Jack tapped his cane against his calf. He gave a half-smile. 'Come, come, Miss Harrison, enough of this flim-flam. You have been overseeing the construction for quite some time. You possess a certain familiarity with the site that does not come from casual visits.'

'My father and I have become close since my mother's death.' Emma put her hand to her throat and hoped.

'With the greatest respect, Miss Harrison, you have failed to answer. The question was straightforward.' His harsh tone gave the lie to his polite words.

She swallowed hard. She had no intention of revealing any more private matters. Exactly how much did he know? It had to be an educated guess, no more. She had been careful. Mudge was sworn to secrecy. He would not betray her father; she knew that. She filled her lungs with air. She had to keep her head and think around the problem.

'He has missed a few days, but I come here every day to advise Mudge on what needs to be done, following my father's orders.' She gave a small laugh, a little self-deprecating wave of her hand. 'I am the go-between, as it were. You know what a stickler my father is. He wants to know everything that happens, even when he is confined to bed.'

'You, Miss Harrison?' Jack's eyes widened. 'What do *you* know about torque and the positioning of stone? What if you muddled the message? The consequences could be disastrous.'

'I am my father's daughter. I grew up living and breathing railways, engines and bridges.' Emma lifted her chin and stared directly at him, daring him to say differently. It had only been in the last seven years, to save herself from the tedium of the sickroom, that she had made any real effort, struggling at first but determined, and gradually relishing the precise work, but he did not need to know that.

'That may be so, but what of the men? How do they respond to a woman issuing orders? How do you command their respect?'

Did he think her incapable of supervising the men? She knew

as much about building bridges as most men—more, even. She had helped her father with the early drawings for this bridge, done the calculations for torque while her father took to his bed. This was her project and her father's dream. Possibly her last chance. Her only chance. She took a deep breath. 'The bridge will be completed as per the contract. Harrison and Lowe have never been late before. We have our reputation to think of.'

'That is not an answer.'

'It is the only one required.' She gathered her skirts in her hand. She did not owe this man any explanation. It was obvious he had already made his judgement. Like most men, he believed the female mind incapable of understanding the complex calculations required. Thankfully, she had finally convinced her father otherwise. 'Your concern is about whether or not the firm can do an adequate job. I assure you that Harrison and Lowe will.'

A scream rent the air. Jack's face froze, and Emma felt a pit open in her stomach. The noise was too close, far too close. She heard the sound of people running.

'Someone has been hurt,' Emma said. 'I need to go.'

'A building site is a dangerous place, Miss Stanton.' Jack put out his hand, held her arm. 'I may be of some small use.'

Emma nodded as her mind raced. Where had the scream come from? She tried to reassure herself that no one could be seriously hurt. The men were not working on anything dangerous, not in this fog. But the cries were alarming. Panic never served anyone.

They hurried in the direction of the moan. Mudge was already there, peering over the precipice and shaking his head.

'I don't know how this happened, Miss Emma.'

Emma winced. Near the spot where she had almost fallen earlier there had been a landslip. One of the young lads lay under several stones. His face was ashen and his eyes shut. Part of the castle wall had collapsed on top of him. Her mouth went dry as she saw another stone on the top of the wall tremble.

'We have to get him out of there, Mudge.'

'The wall's about to crumble, Miss Emma!' Mudge shouted. He made a clucking noise in the back of his throat. He shook his head. 'The weather's against us. Better to shore it up first, rather than risk another injury. Nasty piece of work. We shall have to go around from the back. Slowly, like. The sooner this here castle is razed to the ground, the better for the men. It ain't nothing but a death trap.'

Emma's mouth was dry as she peered down, trying to see what line the men should take. Mudge was right. The safest way was to circle around from the back, rather than going straight down the slope. But in the uncertain light it would take hours— hours that the lad might not have.

'We need to get someone down there. To pull him away from the wall. If more stones should fall…' Her voice trailed away.

She looked at Mudge and the other men, but no one met her eye or moved. She willed them to say something. One man shuffled his feet.

'A block and tackle! Now!' Jack barked as he made his way down the slope, half sliding as the soft mud gave under his feet. 'Why weren't the basic safety precautions taken?'

'It is dangerous work, like,' one of the men commented, rubbing the back of his neck but making no move to help him.

'Go and get what Mr Stanton requires,' Emma said firmly. Finally a man set off, trudging through the mud. 'Hurry!'

'What he's doing—it's bloody dangerous,' Mudge moaned. 'We lost one man today. We don't even know if he's alive. I have to think of the others.'

Jack made an exasperated noise and continued downwards, reaching the boy.

'He's alive.' He put his fists on his hips. 'Now, you men will help me to move him from here. I need rope and wood. Working together, we can save his life.'

Emma started to climb down, picking her way through the rubble. Her foot slipped slightly and she was unable to stifle a small gasp. She froze, her hand digging into the clammy mud.

'You had best stay where you are, Miss Harrison. This is no job for a lady. God help us all if you faint.'

'Mr Stanton, I have never fainted in my life and have no intention of ending that habit,' she said, but she checked her movement and looked for a better route down the steep embankment.

'As you wish.' He shrugged out of his frock coat and stood looking at the fallen lad. 'Once I free him from the stones it should be a straightforward operation. We will lift him out of here.'

'Is he badly injured?' Emma called, fear clawing at her stomach. She disliked the way the stones were lying on the boy's leg. She moved around slightly and saw his distinctive blue shirt. 'That's young Davy Newcomb.'

'It appears to be his leg that is trapped.' Jack bent down and tried to shift the stone with his shoulder, but it didn't budge. Behind him, two more stones crashed down. 'Miss Harrison, you will cause problems. The wall is far from stable.'

Emma reached the bottom and wiped her hands against her skirt. 'You see—nothing to it. I am perfectly safe.'

Jack gave a grunt and his eyes assessed her, but he said nothing. Emma knelt by the boy's side, using her handkerchief to wipe some of the mud from his grey face.

'I'm sorry, Miss Emma.' Davy opened his eyes. 'I took a shortcut, slipped in the mud and fell. Them stones tumbled down on top of me. I didn't mean no harm. I know you said that it weren't safe, like, but it were the quickest way.'

'Hush, hush, young Davy. You need to save your strength,' Emma replied. She held the boy's hand between her gloved ones. The boy nodded and a tear ran down his cheek. 'You are being very brave.'

The men threw down the block and tackle, which Jack caught. Once he had fastened the rope he worked quickly, lifting the stones. Davy Newcomb's leg lay twisted at an odd angle.

'You have been lucky, young man,' Jack said. 'By rights that leg should have been crushed. You may escape with only a bad sprain.'

'That will be something for the doctor to decide,' Emma said.

'As you wish…'

They worked together to lift Davy onto the plank. Jack gave a nod and the men slowly pulled him to safety. Emma gave the lad's fingers one last squeeze before several men hauled him up and out.

'Take him to the hospital,' Emma said, staring at Jack, daring him to say differently. Harrison and Lowe always looked after their men in such cases. It was one of the reasons they commanded their loyalty. 'The company will pay for the setting.'

'Bless you, Miss Harrison,' Davy called.

She turned to face Jack, who was glowering at her, hands balled on his hips.

'I had to help,' she said quietly. 'Someone had to.'

'You should have sent one of the men. You put yourself in danger for no good reason.'

'I saw an easy way down.' Emma dared him to say differently. 'It was important to get his leg freed as quickly as possible.'

She bit back the words condemning Mudge and the other men. He lifted a quizzical eyebrow and his gaze slowly travelled down her body.

'And how do you propose getting back up the slope? In a dress? Weighed down by petticoats?'

'I shall go around the back of the keep. It is an easy enough walk, but straight down was quicker.' Emma adjusted her bonnet so it sat firmly on her head. The sleet appeared to be coming down heavier than ever. She had lost feeling in her fingers. 'You may join me, if you wish. The keep is stunning close up. It is more than the pile of stones Mudge claims.'

'It will give me an opportunity to refresh my memory.' He gave a short laugh. 'You do need to remember, Miss Harrison, this bridge has been a dream of your father's for a very long time. We often used to discuss where it should go.'

Jack put on his frock coat, becoming once again the austere businessman. They walked through the misted grounds of the castle, skirting bits of fallen masonry with the keep rising above them.

'I want to thank you for saving Davy's life,' Emma said.

'I did what any man would have done.'

Emma swallowed hard, but, taking a look at his intent face, decided not to mention that none of the workmen had helped. She bit her lip and concentrated on walking.

'Now you see why the site is a dangerous place...for a woman,' Jack remarked when the office appeared through the mist.

'I always knew it was. I *know* what the risks are. The outer walls are not safe. If you had read the latest survey...'

'I can read, Miss Harrison.' He turned. His eyes became hard. 'Your father and my partners will have to be informed.'

'I fully intend on informing him. No doubt he will write a letter to Robert Stephenson.'

'This accident should never have happened.' Jack Stanton's voice allowed no compromise.

'On that we can both agree.' Emma swallowed hard and looked at her hands.

'How, precisely, Miss Harrison, does Harrison and Lowe intend to prevent more accidents like this one?'

'By making sure the men are supervised correctly.' She waited as the wind lifted her bonnet slightly. She was on firmer ground. She had practised this conversation several times in her head over the last few weeks. If it hadn't been Jack Stanton, it would have been one of the other partners, she tried to reason. They all had links to Newcastle, reasons to travel up from London.

Jack Stanton could not act alone. The other partners liked and trusted her father's judgement. In a few weeks' time, if need be, when her father had improved, she would contact Mr Stephenson and request that he intervene with his partner.

Jack remained silent, regarding her with a steady gaze.

She must not borrow trouble. She had to remain calm and resist the temptation to fill the space with noise.

The sleet swirled around them. Jack eventually cleared his throat.

'What is the precise nature of your father's illness? Your whisper was inaudible earlier. When I worked for your father, he disdained taking to his bed for a mere chill.'

'He will recover in a few days.' She stood, her feet planted firmly, chin held high, meeting his eyes. She was not some young girl who had just put her hair up. She was twenty-five and knew how to speak her mind. He would not intimidate her. 'If you had arrived when you were expected, he would have greeted you.'

'You speak in hope more than expectation.'

Emma gritted her teeth. She refused to reveal her fears, or what the doctor had confided. 'As you have not seen my father in seven years, I assure you that I speak with great authority. The timing of your visit is unfortunate.'

'I arrived when I said I would.'

Emma closed her eyes. She refused to start an argument about that as well. 'Your letter never arrived here.'

'A pity.'

'I trust you have seen enough of the site to form your opinion, Mr Stanton?' Emma tilted her chin and stared directly into his coal-black eyes. 'There is no need for us to stand out in the cold. This conversation, as with our earlier quarrel, has gone on long enough. I wish to visit the hospital before I return home. I want to know the full extent of Davy's injuries before I speak with my father.'

Jack used his gloved fingers to brush a speck of sleet from his frock coat.

'I have business elsewhere. The company is building other bridges. Our rail interests are large and diverse. I am involved with several parliamentary committees on rail safety and other such pressing concerns.'

'That is a pity, as I am sure he would have liked to have seen you. He was quite fond of you…once.'

She heard the sudden intake of breath. Had she dared once too often? But she refused to apologise. His sudden departure seven years ago had cut her father deeply. He had tried to hide it but she knew her father blamed her for losing one of the most promising civil engineers of his generation.

'I can find my own way out, Miss Harrison.' He touched his hat and was gone. 'Give my regards to your father. Once he treated me as a son.'

The mist swallowed the black figure up. Jack Stanton was gone. No doubt to a warm private railway car and a journey back to London. Back to his life.

She was safe. The project was safe. It had to be. And she had come so close to disaster.

Emma stumbled back towards the hut and comfort. She wanted to bury her face in her hands and weep. Why couldn't her tongue be quiet? They had been getting on reasonably well. Then in the space of a few minutes she had brought up the past—twice.

He had never married. No doubt he would. To some young debutante. He had the money and the entrée to society now. Successful engineers such as Stephenson, Brunel and Jack Stanton were welcomed on the marriage market—the peacetime equivalent of the soldier hero. Men who dared to dream the impossible and make it a reality.

She had made her choice seven years ago. She had chosen duty over emotion. At least their first meeting was over and they knew where each stood. It was as well. She would finish her father's correspondence and then return to her old steady life, secure in the knowledge that her first encounter with Jack Stanton had shown there was nothing between them. He would not seek to return.

Her life would continue much as before. The bridge would get finished and she would find a way to save the keep. Her dream.

The past, in the shape of Jack Stanton or anything else, would vanish. A distant memory. All gone.

Emma Harrison wanted him gone. She had engineered the situation to force him to leave as fast as possible. And he had allowed his pride to come before logic. Something he'd vowed he'd never do.

Jack sat bolt upright and turned to look back at the building site as the bells from St Nicholas's Church tolled two o'clock. The castle's ramparts were shrouded in a thick brooding mist. How many more accidents would happen? She had been lucky that the lad had only suffered a broken leg. The project needed proper supervision. Something Emma Harrison and the foreman appeared incapable of giving.

Emma Harrison was hiding something—something important.

She had not known about her father's letter. She distrusted his reasons for being there. He had to believe her when she said that his reply changing the date and time had not arrived. But, equally, her actions were not straightforward. She had set a trap for him and he had walked into it.

He passed a hand over his eyes. He had done what he'd sworn he would not do. He allowed himself to become distracted by thoughts of the past. She had inserted the topic about his marital status. He'd reacted, and she had been able to distract him. Once. Then, seeing his reaction, she had done it again after he had saved that lad. Bringing up the past and getting him to leave. She had never fully answered the question about her father's health.

That was not how he played the game. His rules, not hers. Why had her father sent the letter?

Jack attempted to think. There had to be a way around her—a way to satisfy his curiosity.

Monday. A Saint Monday come to that. Edward Harrison was a man who prided himself on his habits—habits of a lifetime.

Jack used his cane to rap the top of the cab.

'I have changed my mind. Not the Forth Street Station. Hood Street. Quickly.'

He settled himself back into the leather seats.

'Now, let us see exactly how you like my rules, Miss Harrison.'

It had to be here.

Emma shuffled through the report for a third time.

The mantel clock ticked slowly, filling the dining room with its monotonous sound. A fire blazed in the grate. Emma infinitely preferred the red warmth of the dining room to the austere whiteness of the drawing room. The recently installed gas lighting gave a yellowish glow to the room.

The papers Emma had brought home from the site lay spread out over the dining table. A few had fluttered down to the floor. She picked another piece up, made a marking, and placed it in another pile. The answer to saving the keep had to be within one of these surveys and the myriad of calculations, but her mind kept wandering back to Jack Stanton and his reason for appearing. Someone must have said something about her father. Jack had never returned to Newcastle before now. She was certain of that.

Several hairpins had come out, and the hair coiled so neatly earlier now tumbled about her shoulders, while her hands were spotted with ink.

Emma gave a quick glance in the pier glass. Definitely not a lady who expected callers.

She made a face. Looking after her father was proving difficult. He was a far worse patient than her mother, who had positively relished being ill and her life as an invalid.

Her father had chosen not to break the habit of a lifetime, despite his assurance to the contrary this morning. He had risen and gone to spend the afternoon at his club. Emma pressed her lips together. She should never have believed his insistence that a site visit was needed. If she had remained here, he would have found it more difficult to disregard the doctor's orders.

However, then she would have never encountered Jack Stanton. Would have never been there to help save Davy Newcomb. A tiny shiver went down her spine.

She needed to decide how to approach Jack Stanton's visit. There would be no need to bother her father with a blow-by-blow account. Whatever repercussions would come by post, she decided. She would take a view if and when they arrived, but he did need to know about the accident. He would have to speak to Mudge.

'Daughter, daughter.' Her father's strident voice echoed down the corridor.

Emma winced. Strident today, and feeble tomorrow. She had seen the pattern all too often lately. How many cups of punch had he had?

'Papa, where have you been?' Emma rose, and straightened her skirt. She ignored the hairpins flying in all directions. She'd pick them up later. 'I was quite worried.'

Her father came into the room, his black frock coat slightly too large for his frame and his eyes a little watery. 'Monday before St Nicholas's Day. I've been to the club. Do you think I'd miss the final preparations for the dance? I wanted my views known. The punch was far too weak last year.'

'You know what Dr Milburn said, Papa.' Emma signalled to Fackler the butler, who discreetly took her father's coat, and handed him a dressing gown.

'That quack—what does he know?'

'Dr Charles Milburn is a respected member of the Royal College of Physicians, hardly a quack.'

Her father allowed Fackler to help him into the dressing gown. 'I think he comes here to sniff around your skirts, Emma. Now that the widow from Harrogate he was interested in has captured her barrister. You could do far worse than him.'

'Once you wanted a member of the aristocracy for me.'

'That was your mother, daughter.' Her father's eyes crinkled at the corners. 'I was certain that she would not rest until she had made one of her daughters a duchess. She did feel the loss of the title when her father died and it went to her cousin. I wanted you to be happy.'

'I am happy, Father. I chose my lot in life, remember? No

regrets.' Emma waved an airy hand. 'Do you not recall the rate of proposals I received…before Mama became ill?'

'Beggars cannot be choosers. You will be twenty-six next birthday. You should make an effort. If not the doctor, there are a number of men at the club. Perhaps a widower with several children.'

Emma gritted her teeth. There was no use in explaining to her father that Dr Milburn smelt of peppermint and had a damp handshake. She thought they had settled the question of Dr Milburn months ago, but obviously not.

'If I married, who would look after you?'

'True, true.' Her father gave a satisfied sigh. 'You do make a good nurse, Emma. Your dear departed mother often said so.'

Emma ignored the comment. She did not wish to dwell on her mother and her saint-like fortitude throughout her illness. Emma knew the truth—the scenes and tantrums. She had nearly gone mad with boredom, being at her mother's beck and call, until she'd discovered her father's engineering manuals and taught herself higher mathematics and technical drawing.

'If you were well enough to go to the club, you should have gone to the site.' She paused, smoothed her skirt. 'Mudge asked after you. There was an accident—Davy Newcomb fell off the castle ramparts.'

'So I understand. But young Davy suffered no worse than a badly sprained leg. A few weeks off and he will be back. The family needs every penny.'

'How? Who told you?'

'You must not imagine you are the only person to tell me news.' Her father looked at her gravely.

'I am not sure I understand.'

'It was Dr Milburn who drove me in his carriage to the club.'

Her father tucked his thumbs into his waistcoat. 'I could hardly ask him to take me to the building site. He has a new pair of chestnuts.'

She gave a short laugh and shook her head. 'And now he is not a quack? You suffer from a selective memory, Father.'

Her father gave a pathetic cough. 'You are trying to rob me of one of the few remaining pleasures left to an old man.'

'I speak of responsibilities, not pleasures.'

'If I had had a son…'

Emma rolled her eyes heavenwards. She had heard this lament before. 'You have two daughters. One of whom married a baronet, and the other looks after your household and is also trying to make sure the bridge construction goes smoothly until Dr Milburn pronounces you fit.'

'You will never guess who was at the club.' Her father hooked his fingers into his waistcoat and rocked back on his heels, a self-satisfied smile on his lips.

A strange pricking came at the back of her neck. She could almost believe that if she turned around he'd be there, lounging against the doorframe, an elegant curl to his lip. It had to be.

'Jack Stanton.'

'Jack Stanton.' Her father's smug expression faded. 'How did you guess?'

'He arrived at the site while I was there. I showed off the progress. He led the rescue of young Davy.' Emma wiped her hands against her skirt. 'The entire encounter lasted but a few minutes. I gave your excuses.'

A small white lie, but she refused to worry her father. What trouble could Jack Stanton cause? He wanted the bridge built. Harrison and Lowe had been awarded the tender. The incident with Davy would not happen again. The men had been warned.

'Did you, now?' A twinkle appeared in her father's eye. 'And what do you think of him?'

'What is there to think about? He has done very well for himself.' Emma clamped her mouth tightly shut. She had already waded into trouble earlier today, with her light-hearted remarks to Jack. She had no wish to be mistaken twice.

'Done very well for himself? The man's a railway million-aire. Sought after in London. A peerage in the offing for him and Stephenson if they pull this London to Edinburgh scheme off, by all accounts. I would hate to think what he is worth a year, Fifty-thousand pounds or more. Not bad for a charity boy. Not bad at all.'

'I am very pleased for Jack Stanton. Who would have thought it from what he was like when he worked for you? All tight-collared and ready-made clothes. So serious, and with that strong Geordie accent.'

Emma knew her words held more than an echo of her mother at her most snobbish in them. Far too harsh and judge-mental. And Jack's voice only held the slightest echo of a Geordie burr.

'I seem to recall you thought he had fine eyes, or some such nonsense. Your dear mama remarked on it. Then he left abruptly.'

'Papa!' Emma put her hands to her head, dug into her hair, pulling it slightly. She had to remain calm and collected. 'How much punch did you actually drink today? No more of your tom-foolery. Tell me directly, what are you on about?'

Her father nodded. 'Then you will have no objection.'

'Objection to what?' The prickling at the back of her neck had returned with a vengeance. Emma forced her head to keep still. Next she would start believing in ghosts. 'That you snuck out of the house like a schoolboy escaping from lessons? That you have had at least one glass too many of punch? That you will have a bad head in the morning?'

Her father rocked back on his heels, humming a little tune. What mischief had her father done?

'Your father has invited me to lodge with you both.' Jack Stanton stepped coolly into the room.

Chapter Three

Emma stared at Jack in disbelief. She blinked, willing him to be a figment of her imagination. But obstinately he remained, lounging with a lazy grace against the doorframe.

He carried his top hat, and had discarded his cane, but his gaze was as arrogant as ever, looking her up and down, taking in the crumpled nature of her blue gown, the disarray of her hair and finally resting on her ink-stained cheek. He, on the other hand, appeared as immaculate as earlier—the crease in his cream-coloured trousers precision-perfect, and the frock coat barely holding in the breadth of his shoulders.

He had said that he was returning to London but had slunk round to her father's club. Underhanded and devious.

There was no need to wonder any more who had told her father about the accident. Dr Milburn and his pair of new chestnuts, indeed. The only good part was that Jack Stanton had discovered her father in his usual haunt. To think once she had thought him without guile, speaking his mind far too readily.

She forced a smile onto her face. She refused to be the one to renew hostilities.

'Why might you be staying in Newcastle, Mr Stanton? I thought you had other places to go. Projects to complete. Europe and South America beckoned.'

Jack raised an eyebrow and came farther into the room. 'I wasn't aware that I had given you details of my future plans, Miss Harrison.'

'You led me to believe…'

A faint smile touched his lips. 'You merely assumed. Assumptions can lead to fatal errors. It is best to check the concrete details.'

'Jack has agreed to oversee the bridge in my absence.' Emma's father brought his hands together. 'It is a capital solution to the present problem. He has to stay here with us. I would not hear of it otherwise. He was the hero of the hour, after all, saving young Davy. It could have been much worse, and Mrs Newcomb has suffered much this past year.'

'Your father can be very persuasive.'

Emma watched his lips turn up in a slow, sardonic smile, daring her. She forced her lungs to fill with air and refused to give in to the temptation to scream. There was nothing persuasive about it. He had gone to her father's club with the sole intention of being invited here, with the intention of taking over the project. And he knew she knew it—wanted her to know it.

'I long to hear of the bridges he built in South America,' her father said. 'To think a prodigy of mine should have gone to so many exotic places.'

Emma pinched the bridge of her nose. Very neatly done—the carrot that Jack had dangled in front of her father. No doubt he had implied she had been responsible for Davy's misfortune.

'It means that you will not have to go through the drudgery of going to the site,' her father added.

'It is something I enjoy, Papa.' Emma hated the tightness of her voice.

'Your father agreed with my plan. I will undertake his duties while he recovers. The winter air is not good for a man of his age.' Jack's eyes glittered. 'The railway positively insists on it.'

Emma stuffed her fists into the folds of her skirt. She could see the walls beginning to close in on her again, back to the dreary round of calls and having to make unwanted objects for the drawing room. Exactly how many pincushions did one need? How many pieces of netting?

Worst of all, Jack Stanton would rapidly discover that it was not simply a chill her father suffered from. All she needed was for her father to have one of his bad days. On those days even Dr Milburn's tonic seemed to do no good, and he suffered with a wandering mind, and complaints about an aching stomach. It reminded Emma horribly of her mother's last days. Then it would begin—the offers for Harrison and Lowe, the taking of control and stripping her father of all purpose in life.

She forced her head up, met Jack's dark gaze.

'For how long do you intend overseeing the project?'

'As your father has only suffered a slight chill, I anticipate my tenure will be short-lived. Certainly I shall leave before the Christmas festivities.' Jack watched Emma's hand curl around the piece of paper. She looked less than pleased at the news. Good. He did not intend to have her ruin this project out of some misplaced desire to interfere, or to have something to amuse her otherwise dull days, when she did not have the appropriate training.

'There, you see, daughter. It is all settled. I am hoping to persuade Jack to be the guest of honour at Harrison and Lowe's Goose Feast on Christmas Eve.'

'I am sure you will be well by then, Papa.' Emma forced a smile on her face. She would need a miracle if Jack stayed that long. She noticed the paper she held in her hand had been scrunched tight. She hastily put it down.

Her father passed a hand over his eyes and swayed slightly on his feet. 'If you will both forgive me, I fear the good doctor was correct this time. I have overdone it a little. But the punch was excellent.'

Emma moved to help him, but he waved her away. Soon his unsteady clomp could be heard going down the corridor. Jack made no move to go, but stood looking at her with a deep intensity. Would he demand to know the true nature of her father's condition? Or would he also assume too much punch?

The chiming of the mantelpiece clock made her jump, and seemed to break the spell.

'Goose Feast?' Jack raised an eyebrow. 'Is this something I should know about?'

'Harrison and Lowe give their employees and families a feast at Christmas. We hold it on Christmas Eve, when the Goose Club raffle is drawn,' Emma answered, not bothering to hide the pleasure in her voice. It was a topic she could safely discuss. 'Mr Dickens's recent novel—*A Christmas Carol*—inspired my father.'

'I am sure the company will be happy to help.' Jack gave a short laugh. 'We are as keen to keep Christmas as any. Mr Dickens's novel has not only transformed your father's outlook but an entire nation's. We never celebrated Christmas much when I was growing up, but every year more and more seems to be done.'

'Were you a Mr Scrooge, Mr Stanton?'

'Hardly that. I keep Christmas as well as any man. I was merely making an observation. Tell me more about the feast you propose. Perhaps I might have a suggestion or two.'

'This is something that Harrison and Lowe does on its own.'

Emma pressed her lips together. She knew how it was done— a little here and a little there, then suddenly the offer was made and all were expected to fall in with the scheme. No, the Goose Feast stayed separate. Harrison and Lowe needed its independence. She knew how these large railway companies worked— impersonal, letting workers go at Christmas to save a few days' wages. Harrison and Lowe cared about its workers.

'I merely wanted to help.'

'The Goose Feast has nothing to do with the bridge project, Mr Stanton.'

'I understand.' Jack made a slight bow, but his eyes remained inscrutable. 'It is well I am overseeing the bridge-building as now you will be able to concentrate on the feast.'

'One could look at it in that light.' She waited for him to make his excuses and leave the room. There was no need for him to pretend a friendship or even a common cause.

He rubbed the back of his neck, started to say something and appeared to change his mind.

'Was there any particular reason that the book struck a chord with your father?' His voice carried less of a commanding note.

'My mother always loved Christmas.' Emma saw no reason to hide the truth. 'She died three years ago, and my father dedicates a toast to her memory each year at the feast. I like to think she would have enjoyed it.'

'I was sorry to hear of her death when your father told me earlier.'

'Why? It was a merciful release.'

Emma moved over towards the mantelpiece. She concentrated on arranging and rearranging the figurines. There was no need to explain any further. She had no wish to revisit the four years before her mother's death. When she had control of her emotions, she turned back. He was watching her with a speculative gaze.

'Having experienced one invalid it made me determined on my present course.'

'You are right. You have turned into an acid-tongued spinster.' His eyes crinkled at the corners. Emma was surprised how much more approachable he had suddenly become.

'I do try to find the positives in my situation. People are so apt to feel sorry for me.'

'And being able to speak your mind is one?'

'I have little time for polite, meaningless phrases.' Emma crossed her arms in front of her. 'It is a relief to be able to speak my mind.'

'You are correct—spinsterhood suits you.' He gave a short laugh. 'I had never noticed before, but you have quite a determined chin.'

Emma swallowed hard, strove to keep it light. 'Mr Stanton, do you delight in provoking me?'

'Provoking you?'

'You seem intent on revisiting our quarrel of this morning.'

'We both want the same thing, Miss Harrison.' He tilted his head to one side, sending a strand of hair flopping over his forehead. 'We were friends.'

'That was a very long time ago.' Emma lowered her eyes.

The silence between them grew. Emma tried to push away the memories of that other time when Jack had taken to calling at the house. She had enjoyed his laugh and his lively way of talking, of making her father's projects seem interesting rather than deadly dull, as she had previously thought.

'I can find other lodgings if my presence discomforts you.'

'I am not discomforted,' Emma said with a quick shake of her head. She was through with him and she had no regrets. Her mother had been right to advise her against him. 'My father appears quite intent on having you to stay. As he said—he does like to discuss civil engineering.'

'And you, Miss Harrison, what do you discuss? What are your preferred topics of conversation?' His voice was low, and designed to soothe. She wondered how many women had fallen for it. 'What do you want to discuss?'

'Something other than bows and ribbons.' She would go for the grand sweep out of the room—something to show him that she was immune to him and his aggravating ways.

'Miss Harrison?' His low voice called her back, held her.

Emma paused, her hand on the doorknob. 'Is there something I have forgotten? The servants will show you and your man where your rooms are.'

'I wanted to reassure you that the foundations will be laid properly.'

'They were always going to be.'

'With you supervising?'

'If necessary. It may surprise you, but I can read a survey. And directing men is no worse than directing servants.'

'Nothing surprises me about you,' he said softly.

Emma rapidly pulled the door shut, certain she heard laughter on the other side.

She shouldn't have run. She had yielded ground to Jack Stanton.

Emma paced about her bedroom, her nightdress swishing about her ankles. Normally she'd be asleep, but every time she shut her eyes she saw Jack's face, with his quizzically lifted eyebrow. She could not be attracted to the man. Her nerves were overwrought, that was all.

Why, when everything was going as she'd planned, did Jack Stanton have to appear?

And what would happen tomorrow when he went to the site? Would Mudge be loyal, or would he take the opportunity to ingratiate himself?

There had to be a way of keeping the state of her father's illness from him. Something.

A low moan broke her thoughts. Emma went still, heard it again. Her father in the grip of one of his nightmares. His stomach must have resumed its cramps. All too often these days he seemed to experience them, and the night sweats. It reminded her so much of her mother's last days.

She grabbed Dr Milburn's medicine and her candle, praying that Jack had not heard.

'Sleep well, Father.' Emma tightened the shawl about her shoulders and closed her father's door with a click. Her eyes ached with tiredness.

She was thankful she had heard her father's moans before he had woken the entire household up. She had given him a dose of his special tonic, despite his complaints about its metallic taste, and he had drifted off to sleep, leaving her free to return to her room.

Her candlestick threw out elongated shadows as her toes sunk into the thick oriental carpet that ran along the corridor.

'Miss Harrison, is something amiss? I heard someone cry out.'

Emma started and gave a small gasp, sending bits of molten wax flying onto the carpet. Jack Harrison stood in the doorway of his room, his hands gripping the doorframe. His white shirt billowed over his form-fitting trousers.

'Have I disturbed you?'

'No, not at all.' The candle lurched more dangerously to the right. Her fingers felt numb. She tried to think, tried to look somewhere other than at the dark hollow of his throat.

'But I did startle you. If you are not careful you will get burnt.'

He reached forward and took the candle from her hand, his fingers lightly brushing hers. A small shiver went up her arm and she hastily looked away from his intent eyes.

'I was not expecting to see anyone.' Emma hoped her white nightgown would be long enough to hide her feet. Why hadn't she stopped to pull on something more suitable? And why did she always appear at a disadvantage? Her hair was loosely plaited, falling over a shoulder. 'I have quite recovered now.'

'Something is wrong.' His voice surrounded her, low and musical, nearly like a caress, holding her there, pinning her to the spot. 'Confide in me.'

Emma shook her head to clear it. His voice was sending out silken lures, traps for the unwary. She gave a slight shrug. 'There is nothing to confide.'

'There must be a reason for your night-time ramblings.' He looked at her from under hooded eyes, and she reminded herself that he was dangerous, the enemy, the pirate who plundered companies.

'I went to see my father. He called out,' she said, as lightly as she dared.

'Has his chill taken a turn for the worse?'

'His breathing is fine.' Emma's hand played with the end of her plait. 'I suspect he had rather too much punch at the club. I had no wish for him to waken the entire household as he did the last time.'

A crooked smile appeared on Jack's lips. 'Ah, yes, rather a lot of punch was drunk.'

Emma let out a breath. Her shoulders became lighter. He believed her. She ought to go before she revealed anything. Her tongue moistened her lips as she searched her numb mind for the proper phrase. 'If you will excuse me, it is late.'

His eyes travelled up and down her form, lit with something within. 'Very late.'

Emma wanted to tug her shawl tighter around her. This was Jack Stanton, the man she had refused years ago, the man who wanted to destroy her life. He held no attraction for her, and yet she remembered how gentle his fingers had been when he'd helped her in the castle's grounds. 'I will bid you goodnight.'

His eyes danced. His hand smoothed an errant lock from his forehead. 'I promise to take good care of the site for your father and report back on the progress. There should be no more careless accidents.'

'I thought you would. I have, of course, no interest.' She picked up the candlestick. This time she held it firmly, to prevent the flame from wavering.

'You never were a very good liar, Miss Harrison.' He turned on his heel and went back into his bedroom.

Emma resisted the temptation to scream.

Taking small bites of her toast, and keeping an eye on the breakfast room door, Emma attempted to appear nonchalant. It was just possible that if she encountered Jack she could persuade him to take her to the bridge. Somebody needed to explain the situation to Mudge.

'Are you seeking to waylay me and insist on going to the site?' Jack's sardonic voice asked.

Emma crumbled the bread between her fingers, annoyed that her stratagem had been quickly discerned.

'I had no intention of doing that. I believe Mudge will be

capable of answering your questions,' Emma replied through gritted teeth.

'It is good to know you have such faith in the foreman.'

'He has been with my father for six years.'

'But there is something about him that bothers you.' Jack's eyes narrowed. He was a contrast to last night. Last night he had looked untamed, but today he was the picture of the successful businessman. Neither hair nor button was out of place. His white gloves shone against the cane. And his top hat was a brilliant black. But there was something in the way he walked that hinted at danger, the untamed male animal.

'He is insistent on the current course of the bridge. He thinks trying to save the castle keep is a romantic folly.'

'And is it?'

'I don't believe in romance, Mr Stanton, do you?' Emma looked hard at Jack.

'If I did not believe, I would not be building bridges across impossible chasms,' came the enigmatic reply. 'Sometimes you can do nothing but believe.'

He touched his finger to his hat and was gone.

'Have you met him?' Lucy Charlton asked as Emma came into the young matron's drawing room. She had decided, in the light of the circumstances, she was better off doing the rounds of visiting rather than fuming at home. Luckily it was one of her oldest friend's at home days. Several other women, including Lucy's mother and unmarried sister-in-law, were there, delicately sipping tea, doing fine sewing and eating cakes.

'Met who?' Emma felt a prickling at the back of her neck. 'Who is the new victim of the Newcastle gossip mill to be?'

'Jack Stanton,' Lucy said with a decided snap of her mouth. 'I hear he is up overseeing your father's bridge.'

My bridge, Emma wanted to say. *It is my bridge.* Instead she smiled politely as she sank gracefully down on a sofa. 'He is staying with us. You know how my father likes to talk engineering.'

The women in the drawing room gave a chorus of laughter.

'But tell me about him. Is he as handsome as they say?'

'Forget handsome, is he as rich?' Lucy's young sister-in-law, Lottie, clapped her hands together, her china-blue eyes shining, and her crown of golden ringlets bobbing. 'I heard that he had his carriage and a team of matched greys sent up from London by train this morning. More than twenty thousand per year— can you imagine?'

A frisson of excitement ran through the company, and the other women began asking questions all at once. Pincushions, fans and cups were tossed aside as the room hummed with excitement.

'Let Emma speak,' Lucy said with a smile. 'Sometimes, Lottie, I think Henry is correct when he says that you have fewer manners than a baboon.'

Lottie subsided with a practised pout. 'But I only want to know.'

'He is from Newcastle. He used to work for my father. He left about seven years ago, and returned yesterday.' Emma accepted a cup of tea and delicately sipped it, wondering how she would turn the conversation away from Jack. She had no wish to think about the man.

'Emma Harrison, you must know.' Lottie leant forward. 'Tell me every little detail. After all, you were consigned to the shelf long ago—you must know what he was like when he lived here. Mama does not remember a thing, a solitary thing. I need to know. Twenty thousand. Can it be true? Can a man earn that much?'

'I am the same age as Lucy.' Emma regarded Lottie with a steady eye. She refused to allow Lottie's little remarks to annoy her.

'But she is married with two young children. That hardly signifies.' Lottie gave a deprecating wave of her hand. Her lips curved upwards in a mischievous smile. 'Emma is a living relic of a bygone era.'

Emma forced her face to remain bland as the rest of the room gasped.

'Now, Lottie, hush, and stop being rude.' Lucy turned her placid face to Emma. 'Emma, dear, do not mind Lottie. She is a little thoughtless and over-excited this morning.'

'I do not mind Lottie at all,' Emma returned with a smile. 'I have no intention of minding Lottie. She exercises enough minds as it is.'

Harmony was restored as the room burst out in laughter. Even Lottie joined in after she'd puzzled out the pun.

'Now, shall we talk about our dresses for the ball?' Lucy said, clearing her throat. 'I thought the cream silk would be best for Lottie, to show off her complexion.'

'But it has too much lace.' Lottie made a little moue with her mouth. 'I wish it to be much more décolleté. I am sure to be wildly in demand, but I shall save a dance for dear Mr Stanton.'

She lowered her eyes and fluttered her lashes to the sighs of others in the room. Emma contented herself with raising an eyebrow as Lucy led the conversation firmly on to other topics.

The talk ebbed and flowed about her, but Emma's mind kept returning to Jack Stanton and the St Nicholas Ball. She could not go to this ball and see the women fawning over Jack Stanton as if he were some prize to be won. Emma tapped her finger against one of Lucy's pincushions and smiled. She had the perfect excuse—her father's health.

* * *

'Mr Stanton, there is a problem.' Mudge came into the office and stood twisting his cap. 'One of them stone blocks you wanted set up has fallen. Right on top of some tools. It looks as if you will have to let the men go early. It is far too late to do anything about it now.'

Jack lifted an eyebrow. He had expected something like this. If not today, then tomorrow. The men planned on testing him, to see what sort of overseer he would be: whether he knew his job or was simply a man parroting words without any feel for how a bridge was built. He shrugged out of his frock coat and checked his pocket watch. 'There remain at least two hours of good daylight. I believe the problem will be easily solved before then.'

Mudge's mouth dropped open. 'Are you sure you want to do that, sir?'

'I am positive.' Jack looked directly at the burly foreman. 'I think it is about time the men see what I am capable of.'

'You're the gaffer...' Mudge bowed.

'Lead the way.'

Jack regarded the block stone, artfully arranged to look as if it had fallen, but it was too neat and precise. The problem was not difficult, but tricky enough that if a man did not know his engineering he could make a mess of it. Jack smiled inwardly. No doubt Mudge thought he was being very clever—testing the new supervisor. There were two ways to handle this.

Jack picked up a sledgehammer, feeling its balance, and regarded the poorly placed stone. Behind him, he could hear bets being put on. The men never changed. They needed to be shown that he meant business. He lifted the hammer, brought it down with a crack, felt the shudder of the impact, and cleaved the stone in two. It broke beautifully. He closed his eyes in relief and blessed his first foreman for forcing him to learn.

Mudge and the men looked at him open-mouthed. No doubt they had expected him to call for a block and tackle. Or take the wrong approach.

'Once again, the most direct route works,' Jack said, dusting his hands off. 'The tools are accessible.'

'Yes, sir.'

He could see the respect in the men's eyes grow. They were builders. They understood.

He walked back towards the office, then paused, turned around and faced the men. 'I want all the tools and other items that have gone missing on the site while Miss Harrison was in charge returned. No questions will be asked, but I want them back, or unfortunately jobs will be lost.'

He saw the looks of astonishment on their faces, as well as the reddened cheeks, and knew his words had hit their mark. This site would be run properly until such a time as Edward Harrison was able to resume his role.

'You overdid it yesterday.' Emma came in to her father's study to discover him wrapped in blankets with an ice pack on his head. 'Several cups of punch too many.'

'Such a way to greet your dear papa.' Her father removed the ice pack and looked at her with bloodshot eyes. 'Why does the number of glasses of punch I can drink and rise the next morning with a clear head appear to decrease with age? Must the servants' footstep be quite so deafening?'

'Why did you invite Jack Stanton to stay with us? To oversee the bridge?' Emma asked quietly. 'I thought we had agreed.'

'It will be until I get over this cold.' Her father held out his hand. 'After what happened to young Davy, how could I do otherwise? I felt for his mother. It has been barely a year since his father died. Terrible business, that.'

'He's back home now, with his mother and grandmother. Dr Milburn sent word with his account this morning. I thought to visit them.'

'You are a good woman, Emma. Your dear mama would be proud of you.' Her father gave a cough. 'She would be the first to admit that she was wrong about Jack Stanton. She used to say that he would never do anything with his life, and look at what he has accomplished.'

'Papa—'

'You may do all the warning you like, Emma Harrison, but remember I know Jack Stanton wants this bridge built as badly as I do—as we both do.'

'As does Robert Stephenson.' Emma crossed her arms and stared at her father. 'Mr Stephenson would come up and oversee, I am sure, if you asked.'

'Stephenson has other bridges to build. This one needs to be iron and stone. It cannot be simply iron. Stanton is the only one who can supervise the men. I trained him. I trust him.'

What about me? You trained me. Emma longed to shout, but one look at her father's face showed that he would not take kindly to the suggestion.

Her father cleared his throat. 'Now, let us forget bridges and talk about something much more pleasant—the Assembly Rooms' St Nicholas Ball. What is the latest news from the social round?'

'Absolutely not! I forbid it!' Emma crossed her arms and prepared for battle. 'You had a bad night last night. Going to a ball will do you no good at all.'

'But you were excited about the prospect yesterday morning. I distinctly recall hearing about a rose silk dress.'

'That does not signify.' Emma forced her face to remain expressionless. 'You know what the night air does to your chest.'

'Mrs Charlton will be ecstatic. She has been trying to claim a place for Lottie in the top quadrille set for months.'

Emma rolled her eyes. 'You know my feelings about that woman and her odious daughter, Father. I only see Lucy because she is one of my oldest friends and they do not often visit, preferring to leave their cards.'

'But you have seen them recently.' Her father looked at her with a shrewd expression on his face.

'I saw Lucy this morning, and Lottie was there, crowing about her most recent triumphs.' Emma held up her hand, stopping her father's speech. 'But even the thought of denying Lottie does not make me relent. We are not going.'

'It is you who doesn't want to go.' Her father signalled for his coffee to be poured. 'It is a revenge for me inviting Jack Stanton here. You are doing this to be deliberately awkward.'

Emma took a sip of her tea. 'I think only of your health. Last night you were once again in the grip of a nightmare. And you refused to take your tonic. You are being ridiculous.'

'Am I?' Her father reached over and gave her hand a pat. 'I know you well, my daughter.'

'As do I know you, Father. It is my final word.'

'Ah, Stanton,' Edward Harrison said, not bothering to rise from his armchair, where he sat wrapped in shawls and a blanket. 'What is the news of the progress? Are you satisfied?'

'It is as your daughter predicted—your men have returned and are hard at work.' Jack came into Edward Harrison's study. He had spent most of the day at the site. The foreman had nearly fallen over himself in his efforts to be helpful, dropping hints about the state of Harrison's health, but never actually saying anything. His actions only confirmed Jack's suspicions. 'Mudge informs me there is a second survey of the riverbed.'

'You will have to ask my daughter where it is.' Harrison raised a hand, and then allowed it to drop back onto the blanket. 'She does all the organising these days. A remarkably good organiser, Emma. Ask her where anything is, and she knows.'

The last person Jack wanted to think about was Emma. Last night in the corridor he had been struck by her vulnerability. She was not only nursing her father, but also trying to do a man's job.

'I was most impressed with the willingness of your men to work.'

'Once their pay packet ran out.'

Jack laughed, but then sobered. The lines of tiredness were etched on Edward Harrison's face.

He wondered that he had missed them when he'd encountered him at the club. Harrison had not aged well. And, despite Emma's declaration, he knew a woman could not run an engineering firm. Not one as young as Emma.

'Harrison and Lowe has an excellent reputation. If you wish to sell your controlling stake, the company would be delighted to look into the purchase. On favourable terms.'

He closed his mouth and resisted the temptation to say anything more. He who spoke first lost. The clock on the mantelpiece ticked loudly. Jack resisted the impulse to fill the silence, but allowed it to grow until his nerves screamed. He could see from the way Harrison's hand twitched that he felt it, too. Jack willed him to give in, to say yes.

'At the present time I have no desire to sell.' Harrison gave a cough and rearranged his blankets.

'The offer is there, should you require it.' Jack made a show of examining his cuffs. He had done the decent thing. Surely Harrison had to realise the offer was fair, more than fair? Once the news of his illness got out, the vultures would begin to circle.

'I understand, and I will remember it when the time comes, but it has not come yet.' Harrison leant forward, his eyes bright. 'Tell me, what do you think of my youngest daughter?'

'Miss Harrison? We have barely spoken today.' Jack narrowed his eyes. Was this going to be it? A not-so-subtle attempt at matchmaking? He had avoided such lures before. Not even for the prize of Harrison and Lowe would he give up his freedom. There were certain limits.

'May I speak plainly?' Harrison cleared his throat and glanced over his shoulder before continuing. 'I need your assistance in a small matter. It concerns my future and the future of Harrison and Lowe.'

'Please do. I am delighted to be taken into your confidence.' Jack closed the study door with a click and settled himself in the armchair opposite. Harrison had piqued his interest. He was intent on some scheme, and if he humoured him he might be able to get him to seriously entertain the offer.

'My daughter suffers a misguided notion that because she runs my house she can order me about. She has taken it into her head that I am far sicker than I am.' Harrison gave a wan smile. 'In short, she fusses and forbids me small pleasures.'

'This has nothing to do with me. I make it a policy never to get involved in domestic disputes.' Jack started to stand up. He could easily see what had happened. Emma had acquired a taste of power when her father was ill, and now she wished to extend it over his business. She had become a harridan. 'As an unmarried man, I have little expertise in such matters.'

'A pity.' Harrison made a temple with his fingers and peered out over it. 'I regret that until this matter is solved it will fully occupy my mind. I would like to think about your kind offer, but…'

'Tell me about your troubles, and perhaps we can come up

with a solution.' Jack settled back in the chair. He would hear
Edward Harrison out and then politely decline. Emma was
somebody else's problem. Not his.

'She refuses to allow me to go to the Assembly Rooms for
the St Nicholas Ball. I may no longer cut quite the figure at the
quadrille that I once did, but it does my heart good to see the
pretty young things in their dresses.' Edward Harrison gave a
discreet wink. 'There is a widow…'

'I wish you good hunting, but I fail to see what this matter
has to do with me. Inform your daughter that you are going and
have done with it.' Jack held up his hands. Harrison should take
a stronger line. If he truly wanted to go to this dance he should
go, and suffer the consequences. He allowed Emma far too
much freedom.

'It is not that easy. Emma…well, I have no wish to quarrel
with her. She has taken to avoiding such things.'

'Your daughter has sound reasons. I find such things a bit of
a bore myself.' Jack permitted a tiny smile to cross his face.

'Yes, but before my wife became ill Emma loved such pursuits. All gone now. I am not sure she even remembers how to
dance.' Harrison shook his head and gave a heartfelt sigh.
'Sometimes she takes her duty far too seriously. And I fear she
does not entirely approve of the widow.'

Jack tightened his hold on his cane. No doubt the widow in
question did not come from the appropriate background and
therefore was deemed unworthy. Emma had been well indoc-
trinated by her mother.

She needed to learn a lesson. Fast. She could not simply go
on organising people's lives to suit her whims. Mudge had complained about her meddling this morning. Now it was her
father's turn. The woman had to be stopped.

'You want my help so that you may attend this ball and speak to your widow without your daughter knowing? Aiding your suit,' Jack said, carefully watching Edward's features.

'You understand my meaning, Jack.' Harrison took on the expression of a sly fox.

Jack nodded. He understood the code. If he did as Harrison asked and persuaded Emma to attend the dance so that Harrison could pursue his widow, Harrison would seriously consider his offer for the company. The situation might be turned to his advantage. He would enjoy administering a lesson that Emma Harrison badly needed to learn.

'I will do what I can, but it must be Miss Harrison who decides.'

'And, Jack, I never forget a favour.'

'I am counting on that.'

Chapter Four

Emma chewed on the end of her fountain pen and counted for the third time the number of geese they would need for the Goose Club's raffle at the end of the feast. It was always a difficult moment, and she had no wish to get it wrong. The memory of Mrs Mudge's outrage last Christmas, when they'd been one goose short, still rankled.

The problem was that her mind seemed to be wandering today. The lines of figures swam in front of her, twisting and merging into Jack Stanton's saturnine features. Was it her imagination, or did his dark hair curl slightly at his collar? And what would it be like to be held in those long-fingered hands as they waltzed? If they waltzed. She cursed the gossip from Lucy's at home for unsettling her. She had no interest in him, refused to, and there was not the slightest possibility of her going to the dance.

'Miss Harrison, when you have a moment?'

Jack strode purposefully into the morning room without a

courtesy knock. His dark eyes flashed as he surveyed the room with all the arrogance of a lion surveying his domain.

The morning room became much too small. He was far too close, and far too masculine for such a feminine room, with its bows and fussy coverings left over from her mother's reign.

'Is there something I can help you with, Mr Stanton?' Emma kept her voice chilled.

'I do hope so. It is a small matter, and will only take a moment of your time.'

She calmly put down her pen and rose. She straightened the folds of her dress. She could do this—act in a perfectly natural manner. Her breathlessness had nothing to do with him, and everything to do with lack of sleep. She banished the giggling gossips from her mind.

'Did you find everything to your satisfaction with the bridge?'

'The bridge is progressing admirably.'

'Then is there something wrong with your accommodation? I am sure Fackler will be pleased to sort it out.' Emma raised her hand to summon the butler.

'The room is comfortable, and your staff have been welcoming to my valet.'

'But there is something wrong.' Emma kept her head held high.

'A dance is to be held at the Assembly Rooms to raise funds for the St Nicholas Church.' Jack's voice flowed over her, enveloped her senses in its warmth.

'This is the fifth year that such a dance has been held.' Emma tilted her head, trying to assess where the conversation was leading. She would have to work the conversation back round to the bridge. She put her hand on her well-thumbed copy of the latest survey. 'It is quite the thing. Assembly Rooms balls are held in high esteem. Their reputation has only grown since Strauss appeared with his orchestra eight years ago.'

She hated the way her voice caught on the last words. There should be no reason why Jack would remember the first waltz they had shared. The first time he had gone to such an occasion.

She had buried it deep within, half-forgotten until an inconvenient time like today, when the memory sprang full-blown upon her. It was even more poignant than the memory of the last waltz they had shared—the one directly before he'd proposed to her. She regarded the scattered papers.

'Yes, you danced every waltz that night. Always a different partner, always in demand.' There was more than a touch of irony to his look. 'The veritable belle of the ball.'

'I used to live for dancing. Mama despaired about how many slippers I wore out.'

'Indeed.' His eyes narrowed.

'Oh, yes.' Emma gave a little fluttering laugh. 'She used to make a joke of it. How I would need a wealthy husband who could keep me in slippers. Utter nonsense, but Mama was like that.'

'Have you worn out many slippers lately?'

'The state of one's shoes is not something a lady discusses with a gentleman.' Emma tilted her chin in the air.

'We both know my origins, Miss Harrison.' Jack's voice dropped several degrees in temperature. 'Charity boys, even those who have made their fortunes, are rarely considered gentlemen in the best circles.'

Emma pressed her lips together and silently cursed her wayward tongue. His origins were no mystery—father dead at nine, grammar school, and then articled to her father. Everything Jack Stanton had he had worked for. He had acquired the polish of a gentleman, rather than being born to it.

'I attend dances regularly,' Emma said brightly, and knew her words were no more than a polite lie. She did go to the dances. However these days she spent far more time watching her father play cards or chatting to Lucy and the other young matrons than dancing.

Jack drew his upper lip between his teeth. 'And yet I did not discover your name on the list for the St Nicholas Ball.'

Emma released her breath. He seemed content to allow the subject to be changed. 'Is that important?'

'It is a popular dance—the best attended of the year, according to my sources.' A faint smile touched his lips. 'I understand the punch is superb.'

'I don't normally drink punch. Strong spirits are the bane of many an existence.'

'That is too bad. But it is no reason for you to forbid those who enjoy such things.'

The fog in her brain cleared as if it had never been. This had nothing to do with Jack wanting to waltz with her and everything to do with her father's desire to go.

Her father.

Her father had enlisted Jack's aid. Emma crossed her arms. He was not going to get around her that easily. She had made her mind up. It was for her father's own good. The state of his health had to be kept a secret. Dr Milburn had warned her shocks must be avoided at all costs.

'Have you been speaking to my father?' she asked, watching for any sign.

'He mentioned it, and how much he looks forward to it each year.' Jack took a step forward, so close that if she reached out her hand slightly it would brush his. The thought shocked her to the core. She forced her hand to remain in her lap.

'Then you will know that I have forbidden his attendance.' Emma kept her eyes trained on the overly emotional biblical scene that hung on the wall just behind Jack's right shoulder.

She should have known her father would try something like

this. She had to keep calm. She had no wish to relive the humiliation from Lucy's at home. She willed him to leave the room before her words tumbled out and she revealed her true reason for forbidding her father. Even the thought of doing so made her cringe. Pointedly she rustled her papers and bent her head.

'Why, Miss Harrison?' A quizzical frown appeared between Jack's eyebrows. 'Your father has suffered from a chill. Why are you trying to deny him his pleasure? I saw how much he was looking forward to it at the club the other day.'

'I have no wish for the chill to turn into something worse!' Emma fumbled with her fountain pen, dropped it and watched it roll, coming to rest on the toe of Jack's highly polished shoe. Jack reached down, held it in mid-air as if undecided. The anticipation of his fingers brushing hers filled her. Emma knew her cheeks had become flushed, her throat dry. It was some sort of ailment, this inexplicable attraction towards him.

She forced her shoulders to relax, but a small stab of disappointment filled her when he placed the pen on the table and stepped back, his eyes watching her much as a cat might watch a mouse.

'Then you believe he is in danger of becoming seriously ill?'

'Nothing of the sort. I refuse to allow him to jeopardise his recovery. Papa is no longer as young as he used to be. I have lost one parent and have no desire to lose another.'

He raised an eyebrow. 'Your father does not appear in any danger of dying.'

'Not today!' Emma exclaimed, then paused and regained control of her emotions. She had to hope that Jack would overlook the outburst. 'But I have seen what over-exertion can do.'

'Miss Harrison, if he is that weak perhaps he should consider selling his company.'

Emma drew in her breath sharply. She had to keep her head. She had given too much away already. Selling the company to someone with a reputation for making money like Jack Stanton was the last thing she wanted to happen. One hint of her father's long-term health and the price would drop. And would he want to keep on all the men? Some of the families had been with Harrison and Lowe since her grandfather's day.

'That is not what I said.' She forced her voice to sound firm and confident, a contrast to the mass of butterflies and aches in her stomach. 'I wish for my father to return to full health as quickly as possible. The night air will be no good for his lungs.'

'Neither will the river's damp,' Jack countered remorselessly.

'Bridges are my father's life, Mr Stanton.' Emma was unable to conceal the catch in her throat.

'I realise that,' he said quietly.

'I have work on the Goose Feast to do, Mr Stanton.' Emma pointedly picked up her pen again, willing him to go. 'If you only came as an emissary from my father, perhaps you would be good enough to go back and tell him that his stratagem will not work. I am absolutely immovable on the point.'

She nodded towards the door. Jack would now do the polite thing and depart. She waited. He did not move. Instead he settled himself in the armchair and picked up the latest edition of the *Newcastle Courant* and noisily began turning the pages. She sat down at her desk and bent her head.

'Mr Stanton, if you please, I am trying to work.'

Jack Stanton's eyes twinkled as he put the news sheet down. 'Do you mean that as a challenge? Is that why you are holding that paper up like a shield? What are you frightened of, Miss Harrison?'

'I am not frightened of anything.' Emma dropped the paper back on the desk with a thump. She placed her hands in her lap and grasped them together to prevent her from making wild hand gestures.

'I think, Miss Harrison, it is not your father you are worried about, but yourself.' Jack Stanton leant forward as his eyes assessed her. He lowered his voice. 'Could it be that the latest dances scare you? Has the once sought-after Miss Harrison not yet learned to polka? Are you afraid of losing your hard-won dignity? The polka, Miss Harrison, combines all the intimacy of a waltz with the vibrancy of the Irish jig, or so my dancing master assured me when I learnt the steps two years ago.'

Emma rolled her eyes heavenwards. She had to remain aloof, control her temper. 'Polkaing reached Newcastle several years ago, and I do know the steps. As in London, it is wildly popular.'

'Show me.' Jack placed the news sheet down and rose. 'Will you do me the honour, Miss Harrison?'

Emma's mouth dropped open. She looked over to where Jack stood with his hands outstretched. Her mouth went dry. What would it be like to be enfolded in those strong arms again?

'This room is not big enough for a demonstration.' Emma narrowed her eyes.

'Take the risk, Miss Harrison.' He came forward with outstretched hands. 'The only thing that will happen is a few pieces of knocked furniture. Inanimate objects, easily repaired.'

'Mr Stanton, the space is limited.' Emma tried to ignore the tiny thrill that ran through her. Her breath caught slightly in her throat as she remembered his hand brushing against hers last night. 'I hate to think of my mother's ornaments suffering damage. They are a lasting reminder of her.'

'What a pity. But if there was enough space, would you polka with me?' A shadow of a smile touched his lips. 'Speaking hypothetically.'

'Yes, I see no reason in theory why I should not polka with

you. The experience could be quite amusing.' Emma lifted her chin. 'It is nonsense to speculate on such things. It can't be done.'

'All we would have to do is move the tables and chairs. Put a few Dresden shepherdesses beyond reach.' Jack tapped a finger against his cheek. 'There will be space, Miss Harrison.'

He began to move the small table where several Dresden figurines stood, blank-faced and garishly dressed. Her mother's choice, rather than hers. Emma watched, horrified. He intended to make her dance. They would be alone in the room with his hand on her waist, her hand on his shoulder. Heat infused her cheeks.

'Mr Stanton, I must protest. There is no music. Cease this foolishness.'

'I will hum.' Jack start to move about the room, holding out his arms. 'A partner would make this much easier, Miss Harrison.'

'Stop, stop!' Emma shook her head and tried to contain the laughter that threatened to bubble out over her. 'Do you always talk such nonsense, Mr Stanton?'

'Only when it is required.' His eyes sobered as he came to a standstill, no more than a breath away from her. So close she could see the gold stud that held his collar together. 'If not dancing, tell me what you are afraid of. Why are you not going?'

'Why should I be afraid of attending such a thing?' Emma looked away from his deeply penetrating eyes. 'I am as disappointed as my father. My ball dress was ordered months ago. Rose silk with Belgian lace. Quite the thing. Some might even say daring.'

'And you a confirmed spinster.'

'Spinsters dance, Mr Stanton.' Emma swallowed hard. There was no need to say the only people who might consider the neckline daring were aged spinsters. 'I was quite looking forward to it, but then my father became ill. There are certain sacrifices that one has to be prepared to make. But I am unclear if you understand that.'

'As both my parents died when I was young, perhaps I do not understand the nature of sacrifice—is that what you are saying?' Jack's eyes narrowed. 'I can assure you, Miss Harrison, that you are mistaken. I do understand why people feel compelled to look after others.'

'You are putting words into my mouth!'

'Forgive me.' Jack made a sketch of a bow, and the corners of his mouth relaxed slightly. 'I merely wanted to know why you did not want an evening's entertainment. As I recall, the Assembly Rooms held a great attraction once. A parent's health would not have concerned you.'

'Such attractions die when one encounters real life.' Emma gave a little wave of her hand. 'I grew up, Mr Stanton, and realised there was more to life than dancing, society dinners and frivolity. As I said before, my interests now lie in other areas.'

'And real life was…?'

'My mother became ill. I discovered other things interested me far more than dancing slippers.' Emma stood up. She gave her most chilling nod, indicated the door. 'Mr Stanton, this conversation is pointless.'

'Hardly that.' Jack cleared his throat and a superior expression appeared on his face. 'You have yet to say one word that proves to me you are not scared of going to the dance. It is more for your convenience than your father's that you have chosen not to go. You are afraid to polka. You are afraid people might whisper that the incomparable Miss Harrison is on the shelf.'

'I care about my father.'

'Then why have you forbidden him the dance?' Jack ticked off the points on his fingers. 'He is not ill enough to warrant the sale of the business, and you say you are not frightened of dancing, but you decline to prove it. We are at an impasse.'

'You have not told me how your visit to the bridge went.' Emma looked at Jack. The shadows from the gaslight heightened his features. Maybe he was right, and she was using it as an excuse. Her dreams had been full of him last night, standing there, smiling his sardonic smile. She had no wish to feel his arms about her. Not here, in this enclosed space. Her breath was coming a bit too quickly.

'But I have told your father.' A smile transformed his face from planes and shadows. 'I refuse the distraction, Miss Harrison. I am wise to your games. But, as you seem intent on playing, can I suggest an amusing alternative?'

Amusing alternative? Emma swallowed hard. The conversation's direction was clear.

'I suppose the price of obtaining information about the bridge is my guarantee that I will go to the dance and demonstrate I can polka?' she said, refusing to prolong his teasing.

'We begin to understand each other, Miss Harrison. A polka for information. A fair exchange.'

'You leave me little choice.' Emma's throat tightened around the last words.

'It is not a death sentence, Miss Harrison. You used to enjoy the reels, as I recall.' His eyes narrowed. 'But you have not said you will go. One thing I learnt quite early on in my career is to have all the terms of the contract spelt out. It makes it easier for both parties.'

'You have my agreement. I will go, and if there is a polka I will dance.' Emma faltered and tried again, this time with a much firmer voice as she banished all memories. 'Does that satisfy you?'

'For the moment.'

Emma passed a hand over her face as she got a sinking feeling in her stomach. What had she agreed to? She could always find an excuse not to go later, but now she wanted to know. What had he found out at the site? 'Now will you tell me what happened at the bridge?'

Jack's black eyes danced with mischief. 'There is very little to say. Mudge has been most accommodating, and work is progressing.'

'Your words are bland and give precious little away.' Emma crossed her arms. 'I have given you my promise. It is time for you to honour yours.'

'Miss Harrison, this is a most inappropriate conversation to be having with you. I am shocked at your suggestion.' Jack gave a slight bow. 'Shall we wait until after your polka?'

Weak-willed and weak-minded, Emma decided as the carriage stopped in front of the building site.

That was what she was.

Allowing Jack Stanton to manipulate her into agreeing to go to the Assembly Rooms was a mistake of the highest order. She should have stuck to her plan, refused to be manipulated by either her father or Jack. As it was, she would have to face Lottie Charlton and her minions, and hear the giggling gossips.

She could visit the building site whenever she wished. Jack Stanton could not stop her. He would not dare.

Several of the workmen turned and stared at her, almost as if they had never seen her before. A hush fell over the site and all eyes seemed to follow her every movement. Emma hesitated, straightened her jacket and bonnet, and proceeded to the office with firm footsteps.

'Miss Emma,' Mudge said, his eyes widening.

'I have come about—' Emma began.

'I will take care of Miss Harrison.' Jack's smooth voice interrupted her words. Without saying a word, Mudge bowed and left the room. Emma blinked. The foreman had never moved with that much speed before.

Jack came forward into the small foyer. He was dressed in his shirtsleeves, his collar open at the neck and a towel looped around his neck. It looked as if he had been doing physical labour, working with the men. Not what she'd expected at all.

Emma swallowed hard and tried to regain control of her pulse. Her head seemed very light, and all she could concentrate on was that little patch of skin at the base of his throat, glistening slightly. She had thought her dreams last night were bad, but the reality of him was overpowering. She ran her tongue over her lips and struggled to focus elsewhere.

'This is a closed site, Miss Harrison.'

'I am the daughter of Edward Harrison.' Emma tilted her chin upwards and waited.

'There are no exceptions. The work is not at a point that I want the public to gaze and gape. It is far too dangerous. You know what happened to young Davy. One misstep and he fell.'

'I have been to see Davy. He is one of the reasons I am here,' Emma said quietly, thinking about the terrible scene of poverty she had come from. Davy Newcomb had been released from hospital. His leg was not broken, merely sprained, but the Newcombs depended on Davy's wages to make ends meet. That much had been clear from the way Mrs Newcomb would not meet her eyes. She had wanted to do something for them. But Mrs Newcomb had refused. She have never taken charity and was not about to start. Emma had left, feeling dissatisfied.

'How is the lad?'

'He will recover, given time. It could have been so much worse. He knows what he did wrong.'

'I am glad to hear that.' Jack gave a nod. 'Hopefully he will learn from this not to take short cuts.'

'Davy is bright. He planned on going to grammar school.' Emma gave a sigh. 'It is just unfortunate his father died earlier this year. His mother depends on him and his wage. He seems to have given up all idea of learning.'

'It is hard, but it can be done if one has the discipline. The Institute of Mechanical Engineering offers night classes and other opportunities for self-improvement.'

'Hopefully Davy will become inspired, but I am more worried about his family. They need every penny. I have told his mother that Davy's position is safe until such a time as he is strong enough to return.'

Jack crossed his arms. 'What is your business, and why couldn't it wait until I returned to your father's?'

'It is not you I wanted to speak to.' Emma clung onto the remnants of her temper. He should show more concern about Davy. He had saved the boy. She looked up at the grey sky, drew a deep breath. Davy was not his employee. Thankfully. And she had to concentrate on why she was here. She had to discover if what he'd told her father was the truth or simply a polite lie. Mudge would know.

'Then who?'

'Mudge.'

'You will not find him easier to get round, I assure you,' Jack stated. 'Mudge knows who he answers to. Your father is pleased with the progress so far.'

Emma looked over Jack's shoulder rather than meet his smouldering gaze. Her eyes widened as she saw the pile of tools. The levels that had vanished last week were back, as were a variety of shovels. There was no need to ask who had caused their return, or why. The men were probably frightened of him.

'Are you always this tyrannical, Mr Stanton?'

'When the occasion demands…' A faint half-smile played on his lips.

'Very well.' Emma withdrew a sheaf of papers from her reticule. 'I came to see Mudge about the final Goose Club list.'

'The Goose Club?' Jack's eyes widened. 'What does Mudge have to do with this Goose Club of yours?'

'Mudge, as foreman, collects the monies from the men throughout the year. He keeps an up-to-date list. Somehow I only have last year's.' The answer tripped off Emma's tongue. She had been under no illusion that Jack would be easy to get round, but she did want to see what was happening—and gauge how long she had to convince her father and Jack to move the piers. Speaking to Mudge was the best way, as her father had refused to divulge the information, telling her she had to go and speak with Jack.

'You should have given me the message this morning.' Jack regarded Emma, standing before him. Her blue poplin morning dress increased the blueness of her eyes. Her cape and matching hat, with its feathers curling towards her ripe mouth, completed the picture. Her acquiescence last night had been too quick, too sharp. He had anticipated some sort of rearguard action, and Miss Harrison failed to disappoint.

'I did not see you this morning. I only realised the final list was missing when I went through the accounts.' Emma held up the paper with a smile. 'The geese are drawn at the feast. We are missing final payment from six of the members, including Davy Newcomb. But he has paid. I checked with his mother.'

'Do you need the list today?' Jack asked between gritted teeth. This was a ploy of Emma's to get her own way. He had no doubt that she planned to interfere and cause problems. It had taken most of yesterday to undo the damage that Mudge had implied her orders had caused. Her eyes widened, and she looked very innocent, but her expression did not fool Jack. She intended her visit for other purposes. And he had little doubt what would happen in her wake. He had already spent more hours than he cared clearing up oversights and errors. Had he not appeared when he had, the bridge would have been seriously delayed and possibly unsafe.

Jack stepped forward and took the piece of paper from her. The names were neatly written out. She had a fair hand. He had to admit that.

'It is the second of December. The feast is the twenty-fourth. It does take time with ordering. I want plump geese.'

'And while Mudge is checking on the details…?' Jack placed the piece of paper down on the front counter. He could see a certain logic in her statement, but he still did not trust her.

'I had planned to see what was happening with the foundations.' Emma gave a slight shrug and her bonnet shadowed her face. 'There is no harm in that.'

'You cannot think I have so easily forgotten our bargain, Miss Harrison.'

'But we also agreed that I was to look after the feast.' She leant forward. 'The problem with the list is new and unforeseen. Nothing to do with our wager.'

Jack's lips tightened to a thin line. The woman was impossible. It was no wonder she had never married. No man would want such a wife. 'We are at an impasse. Mudge is busy at present. We have begun investigating the castle walls.'

'No, not an impasse.' She gave a small laugh, but her eyes showed shock. 'Hardy that. I am happy to wait while Mudge finds me the correct list.'

'I cannot let you do that. It would be too much of an imposition.' Jack put out a hand, caught her elbow and propelled her towards the door. Emma dug in her heels and, short of carrying her, Jack saw that she was not going to move.

'Are you trying to get rid of me, Mr Stanton?'

'I am trying to do my job in the best way I know how to, and that includes not having any interference from unqualified people. Building a bridge takes more than placing a few piers in the ground and a plank or two over that. Once this bridge is built, it should last.'

'I am familiar with the plans,' Emma said through gritted teeth, hating that he had seen through her.

'Then you will know the hard work and the many mathematical calculations that have gone into perfecting it.'

Emma wrenched her elbow away from him. Glared at the infuriating man before her. He was exactly like all the other men of her acquaintance. She wondered what she had ever seen in him. 'What are you saying? Do you think women are not capable of making complex calculations?'

Jack ran his hand through his hair, making it stand up on end. 'I am certain some women are capable of doing the mathematics.'

'And you think I am not.' Emma continued remorselessly on. 'You think I am only capable of being a decorative object!'

She hated the way her voice rose. She glared at him and struggled to regain her temper.

Jack looked away first.

'Bridge-building is not a hobby for bored women,' he said at long last, turning back to face her. His voice held that very calm and reasonable note, the one that made her want to scream. 'You could do more harm than good by inferring with things that are beyond your comprehension. There must be a thousand worthy causes that need your attention.'

'Is this what you think my interest in the bridge is— interference?'

'Miss Harrison, we have an agreement. You have yet to fulfil your part of it. Until that time I would suggest you let me get on with my job.'

Emma rolled her eyes heavenwards and clung onto the last remnants of her temper. 'The reason I came is important as well.'

'And you will have your precious list, and the correct number of geese you need. Order several more than you need. I am quite willing to foot the bill. Problem solved.' Jack smiled, the sort of smile that lit his eyes and no doubt had the power to make women go weak at the knees. 'Now, if you will let me get on with my work…'

Emma stiffened her back. 'You are leaving me no option.'

'I am not.'

He escorted her back to her carriage and saw that she was comfortably settled, tucking the carriage robe around her. Altogether the solicitous gentleman, despite his attire. 'If you will excuse me, I have a bridge to build. No doubt you will have some social calls to make.'

'As a matter of fact, I do.'

Emma pressed her head against the seat and closed her eyes. The memory of his fingers brushing hers lingered, grew. She did not want to like Jack Stanton. She wanted to hate him. But she found herself growing increasingly attracted to him.

Chapter Five

Jack paused in the doorway of the dining room. The gaslight lit a charming domestic scene. Emma was curled up on a sofa, reading, while her hand absently stroked a black cat. It was perfect. Almost too perfect. Jack felt a pang in his insides. He tried to hang on to the illusion for a while longer. He had forgotten how much he had once longed for a family, and how cruelly she had snatched the hope away. He forced himself to remember that as well.

'Miss Harrison.' Jack gave an indulgent smile. No doubt she was reading a Minerva Press novel. He could see a half-sewn pair of slippers lying abandoned next to her.

She glanced up and stuffed the book behind a cushion. Her hands went to her hair, automatically adjusting the pins.

'Mr Stanton, I didn't hear you come in.'

'I am sorry to interrupt such a charming tableau. Pray continue with your reading.'

Jack thrust his hands into his jacket pockets. There was no

reason to keep thinking about this woman. She wasn't even pretty—not in the conventional sense, not any more. Her nose was too long, and her cheeks far too pale for the china doll prettiness favoured by society. Her eyes had taken on a serious glint, and there was determination in her chin, but once he started to look at her he found it difficult to draw his eyes away. All day he'd found his mind wandering back to her, wondering what her next move would be.

'Did you wish to speak to me about something?' She tilted her head to one side. 'Another attempt to induce me to polka? Or is it something more ridiculous?'

With a start he realised he was staring at the shape of her lips. Quickly he crossed over to the fire and gave the coals a stir. The fire leapt back into flame, consuming the coals with orange tongues. Bright, brilliant, but over in an instant.

The thought shook him. He had sworn never to have anything more to do with this woman after the way she had treated him. But that was in the past. He had put the past behind him, so why had he returned to her?

'That list you gave me this morning—I presume it was in your own hand?' he said, when he had regained control.

'It was.' A frown had appeared between her brows. 'Mudge will find the correct list, I am sure, and your company will not have to provide the extra geese…if that is what concerns you.'

'Which you have ordered?' Jack said.

'It had to be done.' She raised her chin and the blue flecks in her eyes fairly danced. 'I asked for the largest they had.'

'I feared you might have done so.'

'You are not telling me that you now wish you had never made the promise?' She tilted her head.

'I always keep my promises, Miss Harrison, foolish or otherwise. And I fail to see how anyone could consider giving a few geese at Christmastime foolish. But I thought to order turkeys. They are larger birds, and their meat goes further.'

'That is true, but it is too late. The order has gone in and I would be loath to change it.'

'But I did not come to speak of this.'

'If you did not come to tell me about the Goose Club, why have you invaded my bower?'

Jack waited. Now that he looked closely he could see the piles of notes, and a pen. Miss Harrison had not been reading a Minerva Press novel. She had been doing calculations. Something about the bridge concerned her.

'You have a distinctive way of forming your "e"s.'

'I had an eccentric governess. She taught me a little of this and that, but nothing of any real substance.' Emma gave a brief self-deprecating laugh. 'It was not until my mother became ill that I really learnt to apply myself.'

'It can be tedious being at the beck and call of an invalid when one is used to going out in society.'

'I managed.' Emma held her breath. She had no wish to explain about the relief she'd felt when she did not have to make meaningless small talk any more or strike attitudes, a living picture to be admired.

'You did one or two of the sketches for the bridge.' Jack looked at her, daring her to deny it.

'I may have done. My father wanted to see if I could draw properly,' Emma replied cautiously. She watched his face for any sign that he had guessed what she had done, any opening so she could explain without accusing her father. 'My drawing has always been a great comfort to me.'

If he suspected the main design had been done by her, rather than her father, she could well imagine the eruption. He would insist on the whole design being redone, rather than simply moving the line. She had to face facts. If she wanted this bridge built, she would have to keep silent, downplay her role. The design was correct. It was the position that was wrong.

'They are very charmingly executed. I notice yours have the keep in the background.'

'I think it is important to retain the past.' Emma met his deep black eyes, eyes that assessed but showed little warmth. Tried to ignore the sudden butterflies in her stomach. 'The castle is central to the city. It is where it gets its name.'

'The castle belongs to the city's past.' Jack banged his hands together. 'It is the city's future I am concerned with. If the bridge becomes too expensive to build, Newcastle will cease to have its position as one of the premier cities in the Empire, if not the world. How then will the citizens of Newcastle fare? The workers and their families?'

'But…' Emma tried to think of an argument that would sway him. He had to understand that tradition was important to people.

'You should not have false hope, Miss Harrison.' Jack tucked his thumbs into his waistcoat. 'The ground farther down the bank is poor. Your father's precise calculations have shown that. It can't be done. Not without causing the foundations to go down much deeper.'

'It can't be done?' The corners of her mouth quirked upwards. 'I thought the motto of the modern British engineer was it *can* be done.'

'One cannot fight the laws of nature.'

'It is impossible to work outside the laws of nature. Even a woman like myself knows that.' Emma fought to keep the exasperation from her voice. 'It is just…'

'Just what?'

Emma regarded her hands. How could she confess that she

was certain some of her father's calculations were wrong, dangerously wrong? She had worried before, but after what she had read today she knew. She wanted a little more time to recheck. But how could she have missed it before? How could her father have made those errors? 'A few more experiments have been made, a new survey…it leads to slightly different conclusions.'

'A survey you ordered? When your father was laid low by his chill?'

'Yes.' Emma kept her head upright. There was no need to explain about her discovery that several of her father's calculations were wrong. He had transposed several of the numbers. An honest error, but one that needed correcting. 'I thought it prudent.'

She waited for his answer. This was probably her one chance to get him to see about the bridge. And once she had done that she would have no need to go to the dance. Her lips curved up into a tiny smile.

'Miss Harrison, this is the most inappropriate conversation.' The corner of Jack's mouth twitched.

'Inappropriate? Why?'

'You very nearly had me discussing the bridge.'

'Is there something wrong with that?' Her eyelashes fluttered. 'It is something we are both interested in.'

'You forget our contract—we have yet to dance, to polka. You have but to say the word and we could dance in this very room.' He tilted his head, his eyes assessing her. 'No, Miss Harrison, I fear you think me only funning you.'

Emma struggled to keep a straight face. 'Are you not?'

'I am deadly serious about it. I never neglect a contract.'

'Are we not to speak until then? Or only discuss the weather?' She lifted a hand. 'I do not need to tell you how much speaking about the weather bores me.'

'What do you wish to speak about?'

'Your travels.' She gave a decisive nod. She would work the conversation around to the bridge. 'Tell me about Brazil and your work there.'

He laughed, the sort of deep, rumbling laugh that flowed over her, enveloping her in its rich enjoyment of life. 'I can tell you about the places I have visited, but not about the bridges or how they relate to the one I am currently constructing. Tell me, what is it about going to the ball that you fear most? Why do you seek to hide?'

'I don't fear anything.' Emma curled her hand. She lied. She feared Jack Stanton and his ability to see through her. She feared the stories she had heard of his business practices. How had he made so much money, so quickly? She had a duty and responsibility towards her father's employees. She could not simply lose her reason because he was near.

'Papa, I want to speak with you.' Emma paused in the doorway of her father's study. She had gone over and over in her mind how best to approach this. Dr Milburn had been quite insistent the last time her father had had a fit—nothing was to be said to upset or alarm him. He took such pride in his work and his accuracy. The shock could kill him.

A large snore emanated from under the red handkerchief.

'You must wake up, Papa. It is important.'

Her father sat up, blinked his eyes open. 'Huh? What? Oh, it's you, Emma. What domestic crisis are you going to tell me about now?'

Emma took a deep breath and plunged ahead. She had to keep calm. She would even say that it was her fault, take the blame. He had to understand the importance of what she had discovered.

'Papa, it is about the calculations for the bridge. I couldn't understand why the two surveys were so different, but I think I have uncovered the reason.'

'Say no more, daughter.' Her father held up his hand. 'Stanton has already told me about your agreement. I am not going to aid and abet you. All the calculations in the first survey are accurate. If Stanton is half the engineer I think he is, he will recheck the calculations. But, daughter, he will find them accurate. My calculations always are.'

'Papa, I only came to ask…'

'Mudge discovered the list, if that is what you wanted to know. Came to me about it earlier, with his cap in his hands. Mrs Mudge had put it in a disused teapot and forgotten it.' Her father raised his paper. 'All this fuss about a pair of geese.'

'It was more than that, and you know it. It is the principle of the thing. I had no wish for the Goose Club to be a disaster like last year.'

Her father ran a finger around his collar. 'There were reasons for that.'

'And I swore this year would go smoothly. Jack Stanton refused to let me speak to Mudge! He threw me off the site.' Emma struggled to take a breath, and waited for her father to agree with her.

'The plain fact of the matter is that you can't stand to lose.' Her father put his hands behind his head and leant back. 'And you know Jack Stanton has bested you. Well, my girl, I have held the lines too slack since your mother died. And it is about time somebody took you in hand—stopped you from becoming like my great-aunt Agatha, who kept cats and painted rather poor watercolours of dreary landscapes.'

'I have never been tempted in any way to be like Great-Aunt Agatha.' Emma looked at her father in horror, remembering the eccentric woman who had smelt distinctly musty and had

had a booming voice. She rushed to the pier glass and regarded her face. It was still hers, and not Great-Aunt Agatha's
hooked nose and squint eyes. 'You must not say such things.'

'I see I have found your weak spot—Great-Aunt Agatha.' Her
father chuckled and turned the page of his news sheet. 'I shall
have to remember that.'

'But, Papa, this is serious.' Emma turned from the glass. She
clasped her hands together. She had to make one last effort. 'The
line of the bridge will have to be moved. It is imperative that it
is moved. You must let me show you why.'

'Emma, we have been over this before. I know how much
time you spent, and what a help you have been, but Jack Stanton
is here now. If there is an error, which I highly doubt, he will
find it. I trained him to the highest standards. There is no one I
trust more to do a proper job.' He made a chopping motion with
his hand. 'The only way you will be able to discuss the bridge
is to go to the St Nicholas Ball.'

Emma pressed her hands to her face. She would have no
option but to go to the ball and face Lottie Charlton and her
cronies. Mentally she lowered the neckline of her ballgown. An
inch and a half would serve better. A living relic, indeed.

Several hours of boredom was worth it if she achieved her
goal in the end.

Jack was right—she could not change the laws of nature, but
she could work within them. She would go to the ball and
triumph. And then Jack would have to listen to the reason why
the line of the bridge must be moved. It would be done without
revealing the state of her father's health or who was to blame.

Butterflies attacked Emma's stomach, swooping and swirling.
It was one thing to plot and plan, and quite another thing to
execute. She could not help wondering if perhaps she had made

the neckline of her ballgown a fraction too daring. And while the new hairstyle was certainly becoming, did it make her seem altogether too frivolous?

The urge to demand the carriage turn around and go back to the house filled her.

'Is there some problem, Miss Harrison? You look perturbed.'

'Nothing.' Emma shook her head a little more vigorously than strictly required. Her earrings swung against her jaw. She would not concede victory to Jack Stanton. She needed to hear what was happening with the bridge, particularly as her father had taken to dropping small hints about the progress and then refusing to yield any more information. She believed he took a great deal of pleasure in doing so. 'I wondered how long until the carriage arrived at the Assembly Rooms.'

'We have joined the queue. It won't be long now.' Her father stuck his head out of the window. 'I can see the Charltons have two new bays. And whatever is Fanshaw doing with a livery painted on the side? You would think he would know by now.'

'Hush, Father. You sound as bad as Mama.'

'Nobody could be as bad as that.' Her father gave an indulgent smile. 'Poor woman, she was absolutely obsessed with social position. But she had a full life. Unlike Great-Aunt Agatha.'

'Please, Father, no homilies about marriage. Not tonight.'

Emma gave a hurried glance over to Jack, who appeared to take no notice of the exchange but directed his studious gaze out of the window.

The faint strains of a waltz emerged from the Assembly Rooms as the carriage finally reached the covered entrance. Its fabled chandeliers blazed, making a welcome pool of light in the dark. Emma shifted away from Jack. The close confines of his carriage, and her father's insistence, meant they had shared the same seat.

Emma swore her father's eyes twinkled as he alighted. His intent became clear. Matchmaking. Her father had used her interest against her. She had played directly into his hands. She should have guessed. But Jack had no interest in her. He had set up this silly contract simply to force her to go to the ball, to please her father and to teach her a lesson about interference.

'You will survive the dance. I promised you that.' Jack's hand briefly touched hers as she alighted from the carriage. The kid gloves he wore were neither shining white nor faded, but had an expensive sheen to them. In fact everything about Jack tonight, from the cut of his evening clothes to the gold stickpin in the centre of his stock, proclaimed that here was a successful man, a man of great wealth and taste.

'I planned on it. Like you, I do try to keep my promises, even if they are foolishly given.' Emma inclined her head. 'Did you think I would find an excuse?'

'The thought had crossed my mind—several times. But you appear determined to discover what is happening with the bridge.'

'The company belongs to my family. I have an interest.' Emma concentrated on rearranging her cloak.

'You should leave such things to the experts.'

'You mean to you,' she said quickly.

'And your father.' He nodded towards where her father was greeting several of the town worthies. 'He is well respected.'

'And you think I should have no interest in such matters?'

'What I think has very little relevance, as I did make a promise. Had I really wanted to keep such things a secret, I would never have made the promise.'

'Then this was purely an exercise to get me to go to the dance.'

'To get you over your fear.' He gave a wide smile 'The

prospect of the evening seems to have improved your father no end. He seems as giddy as a schoolboy.'

She had to admit, from the way her father jumped down from the carriage, he was far more sprightly than she had thought. However, he had taken to refusing his tonic, complaining that his stomach cramps were always worse after it than before. And goodness knew when his other symptoms would return. It was only a matter of time. She had to face facts. Dr Milburn had been quite clear on that. She had to be practical, but she also had to ensure Harrison and Lowe would survive.

'As I said—it was a chill. He is inclined to overdo things at times. Mama used to complain about it regularly.'

'The evening will do your father good. There, now, you can relax. He has made it to the door. He is safe from the night air.'

Emma pressed her lips together. Jack was making it sound as if she acted like her father's gaoler, or an overly-protective nanny. 'I have no wish for the chill to return. It was…frightening to see my father in bed.'

'You will be gratified to know that he has decided to be sensible and allow me to oversee the bridge until at least Christmas.'

'But I understood you had a number of projects…' Emma said with dismay. She had hoped she'd be able to persuade her father without involving Jack. She was not sure if she was ready to explain that it had been her father who had made the mistakes. She had clung to the hope that Jack would tire of this game and depart, now that her father appeared to be getting better.

'None as pressing as this one. I am not satisfied with the riverbed. The second survey—' He stopped, and his lips turned up. 'Ah, but I shall say no more until after I have seen you polka.'

'You enjoy teasing me. We are here now.'

'But a contract is a contract, Miss Harrison.'

'I shall hold you to your promise,' Emma said, and allowed the maid to take her cloak and muff. Her hands smoothed the rose silk, making sure it fell smoothly.

Jack's eyes suddenly darkened as the full glory of her ball-gown was revealed. The rose silk and Belgian lace set off her complexion nicely, she thought, and the spaniel curls at the side of her head made the planes of her face seem less angular, younger somehow, but she had definitely lowered the neckline a little too much. She resisted the urge to pull it higher.

She lowered her lashes and quickly scanned the list of dances. 'There is a polka first. Or one immediately after supper.'

'I had wondered if you would mention it.' Jack took the printed sheet from her. 'Normally a lady waits to be asked.'

'We have an agreement. Unless you mean for me to dance with someone else?'

'How did our contract go?' His voice rippled over her, holding her in its warmth. 'Remind me of the exact terms. Did we specify who you were to dance with?'

'I…I can't remember.' Emma hated that her voice faltered, that her mind appeared to be more intent on the shape of his mouth than on the terms of their agreement. She straightened her shoulders. It was humiliating to think that he did not really want to dance with her. He knew that they had agreed on a polka, and that was the first dance. It only stood to reason. Maybe he wanted to wait until the one after supper, see her sit on the sidelines, waiting to be asked? Emma forced her spine upright. This was not going to be the first time she had spent most of a dance seated.

'My father has entered into the spirit. He refuses to divulge any information.'

'I believe he can sense an opportunity.' Jack's hand touched the small of her back, guiding her forward and up the stairs. 'You are now here, but can you polka properly? I have no wish to cause you embarrassment. Or would you prefer a waltz?'

A waltz. Emma moved away from his hand. He had no idea what the two words did to her insides, making her remember what it had been like all those years ago here. They had waltzed then. He had been light on his feet, and a warm cocoon had surrounded her. What would it be like to waltz with him now? Emma's mouth went dry. She thought she had buried such thoughts a long time ago.

She noticed Jack was watching her with speculation in his eyes. He had probably forgotten. Emma straightened her skirt, lifted her chin, and became determined to look forward. 'I can polka, Mr Stanton. I am quite determined to polka.'

Emma did not want to think about how many times she had practised the steps in her bedroom this afternoon. She'd been determined not to make a fool of herself. And now it appeared that Jack had simply used it as a way to get her to attend the dance. She need not have bothered.

A tiny smile appeared on Jack's face. 'I never doubted that for an instant.'

'Ah, Miss Harrison, what an unexpected pleasure.' Dr Milburn's strident tones echoed around her, causing her to jump. 'Is your father here as well? He looked peaked the last time we spoke. I fear it can be but a matter of time before we are called to increase the amount of tonic your father takes.'

Emma winced and turned from Jack's suddenly narrowed gaze. She should have planned for Dr Milburn. She could only hope that he did not mention her father's illness.

'My father has disappeared into the throng, yes.' She waved a vague hand towards the ballroom. 'He has probably gone to the gaming tables. You know his addiction to whist.'

'You are taking a risk, Miss Harrison, a definite risk.' Dr Milburn shook his head, his blond locks slightly swaying. 'I trust you made sure he was well wrapped up before you both ventured forth?'

His eyes lowered to her neckline. Emma felt her flesh crawl. She wished she had brought lace with her, but to retreat now would be to admit she had made a mistake.

'My father has improved a good deal recently.' Emma raised her chin, and ignored the tiny pain in the back of her eyes.

'I put it down to stimulating dinner conversation myself,' Jack remarked, straightening his cuffs and moving so that he had subtly placed his body between Emma and Dr Milburn.

Dr Milburn looked him up and down with a raised eyebrow. 'And you are?'

'Jack Stanton. I believe we knew each other in our younger years at school. You are Charles Milburn.'

'Ah, yes, I can place the features. You were a charity case. I heard you were working for Harrison and Lowe again.' Dr Milburn's voice was cold. 'I suppose it explains why Miss Harrison has arrived with you.'

'Mr Stanton is one of the foremost civil engineers of our day, Dr Milburn.' Emma kept her voice steady.

'Indeed, Miss Emma.' Dr Milburn gave a cough. 'I must have heard the latest gossip wrong. I could have sworn that he had returned to his old post.'

Emma bit her lip. The insult to Jack was unmistakable. She could tell from his stance that the barbed comment had hit home. After all he had achieved, he remained vulnerable.

'Mr Stanton is looking after the project while my father recovers,' Emma said. 'He is Robert Stephenson's new partner, and has been entertaining my father and me with his tales of railways in far-flung places.'

She waited, and saw Jack's shoulders relax slightly, and Dr Milburn's frown increase.

'Hopefully you are making sure he takes his tonic, Miss Harrison. You must not underestimate its importance for a man in your father's condition. I have seen so many like him—fine one day, and the next they are at death's door. I am sure it is not a fate you wish on your father.' Dr Milburn drawled the words.

'No, indeed.' Emma cringed. The last thing she needed was Dr Milburn dropping hints about her father's health in the presence of the man most likely to exploit the information. And she had to remember that Jack was the enemy, not Dr Milburn.

'Edward Harrison needs medicine for a chill?' Jack asked. 'What is wrong with him?'

'I recommend all my elderly patients take my tonic.' Dr Milburn puffed up. 'It does wonders for them. I am sure it helped prolong the late Mrs Harrison's life.'

'My father has a very independent mind.'

'I know, but I am counting on you, Miss Harrison. You will save a dance for me, won't you?'

'But not a polka. She is already spoken for with that dance,' Jack said smoothly, but his eyes were cold.

'Perhaps the Sir Roger de Coverley. It is a fine dance, very respectable.' Dr Milburn indicated that he considered the polka to be beneath him. 'The committee have decreed, in accordance with tradition, that the reel will be the last dance. A festive way to end this holiday ball.'

Emma glanced from Jack to Dr Milburn. Jack Stanton appeared close to creating a scene. What had happened between these two in the past? She hid a smile. Dancing with Dr Milburn would show Jack that she was not without partners.

'Yes, I believe I am not engaged for that one.'

'I look forward to it with great eagerness, Miss Emma.' Dr Milburn made a bow and was gone.

Emma breathed a sigh of relief. Nothing untoward had happened. She started to go towards the chandelier room, but Jack's fingers held her elbow. She turned to see his intent face—black hair framing even darker eyes.

'How long has Charles Milburn been your father's doctor?'

'For the last five years or so. He was wonderfully kind when Mama was dying.' Emma tilted her head. 'Dr Milburn serves as Papa's personal physician and the company's doctor.'

'We knew each other at school.' Jack forced his jaw to relax, forced his mind not to revisit the petty cruelties Milburn had inflicted on those unable or unwilling to stand up for themselves. 'I had always wondered who Milburn reminded me of, and now I know.'

'Who?' Emma tilted her head, and her curls touched the white column of her throat.

'A man I was unfortunately acquainted with in Brazil.' Jack chose his words with care.

'And this person was not someone you were overly fond of?'

'He was a conman and murderer,' Jack stated, and watched Emma pale.

'Dr Milburn kept my mother alive.' Emma's voice became chilled. 'Mama lived for his visits. He has been helpful with my father, who is not the best of patients. People change. You have.'

'As you say, people change.'

'Father would have a match between Dr Milburn and me, but I suspects he says it in fun.' Emma gave a little laugh. She could hardly confide her unease to Jack. Dr Milburn was fine as her father's physician, but as a husband—never! 'He knows I am determined on my spinsterhood.'

Jack's eyes travelled down her face, finally resting on her

neckline. A bold, caressing gaze that caused a strange warmth to grow inside her. Emma resisted the urge to pull her neckline higher. 'In that dress, you look anything but a spinster.'

'I shall take that as a compliment.' Emma looked at him from under her eyelashes.

'It was an observation, Miss Harrison. Pray do not mistake the two.'

Several men claimed Jack's attention before Emma had time to give a suitable retort. She glared at his back.

Chapter Six

'Emma Harrison!' Lucy's laughing voice called out from the increasing throng of people. 'Of all the things!'

Emma spotted her friend, sitting with the other young matrons as the dancers swirled around them. The room baked in the glow of the crystal chandeliers. The committee had ensured the rooms were festooned with greenery, giving it a very festive look.

'Is there something wrong?' Emma asked, as she noticed Lucy's brows puckering.

'I haven't seen you wear a dress like that in years...not since...well, since your mother became seriously ill,' Lucy replied, holding out her hand. 'Are you going back on the marriage mart? Giving up on your determination to lead the solitary life?'

Emma shook her head. 'I made an unwise bargain.'

'A bargain? Do tell me more.' Lucy patted the seat beside her and Emma sank gratefully down. She had forgotten how many petticoats a ballgown required, and how much the weight increased. 'If you look now, you will see that my sister-in-law is seething.'

'Why?' Emma looked with interest to where Lottie Charlton stood, listening to Dr Milburn. 'She does appear to have swallowed a rather nasty plum. Perhaps she is not enamoured of Dr Milburn's conversation.'

'You upstaged her entrance. Lottie had consigned you to the shelf, and you—you have leapt off it in spectacular style tonight. That dress, Emma!'

'I have done nothing of the sort.' Emma gestured with her fan towards the increasing crowd of men who surrounded Lottie. The petite blonde was half hiding her face behind a fan, and laughing flirtatiously at something Jack said. Emma ignored the stab of jealousy. 'She is quite the picture. You can see from here the officers lining up to beg her acquaintance from one of the stewards. You will see. I shall have my normal place at your side for most of the dances while she is the reigning belle.'

'Reigning belle she may be, but Lottie is also a minx. She has enticed Mr Higgins to put mistletoe up, and is determined to catch your Jack Stanton under it.' Lucy nodded to where the kissing ball presided in the centre of the room. 'It's also hidden in the garlands. She will come to no good one of these days, and be married off to the wrong man.'

'He is not *my* Jack Stanton,' Emma retorted, and then worried that she had said the words too quickly. She should have concentrated on Lottie's misdemeanours—a much more suitable subject, and having little or no peril.

'You arrived with him, and there's a sort of glow about you tonight that I haven't seen in many years.' Lucy folded her hands in her lap and gave a very superior smile. 'It makes you look years younger, less like a dried-up prune.'

She ignored the glow, and the prune comment. Lucy had obviously mistaken strain and heat from the chandeliers for something else. And her clothes were suited to the purpose.

'Only because Jack Stanton forced my hand,' Emma said between gritted teeth.

She restrained her fingers from fiddling with the pearl button of her glove. *A lady does not fidget*—words her mother had tirelessly repeated rose up again. Her life now was very different from one that her mother would have considered proper.

'Forced you?' Lucy put her hand over her mouth, but Emma saw the amused glint in her eyes. 'I find it hard to believe that any man could force you to do anything. You have grown formidable, Emma.'

'You have been a friend for a long time, Lucy, and I shall allow that remark to pass.' Emma lifted her fan to hide her expression. It was all right for Lucy to talk. She had chosen Henry Charlton six years ago, after she had been out for a while but before her star had started to wane. It was not a love-match, but one in which Lucy professed herself content. 'But even old friends should not presume to take liberties.'

'Stuff and nonsense, Emma, we have been friends for ever.' Lucy laid a gloved hand on Emma's arm. 'What I worry about is what will happen if your father remarries.'

'I don't think that is a possibility.' Emma gave an arch laugh and hoped. She had not confided in Lucy about her father's illness and her fears.

'You do need to think about it.' Lucy's hand tightened. 'He is not that old, and he is possessed of reasonable fortune. See how that farmer's widow from the Tyne Valley circles.'

Emma shifted uncomfortably as a cold chill passed down

her. She had been in charge of the house ever since her mother became ill—seven long years. If her father did remarry she would be delighted for him, but the house would cease to be her domain. 'I can always be a companion.'

'Emma, you are not one of life's companions—ready to fetch and carry, read aloud dull religious tracts and do endless tatting and netting.'

'You didn't think I would make a good nurse either,' Emma reminded her. 'You made many dire predictions and told me that I would abandon Mama and wed before the year was up.'

'Sometimes I think you persisted simply because you delight in proving everyone wrong.' Lucy's brown eyes twinkled. 'I have known you for a long time, Emma Harrison.'

No, I persisted because my heart ached. Emma caught her lip between her teeth. Where had that thought come from? She banished it. She was happy and content with her life. Her sole concern was her father, and keeping him alive. 'There may be something in that, Lucy.'

'Miss Harrison.' Jack's warm voice washed over her. 'Here I discover you. You appeared to have been swallowed up by the crush.'

'I did not know you needed to discover me.' Emma slowly lowered her fan, placed it in her lap, but her insides trembled. She had hoped that Jack would be content with her simply appearing at the ball. 'I thought I was visible from all angles.'

'Have you forgotten? We are to polka.' His manner was light but his eyes were cold. 'The first dance is the polka. I do not see any point in wasting more time. And you do not appear engaged for the dance.'

Emma's heart sank. Now that it came to it, she was less than certain that she could do it. She knew the steps. But to be out in the middle amongst all those people—people who could remember when she'd been the belle of the ball instead of being led out onto the floor for the Sir Roger de Coverley at the very end. 'I had thought I would have longer.'

'Longer? Longer to get up your nerve, or to find an excuse as to why you are suddenly afflicted with pains in your legs and cannot dance?'

'Emma, you never said that Mr Stanton had asked you to partner him for a dance. You silly puss.' Lucy's eyes twinkled with mischief. 'And here I thought you were to keep me company until Dr Milburn claimed you. Pray, take her away, sir. She does precious little dancing these days, not like when we were young. I should like to see her polka.'

'She *claims* to know the steps, but I have my doubts.' Jack's gaze challenged her.

'You doubt my word, but I am no liar, Mr Stanton. I do know the steps.'

'She is shocking, isn't she?' Lucy put her finger to her lips. 'I trust she will not tread on your toes.'

'I have never trodden on anyone's toes.' Emma put her hand on one hip. 'Really, Lucy!'

'Emma is far more interested these days in silly calculations about wind speeds and tides,' Lucy continued, as if Emma had not spoken. 'For ever going on about them. I mean, who would be interested in such things as a topic of polite conversation?'

Emma's breath stopped in her throat. She was torn between the desire to shake Lucy and the pride she took in her own ability.

'Indeed? I had not realised her interest in civil engineering extended as far as that.'

'Oh, yes. You should see her designs for the new bridge. I saw the early sketches, and then how—'

'Lucy Charlton, you are allowing your tongue to run away

with you,' Emma said quickly. 'Sometimes I don't think you know what you are saying.'

'But I do know what you are trying to do, Emma Harrison! And I quite agree with Mr Stanton that you should not be allowed to sit on the sidelines when other lesser dancers take to the floor.'

Lucy's elbow dug into Emma's back, forcing her to stand. Emma shot a black look at her friend.

'Tell him,' she said in an urgent undertone. 'Tell him you were teasing me.'

'I am funning, Mr Stanton.' Lucy fluttered her fan. 'She has been sitting here tapping her foot to the music. She is the same old Emma Harrison that she was years ago. You have come to her rescue not a moment too soon. She was using her hand to stifle a yawn.'

'And I thought you enjoyed my company, Lucy,' Emma protested, but she gave her friend a grateful look. She had to tread very carefully where Jack was concerned.

'Miss Harrison.' Jack held out his hand. "The dance is about to start. Try to look as if it is not a death sentence.'

'A death sentence? Hardly that, Mr Stanton!' Emma struggled to contain her nervousness. Mentally she rehearsed the steps again. She only hoped the tempo would not be too fast.

'Your face seems to have paled significantly.'

'I stood up too quickly.' Emma forced her lungs to fill. 'My stays…'

'Yes, of course. That would explain it.'

'Shall we go?' Emma held up her fingertips.

'Have no fear, I shall endeavour to entertain you with quips about wind speeds and the height of floods, as your friend suggested.'

'I don't think this is quite the appropriate place for an in-depth discussion.' Emma straightened her shoulders.

'No? You should have thought about that before you agreed to our little contract.'

'You don't mean to cheat, Mr Stanton, do you?' A cold shiver ran down Emma's spine. She might as well cause a scandal and abandon him on the dance floor if all the information he was prepared to give her would be contained in the length of the dance. She needed longer, but she would begin her explanation now, while she had the chance. 'I desire a full account of what has been happening. I had grown quite used to it. The bridge-building has become an obsession with me. Lucy was right about that. I'd like to speak with you about the line of the bridge and the new survey. I believe I have discovered why it is different from the earlier one.'

'You should know, Miss Harrison, that I never cheat where business or ladies are concerned. And I never combine the two.' He gave a half-smile. 'I only thought to tease you a little, but I see now you resist such things. Shall we indulge in a light flirtation instead?'

'I think we should polka,' Emma said firmly. The last thing she wanted was a flirtation with Jack. She had to remember that he was the man most likely to ruin her world.

'As you wish…'

Emma gulped, lightly placed her fingers in his and allowed herself to be led out onto the floor with the other couples. She ignored the viperous glance that Lottie gave her. Jack put his hand on her waist and gave a nod. The music rose up and surrounded them.

'Heel and toe and away we go,' Jack said, before they began.

'Excuse me?' Emma resisted the impulse to laugh.

'It is the way I was taught the polka. The little rhyme helps. You had a worried frown on your face. Are you sure you have danced the polka before?'

'I know the theory.'

'There is a world of difference between theory and practice, Miss Harrison. Both in the fields of dance and civil engineering.'

Emma stumbled a few steps, but then found her rhythm. Unlike the smoother and slower waltz, which attracted all sorts of participants, the polka was mostly confined to the younger generation. Jack proved an able partner, guiding her around the floor with expertise, but not so good that he danced like a dancing master. Emma began to relax, and began to notice little things—the way his hand rested lightly against her back, the slight curl of his hair, his crisp masculine scent, and most of all the shape of his lips.

Emma missed a step and stumbled against him, her body colliding with the starched white linen that covered his broad chest. Her breath hissed through her lips. Jack smoothly manoeuvred them so it appeared as if her stumble had been planned. Emma regained her footing and they galloped around the room once more.

'I'm sorry,' she mumbled, and felt heat surge through her cheeks, praying that he would think it was from the exertion of the dance.

'It was undoubtedly the floor's fault, as someone once said to me.' The words were quietly spoken.

'They have not improved it in eight years,' she said, her breath catching in her throat. All too clearly she remembered when they had first waltzed as Strauss played, and she had said those very words to him. It had been the start of her awareness of him. Then, about a year later, he had asked and not waited for her answer.

'No, obviously not.'

She glanced up and saw his dark eyes had softened slightly,

and his face had become serious. She had forgotten the exact curve of his lips. What would they feel like? Soft or firm?

"The music has stopped.' She withdrew her hand, but her feet refused to move. 'You must have other partners waiting. A waltz is next.'

A strange smile crept over his face. 'Miss Harrison, it is an intriguing place that you have ended the dance at.'

Her gaze travelled upwards and saw what they had stopped under. Mistletoe. Lottie's little mischief-making. She should have thought and found a way to steer clear of it.

His finger lifted her chin and his eyes searched her face, coming to rest on her mouth. 'The prospect is tempting, but not here, I think. It wouldn't be a good idea. It is far too public.'

'No, it wouldn't.' Emma agreed with his assessment, despite the faint ache of her lips. Already several of the old ladies were turning their gimlet eyes towards them, pince-nez poised for a better look. The room would buzz with gossip if he brushed her lips. But then if he left her standing there without even a peck on the cheek the room would echo to whispers that he had spurned her. Silently she cursed Lottie Charlton for her little innovation. 'I can see my father signalling…'

'Are you trying to run away, Miss Harrison?' His hand tightened on hers, turned it over. Capturing her. 'You need to pay a forfeit.'

'Not at all. I had not intended to stop here. It was happenstance.' The words were a mere breath. Her lips tingled as if he had actually touched them, instead of simply fixing them with a gaze.

'Some might say otherwise.'

He raised her hand and lowered his head. She fixed her gaze on the curls at the base of his neck, tried to ignore the sudden warmth flooding through her.

'Please,' she whispered, hardly knowing what she was asking for.

'I am always happy to oblige.'

His mouth touched the inside of her wrist, where her glove gaped slightly, touched naked flesh, lingered, and somehow it was much more intimate than she'd thought possible. And over in a breath.

'Until the next time.'

'The next time?' Emma whispered, looking up at Jack.

If he danced with her again tonight the gossips would be linking their names together. Her limbs trembled. She wasn't sure she was ready for that. What was past was past. She was no longer the girl of seven years ago. She no longer laughed as much, and she certainly knew pain and hardship far more than she had done.

Who did Jack see when he looked at her?

'Is there to be a next time?' She had meant the words to be sarcastic, but they came out plaintive, like a child asking for a sweet.

He gave a nod. 'And a waltz, I think, rather than a polka. Your servant, Miss Harrison.'

Emma put her hand to her cheek, felt the coolness of the kid leather against the flame. The mark of his lips seemed to be imprinted on the inside of her wrist. Such a simple act, but it had appeared to be far more intimate than a brush of lips against her brow. She watched his broad-shouldered figure disappear into the crowd.

'Stanton—here I discover you. I thought you would have been at the gaming tables.'

Edward Harrison's voice interrupted Jack's thoughts as he watched Emma taking part in a country dance. Her skirts swayed and he caught a glimpse of a slender ankle, saw Milburn looking as well, and fought against the urge to slam his fist into the doctor's smug face. He pointedly turned away from the dance floor.

'I make it a point never to gamble. I prefer to take calculated risks.'

'Which explains how you have acquired so much money so rapidly and seemingly effortlessly.' Harrison held out a cup of steaming punch. 'You predicted the phenomenal growth in the railways. I wish I had taken your advice then. You were right.'

'I like to think so.' Jack took a small sip of the lamb's wool punch—so called because the mashed roasted apples floating on the surface bore a marked resemblance to newborn lambs' fleece. The heady combination of steaming brown ale, sweet white wine, cinnamon, ginger and nutmeg always reminded him of the Christmas season.

'I know so, Stanton. I know so indeed. Who would ever have imagined that railways would become such a necessary part of the Empire in such a short span of time?'

'Harrison, did you find your widow?' Jack nodded towards where several older women sat, gossiping, at the edge of the floor. 'Does the course of romance run smoothly?'

'She is in a tolerable frame of mind.' Harrison rocked back on his heels. 'It was lovely to see you circling the room with Emma. Your dancing has improved over the years. I remember how you once used a surveyor's level to practise your waltzing.'

Jack gave a tight smile. This ball appeared to be dredging up old memories, feelings he'd thought long-dead. The hours he had put in practising bore little relation to the actual feel of Emma Harrison in his arms. Then. Or now.

'Thank you, the pleasure was all mine.' Jack inclined his

head, pulling his mind away from the past. 'Your daughter is very light on her feet.'

'I had hopes for you and my daughter once.' Harrison waved his hand in the air.

'That was a long time ago,' Jack replied carefully. He had not expected to feel anything when he took Emma in his arms, but his body had responded to her nearness. He had wondered what her lips tasted like. Ripe cherries? Syllabub? It was as if the years had melted away, and yet he knew he was not the callow youth he had been.

'I would like to inspect the works tomorrow—see what is going on,' Harrison said, bringing Jack back to the present with a crash.

'That can be arranged, I am sure. I look forward to showing you around. There are a few questions I have about some of the calculations.'

'They are all accurate on the first survey. I checked them myself.' Harrison's mouth turned down. 'I may be getting on in years, but my mind works admirably, Stanton.'

'I like to double-check, Harrison. I hope you don't mind. I am only following your teaching.' Jack regarded Harrison with a steady gaze. There was more to this situation than he had first thought. 'If I am working on a bridge, I want it to last.'

'And, Stanton, I think we can bring my daughter along—if she isn't too tired from her dancing.' Harrison gave a proud smile. 'Now, if you will excuse me, I must go and entertain my widow. She is to partner me at whist.'

Harrison sauntered away, and linked arms with a woman only a few years older than Emma. The woman gave a huge sigh and fluttered her eyelashes. Harrison turned a light shade of pink.

Jack narrowed his eyes. Emma might feel safe and secure in her position as her father's hostess, but what would happen when he remarried, as he appeared intent on doing? He doubted she would like a position as a companion, serving at the beck and call of an aged relative. He found he could take no pleasure in the thought.

There was something alive and vital in Emma that called him tonight.

One of the dancers knocked against the greenery, sending a sprig of mistletoe tumbling to the ground. Jack reached down, picked it up, intending to return it to its place. His gaze narrowed as Emma circled past in the arms of one of Her Majesty's soldiers. Her skirts swayed in time to the music. She appeared to be every inch the social butterfly, but he knew that was a lie. There was a new seriousness about her, something that had not been there before.

Their eyes met, held for a brief heartbeat. She was the first to look away.

'So, Emma, your father wants me to take you to the bridge, rather than discuss the situation with you in the drawing room. Did you enlist his aid? And who are you trying to protect?' Jack said softly, as he twirled the sprig between his fingers. 'How far are you prepared to go to realise your desire?'

Chapter Seven

The chandelier candles had burnt low, and the ballroom was bathed in a golden glow. The wooden floor had become splattered with candle wax. A molten drop narrowly missed Emma's shoulder as she circled around the dance floor with one of Lottie's officers.

'Miss Harrison, you are not attending,' the Major said.

'I am sorry. I will endeavour to be a more gracious partner.' Emma gave a quick smile and forced herself to stop looking for Jack's broad shoulders.

Every time she went out on the floor she looked for him. He was different from the man she had so very nearly given her heart to seven years ago. Outwardly he looked similar, but she sensed an intense drive, a desire that had not been there before. He had pursued his dream and won.

What was worse, she knew that, given the choice between dancing with him again and finding out about the bridge, she would be tempted to forget her duty and choose the dance.

'Miss Harrison, I believe I have the pleasure of the next dance.' Dr Milburn's voice interrupted her thoughts and she found her nostrils assaulted by peppermint. Dr Milburn's cod-like features swam into view.

'Dr Milburn, I had not realised the end of the ball had arrived.' She held out a slipper and gave a rueful smile. 'I fear the worst for this pair. I have hardly been able to sit since the polka.'

'I noticed you were much in demand.' The doctor inclined his head.

'It makes a change. I had quite forgotten what it was like to dance all night.'

Dr Milburn frowned. 'You know, I worry that your father is involved with Jack Stanton.'

'My father has known him a long time,' Emma said carefully. 'He gave Mr Stanton his initial training.'

'We were boys together.' Dr Milburn gave a braying laugh. 'He was a charity pupil and had much to say for himself. Breeding will out.'

There was something unpleasant in Dr Milburn's tone. Emma took a deep breath. What was Dr Milburn implying—that Jack was not entitled to his money because he had been a charity case? That he had somehow acquired it illegally? Her mind shied away from the thought. Impossible.

'He has done well from the railways.' Emma crossed her arms. 'All of them have—Brunel, Stephenson, and the rest.'

A look of annoyance crossed the doctor's face. 'You know in my charity work I go to the homes of workers. Poor places they are. Foul. Sometimes I wonder about this Industrial Revolution they are always going on about. Is it making the world a better place?'

'What does this have to do with Jack Stanton?'

Dr Milburn gave a shrug. 'I hate to think of what must have

happened to those poor devils he bought out. How do they feel about his wealth? And the women he has romanced but not married? You must be careful, Miss Harrison.'

'I believe I understand the measure of the man. He is over-seeing the bridge—that is all.' Her wrist tingled slightly where Jack's lips had brushed it. 'I have no interest in the man.'

'I am relieved to hear it.' Dr Milburn made another bow. 'I believe the reel is about to begin. Shall we?'

Emma let him lead her out on the floor. As they lined up, ready to begin, she saw Jack in the next line. Jack's eyes were on her, cold and hard, speculating. Something she had never noticed before. A shiver ran down her spine. What did he have planned for her? Was Dr Milburn right about his business practices?

'Miss Emma, the dance has begun,' Dr Milburn complained.

Emma looked down at the floor, trying to pay attention to her dance steps and banish all imaginings from her clearly over-taxed brain.

'I shall now retire to my room a happy man,' Emma's father pronounced when they arrived back at the house. 'I am not getting younger, but these balls do my heart good.'

Emma made a move to follow her father up the stairs. Her feet ached, and she was certain a blister was developing on the base of her right foot, but a happy glow filled her. She had forgotten dancing could be this much fun.

'A word, Miss Harrison, if you please.' Jack gestured towards the drawing room.

Emma swallowed the quick retort. Her body quivered as if his hand had brushed hers. She forced the tiredness down. Surely Jack could not want to have a discussion about the bridge at this hour? She had counted on it being tomorrow morning. As it was, she had probably had one cup of punch too many. It was the only thing that could account for this lighter-than-air feeling. In the morning she expected to feel every inch of her twenty-five years again.

The embers of the fire gave out a golden orange glow, giving the normally sedate room a mysterious allure.

'Is there something wrong?' Emma asked as she moved about the room, straightening all the cushions. Her heart thudded in her ears as Jack shut the door with a click.

'I have been remiss.'

'Remiss?' Emma's hand froze, hanging suspended in mid-air, hovering over a cushion. 'You have been most pleasant all evening. I can find no fault with your behaviour. You even shepherded old Mrs Armstrong into supper. Goodness knows that was above and beyond the call of duty. She assumes everyone is deaf and in need of an ear trumpet.'

'She is pleasant enough, but my choice of dinner companion is not what I want to speak about.' The darkness of Jack's hair contrasted sharply with the whiteness of his shirt-front, giving him a dangerous look.

'The bridge? You wish to discuss the bridge now?' Emma held out a cushion as her mind struggled. She was over-tired from dancing and would have to guard her tongue. Where to begin? How to begin?

He took the cushion from her and replaced it on the sofa. The air was suddenly tinged by his very masculine citrus scent, holding her, enveloping her. Within the space of a heartbeat the room had shrunk. Emma's tongue wet her dry lips as her pulse began to race. They were alone, and it was unlike the last time they had been alone. Then, the servants had been about; now the house was hushed. Above her, she could hear the distant sounds of her father getting ready for bed.

'I promised you another dance—a waltz, I believe—but I became entangled in other matters.' The fire cast shadows over his face, concealing his expression. 'And you...were busy.'

'After our polka I was not a wallflower.' Emma's voice sounded breathless. She concentrated on the mantelpiece clock, ignoring the way her body became alert, as if it expected something to happen—wanted something to happen.

'I dislike saying something and not doing it.' Jack took a step closer. If she reached out a hand she'd encounter his shirt-front. Her palm itched to touch, and she barely restrained it.

'There is not another ball between now and Christmas. Put it out of your mind. I have.' Emma knew it was a lie. All the time she had waltzed with the other men she had thought about what it had been like to be in Jack's arms. How safe and familiar it had felt, like returning home. She struggled for control. 'Shall we speak about the bridge? It is another promise you made. I am eager to hear your progress.'

'If a polka was worth a discussion, might a waltz be worth a site visit to see how things are actually progressing?' His voice dropped an octave, became thick rich velvet that stroked her skin.

She struggled to remember what was important.

'It might be. But we are discussing theory only, Mr Stanton. I told you there was no ball between now and Christmas.' A pang of disappointment ran through Emma. Against all reason, she wanted to be in his arms again. The reason did not matter.

'What if I hum?' He held out his hands. His eyes were shadowed. 'Would you dance with me? Here, now, in the fire-light?'

She attempted to draw a breath, but her stays were pulled far too tightly. To dance here... A tingle of excitement rippled down her spine.

'You are teasing me, Mr Stanton. Waltzing in the drawing room? Without music?' Emma tried a laugh, but it died in her throat as she saw his expression. The light from the dimmed gas gave him a dangerous look, his face all planes and shadows. And his evening dress did nothing to tame him. If anything, it showed that the merest veneer of civilisation covered him.

'I have never been more serious.' He moved over to the fireplace.

Emma stared at him, took an involuntary step forward, gave an imperceptible nod.

Tomorrow she would be sensible. Tonight she wanted to feel his arms about her waist. She had drunk a cup too many, and even her blood seemed to be tingling.

'Once around the room and that is all.'

'As my lady commands.' He put one hand on her waist, and the other clasped her free hand. Emma's fingers trembled as they touched his shoulder, felt the muscles rippling underneath.

He began to hum loudly, a definite waltz, a Strauss waltz like the one that they had first danced to all those years ago. Was it deliberately chosen? Or simply the one waltz tune he knew? Emma hesitated, longed to ask but decided against it. She had no desire to alert him to the fact that she remembered. She dreaded to think what construction he might put on that piece of intelligence.

At his look, she joined in. Her hum matched his. He nodded, and his hand rested more firmly on her waist, pulled her body closer to his. His hand seemed to burn through her dress.

They circled the room once. Their feet slowed, the humming faded. Stopped.

Her gaze tumbled into his, caught, held. Emma knew she should step back. Propriety demanded it. But her limbs were powerless to move.

She wanted to stay where she was—in his arms. Safe. The desire to lay her head against his chest and hear the steady thump of his heart threatened to overwhelm her. She made one last effort towards sanity. Pushed back against the circle of his arms.

'I should go.' She looked towards the closed door. It seemed an age away. She had no idea how she would make it there without stumbling. Her legs seemed to be made of jelly.

He made no reply, but his mouth swooped down and captured hers. Lips touching lips. His hand came and cupped the back of her head. It seemed as if her entire world had come down to this one thing—the pressure of his mouth against hers.

Firm, but gentle.

A warm ripple coursed through her. She had been kissed before, quick pecks, and once someone had kissed her full on her lips. But nothing like this lingering possession of her mouth, this kiss that threatened to unravel her senses. She should move back, but her spine appeared to have melted. She wanted the moment never to end. The kiss changed, became more seeking, more urgent, devoured her lips as his arms tightened and drew her closer, crushing her against his hard body.

The clock chimed, striking midnight, and Emma jumped away from Jack. Her face showed panic, but her lips were a little too full, too red. He made no move to keep her there.

He had meant to test her, to see how far she'd go and to pull back at the last possible moment. Then this had happened. He had tasted her lips, felt them curve underneath his, yield, and it had taken all his self-control not to go beyond that. Even now his hands itched to reach out and press her warm body back against his.

'Forgive me, Miss Harrison—the mistletoe.' His breathing was laboured, as if he had run a long distance. He forced his lungs to fill with air, his hands to remain by his sides, his head upright.

'There is no mistletoe here.' She crossed her arms and narrowed her eyes.

He raised an eyebrow. 'You surprise me with the boldness of your assertion, Miss Harrison. There is a sprig in your hair.'

Her cheeks flamed red as her hands explored the knot at the back of her head. 'Where? How did I not notice? Do you know how long it has been there? Imagine what the gossips will be saying!'

'Not so very long.' Jack reached out and plucked the sprig from where he had placed it as they were dancing. A mild deception, but surely better than the accusing stare. And her lips had tantalised him all night. 'You should be more observant.'

He kept his face perfectly solemn and waited.

The corners of her lips twitched.

'I am sure that wasn't there before.' Her eyes danced as a tiny bubble of laughter escaped. 'I am positive. It couldn't have been. Lucy Charlton would have said something when we parted. You put it there.'

His laughter echoed hers.

'Are you accusing me?' He raised an eyebrow and dared her to carry the flirtation further.

'Maybe.' She lowered her lashes and developed a sudden interest in the pattern of the Turkey carpet.

He hesitated, waiting.

The ticks of the clock grew louder, reverberating through his body. He forced his hands to freeze. Years ago they had once shared a flirtation, and he had rushed things. And had lost her.

He refused to lose again.

Jack shut his eyes. Seven years ago he had vowed to start afresh, not to look backwards. He should not break his resolution simply because the woman he had held in his arms was Emma Harrison.

'Then perhaps I did have something to do with it. Now, say you forgive me.'

Her cheeks flushed, and her mouth became redder. A small sigh escaped, but the carpet still held her interest.

He waited, wanted her to offer her lips again, wanted to plunder her mouth. He had felt her quivering response.

Her small white teeth caught her bottom lip and she turned her head. 'There is nothing to forgive.' She gave a small trill of laughter and trailed her hand along the mantelpiece. 'As you said, it was the mistletoe's fault. It could have happened to anyone.'

Her eyelashes swept down, forming black smudges on her cheeks, making her look like she'd used to. Jack's hand curled at his side.

He had to remember what she was capable of—how he had poured out his heart to her in that letter and she had cut him dead, never answering, never acknowledging it. He had used her silence as a spur to make something of his life rather than settling as a junior civil engineer.

With the death of one dream came another.

But there was something different about Emma. Something that called to him, urged caution. All was not as it seemed.

'Why did you dance with me?'

'I told you that I was very interested in the bridge. I wanted…wanted to go on a site visit.' She tilted her head to one side. 'You did promise.'

'And why is that?'

The words seemed to resonate throughout the room. Emma could hear the warning behind them. Danger. She had nearly forgotten who Jack Stanton was, and how much depended on him not guessing the truth about the bridge and its design. She had to find a way to alert him to the errors in the calculations without explaining about her father.

She had to think about more than the way his arms had felt against her, or how she'd wanted to lay her face against his chest and confess her fears about her father, about her future. She could not explain. Not even now, after they had shared a kiss. Especially after they had shared a kiss.

A kiss.

No one had walked in on them, but the possibility had been there. What would her father have said? Would he have forced the issue? The worst thing was that she wanted to feel the pressure of Jack Stanton's lips again, be encircled in his arms. She wanted all this.

'Tell me, Miss Harrison.' His words coaxed her, but she saw his intent expression. 'Tell me, Emma.'

'Because—' Emma bit back the words to explain about the mistaken calculations. Now was not the time to discuss such matters. She wanted to enjoy the romance of the night. 'Because I like to take an interest in the things my father does. It gives us something to discuss besides the weather.'

Even as she said the words she knew how false they must ring. She covered her mouth with her hands and hoped.

Jack's face hardened. He reached over and lit three candles, making the room suddenly bright. 'Hopefully one day, Emma, you will trust me enough to tell the truth.'

'And hopefully one day you won't need to cheat. Mistletoe in my hair, indeed. To think I trusted you. You are worse than a rake.' She drew herself up, picked up a candle to light her way, and gave a nod. 'I expect the site visit tomorrow morning.'

'But—'

'You should have read the fine print of our contract, Mr

Stanton,' she said firmly. 'Goodnight. Annie, my maid, will be expecting me. I have no wish to keep her waiting.'

She hurried out of the room before her legs gave way. Before she begged him to let her stay.

Jack let her go, despite the temptation to haul her back and kiss her again, to properly taste her mouth. He was sure she would return.

Her footsteps echoed as she mounted the stairs quickly.

He poured a brandy out of the decanter, held it up to the light, swirled it and saw the colour of her hair in the glass. He downed the liquid in one great gulp.

'The game is not over yet, Miss Emma Harrison.'

Chapter Eight

'Emma, I must say I think the way your hair is done today suits you,' her father remarked the next morning, as Emma sat nibbling at her bread and butter. 'Much better than the old way, which made you look as if you were attempting to become a younger version of Great-Aunt Agatha. The resemblance is not quite as marked today.'

Emma bit back the words to inform her father that she would wear her hair how she pleased, and that she had never, ever looked like Great-Aunt Agatha in her life. She had decided to agree with Annie and keep the spaniel curls at the sides of her head. They did soften her profile. Emma glanced at the small marble mantel clock, and then back at her father.

'Father, what are you doing down so early? It is barely even light.'

He was dressed in his frock coat, and his large gold pocket watch gleamed from his waistcoat. She had not seen him dressed

like this since the Saturday before last, when they had expected
Jack to arrive. Then it had been only at her insistence, and they
had arrived at the site in time for the eleven o'clock break, not
before.

Her father calmly settled himself at the breakfast table, signalling for his breakfast and coffee. Fackler moved silently and
swiftly, arranging her father's napkin and getting the food he
required almost before he asked for it.

Emma reached behind her and pulled out his tonic, but he
waved it away.

'I want all my wits about me today.' He wrinkled his nose.
'The taste bothers me, and it makes my head pound. You
worry too much.'

'You don't want to have another attack.' Emma tightened her
grip on the bottle. She hated to think what would happen if her
father did have a full-blown attack while Jack was here.

'You let me be the judge of my health, daughter. I have everything under control. I know the risks. I have done the calculations. Sometimes it would seem that you credit me with little
sense, Emma.'

'That is an unfair accusation.'

'The truth is never an accusation.' Her father's blue eyes met
hers in a steady gaze. 'Now, the day's a-wasting. Where is that
young Stanton?'

'Why, Father? What are you planning with Mr Stanton?'

Emma tried hard not to smile at the description of Jack as
young. She could well remember when her father had used to
call him that. He used to speak of him regularly at the dinner
table until her mother had clicked her tongue and moved the
conversation away from business.

Jack was not 'young' Stanton, not any more. Just as she had
grown and changed, so had he. He had become more danger-

ous, sophisticated and…desirable. He was a mature man. There was nothing boyish about him.

Her hand trembled as she set the coffee down, sending the liquid spilling over the edge.

'A surprise is planned.' Her father rubbed his hands together.

'You are definitely up to something. I can see the gleam in your eye.' Emma leant forward. 'Confide in me, Father, you know you want to. What mischief?'

'No mischief. You are going to inspect the bridge today, and I am coming with you.' Her father began attacking his eggs with great vigour.

'Yes, I know I am going. That is hardly news.' Emma stopped and her eyes narrowed. She stared hard at her father. 'How did you know I was going to the bridge? When did you see Mr Stanton?'

Her breath caught in her throat as tiny wings of tension filled her. Jack had gone to see her father this morning. But about what? She tried to calm the sudden butterflies. It was all too quick and new.

Her father gestured with his bread and butter. 'I had a little word with Stanton at the Assembly Rooms last evening. Thought it would be a capital idea. You have been moping about the place long enough. Have no idea why you have taken to that bridge, but you have. And that's all there is to it. It must be in the blood. Never thought I'd see a female interested in such things. Your mother's eyelids grew heavy with the merest mention of a mathematical formula.'

'But you enjoyed her conversations and amusements. You encouraged her.'

'She was right. I did spend far too much time speaking about work. It astonishes me that my youngest daughter should share the same sort of passion. You had a fit of the blue devils last week when I refused to tell you about the progress.'

'I do not mope,' Emma retorted quickly, before her throat became tight. She'd had no idea her father was that perceptive. She'd have to be far more careful about choosing her words. How she explained the mistake—particularly if he was not taking his tonic. 'I have been seeing to the preparations for the feast, filling the boxes for the poor and making sure my ballgown was fit to be seen. I have had a thousand and one things to do.'

'I knew how much you had been missing it. Stanton agreed with me when I spoke with him at the ball. You were dancing with some soldier.'

Emma stared at her father as her mind went back over what had happened last night. Her mouth became dry and the coffee tasted like ashes. Jack had known! He had already agreed. He had manipulated her into the dance and the kiss! The kiss that she had wanted to go on and on need never have happened.

And, what was worse, it was she who had initiated the kiss. She had been the one to lift her mouth, to have her feet stop, and to stare up into his deep dark gaze and will him to lower his mouth.

A shiver ran down her back. She should feel ashamed, but she didn't. The kiss had been something special, something time out of mind. But it would not be repeated. Ever.

It need not have happened. If she had but known. Jack had toyed with her. He had always intended on taking her to see the bridge. Shame washed over her.

'You? You arranged this day?' She banged her fist on the table, giving vent to her frustration. 'How could you do such a thing without consulting me?'

'What was it that you said? I swear my hearing gets worse and worse. Soon I shall need an ear trumpet.' Her father put his hand over hers. 'I shall go on my own. You need not worry about

coming up with an appropriate excuse. Jack Stanton will understand. Your interest in the bridge was short-lived. You have
found something new to occupy your time.'

'You deliberately mistake me, Papa. I do want to go,' Emma
said quickly. 'It will be the highlight of my morning. I am happy
that you feel well enough to go. Dr Milburn's tonic must be
working its usual miracles.'

'That's my girl.' Her father tapped the side of his nose. 'I
haven't been taking the tonic. That's why I waved it away this
morning. Didn't want Stanton to see how ill and namby-pamby
I had become.'

Emma's answer was stopped by Jack's arrival into the breakfast room. Not a hair was out of place, and his cream-coloured
trousers had perfect creases in them. Everything about him proclaimed gentlemanly elegance, but her mind kept remembering
the way his mouth had felt against hers. The way he had held
her. The way he had tricked her.

She twisted the napkin in her lap between her fingers and
willed herself to forget. He had used her. She had to hang onto
the thought. His sole interest was the business. He did not care
about Harrison and Lowe and its employees. All he saw in her
was a means to an end.

'Everyone is up,' he remarked, and his dark eyes shone with
a hidden fire. 'Are you intent on coming to the bridge this
morning? It can be postponed if you desire.'

'Yes, we are. I am determined to see the bridge today, and my
father is as well.' The words came out more forcefully than
she'd intended. Jack raised an eyebrow.

'I had never intended it would be anything but a chaperoned
excursion. I am well aware of your dedication to the social
niceties, Miss Harrison.' There was a hint of mocking laughter
in his words.

'Yes, even though I am on the shelf, I do find it easier to conform to social convention.' Emma pressed her lips together and attempted to look stern. 'There has never been any whiff of scandal in this family. My mother raised my sister and me properly.'

'I am pleased to hear it,' Jack said, his dark gaze directly on her mouth. His velvet voice flowed over her, reminding her of their dance and subsequent kiss. 'I am sure you will enjoy the outing.'

Emma frowned, then pulled herself together. She had to remember what he was, and how he had tricked her last night.

'That remains to be seen,' she returned tartly.

Jack and her father exchanged glances. Emma narrowed her eyes. Her father was up to no good. It wasn't matchmaking. She did not think he would be underhanded enough to try that. Not after what had happened seven years ago.

She simply did not know what her father was up to this time and it bothered her. If Jack Stanton was involved, she doubted that it would be to her advantage.

The building site sparkled in the sunlight. Heavy overnight frost lay thick, covering everything. The puddles were lightly crusted with ice and crunched slightly when she stepped on one. Two of the young lads were playing at sliding along the length of the site, but with one look from Jack they stopped their game, picked up some stone and began working again.

Emma snuggled her hands deeper in her muff as she watched the plume of air rise like a cloud around Jack, obscuring his features.

During the carriage ride she had done everything possible to keep her skirts from touching him. He had seemed to take a delight in provoking her, moving his foot ever so slightly towards her when the carriage rounded a bend. And still she couldn't stop thinking of that kiss!

'The site appears to be covered in ice,' she said, to cover er dismay.

'I have no wish for you to fall.'

'I am quite steady on my feet.' She managed a smile. 'All my artners' toes remained unbruised last night.'

'You may be an excellent dancer, but black ice is another natter. Caution is called for.' An amused smile touched the orners of his lips as he put his hand under her elbow to guide er around an icy patch.

Emma pressed her lips together. He had deceived her last night. The decision to bring her here had been decided long before they poke in the drawing room, long before his hands touched her vaist, long before… She wrenched her mind away. 'I am not nade of porcelain, Mr Stanton. I can stand on my own two feet.'

'You appear perturbed this morning, Miss Emma.'

The amusement in his eyes deepened. His fingers remained lovering just below her elbow, tantalisingly close. Her whole rm quivered with anticipation. Then she saw her father's eyes gleam, and a tiny smile appear on his lips. A rush of ice water vent through her veins and Emma forced her body to move away from him. Jack's actions were for her father's benefit. He lad engineered the whole situation. He had enlisted Jack's aid, out surely he had to see that Jack was playing a game of his own. Now Jack had to realise that she understood the rules, understood what he was trying to achieve.

'You tricked me!' she said, when her father had disappeared from earshot. 'You had every intention of taking me here today. There was no need to waltz. No need at all.'

'It was you who insisted. I merely enquired. And very enjoyable it was, too.'

'I? You—!' Emma stopped, raised her eyes heavenwards as ushing heat washed over her.

'You react very well to teasing, Miss *Emma*.' His eyes dance
with hidden lights. 'You always did.'

Her breath was drawn in with a hiss as she noticed the change
in address. Not Miss Harrison, but Miss Emma. The way he'c
used to say it all those years ago, with an emphasis on the
'Emma'. She had to admit she rather liked the sound of her name
on his lips, but that was beside the point. He was using he
Christian name.

'Normally a gentleman asks a lady's leave before addressing
her so familiarly.'

'We have already agreed that I am no gentleman. My birth
precludes that.' His eyes hardened. 'You would do well to
remember that, particularly in drawing rooms at night.'

'What are you, Jack Stanton?' Emma asked slowly.

'A civil engineer who happens to be a very good business
man and who also happens to be taking you around his lates
project.'

'It is my father's project,' Emma said, her heart beating fast
He had been here little more than a week, and already the bridge
belonged to him. She could see it in the way the materials were
stacked, and the way men saluted him. Soon he would be using
his business practices and methods, rather than the ones her
father always used.

'What do you mean by that statement?' His eyes narrowed.

'Harrison and Lowe are building this bridge,' she said
crossing her arms and staring directly at him.

'Harrison and Lowe are building the bridge for Robert
Stephenson and Company, so it belongs to both of us.' He made
a bow and gestured towards the river, where bright sunshine
glinted. 'I am determined to show you what I have accomplished. I think you will notice a change even in the short time.
I hope you will approve.'

'It is not up to me to approve or disapprove.'

'But it would make things much easier if you did,' Jack said quietly. If he was to discover the truth, Emma would have to trust him. She would have to help him understand why her father had made elemental errors. He wanted her to see that it was in her and her father's best interests to help him gain control of the company. Harrison had a reputation to protect, and he had a bridge to build.

'It is my father you should be showing around.'

'You are his daughter.'

Rather than continue to meet Jack's penetrating stare, Emma's gaze swept around the site. Despite the cold, there were a good number of men here, working away. She gasped slightly as she saw Davy Newcomb clumping across the yard. The young boy gave a cheerful wave.

'What is he doing here?' Emma turned to Jack in astonishment as Dr Milburn's warning crowded back into her brain. She had been so caught up in last night that she had nearly forgotten who Jack was, and how he'd earned his reputation. 'Surely he is injured?'

'I have found him work to do.' Jack gave a slight shrug, as if the boy's condition mattered little. 'This site has no place for slackers or layabouts.'

Emma struggled to control the indignation growing in her breast. Davy Newcomb should not be here. It was wrong of Jack to force him to work. Did Jack consider this appropriate business practice? Forcing injured men to work or become unemployed? 'But he sprained his leg. He should be resting. You should not have had him back here. He is in danger.'

'His family cannot afford for him to rest. He is the only breadwinner, although his mother does take in laundry.' Jack stared at her, his dark eyes hardening. 'What would you have me do—

make sure his family starve at this time of year? You surpris
me, Miss Harrison, with your unchristian spirit.'

'That is not what I said.' Emma put her hands on her hips, pre
paring to argue. She did not want to think about his sudden re
version to the more formal use of her name. All she knew wa
that Jack Stanton was in the wrong. Davy Newcomb should no
be here. He was a danger to himself and to the other men. 'It i
not the way my father runs his business.'

'I am in charge here, until your father recovers enough to tak
back the reins. Permit me to run this building site as I see fit.
Jack turned on his heel and strode away towards the office.

'But…but…you have to understand about the men's goo
will,' Emma said to his uncompromising back. She gritted he
teeth. High-handed. Arrogant. And totally sure of himself.

He had to see that having the lad back was folly of the wors
sort. Bad for morale. Bad for Davy Newcomb. Bad for Harriso
and Lowe. Emma bit her lip, torn between following him an
continuing her protest and finding out the truth. There was
chance that she could undo the damage he had inadvertentl
caused.

'I will speak to him and let him know that his position is safe
Let him know how Harrison and Lowe truly treats its employ
ees,' Emma called after him.

Jack stopped and slowly turned. His face was hewn from
granite and his eyes were cold. 'As you wish.'

Emma hurried over to where Davy had stopped to readjus
his crutch as he balanced a sheaf of papers in one hand. 'Are
you all right, Davy? Is your leg healing?'

'Yes, Miss Harrison, I fare well enough with this here crutch.
The boy pushed his cap back and gave her a cheeky grin. 'I don'
aim to fall down no more cliffs, ma'am, if that was what you
were worried about. Right brave I thought you were, to climb

own as well as the gaffer. 'Course I didn't know he was the gaffer then, like.'

'Your leg, does it pain you much? Particularly after working ere?'

'Could be better, could be worse,' Davy replied with a shrug.

'But why are you here? Surely you should be at home, recovering?'

'The gaffer has given me some jobs to do. Important ones they re, too!' The note of pride in Davy's voice was unmistakable. Ie shifted his weight and stood a little taller. 'He came by the ouse t'other day and had a little chat with me mam. Told her vhat a fine young man I was shaping up to be.'

Emma glanced over towards Jack, who was busy issuing rders to some of the men. Her fist clenched around her reticule. Ie had taken it upon himself to go see Davy and his family. It /as not the way her father ran his business.

'You should be at home,' she tried again. 'Your leg needs to eal properly before you come back to work. You and your nother must not worry, Davy. There will be a place for you here vhen your leg is better. The Newcombs have worked for Iarrison and Lowe for as long as I can remember. First your randfather, then your father, and now you.'

'Miss, please don't send me away.' Davy caught her sleeve nd looked up at her with pleading eyes. 'We need the money, ke, and it is far warmer in the office than it is at home.'

'I am sure the company can arrange something.' Emma moothed her skirts. 'My father is here today. I will have a quiet /ord with him. You will not starve.'

'The Newcombs don't accept charity.' Davy drew himself up his full height. 'I knows you mean well and all, miss, but the affer and I have it sorted.'

Davy clumped away down the hill. Emma watched him go

with mixed emotions. Had she made a mistake? Had she been too quick to judge? She pressed her fingertips into the bridge of her nose, trying to think. She needed to have answers, and fast

'Did you learn anything from your conversation with Davy?' Jack said as she went into the back office. He did not move from his place behind her father's desk. His eyes could have been smooth black marble, and his voice held a distinct chill to it.

'We have been having a discussion. The lad is as obstinate as you.'

'I shall take that as a compliment.'

Emma crossed her arms, stared back at him. She would get to the truth of the matter. 'Why is he here? The boy is injured He should be home, resting!'

'Have you tried to make him rest? Do you know why he is here? Do you care about that? Or did you simply leap to conclusions and find me guilty? Pretty little assumptions that fit neatly into your view of the world.' He placed both hands on the desk and stood up. His eyes burnt. Emma took a step backwards as she became aware of the anger he was holding back 'Let me know when you are ready to listen, and then maybe we can speak.'

'No... I....' Emma put her hand to her throat as she remembered Davy's words—he would not accept charity. She had gone about this all wrong. She dropped her gaze and concentrated on her glove's pearl button. She swallowed hard, aware his burning gaze was on her. 'I am sorry. You are right. I have no idea why Davy Newcomb is working here today. But he should not be here. It is not the way my father's company does business.'

'Emma Harrison, you are the most infuriating woman!'

'I know. I have to be.' She put her hands on her hips. 'My father's workers matter to me. They are part of the family. We ave a duty towards them. I have no wish for that boy to be rippled for life. He has a mother and siblings to support.'

Suddenly his face softened; the lines became less harsh. 'Miss Harrison, can we talk about this sensibly? Shouting like fish-vives will do neither of us any good.'

She tilted her head to one side. A fishwife! Was that how he saw her? 'No, you are right. I have no wish to be regarded as someone vulgar. No doubt Mudge and my father can hear us.'

'I suspect they can hear you down on the quayside with great ase.' A smile broke over his face. 'And me as well.'

Her breath caught in her throat. No man had the right to look hat handsome or be that infuriating. She had to meet him halfway. She had to show him that she could listen. It was her only hope of getting him to understand about the necessity of hanging the bridge's line.

'I will listen,' she said quietly. 'I am ready to hear your ex-planation.'

Jack pressed his palms against the desk. When he spoke, he poke clearly, emphasising each word as one would to a child.

'Davy Newcomb is here because he wants to be here. It is his hoice, freely made.'

'But he is in pain. He cannot serve as an apprentice with a urt leg. You should never have allowed it.'

'We came to a mutually beneficial arrangement.' A very uperior expression crossed his face. 'It has solved several roblems.'

'But he can't work. You are asking the poor lad to fail, and if e fails he will find it difficult to get other work.' Emma strug-led to keep her voice calm. She had to put her objections in a manner that Jack would understand. 'The company cannot fford to carry someone who does not work properly. He will e a danger to himself and to others on the site.'

'And I say he can work!' Jack struck the desk with his open palm. 'Allow me to decide who is and who is not a danger on this site. I run this site my way.'

She swallowed hard. She'd have to leave the argument for later, but she knew she was right. Davy should be at home resting. 'I will *naturally* have to defer to you. You are currently in charge here.'

'You will.' His eyes softened. 'If it makes you feel better, Davy has left Harrison and Lowe's employ.'

Emma stared at him, uncomprehending. 'He is here on site working.'

'He works for me and me alone.'

Chapter Nine

'I am not sure I understand,' Emma said carefully as she stared at Jack. One part of her mind took in the small details, like how his long fingers rested against the desk, the slight curl of his black hair and the intent expression of his eyes, while the other part kept turning over and over the information. He had given Davy Newcomb a job. A job! 'He already has a job. He works for Harrison and Lowe as an apprentice.'

'No, he doesn't.' Jack stood up. He hooked his fingers into the pocket of his waistcoat. 'As you rightly said, Harrison and Lowe has no position for someone who is injured. He would be a danger to the others.'

The ribbons that tied Emma's bonnet threatened to choke her. He had dismissed Davy, and then hired him. Why? It made no sense. She wanted to hate Jack, but Davy was here, and clearly loving what he was doing. 'Why should you want to employ him? You already have a valet.'

'He is not my valet. Nor is he my personal servant.'

'Then what is he?'

'My personal assistant.'

'You have taken Davy on as your personal assistant?'

'I need assistance here. Little jobs. Jobs that require a quick mind and willing hands. It seemed the perfect solution to the problem.' His lips curved upwards. 'To both our problems. I went to see him the day you came to the site about the goose list. You were right that day. I should have gone before.'

Emma flattened her hands against her skirts as her insides twisted. She had done him a grave injustice. His solution for Davy Newcomb was extremely practical. The boy and his family would not accept charity, and yet he could not do heavy building work. Sensible. Practical. 'I misjudged your intention, Mr Stanton, and I deeply regret my earlier words. They were thoughtless. Please forgive me.'

'Sometimes the solution to a problem comes in unexpected ways.' He held out his hand, a strong hand, with tapering fingers. 'Shall we start again, Miss Harrison? Shall we be friends? Work together instead of against each other?'

'Start again?' She put her fingertips against his, felt his fingers curl around hers for a brief instant before she withdrew. Friends. That was all, and she would have to remember that. "I think can agree to that. I welcome your friendship.'

He gave a smile. 'It is good to know that you have decided to trust me and my judgement.'

Her insides squirmed. If she truly trusted him she'd tell him about the mistakes in the calculations, and her father's illness, but to do that would mean exposing everything. How would he react? What damage would it do to her father's reputation? D Milburn's warning about Jack's underhanded business practice still resounded in her ears. Could she really trust Jack Stanton to behave honourably when serious business was involved? She'd wait and see if there was an opening, a way she could explain. See how their friendship grew.

'What exactly are Davy's duties?' she asked with a bright smile, changing the subject. Once she knew more, she could decide. 'He appeared laden down with equipment and charts.'

'There are measurements that need to be done. Experiments I want rechecked. Davy is ideally placed to do them. He is bright, and willing to work.' He nodded towards Davy, who had reappeared with several different instruments. 'If he proves as able as I think, I am quite willing to help him train as a mechanical engineer. The Empire needs more. Progress demands it.'

'Why do you need to do experiments?' Emma forced her voice to stay calm.

'I have found it best to make sure of everything. Both Brunel and I agree on the matter. Attention to detail ensures the success of a project.'

Emma's breath stopped. Was this a solution to her problem? Could she explain where her father had gone wrong without seeming to criticise him? Ask that Jack repeat the experiments, repeat the calculations?

'I...that is...my father undertook a series of experiments before the bridge was designed. Wind speeds, flooding, and looking at the bedrock.' She hesitated, wrinkling her nose. There had to be a way of explaining this. 'It is possible that one or two needed more data. My father was ill earlier in the year...'

Jack schooled his features. Emma had helped with the experiments. That piece of information did not surprise him in the least, particularly not after what he had read. The question was, who had made the errors? They were simple, and easily made, but the fact remained that Edward Harrison should have caught them. Unless... He dismissed the idea as preposterous. Had

Harrison been the one to make the mistake, and was Emma covering for him?

It would appear Emma Harrison had definitely developed an interest in civil engineering. She knew the correct terminology, and the bridge design did show her distinctive handwriting.

'I was not happy with everything I read,' he said carefully. 'It would appear a few mistakes were made. Perhaps not enough attention was paid…'

'The greatest care and attention was paid to the experiments.' She tilted her chin upwards, the blue in her eyes deepened to a flame. 'It is the way my father has always done things.'

'I am not accusing your father of anything.' Jack held up his hand, stopping her words. She had raised her defences. He would have to find another way to get to the truth. 'Through long experience I have learnt to conduct my own, rather than rely on another's interpretation of the facts. Mistakes happen when one least expects it. Numbers can get transposed.'

She started, and her eyes became wary. She trailed the toe of her shoe along the dusty floor. 'It could happen.'

'I think it might have here, but I have to be certain. Much depends on getting the location right. I have decided to take the cautious approach. The current weather has given us time.'

'You are going ahead with the present course, then?' Her voice was quite small.

'Yes, for the moment. But you were right to ask for another survey. It does show that the ground might be better if the line was moved away from the castle keep. A few simple calculation errors in the original document.'

Jack watched Emma's face become animated. It was as if he had given her a diamond bracelet. Or a load had rolled off her back. He had not been able to sleep last night, and he had read the report. He had also seen the neat notations Emma had made in the margins. Those calculations were accurate, unlike the ones he had questions about.

Exactly who had made those first calculations? It seemed incredible that the Edward Harrison he knew would make such a basic error.

'Do you mean that?'

'Nothing is certain.' Jack ran his hand through his hair. More than ever he wanted to make her smile like that again, but this time at him, because of him, not because of the bridge.

'But you will retain the keep? It is important. It is a symbol, and symbols matter.' She had pressed her hands under her chin, and her eyes were shining.

'I cannot promise anything, but the river appears slightly narrower, and it is possible that we could have seven piers in the water instead of the nine that your father originally planned. Nine is just too many. It will add to the cost enormously.'

'I see.' Emma spoke around a tight lump in her throat. She should be happy that Jack was even considering moving the bridge. But he was also changing the design, and it appeared that he planned on being here much longer than she had first anticipated. Was this something else that he'd forgotten to tell her?

Exactly what did her father and Jack have planned? She should be furious, but her heart was rejoicing. She wanted to spend time with Jack. After last night, when she had danced in Jack's arms and then his lips had touched hers, it seemed as if the world had become a different place, bright—sparkling with the possibility of adventure.

She had lived too long in her own safe world, with limited horizons. Suddenly her future horizons appeared vast and enticing. She concentrated on filling her lungs with air. She had to be cautious and not say too much. The last thing she wanted was to reveal everything, to ruin everything.

She had to remember that Jack Stanton had the potential to be her enemy. She had been wrong about Davy, but she had no firm idea about his intentions towards Harrison and Lowe. One wrong word, one slip, and she knew the vultures would start to circle. How many companies had he swallowed on the way to his fortune? But he was moving the line of the bridge.

'Seven arches instead of nine, but the design would remain the same?' she said, struggling to keep the excitement from her voice.

'It is a good solid design, despite the unusual combination of iron and concrete.'

'It is important to get this bridge right.'

'I plan on having it standing…' Jack paused and his smile broadened '…for at least the next one hundred and sixty years.'

'One hundred and sixty years?'

'Yes. Think of what someone might think in 2007 as their train passes over this bridge.'

Emma stared across the grey water moving under the low-level bridge. She tried to see her bridge and think what Newcastle might look like then. She screwed up her eyes and shook her head.

'I can't think that far ahead. It is beyond my capability to think that far in the future.'

'Think of your great-great-grandchildren riding on a train crossing the bridge.' He leant forward, pointed, his eyes alight with a hidden fire. 'Can you see it now, Miss Emma? The lit carriages? The girl with her nose in a book? What do you think she is thinking about? Do you think she even wonders how the bridge got here, or suspects you might have had something to do with it?'

Emma looked, but all she noticed was how close Jack was, and the shape of his mouth. One kiss stolen and she was hinking about more. She had to stop building bridges in clouds. Bridges needed firm ground and strong foundations. With Jack, here and now, she felt as if she were about to slip over a precipice.

'I am unmarried,' Emma replied quickly. She was a spinster. There would be no children, let alone great-great-grandchildren. The thought depressed her. She had wanted children once.

'Miracles do sometimes happen.'

'Not those sorts of miracles, Mr Stanton.'

Emma toyed with her glove. If she allowed herself, she would start to build iron bridges in the air. Marriage was something she had given up hope of long ago, when she had decided it was far more important for her mother to spend her last years being looked after by someone who loved her. And by the time she had died Emma had become aware that such opportunities had passed her by. Men were interested in younger, prettier women, not women who read books on civil engineering and were inclined to speak their mind.

'Are you not being hard on your prospects? You may meet someone one of these days. Such a thing is not beyond the realms of possibility.'

'As I have said before, Mr Stanton, I enjoy being a spinster. It gives me freedom.' Emma raised her chin and directly met his gaze. 'I am not looking for anything beyond friendship.'

'Who are you trying to convince, Miss Harrison?'

The wind ruffled his hair slightly, sending it across his forehead. Emma's fingers itched to touch it. She forced her body to turn. She gazed out at the swiftly moving river.

'You are relying on Davy's help,' Emma said firmly. 'Are you sure he can do this with his leg?'

'He has a very quick mind. I think he will make a first-rate civil engineer if he gets the schooling he needs.' Jack put his hands on his hips. 'I intend to impress on him the benefits of education, night school. He can work and learn.'

'Are you planning on remaining in Newcastle for a long time, then?' Emma disliked the way her insides trembled. She was torn. She wanted him to stay, but not at the risk of losing her father's company.

'Somebody has to oversee the bridge and co-ordinate the building of the central railway station,' came the enigmatic reply.

'But my father will be well soon.'

'I do hope so.'

Emma watched a plume of breath come from Jack's mouth. 'I have some books—old schoolbooks. I could give them to Davy. They are cluttering up the schoolroom my sister and I used.'

'He will refuse anything that gives the slightest impression of charity. It would have to be skilfully done, but it is a good thought.'

Emma bit her lip as she watched Davy determinedly cross the yard. 'What do you suggest? I would like to do something for him, to encourage him.'

Jack was silent for a moment. The sun sparkled off the white frost, dazzling her eyes. Emma pulled her bonnet more firmly on her head.

'Are you familiar with German Christmas trees?' he asked at last.

'Yes, they have reached Newcastle—just.' Emma gave a small laugh. 'My father and I put one on the table in the drawing room last Christmas Eve. I have ordered one from the confectioner's already for this year. It is to have oranges, lemons and sugar-iced grapes on it. But what do Christmas trees have to do with Davy not accepting charity?'

'A party I attended at the London Mission Hall last year had an exhibition of German Christmas trees—trees of love. At the end of the party the presents adorning the trees, and one or two below, were handed out.'

'It is just perfect.' Emma clapped her hands together, her mind quickly turning the idea over. She could almost see the scene before her. 'Why hadn't I thought of it? I can remember reading about it in the *Illustrated London News*. Is there time? The feast is less than two weeks away.'

'If you will find the presents, I believe I can find the tree. And I think a tree as large as the hall at the Institute of Mechanical Engineers can take, rather than a series of small pinetops. Shall we do it, Miss Emma? Will you work with me on this project?'

'Consider it done.' Emma's mind raced. She tried to list everything that needed to be done. She had been wrong. He had changed. It was such a lovely thought to do that for Davy and the others. It would allow them to accept a bit of charity. 'I will get a list from Mrs Mudge and Mrs Newcomb. They will have an idea about what the children might need.'

'It would not have to be elaborate. Nuts and fruit go down well.'

'And I can ask my father to play Old Christmas now that he is more fully recovered. He can hand the presents out. There is a green robe somewhere in the attic, and I can easily find a Yule log to strap to his back. I am sure Mrs Newcomb can fashion him a holly crown.'

'I can see your father as Old Christmas somehow. His hair is the right colour, and he is thin enough.'

'I can't think why I did not think of this before. It will make a capital end to the feast.' Emma clasped her hands together, resisting the urge to throw her arms about him.

'Sometimes we need others' help to achieve our dreams.'

Emma stared at him. His eyes glittered with banked fire, though his hand was loosely wrapped around the ebony head of his cane. The words had a deeper meaning. Did he understand about the bridge?

'This was supposed to be a tour of the site.' Her voice sounded strained to her ears, and her insides trembled.

'Why don't I show you some of the experiments? Unless you find such things deadly dull?'

'I would like that.'

Jack's fingers brushed her elbow as she scrambled down the bank. A bolt of heat seemed to pass from him to her. Emma went still, concentrated on breathing. The wind blew the ribbons from her bonnet across her face. She pushed them away, and nearly turned into him. She could see his pearl collar stud. She became aware that they were alone here, without her father. The shouts of the workmen were distant sounds. Her lips ached.

A seagull rose from the river and the spell was broken. She hurried down to the river on her own.

In the cold, the river moved sluggishly, and a faint layer of ice was apparent in the shallows. Emma's eyes widened at the array of instruments. Some of the experiments she had not even considered necessary, but once Jack explained the reasoning, she knew they had to be done. She asked a few questions, and heard the growing note of respect in Jack's voice.

'Some people consider a bridge to be stationary,' Jack said. 'But it is not. Bridges are constantly moving. They need to be able to withstand the stress of changing forces.'

'I know that.'

'There is a world of difference between the practical and the theory. What works in theory may not work in practice.'

'Are you trying to tell me something?' Emma went over and

righted one of the sticks being used to measure the height of flooding.

'Making an observation, that is all.'

'I do understand the practical side of bridge-building,' Emma replied.

'You say you do, but I wonder…'

'You wonder what?'

His eyes flashed with hidden fire, and a mischievous dimple appeared at the corner of his mouth. Emma realised with a start that she had forgotten about the dimple, and the way it showed when he was very pleased about something. 'Would you like to go to the theatre with me?'

'What does the theatre have to do with bridge-building?' Emma's voice sounded breathless. She glanced over her shoulder and saw that they were quite alone by the river. The shouts and cries of the men were distant noise.

'There is an educational pantomime at the Theatre Royal, looking at several bridges and points through history as well as other sights for the amusement of onlookers. We could discuss them.'

'You wish to take me on my own?' Emma said the words slowly. The treat was tempting, but impossible. Surely Jack knew that. They were not even courting, let alone engaged. There was no understanding between them. Exactly what was her father playing at? Having failed with Dr Milburn, was he trying his matchmaking skills again? The temptation was there, but the obstacles were insurmountable.

'I have discussed it with your father. A party will be going. Your friend Lucy Charlton and her husband are included. You will be properly chaperoned.'

'I had no idea you were that well acquainted with Henry Charlton.'

'He has a business that he wishes me to invest in. For old times' sake I have agreed to listen, to hear what he says.'

'But you have your doubts.' She could well remember the drawling tones of Henry when he had first encountered Jack, and the way he had once humiliated Jack over his ready-made suits and strong Newcastle accent. She had been surprised when Lucy had married Henry, but—as Lucy said—she had chosen security and contentment over happiness.

'Why would you say that?' Jack's eyes had taken on a granite look.

'You were hardly friends. It surprises me that he seeks to draw on past acquaintance in that way.'

'I thought you had forgotten everything that happened seven years ago.' He tilted his head to one side. 'I had barely any recollection of him.'

'I had put it from my mind, but I do remember the way Henry Charlton behaved. It bothered me how some of them treated you. I never liked him very well after that. It is only because I am so fond of Lucy that we remain friends.'

'I cannot change the past, Miss Harrison. But I can change the future. It is the future that concerns me, not the past. I will invest if the business plan shows promise.'

And where do I belong? Emma longed to ask. *What we shared last night—was that linked to the past or the future?*

Instead she swallowed hard and pressed her gloved fingers together. She had to contain her emotions. She had to look at this dispassionately, as no doubt he was.

'You have discussed this trip and the pantomime with my father and others. Is there anything else you have committed me to that I should know about?'

'I am not in the habit of betraying confidences, Emma. Perhaps you can enlighten me. What else should I be planning to do?' His eyes twinkled with some unseen mischief. 'Put mistletoe in your hair? Forgive me, Emma, but I don't think you would take kindly to that happening to you twice.'

'I have no idea.' Emma clutched her reticule more tightly and resolutely turned her gaze from his mouth. Even the mere mention of the kiss caused a ripple of warmth to infuse her body. 'I shall have to see if my father is too ill…'

'Your father has recovered quickly for a man of his age and disposition.'

'He loves speaking about engineering. I am sure your being here has helped with his recovery.'

'His enthusiasm is infectious. I know I caught it from him many years ago,' Jack replied. 'Now, will you give me your answer? Will you cement our new-found friendship with a trip to the pantomime?'

Friendship. She could trust him with a trip to the pantomime. Emma closed her eyes. But she could not explain about her father and his attacks. Jack still saw him as strong and vigorous. She wanted to trust him, but first she wanted to be sure her instinct was correct. He was very different from the man she had known seven years ago. She had to think about people other than herself. It could wait a little while yet. 'That is the reason you are asking me—friendship?'

'What other reason could there be?' His eyes searched her face, stopped at her mouth. 'I wish this war between us to end.'

'Hardly a war.'

'You appear intent on seeing the worst in me.'

'Not the worst.' Emma tightened her hand around her muff. 'I have apologised about jumping to the wrong conclusions about Davy.'

'If you have no objections to my personage and my offer of friendship, why don't you want to go?'

She was very neatly trapped. Keeping her father's illness a secret was far more important than wondering why Jack had invited her. Emma inclined her head. 'In the spirit of friendship and new starts, I will go. You have given me the assurance that I will be properly chaperoned, and it has been a while since I have seen a pantomime at Christmas.'

The dimple reappeared by Jack's mouth. 'Look on it as an educational experience, Miss Emma. A way to improve your mind. You might learn something.'

'Father, what game are you playing?' Emma asked Edward Harrison the minute they climbed in the carriage and the wheels started turning. 'Why did you leave me alone with Jack Stanton? Surely Mudge did not need you for that long? This is not another of your matchmaking schemes, is it? I have told you before, I am quite happy with my life.'

'I have no idea what you are talking about.' Her father turned his mild blue eyes towards her. 'Daughter, did you not enjoy your tour? You were gone a long time with Jack Stanton, and I waited for you, not the other way around.'

'We were looking at his experiments.' Emma laid the muff on her lap. 'He is not satisfied with some of the calculations and wants to do them himself. They may take some time.'

'He wants a reason to stay in Newcastle.' There was a smug curve to her father's lips. 'He knows I always take great care over my calculations. They have never been wrong before.'

'I fear you are right, Father. I worry that he wants to take over the bridge construction.' She had said the words, and now she waited for her father's denial.

'There are worse men I could think of,' her father replied, with maddening complacency. 'But I do not believe that is his intention at all.'

'Then what is it?'

'He means to court you, Emma.'

Emma stared in disbelief at her father, willing his eyes to twinkle or the ghost of a smile to appear. Something, anything to show he was in jest. Surely he could not have forgotten about what had happened all those years ago? But his face stayed serious.

'You must not say such things, even in jest. It is impossible. Everything is finished between Jack Stanton and I. It finished years ago.'

She willed her father to believe her. Jack Stanton was not interested in her. He had kissed her last night to prove a point. And he was inviting her to the pantomime because he thought she spent far too much time alone and was frightened of facing society, having suffered from a humiliation.

'This is no joke, nor a merry jape to make the journey home pass quicker, daughter.' Her father's hand enfolded hers. 'I am perfectly in earnest. Do you think I would have left you alone with him last night or today if I'd had the slightest suspicion that his intentions were less than honourable?'

'But he has no intentions. Business occupies his every waking thought.' Emma withdrew her hand, slid it into her muff and clenched her fist. 'Sometimes I wonder if your illness clouds your mind. Soon you will swear you hear wedding bells, when all the sound will be is the bells in St Nicholas's lantern chiming the dinner hour.'

'Daughter, what a thing to say! I can read the signs very well indeed. My mind is as strong as ever it was. You are being purposefully blind.'

Emma tried to ignore the trembling in her stomach. She had to make her father see. He should not harbour such fantasies. She was very glad he had no idea what had passed between Jack and her last night. Luckily it had not gone further.

'Mama's mind wandered at the end.'

'Shall we leave your mother alone? Her affliction was her own, and quite different from the mild chill I suffered.' Her father rapped his cane on the carriage floor. 'No, I am as sound as I ever was, and you, my daughter, are being stubborn.'

Emma looked out of the carriage window at the scene unfolding—the children sliding on the ice, the women hurrying with parcels, the men striding along. A few of the broadsheet salesmen had started their Christmas patter songs. A lump grew in her throat and she swallowed hard, forcing it down. Certain things had to be said before her father utterly ruined her life.

'Have you forgotten, Papa, Jack Stanton left seven years ago without a word?'

'Daughter—' Her father cleared his throat several times.

'Surely I meant more to him than a half-hearted proposal.' Emma turned her gaze back to the scene outside the carriage. 'It was you and Mama who counselled me to wait and see, saying that if he was serious he would send word. He never sent a letter, never gave me the chance to explain about Mama's illness.'

Her father's eyes slid away from her, and he developed a sudden interest in the carriage seat. 'Your dear mama did it for the best, Emma. Sometimes, though, I have lain and wondered what if—particularly in these later years, when you have developed such a gift for engineering. It is too bad that you were not born a man, my daughter. What a civil engineer you would have made!'

'What did my mother do?' Emma bit out each word, and resisted the urge to shake him. She would not be distracted by his civil engineering remarks. She had to know what her mother had done! How had she discouraged her unsuitable suitor? Was there far more to what had happened seven years ago than she first thought?

'Such things are best not spoken of. One never criticises the dead, Emma. Remember that.' He reached out his hand, but Emma ignored his fingers. 'What happened is water under the bridge or grains of sand between the fingers. One can never turn back the hands of time.'

'What did she do? You must tell me!' Emma clasped her hands together in her lap. She wanted to shake her father, to get him to tell her what her mother had done.

'Emma Harrison, keep your voice down. Both the driver and the footman will hear!'

Emma closed her eyes and concentrated on her breathing. By the time she felt she could speak without raising her voice the carriage had arrived back in Jesmond, and Fackler had come out to greet them. She waited until her father had sat down in front of the drawing room fire. She began to pace.

'Emma, you seem disturbed.' Her father held out his hand. 'Did you see something amiss at the site? I must confess Jack Stanton keeps it in better order than ever I dared hope.'

'What did Mama do, Father? You will not fob me off by speaking about the bridge. I know you too well.' Emma stood in front of him and placed her hands on her hips. 'I have a right to know.'

'Her sole thought was your future happiness.' Her father did not meet her eyes. 'She had no inkling, of course, about who Jack Stanton would become. Neither of us did. She thought him a fine enough young man, but beneath her daughter. You have to remember that Claire had just married a baronet. She had high hopes for you—very high hopes. A member of the aristocracy, or failing that someone who had land and wealth. Someone who would keep our youngest in the style she should have been. Someone to appreciate you.'

'She thought of no one but herself.' Emma put her muff down

on the small table. She tried to control the cold anger that flooded over her. Her father might like to pretend, but she had known her mother's faults. She had still loved her, but had known what she was like. 'You know how selfish she was, how ambitious. It was never for me or Claire, but for her own position. She wanted a title. She never forgave you for being a second son.'

'You should not speak of your mother in that way! She loved you, and wanted the best for you. Her daughters meant everything for her. The sacrifices she made…' Her father's eyes held a slight glint of tears. 'She had her faults, but she loved you.'

'We both know what a snob she was, Papa.' The words came tumbling out of a place deep within Emma, a place she had thought hidden well, but once she had begun she had to continue. 'Why try to deny it? She may have loved Claire and me, but ultimately she wanted that title. She never asked me what I wanted.'

'It is the job of parents to make sure their offspring marry the correct people—people they would be suitable for, not ones for whom they have a passing fancy.'

Emma breathed deeply. Perhaps her father was speaking the truth. She knew her parents' marriage had been a love-match, but one that had not lived up to her mother's expectations.

'Tell me what she did, Papa. Why do you feel guilty? You know I loved my mother, but I wasn't blind to her faults. And I loved her all the more because of them.'

'I grow weary, Emma.' Her father passed a hand over his brow. 'I fear this morning's inspection took a great deal out of me. You were right earlier. I was foolish to abandon the tonic.'

'I shall get some right away.' Emma rang for the butler, obtained the tonic, and poured out the correct dose. 'You must be careful, Father. You must do as Dr Milburn says.'

'You are a good daughter, Emma.' He patted her hand. 'We shall speak no more of this. Your mother did what she felt she had to do.'

Emma gritted her teeth and allowed the conversation to drift. There had to be another way of finding out why her father felt guilty. It was something to do with Jack's proposal of seven years ago.

Chapter Ten

A fter her father had settled down with the day's papers, his tonic and a glass of sherry, Emma left him in the drawing room and hurried into the morning room, where her mother's old desk stood. She tapped her fingers against the rosewood. Her father was definitely hiding something—something that her mother had done.

She had gone through her mother's letters when she died, and there had been nothing about Jack Stanton there. She would have remembered. Her mother had been meticulous about noting everything down, keeping a log of correspondence. But her father felt guilty about something—guilt that Jack's return had sparked.

Had Jack sent something? A letter explaining why he'd left without waiting for her final answer, perhaps? It could explain so many things.

She made a wry face. If he had, it had vanished a long time

ago. A small fire crackled in the fireplace, sending out a little bit of warmth. It would not yield up any secrets. She hated to think how long ago the ashes from any letter would have been taken out.

A surge of anger swept through her. What right had her mother had to make that sort of decision? Emma had been eighteen when Jack had made his offer. She should have trusted her.

Emma pressed her hands against her forehead. She had chosen the course of duty. Chosen it before Jack had asked. Her mother had been ill, deathly ill. They had only expected her to last a few months, but she had lingered for years. Her mother had had the right to expect a nurse, someone who loved her, and Claire had already been married.

Jack had simply not waited for an explanation, just stormed off. And if he hadn't been able to bear to wait for that, would he have waited for her? The 'few months' her mother had had left had turned into years. Long years where she had learnt the value of using her mind and thinking—something her mother had encouraged her to do, as it kept her near at hand. She might have resented her mother, and her demands, but they had grown closer, and in the end her mother had approved of her chosen path.

Emma slapped her hand against the smooth wood of the desk. She lived in the real world—one not populated by romantic imaginings but punctuated by precise calculations.

Her hand had hit a tiny carved rosebud on the back of the desk, and Emma was sure she'd heard a distinct click. She opened the top and looked. A panel was slightly pushed out. She started to push it back, and then paused, got out a paperknife, and pulled.

A bundle of papers fell out, tied in a blue ribbon. Like a ghost, the faint lavender scent of her mother's perfume wafted through the room, tickling her nose and making her recall the sound of her mother's laughter and her lightning-quick wit. Emma's heart constricted at the unexpectedness of the memory.

Emma's hand trembled, and she concentrated on the letters. She sorted through them quickly, searching for Jack's signature. Then smiled at her own actions. What had she expected? A letter like in some penny-blood? They were all simple correspondence between Mama and her best friend. But why had she shoved them in the secret compartment? What secret had she wanted to hide from Emma?

Emma rescanned the letters—mostly domestic happenings and crises that had once seemed insurmountable and insoluble. A single sheet of paper was dated from seven years ago. The writing was crossed to save money. Emma turned the paper to read the continuation of the letter.

Her eye stopped, and she reread the next to last paragraph.

You did the right thing, Margaret, with that letter—what the heart doesn't know, the heart doesn't grieve over. Emma will get over Jack Stanton in a few months' time. You did what you had to, my dear. Be proud of it. Your daughter will thank you, given time.

Emma rechecked the date. It was a few weeks after Jack's proposal, after she had asked for time to consider. She had had no other serious offer at the time. Jack must have sent a letter, and her mother had intercepted it.

For a long time, Emma sat stunned. Then she noticed the cold creeping up her fingers as the fire burnt down to a pile of ash and the daylight started to fade.

Jack obviously thought she had received his letter and decided not to reply.

Emma looked at the wavering words again. What could she

ay? She had no idea what she would have done if she *had* received the letter. Had her mother even broken the seal, or had he simply recognised the handwriting and burnt the letter?

There was little point in asking her father. She did not want to risk another scene. She had no desire to bring on an attack, have her father gasping for breath and Dr Milburn called to administer his pills. No, she refused to take the risk.

There was no point wasting time wondering what might have been. Because it wasn't—never could be. She had to live in the present, not dwell in the past.

Emma pressed her hands to her forehead. She had to consider that seven years was a long time. The girl she'd been then bore little relation to the woman she had become. The Jack Stanton who had shown her around the building site was not the man who had asked her to marry him and then left without a word.

'Emma, what are you doing sitting alone? Has your father taken a turn for the worse?'

Emma hurriedly stuffed the letter under the blotting paper as Jack came into the room. He had changed from his work clothes, and his cream trousers once again showed the perfect crease. His cravat was immovably tied. The casual observer would think him a man of leisure, never suspecting that he had been clambering over stone and rock earlier.

'I was thinking.' Emma covered the letter with another sheet of paper. She would burn it later. There was little point in keeping it, or the dressmaking bills her mother had stuffed in the secret door.

'About anything in particular? There is a crease between your eyebrows. Have you found something else in the Goose Club list to perplex you?'

'Nothing important.' Emma smoothed her forehead. 'I had a bit of a pounding head earlier and took a tisane.'

'You look as if you have been crying.'

Emma scrubbed the back of her hand over her eyes. 'A trick of the light.'

She moved to go out of the room. Her nerves were too raw. She wanted to blurt out what she had learnt, but it would only make matters worse. And how could she excuse her mother's behaviour? The inescapable fact remained that their courtship had been doomed from the start seven years ago.

'If there is anything I can do,' Jack said quietly. 'I am willing to help. Trust me.'

The words were tempting. Emma longed to lay her head against his chest and confess all—confess to the wasted years and the times when she had longed to be anywhere but here. Except it was not possible. She could not betray her past or her mother's machinations. Her mother had acted the way she had because she'd felt it right.

Jack raised an eyebrow, and Emma realised that silence had grown between them. Something needed to be said before she blurted out the sorry tale.

'The cook will shortly have supper ready.' Emma opted for a brave smile. 'I trust you will be joining my father and me?'

'I would like that very much.'

Still he did not move, but stood there. Emma remembered the way his hands had held her last night, and the way he had taken the time to describe his experiments this morning. She could feel the heat increase on her cheeks and hoped he would think it was because she was standing close to the fire.

'And, Mr Stanton…I am looking forward to the pantomime.' She smiled and lifted her shoulders slightly. 'It strikes me that I may have sounded ungracious before.'

He was silent for a while. 'I have never thought you ungracious.'

'You lie exceedingly charmingly. I was certainly ungracious when you appeared the other day.' Emma tucked a stray lock of hair behind her ear, fought against the warmth building inside her. 'I was preoccupied, not to mention annoyed at being caught in one of my oldest dresses.'

'It most certainly did not show off your charms as well as the ballgown you wore last night. Had I seen you in that first, I would never have believed you an acid-tongued spinster.'

'But now you do?'

'I know you for what you are.' Jack's gaze held her. She noticed how his eyes had taken on a slightly deeper, richer hue. They were the sort of eyes a person could drown in.

She forced her gaze onto the blotting paper, reminded herself of what lay underneath and why there were so many things between them—too many things. 'But you thought me a terribly interfering biddy when we first met at the bridge.'

Jack gave a short laugh. 'You were doing your best under difficult circumstances.'

'And you were right to step in. The building site positively rang with activity this morning.' The words seem to stick in her throat. Did he understand how much it cost her to say those words? 'I am grateful you are looking again at the line for the bridge. The bridge means so much to my father. Since my mother died, it is all that he has to occupy his attention.'

Jack's face betrayed nothing, but Emma thought she detected a slight softening of his eyes.

'The men reacted to your father's presence. They know who signs their pay cheques. He appears well recovered from his chill. One of these days he may consider remarrying.'

'My father?' Emma stared at Jack in astonishment. First Lucy at the ball, and now Jack. Surely they had to realise that her father had no intention of doing such a thing? But that fact

would be impossible to explain without telling them about her
father's illness and how Dr Milburn had said that there was very
little hope. She regarded her hands. 'My father has no plans to
remarry—none whatsoever.'

He paused and his eyes grew warm. 'Should you ever need a
friendly ear, Emma...'

'I shall remember we are friends,' she said slowly, compre
hension dawning. He thought she was upset because her
father wanted to pay court to some woman and her own
position in the house might be in jeopardy. It was ironic, but
it saved her from having to explain the truth. She made sure
her back was rigid. 'I value your friendship highly, Mr
Stanton. I always did.'

'Yes, friends.' There was a bittersweetness to Jack's smile. 'I
think you may say we are friends once again, Emma.'

'It is good to have a friend...Jack.' She felt very daring as she
said his name, but it would go no further than that—light flirtation between friends, never anything beyond—as much as she
might wish it. There was too much history between them, too
many secrets. Even last night belonged to the past, and she had
to keep her face to the future.

He paused with his hand on the doorframe, his dark eyes inscrutable. 'And, Emma, don't look back. Keep your face forward. The past is done and the future is yet to be.'

'Papa, are you sure you will be fine? Fackler has orders to
send for me if anything should go amiss, or if you should start
to feel under the weather.' Emma fastened a short cloak around
her shoulders in preparation for her visit to the theatre. She was
tingling with anticipation. The theatre—and most of all Jack.

Her father stood in the hallway, dressed in his silk dressing
gown and carrying the latest news journals in his hand. Emma

frowned. His face seemed pale, but it could be because he was wearing a burgundy silk dressing gown.

'Stop your fussing, Emma. I am as fit as I ever was. The cold was a blasted nuisance, but you shall see in the New Year…' Her father gestured towards the door with his paper. 'Go out and enjoy yourself. You know I dislike having several nights out in a week. I trust Lucy Charlton and that husband of hers will prove more than adequate chaperones.'

He gave a slight cough and pulled his dressing gown tighter around his body.

'Perhaps you should not have gone to the bridge two days ago.' Emma tilted her head. 'I could have reported back.'

'Perhaps you should pay attention to your own business. I wanted to see what Jack Stanton was up to. Satisfy my curiosity. See if he remained faithful to the ways I taught him.' Her father tapped the side of his nose. 'Besides, it would not have been proper for you to go on your own.'

'You let me go before.'

'I had no choice. And I had assumed you took Fackler or Annie. A woman's reputation reflects on her family, and in this case on the company. A man's private life shows the world how he conducts himself.' Her father held out his hands. 'Emma, I do want what is best for you.'

What *was* best for her? What she wanted, or what her father considered best? The clock struck eight, and Emma knew she did not have the time to argue.

'And do you approve of Jack Stanton's methods?' she asked, changing the subject away from her future. 'I thought the site looked clean and industrious.'

'There is not much one can do in the frost, but Stanton seems to have found work for everyone who wishes it.' Her father went over to the barometer, gave it a tap. 'If it gets much colder there will be snow, and skating on the pond. You used to enjoy such things. I can remember you and your sister coming back with rosy cheeks and pink noses.'

'That was a long time ago.' Emma's hand stilled, and she regarded her father in the looking glass.

'But I remember.' Her father put a hand on her shoulder 'Here is Stanton. His tailor does right by him, don't you think?'

Emma turned her head and saw Jack coming down the stairs. No man had the right to look that good. It was not the clothes making the man, but the man making the clothes. The deep black of his evening suit fitted his colouring perfectly.

'Ah, Miss Emma, you are ready for your *educational* evening?'

'As ready as I will ever be.'

'You will find it amusing, I promise you.'

The pantomime *had* been amusing, and Emma had to admit that the company had been entertaining. She had not realised that Henry Charlton knew quite a bit about engineering as well as finance. His plan for a new engine was sound. He and Jack had spent a good deal of time discussing it, and possible modifications. Jack had agreed to look at the plans in greater detail if Henry supplied them.

'You look pensive,' Jack said now, as they waited in the Theatre Royal's portico for the carriage. A few of the Christmas broadsheet patterers could be heard singing out the verses of carols, hoping to entice the theatregoers to buy their wares. 'God Rest Ye Merry Gentlemen' vied with 'The First Nowell', a raucous but not discordant noise, somehow giving the usually austere portico a taste of the festive spirit. 'Or have you laughed too much? I know I heard a distinctly unladylike snort coming from your direction when Punch appeared.'

'There may have been.'

Emma's smile turned to a frown as she watched a ragged girl offer a sprig of holly to several of the theatregoers. Most were too busy adjusting their coats and bonnets to pay much attention.

'Something is troubling you.'

'How do you know?'

'Your brow has become furrowed and your expression intent.'

'It seems a shame that so many have so little.' Emma nodded towards the little flower girl.

'You cannot save the entire world.'

'I don't intend to, but it makes you think. Particularly at this time of year. I can see the first snowflakes falling.'

Jack gave the girl a coin, and then handed the sprig to Emma with a flourish. The little girl clutched the coin and ran off as fast as her little legs would carry her. 'There, now, does that make you feel better?'

'How much did you give her?'

'Enough to make her evening. She should be able to buy a hot meal or two.' His fingers touched her cheek, making a warmth grow inside her.

'I wish there was more I could do.'

'You are doing something. Or rather your father's company is. The railway bridge is vital to the future prosperity of this city. Without it you would see more children like that little girl. With it, and a proper station, the city prospers.'

'I suppose you are right.' Emma looked after the girl, but she had disappeared into the night.

'I know I am right. Progress will bring prosperity. It is the only way. Think about how far we have come in the last few years.'

'But we could be doing more.'

'At least you saw the girl. You did not pass her by, and you did not offer her charity.'

There was something in Jack's voice that made Emma pause.

'Is that really so important?'

'Yes, charity can destroy the soul. People want to feel valued. That they have given as well as received.' His fingers touched her elbow. 'Ah, here is the carriage.'

Emma kept her skirts carefully away from Jack, and chatted about inconsequential things as the carriage wound its way back to Jesmond, but her body hummed with anticipation. Would he attempt to take her in his arms? What should she do if he did?

In the dim light she could see his hands resting loosely on his cane, his eyes watching her face, watching her mouth. He had to kiss her. She wanted him to. Emma leant forward, her lips parting as the carriage swung into the drive. He put out an arm to stop her falling. Her body brushed his—but she pushed away as her attention became fastened on the light flooding the carriage.

'There's something wrong,' Emma said, and a shiver went down her spine. 'Something is dreadfully wrong.'

'How do you know?'

'Father would never have the lights blazing this brightly at night. He is very mindful of the cost of candles and gas.'

'I am sure it isn't anything.'

Emma leapt from the carriage without waiting for a hand and rushed in. Fackler was there, shaking his head and wringing his hands.

'Something is wrong!' Emma did not bother waiting for any pleasantry. 'What has happened here tonight? You should have sent the carriage for me.'

'We have had to send for Dr Milburn,' Fackler said. 'Your father took a turn for the worse soon after you left. He called for his tonic, drank it, then went rigid.'

'Emma, Emma—are you all right?' Jack's concerned voice broke through her misery. 'Give Miss Emma some space,

Fackler. She needs air. Your news has been a shock, a great shock.'

He put his arm about her shoulder and led her into the parlour. The simple act calmed her, made her see that she had to take control of the situation. She could not give in to temptation and weep.

'My father has taken ill. The servants have summoned Dr Milburn.' Emma was amazed at how calm her voice sounded. But how faraway and distant. She shrugged his arm away, stepped from the warm circle of his embrace. 'I must go to him.'

She staggered a few steps, and was amazed at how light her head seemed. She should have eaten more at supper, but her nerves had been too great. The staircase appeared to grow with each step she took.

Then suddenly she was there, at her father's door. She peered in and heard the steady sound of her father's breathing, saw his form on the bed. At her footsteps, Annie looked up from where she sat and came hurrying over.

'How is he, Annie?'

'Sleeping, miss. Praise be to God, the worst appears to have passed.'

Sleeping. Emma dared breathe again. Her father was sleeping. The fit had passed. She had seen them so many times over the past few weeks. They were always the same. First the fit, and then the long sleep, as if life itself had exhausted him. But afterwards, when he had taken the pills Dr Milburn prescribed, he could remember little of it, and insisted that he was fit and well. 'Thank you, Annie.'

Annie's face creased. 'But, miss, he mustn't see you like this. You are as pale as a ghost. You know how it upsets him if he thinks you are perturbed, particularly after one of his turns.'

Emma put out a hand and held onto the doorframe. 'I am fine. Truly.'

'She is far from fine. She has had a shock and needs to sit down,' Jack said, and his strong arm went around her shoulder, led her out of the room. 'You may come down to the drawing room when you are certain he is settled, Annie, and tell Miss Emma all about it.'

Emma wanted to protest, but her knees were beginning to feel like jelly. She allowed Jack to take her down the stairs. When they reached the drawing room she paused and tried to pull herself together. 'It was the shock of it all. There is no need to fuss and fret.'

'You will do your father no good if you collapse as well. When you have recovered your breath you may go and sit with him for as long as you like.' Jack propelled her to an armchair. 'Fackler, get Miss Emma a brandy.'

'I never drink strong spirits.' Emma put a hand to her head.

'You need something to bring back the roses in your cheeks.'

Jack pressed a crystal balloon glass into her hand, and gave a stern nod. Emma was tempted to refuse, but she did need something. She took a small sip and felt a fiery trail go down the back of her throat. Her nose wrinkled. 'I can't say that I am over-enamoured of it. But I shall look on it as medicine.'

'It will do you good.'

'I suspect I might do better if I took some of Father's tonic.' Emma gripped onto the armchair, ready to stand.

'What exactly is wrong with your father?' Jack's eyes burned into her soul. 'And do not try to tell me that it is a simple chill. It is much more than that. Trust me with your secret, Emma.'

Chapter Eleven

Emma put her hand to her head and sank back down into the chair. The room gently swayed, merged, and then became clearly focused again. All the while the awful truth kept repeating in her head.

He knew!

Jack Stanton knew her father was ill. And he had known for some time. She had thought she was being clever and he had seen through her, toyed with her much as a cat played with a helpless mouse, waiting to see if she would confide in him.

Emma gulped air and tried to fill her lungs. She had to keep her wits and not give way to blind panic. Panic never served anyone. She had always known that she might have to face this one day, and that day had finally arrived. But all her explanations and half-truths vanished. Only the full truth would do.

'Yes, it is,' she said in a small voice. 'Much more than that.'

Her hands gripped the arms of the chair. She looked over his shoulder at the clock ticking. There was a muffled noise as the clock struck the hour, but beyond that silence grew. She tried to explain, but her voice refused to work. The prick of tears behind her eyelids grew stronger. Jack had to understand what she couldn't say. He had to see.

'I want to learn,' Jack said into the silence. 'I want to know, Emma. I want to know what I can do to help.'

Emma averted her head from his penetrating stare, focusing on one of the rivets that held the upholstery to the armchair. Help? Would he be so willing when he knew the full extent? Or would his predatory instinct come out? Her heart whispered that she could trust him. She had seen what he had done for Davy and the little holly-seller. He was a man with compassion in his soul. But her mind recoiled, remembering Dr Milburn's stories of how Jack had obtained his wealth.

A single tear rolled down her cheek. She brushed it away with impatient fingers.

'I am afraid. I have buried one parent in my twenties, and now it appears I shall have to bury my father,' she whispered, trying to keep her teeth from chattering. She looked up and saw compassion mingled with sorrow in his gaze. She swallowed hard and turned her face away, forced her voice to continue on. 'It has been awful living with the knowledge…keeping it from him, from you. I have felt dreadfully alone. There was no one I could turn to.'

'I waited for you to turn to me on your own, but you will have to trust me now.' Jack stood there, solid and real in his evening clothes. 'What ails your father precisely, Emma? Stop shielding him. You are doing him no favours.'

'He has turns.' Emma pressed her hand against her eyes and strove for control of her voice. 'Sometimes he goes rigid and his muscles shake. Afterwards he says that he remembers nothing, and chides me for being overly concerned.'

'When did these turns start? Is there any pattern to them?'

'Oh, God, I don't know.' Her hands curled around and held onto the arms of the chair as her body shook. Then the storm appeared to pass, and she regained control. She knew she could speak.

'Take your time, Emma.'

'They started just after my mother died.' Emma closed her eyes, remembering her terror at discovering her father slumped at his desk that afternoon. The papers, the pens and the empty tonic bottle strewn about the top as if some child had been playing. Her father was always precise in where everything went on his desk, always knew where everything was. He had been lying there, the man who had always been strong and who liked to boast that he had never been sick a day in his life. 'The first one came without warning. It was a bad one, and I called Dr Milburn.'

'And then what happened?' Emma could hear the tension in Jack's voice.

She forced her hands to relax. 'Back to his old self once he learnt that the bridge was a reality instead of a distant dream. He lives for that bridge. It occupies his mind, keeps him from dwelling on what could be.'

'And these fits—do they occur regularly now?' He leant forward. 'Think, Emma. Has he been doing anything in particular before they happen?'

'Most of the time he is fine, but occasionally he is vague, uncertain where he is. Dr Milburn keeps increasing the dose of the tonic and it seems to help for a little while.' She paused, and then continued in a trembling voice as she concentrated on the pearl button of her glove. She glanced quickly up into his eyes and then back at the button. She had to tell him. She had been a coward before. 'He makes mistakes, though.'

'Like the calculations for where the bridge should be. He was the one to make the errors, not you. You were covering for him.'

He slammed his fists together, making her jump.

'You knew!' Emma's mouth dropped open as her mind raced, grasping for bits of information, impressions. He had known, known and not said a word. When had she betrayed her father? She had been willing to take the blame. 'How did you? When did you?'

'I told you that you have a distinctive way of making your "e"s and equally your numbers. I told you I always recheck everything. I did so the night of the ball, when sleep evaded me.' His eyes darkened and his voice became hard and uncompromising. 'The figures in your handwriting were correct. Several in your father's hand were wrong, potentially dangerous.'

Emma put her head back against the chair as a great wave of tiredness washed over her. He knew, and he had never said a word.

'Why didn't you say?' She struggled to sit up. 'Have you told my father? It could kill him if you approached it in the wrong way. Things have to be put in a certain way, otherwise it agitates him. Dr Milburn explained this to me after the first fit.'

Jack made no move towards her, but continued to look at her with his deep black eyes. His hands were thrust into the pockets of his waistcoat. Uncompromising. 'Spare me Milburn's homilies.'

'He is a good doctor. He cares about his patients.'

'I had been waiting for you to explain,' he said quietly, 'but then I saw the relief in your eyes the other day, when we were at the bridge, and I knew there was more to it.'

'I only discovered the mistakes the day you arrived. I never thought my father would make errors like that.' A shiver went through her as she remembered her horror at the discovery. 'A first I did not want to believe it. I tried to tell you, but you thought it was my fear of the ball and Lottie Charlton. And then…then that day at the bridge I was too much of a coward. You were checking the calculations I had concerns about, and I had no wish to borrow trouble.'

'You thought I would blame you?'

'Never that.' Emma brought her head up. 'I was worried about what would happen to my father's business if the truth became known. I thought I could get the line of the bridge moved without….without explaining everything. I was willing to take the blame. That is the unvarnished truth.'

Her breath caught in her throat. He had to believe her. There was no sound in the room except the slight popping of the fire.

'Are you sure your calculations are correct?'

'I have gone over and over them. I don't understand where he got the information or how he did the calculations. It makes no sense.'

'Emma, I am checking all the experiments your father did. Your father taught me that—to check and recheck,' he said, breaking the silence. 'We shall see what went wrong. I blame no one at this point.'

'He was a great civil engineer.'

'You cannot change the past.' Jack made a chopping motion. 'But enough of this. The fact remains you were prepared to risk the fortunes, the lives of others, to preserve one man's vanity.'

'It wasn't like that at all. His turns have only just started to become more frequent. And I did discover the errors. I was trying to put everything right!'

'And if you hadn't done…'

A cold chill passed over Emma. She regarded her hands. It did not bear thinking about. All those lives, innocent lives. He was right. She had not properly considered the consequences.

A life was more important than a reputation. It had to be. But the problem had been solved. Steps had been taken. She refused to dwell in the land of might-have-been.

'We are discussing what ifs and theory while my father lies immobile up in bed. I must go to him.' She rose, started forward. 'He will be devastated when he realises what he has done. The knowledge could kill him.'

'You should have tried harder to tell me.' His voice bounced off the walls.

'Me?' Emma stared at him in astonishment, anger growing inside her. 'I tried! It was you who encouraged my father to play that silly game of forcing me to go to the ball. I had to dance with you before you would even entertain any notion of speaking about the bridge.'

'And what of it?' A muscle jumped in his jaw, but he moderated his voice.

'You treated me like a brainless ninny. You made assumptions about me that were false.' She glared at him, daring him to say different.

'I have never thought you brainless.' A half-smile appeared on his face. 'Misguided, perhaps, but never brainless.'

'And that is supposed to placate me?'

'I hope so.' He held out his hands. 'What is done is done, Emma. The past is written in stone, unchanging. It is the future that is yet to be.'

'But you do believe me, believe that I tried?' Emma leant forward, staring into the abyss that was his eyes. He had to. He had to understand she had tried.

'God forgive me, but I do,' Jack replied after a long moment. 'You should know that I made an offer for Harrison and Lowe before I knew the full extent of your father's illness. I have every hope of him accepting it. You must make sure he accepts it.'

Emma stared at him as her stomach flipped over. He had made an offer. She should have guessed before. And now he would decrease the offer. She knew how these things worked. She knew what vultures businessmen could be. Friendship meant nothing in the world of finance. She doubted he would let friendship stand in the way of acquiring a company like Harrison and Lowe.

'I know what your business practices are like.' Emma looked at him with a level gaze. She knew what was coming next. He would lower the price. It was what she had feared. And the whole awful round of negotiation would begin, until they had nothing and he had everything. This night, which had started beautifully, was rapidly becoming a bad dream.

'You know nothing about my business practices!' Jack thundered, his fist hitting the table, making the Dresden shepherdess jump. He caught it before it tumbled off. 'How could you say such a thing? Think such a thing?'

'I have heard rumours…I have been interested in your career.' Emma pressed her hands together to stop them from trembling. She had to say it now. Before it ate into her soul. If she knew the truth, then it might serve to end her attraction. 'No one amasses that great a fortune without cutting a few corners.'

'Or without making a few enemies.' His eyes were hard lumps of black glass.

'Then how did you do it? How did you make it?' Emma pressed her hands against her stomach. She hated to ask the question. She wanted to believe Jack. But she had to know.

'I have been lucky. The right place at the right time with the right amount of grit and determination.'

'You make it sound like something anyone can do.' Emma gave a little laugh, more of a hiccup. 'No one amasses such a great fortune easily.'

'It was not easy. I gave my blood, sweat and tears.' Jack's fac
was grim, his lips white and his eyes shadowed. 'Do you thin'
I would have lasted long if I had cheated men? Would men such
as Stephenson have made me their partner?'

Emma shook her head slowly.

'I build my bridges and levees to last. I have done the sam
with my business. Its foundation is integrity, not deceit.'

Emma regarded her gloves. She had not really considered i
in that light before, but she could understand what he wa
saying. She wanted to believe him. 'But your reputation in th
press…'

'A man gets a certain reputation. I drive a hard bargain, yes
but it is always an honest one.'

Emma looked at him. Her heart whispered that she knew wha
sort of man he was. She needed no proof. 'What you say make
a certain amount of sense, but then I *am* an acid-tongued
spinster.'

A ghost of a smile appeared on his lips. 'Thank you for that.

'But this offer you have made my father—does it stand now
that you have discovered the truth?'

'It is a fair offer. More than generous in the circumstances.'

Jack named the figure. Emma raised her eyebrows and he
lungs filled with life-giving oxygen. Dr Milburn had been
wrong. Jack was not about to cheat her father. 'And after wha
you have learnt tonight?'

'I want you to know that it stands whatever happens tonight
I put the offer in writing when I first arrived here. It won't be
rescinded simply for me to make money in the short term. It is
the long-term health of my businesses that I care about.'

Emma stared at him, allowing his words to sink in. He knew
about her father's illness but did not intend to lower his price
Relief washed over her. Her shoulders eased. She hadn't realised

hey were tight. The burden she had been carrying for so long, ver since her father's first turn, had gone. Her head seemed ositively giddy. Words failed her, and she stared at Jack.

'Thank you,' she whispered, reaching for his fingers and queezing them as his eyes softened.

It seemed to be enough. Suddenly she knew she had the trength to climb the stairs and face her father, face whatever rdeal lay before her.

'Miss Emma, Miss Emma.' Annie came hurrying into the oom. Her cap was askew and her apron crumpled. Emma was ard pressed to remember when she had ever seen Annie nything but perfectly turned out. 'We have been so worried. But he master would have none of us calling for you. He wanted ou to have fun, to enjoy the pantomime. You have little enough f that sort of thing, he said.'

'Tell me everything, Annie. Don't spare me.' Emma pushed er curls behind her ears. 'I should never have gone tonight.'

'It were a right to-do, like.' Annie's placid face creased, and ears threatened to spill from her eyes. Emma put her arm around he distressed maid. 'I never heard the like. It was right after he inished his bottle of Dr Milburn's tonic, or so Fackler says. urned all purple and gasping for breath. I was certain he was a oner.'

'Miss Harrison needs to know his exact symptoms, Annie,' ack said. 'Tell her in plain, simple language. We know that Mr Iarrison is still alive and sleeping. We both saw him resting.'

'You are right, sir.' Annie bobbed a little curtsey. 'As I was aying…'

Emma listened intently while Annie related the evening's vents. From the recounting, it appeared her father's fit had ollowed its usual terrifying course.

'I will sit with him for a while.' Emma started towards the stairs.

'He is sleeping like a lamb.' Annie held her nose and wafted the air with her hand. 'But his breath smells of garlic, like. And he ain't had any garlic. I checked with Cook. He barely touched his food today. His stomach was paining him that badly, and he said his mouth tasted like he ate steel. He finished his tonic tonight, no questions asked. Drained the bottle. It was then the attack happened.'

'That settles it,' Jack remarked decisively, his face suddenly wearing a very determined look.

'Settles what?' Emma asked in surprise. 'What are you talking about, Jack?'

'Do his turns always happen after he has finished a bottle of tonic?'

Emma tilted her head to one side, thinking back to the attacks. 'Yes, I think you are right. Does it signify anything?'

'It might do, but I need to know more.' Jack started to pace the room. 'Tell me everything you can remember about his most recent attacks.'

Emma explained, going back over the symptoms several times. When she had finished, she looked at him. His brow was furrowed. He had made several notes on a piece of paper and was reading them over. Did he really care about what happened to her father?

'What should we do? Can I go up and see my father?'

He jumped slightly, as if he had forgotten she was there.

'Do? You go up and see your father. Put your mind at ease. Leave Milburn to me.' He crossed his arms. 'I have some questions I want answered. Once they are answered, then the doctor can see his patient.'

'But…but…' Emma hesitated on the bottom stair.

'For once in your life, Emma, please do as I ask.' His hand enveloped hers. 'Trust me.'

Emma stared at him, met his intense gaze full-on, but hers was

he first to falter. She had to trust him. She wanted to trust him.
Send Dr Milburn up when he arrives.'

Emma gathered her skirts and raced up the stairs, taking them
wo at a time.

Jack watched her go, then rang for Fackler. He would do
vhat was necessary. Dr Milburn would only see Harrison once
ack was certain. 'Do you have the tonic bottle? The one Mr
Harrison finished tonight.'

'It can be found, Mr Stanton.' The butler's face was perfectly
chooled.

'With all speed and diligence, Fackler.'

'With all speed, sir.'

Jack smiled inwardly. Fackler thought him slightly unhinged,
ut it was important to follow his hunches, and the signs pointed
o the tonic. Nothing happened without a reason. Everything
beyed the laws of nature. Everything.

The bell sounded—harsh, insistent. Jack stared at the solid
loor.

'I want to see Dr Milburn first.' Jack met the butler's stare.
Miss Emma is not to be disturbed. She has had but a little time
vith her father.'

'Very good, sir.' Again the butler's face gave no indication that
ie thought the request odd or out of the ordinary. 'And if I
night say so, sir, I don't put a huge store by medicine pedlars.
A great big bunch of tomfoolery, if you don't mind me saying
o.'

'Thank you, Fackler. I had thought that as well. Some tonics
ire good, and others—well, it doesn't bear thinking about.' Jack
·lenched his jaw. He was determined to give Dr Milburn a fair
iearing, and as Harrison was now asleep, it would make no dif-
·erence if he was examined in the morning or now.

'I have come from an important supper,' Dr Milburn pronounced when Fackler barred his way. 'And this man says that I am not required.'

'Please forgive the servants, Milburn, they overreacted.' Jack went to the door. The first few snowflakes drifted down, landing on Milburn's black coat. 'Harrison is resting comfortably after experiencing indigestion at supper.'

Dr Milburn carried his black leather bag in one hand and had a white silk scarf wrapped around his neck—the very picture of a successful doctor. His eyes slowly travelled up Jack's form. A tiny smile played on his thin lips.

'My patient is ill, Stanton.' He made an imperious gesture. 'Stand aside.'

Jack braced his feet and met Milburn's glassy gaze. With effort, he retained control of his temper.

'Your patient is resting. From what I know, sleep is often the best healer.'

'And what are you now? A doctor as well as an engineer?' The sneer on Milburn's face increased. 'For a charity boy, you express your opinion on a wide range of matters.'

'Out in the wild, you have to. Your men's lives depend on it,' Jack answered, allowing the charity remark to pass. He had proved his worth a thousand times over; no jumped-up doctor would take that away. Milburn wanted a reaction. 'I know what I am on about. Do you?'

'For the love of God, man, let me pass,' Milburn said, his voice thundering. 'I have work to do. A man's life depends on me and my skill.'

'I think not.' Jack lounged against the doorframe, giving the impression of great casualness, but in reality every muscle was ready to spring.

'What did you say? Are you threatening me? *Me*? A member of the Royal College of Physicians? How dare you?'

Milburn raised his bag, but Jack reached out and grabbed his
rist, holding him there.

'I dare all right.' Jack pushed the arm away. 'You forget
ourself, Milburn, and you forget who you are dealing with.'

Neither man moved. The sound of his breathing, of Milburn's,
choed about him. Then Milburn blinked and lowered his bag,
s shoulders slightly hunched.

'I have been summoned.' He tried again, his face flushing
ightly. He spoke each word as if he were speaking to a
ackward child. 'Miss Harrison desires me to see her father.'

'You were summoned mistakenly. By the servants. Miss
arrison was with me this evening.'

'With you?' Milburn opened and closed his mouth several times.

'At a pantomime. The Charltons were in the party.'

'No one informed me of this,' Milburn muttered out of the
orner of his mouth.

'I did not know either of the Harrisons were in the habit of
lling you their social engagements,' Jack said through a
enched jaw.

Milburn blinked. A cold smile spread over his features. 'You
e quite right, of course, Stanton. I have no claim over Miss
arrison…yet. But I do have hopes. Miss Harrison, despite her
ain looks, would make an admirable helpmate for a doctor,
on't you agree?'

Jack stared at Milburn. Emma? Plain? Infuriating. Mad-
ening. Obstinate. But not plain. Her beauty might be uncon-
entional, but he found it very pleasing to the eye. And her
ind was first-rate. She had matured into an excitingly attrac-
ve woman. She deserved someone who appreciated her.

'If Harrison's condition has failed to improve by morning I
ill personally come for you. Until then, I suggest you go
ome.' Jack restrained his fist with difficulty.

'You are playing a dangerous game, Stanton.' The doctor' sneer resembled that of a snake. His eyes glittered. 'Harrison's condition is complex and complicated. I would hate to think anything untoward had happened to him because you refused me entry.'

'It is a risk I am prepared to take.' Jack moved solidly in from of the door. He clung onto his temper, dared Milburn to make another move.

The sneer on Milburn's face increased, became more pronounced. 'It is on your head, Stanton, if Harrison dies since you play at doctoring. I will be quite happy to say as much to the authorities.'

'I welcome the responsibility.' Jack stared hard at the arrogant doctor. Emma as a dutiful helpmate to *him*! Impossible Ridiculous. He refused to allow it.

'Until the morning, then. I pray to God that the patient last that long.' Dr Milburn stalked off to the waiting carriage.

'Old crow,' Fackler muttered under his breath as he banged the door shut. 'As you said, Mr Stanton, there weren't no need to call him out. I should never have listened to that Annie.'

'Miss Emma seems to set store by him.' Jack tried to keep his voice light. 'Their names have been bandied together.'

'Miss Emma?' Fackler shook his head. 'She don't like him Not in that way. It were the late mistress, Mrs Harrison. She did set store by him. Called him her ministering angel. Wouldn't hear a word spoken against him. Not by nobody.'

Jack squared his shoulders and faced the butler. 'Mrs Harrison is dead. It is Mr Harrison and his daughter I am concerned with

Chapter Twelve

Her father lay in the centre of the double bed. His face pasty but peaceful against the white sheet. No rattling, no wheezing, just the steady breath of peaceful sleep. Annie was correct. His breathing was even and regular. There was no reason to disturb Dr Milburn. Emma offered up a prayer of thanksgiving.

Whatever her father had had, it had passed—just as it had done every other time. The fit had gone and he would be restored to the land of the living. But for how long? When should she tell him that he was dying? That Dr Milburn held out little hope? That she had confided everything in Jack? She would have to say something. Or Jack would.

She drew a sharp breath. Everything she had worked for these last few months gone. Her father had to survive—that was the main thing. Everything else could wait.

She was not ready to become an orphan.

'Papa, stay with me. Don't go to Mama.'

Emma stumbled forward and laid her head against the coverlet
her strong fingers curling around her father's limp ones.

'I have seen the good doctor,' Jack said, coming into the
room.

Emma jumped up and made a show of securing the coverlet
more tightly around her father. She brushed away the glint of
tears and straightened her crumpled dress.

'Where is he?' Emma peered around Jack, trying to see the
doctor's looming figure. 'Dr Milburn should be here by now.
distinctly heard the bell earlier. Why is he taking his time
Generally Fackler sends him straight up.'

Jack came closer. In the firelight, a pair of scissors gleamed
in his hands. His face wore that same determined expression
he'd had when he rescued Davy. 'I sent him away. His services
were not required.'

'Sent him away?' Emma rolled her eyes heavenwards, choked
back the anger. She had to remain calm. Shouting at Jack was
going to make matters worse, but right now she wanted to
throttle him. Of all the high-handed—! 'Why did you do that
How could you do that?'

'Your father is resting comfortably. After the shock he had
it is probably the best thing for him.' He paused and looked at
her father's bedside table, where a variety of bottles and boxes
stood along with a half-used candlestick. 'If needs be, Dr
Milburn can call in the morning. I will personally fetch him.
think he is hoping to be able to say I told you so.'

'Will he?' Emma crossed her arms and narrowed her eyes
"My father is not a bone to be fought over by two men who have
borne grudges since school. This is a man's life we are talking
about. My father's life.'

'I doubt it. Your father is over the worst. He will live.' Jack
nodded towards where her father lay. 'See, his breathing is easy

here is no sweat on his brow. You said that every fit he had, he had when he'd reached the end of a tonic bottle?'

'Did I? I don't remember.' Emma paced the room, clasping nd unclasping her hands. She found it difficult to think beyond he immediate room. 'Yes, I suppose that is correct.'

'Think. Take your time about it, but do you ever remember a it that happened when he was in the middle of a bottle?'

Emma shook her head. 'It could be coincidence. Or perhaps ny father tries to eke out the bottle. He has a great dislike of alling for the doctor.'

'I do not believe in coincidence. Nobody operates outside ature. A bridge falls down because of the forces exerted on it. eople become ill for a reason.'

Emma swallowed hard, torn. Every instinct she had told her to rust him. It was a basic tenet of civil engineering—the forces of ature controlled everything. Every fit her father had had, had appened when he'd reached the end of a tonic bottle. She was ure of it now. She had never thought about it before. Jack was orrect. Coincidence was highly unlikely. 'What do you intend on loing?'

'Following my hunch.' He gave a crooked smile. 'Check and echeck everything before coming to any definite conclusion. It s what I am good at. Details are important.'

'What sort of details?' Emma asked cautiously.

She glanced again at her father. He was sleeping comfortably. t would be a shame to wake him. She wrapped her arms about er waist and kept her mind away from what might happen.

'When he has the attacks, is there anything Dr Milburn gives im?' Jack paused and tapped the scissors against his thigh. What does Dr Milburn do? Does he bleed him?'

'No, not that. He has other methods.' She swallowed hard. 'I lisapprove of bleeding. I think it made Mama weaker, despite

what the doctors said. It is one of the reasons we changed to D
Milburn. His methods are more modern. He believes i
medicine-pills and tonics.'

'What methods? Think carefully, Emma. How does he contro
your father's attacks?'

'He has some special pills that my father is supposed to take i
ever he is starting to feel dizzy. They seem to cure it, or at leas
make the fits less.' Emma rummaged through her father's to
drawer and pulled out a glass bottle. She squinted at the spidery
writing. 'Charcoal and sulphur. They are all gone. Is it signifi
cant?'

'Yes, I thought they might contain those two ingredients. I
all fits.' Jack went to her father, snipped a lock of hair from hi
head, then captured it in a handkerchief before carefully trans
ferring it to an envelope. He handed the envelope to Emma
'Seal it.'

'I trust you,' she said.

'I would feel safer if you used your father's wax and ring t
seal it. I want everything to be correct. You never know when i
might have to be used in a court of law.'

Emma took the envelope and went over to her father'
dressing table. She quickly sealed the envelope, pressing the ring
into the warm red wax. Jack took it from her nerveless fingers
'What will you do with it?'

'I will send this away, along with the empty bottle of tonic
to make sure my hypothesis is correct.' Jack ran his hand throug
his hair. She could see tiredness around his eyes. 'Milburr
knows there is something in the tonic. Sulphur and charcoal ar
given for one specific reason. He knows what is causing thes
fits, even if he is not telling you.'

'Dr Milburn knows the cause?' Emma stared at where he

father lay. Questions crowded in her brain. 'But he would dearly love to know. It would make his fortune, he says.'

'I suspect your father is suffering from arsenic poisoning. He has all the symptoms—confusion, garlic breath, metallic-tasting mouth and stomach cramps. Luckily Edward Harrison has a strong constitution.' Jack turned the empty pill bottle over. 'The cure for an accidental overdose is charcoal and sulphur. When your father feels up to eating he will need to have eggs and onions—foods that contain sulphur.'

'Poisoning?' Emma stared at Jack, incredulous. Her body became numb. Poison. Her father. Impossible. 'Who would do such a thing? How would he get arsenic?'

'Milburn's tonic most likely contains some,' Jack said quietly. 'A good many tonics do. In small doses it is supposed to be helpful in certain cases.'

'Dr Milburn is poisoning my father?' Emma looked at Jack. 'How could he do such a thing? Why would he do such a thing? If he knew, why would he have my father continue to take the tonic?'

She backed away from the tonic bottle as if it might bite her, trying to make sense of it. Dr Milburn was poisoning her father.

'I am sure it was not deliberate, Emma,' Jack said carefully. 'It is possible that the arsenic settled after being left too long. It needs investigating. We need to be certain before deciding what to do next.'

'You don't sound convinced.'

'I want to wait and weigh the options. I may not like the man, but I doubt Charles Milburn is a cold-blooded murderer. You say that he kept your mother alive. I have to trust your judgement.'

'Yes,' Emma breathed, and the word came out as a half-choked sob. Emma fumbled for a handkerchief but could find none. She gazed up at the ceiling. Why did she always get the

temptation to cry when she was not in possession of a handkerchief? She blinked back tears and swallowed hard. Regained
control of her emotions, then continued in a stronger voice. 'He
saved Mama's life. I am convinced of it. We kept her going for
as long as possible.'

Jack was standing right beside her. Emma turned slightly. His
strong arms went around her, held her close in their gentle
embrace. She laid her cheek against his starched white shirt-
front and heard the reassuring thump of his heart in her ear.
Nothing lover-like, a place of comfort. Safety. She swallowed
hard. They were friends, and she had to be content with that.

'How long will it take until we know for certain?' she asked,
fixing her gaze on his second shirt button down.

'I will have the answer before Christmas. Before I depart
from Newcastle.' He spoke into her hair.

He loosened his arms and stepped away from her. The cold
air rushed around her. She forced her lips into a brilliant smile.
'I imagine these things take time.'

'You won't have to wonder for long.'

All the while her mind kept echoing his words. Christmas.
Christmas was when Jack would be leaving. He planned on
going despite his new knowledge. Only a few days ago she
hadn't been able to wait until he went, and now the thought of
him going filled her with dread.

'What am I supposed to do in the meantime?' She struggled
to keep her voice steady.

'Wait and watch. Hope.'

'And what of Dr Milburn?'

'I think it best if your father finds another doctor.'

'You may be correct.' Emma hugged her arms about her. She
hated to think it had been she who had insisted her father take
his tonic. She had thought that it was doing him some good, and

instead she had been poisoning him. Her mind recoiled. She wanted to sink to her knees and weep. She forced her body to stay upright. 'Papa, you are not dying. We are going to get you well. You will live to see this bridge across the Tyne built. I promise you that.'

She heard the door click, and saw that Jack had quietly gone. 'Thank you,' she whispered to the emptiness he'd left behind.

'Fathers!' Emma closed the door to her father's room with a satisfying bang the following morning. 'One would think they enjoyed turning the entire household upside down and inside out.'

'You seem perturbed this morning, Miss Emma.' Jack lounged against the doorframe. 'Hopefully your father has not become worse in the night.'

'He agrees with you!' Emma put her hands on her hips and tried to forget that she looked a fright. Up most of the night, and with her hair hanging down her back in a loose plait, and more than likely dark circles under her eyes. Her only consolation was that he had seen her worse. But she wanted him to think her attractive. As excitingly attractive as the women in London or Paris.

'Agrees with me about what?' A faint dimple showed in the corner of his mouth.

'"There is no need to send for the quack."' Emma put her hands on her hips and mimicked her father's tone. '"Nor to take any more of that quack's medicine." Hooray! Hoorah! "Always knew it wasn't good for me," says he.'

'I thought we had decided not to send for Milburn anyway.' Jack reached out and grabbed her arm. 'We agreed to wait for the results.'

Emma stepped back and his hand released her. She held her

elbows and did not meet his eyes. 'I thought maybe one of the other doctors, but Papa is refusing even that. He approves of your methods and is willing to wait for the results.'

Jack gave a satisfied nod. 'I would say that is a very positive sign.'

'Positive? It is infuriating!' Emma began to pace up and down the hall. 'This is the first time in a long time that my father is not being sensible, and you are encouraging him in this foolish behaviour.'

Jack came forward, blocking her way. He reached out and gathered her hands in his. Emma found it difficult to breathe, her mind spun. She kept her gaze on his embroidered silk waistcoat.

'Emma,' he said, and his finger lifted her chin. 'Listen to me. Believe in me. Your father is recovering.'

'I am. I do. He must be.'

With the greatest of efforts she tore herself away from his hands. Took a deep breath. Her lips ached. In another moment her hand would have curled around his neck and pulled his mouth against hers.

There were too many servants about, and she hated to think about the scandal. And what it would do to her father. She had to be realistic. This was a flirtation for Jack. He had said when they first met that he was not interested in marriage. Nothing he had done since gave the slightest indication his mind had changed. Whatever chance they'd had, had been destroyed a long time ago, when her mother had not given her the letter. No. If she was honest, it had gone before then—when Jack had left without giving her a chance. His departure had nearly broken her heart. He would not have a second chance. And this time her heart was immune.

It had to be.

Jack made no effort to recapture her. He raked his hand through his hair.

'If your father was not feeling right within himself he would want to see the doctor. He'd welcome your suggestion.'

'He is talking about what will happen once he is in charge at the bridge.'

Jack's face betrayed no emotion. 'I would say that is a good sign.'

'He may change his mind about your proposal…I mean offer.'

Emma wanted the earth to open up when she realised which word had escaped.

'My proposal?' He lifted a brow. 'And which proposal would that be, exactly?'

Emma felt a tide of burning wash up her face. 'I was speaking about your offer for Harrison and Lowe. That is the only proposal I know about. Is there another one?'

'Not that I have heard of.' His eyes glittered slightly, and a half-smile appeared on his lips. 'I thought maybe you could enlighten me. Exactly what is your proposition, and will I enjoy it?'

Emma smiled back at him, feeling on firmer ground. Light-hearted remarks with no substance she had learnt to deal with years ago. 'I don't have time to stand here bantering with you. There is work to be done.'

'On a day like today? Have you had a look out of the window?'

Emma hurried over to the window on the landing. Snowflakes were coming down in great piles, as if there was a gigantic pillow fight in the sky. The garden was rapidly filling up with huge white flakes. The muddy patches, the bare trees and bushes and the Greek goddess statue that had been her mother's pride, were all covered in a blanket of wet snow.

'You are right. There will be no work on the bridge.'

'It would be impossible,' Jack agreed. 'The men will work all the harder when the thaw comes and the ground is soft.'

'I pray when it comes the thaw will not be too rapid.' A shiver ran down Emma's spine as she thought of what the Tyne was capable of. Her father's previous project before this one had been strengthening the flood defences along the Tyne, and she prayed they would not be needed.

'You are too tender-hearted, Emma. The thaw needs to be rapid. We need to see what happens when the Tyne is in full spate. When I build a bridge it stands for all time, not just until the first one-hundred-year flood.'

'But think on the potential for devastation, the lives that would be ruined, the property.'

'If we can understand the pattern and the effects, we can save lives and ensure the bridge stands. The Tyne has washed bridges away before now. Every single bridge was lost last century due to a flood. It will not happen to my bridge.'

'Another of your it-can-be-done projects?'

'I am interested in taming the forces of nature, making them work for us rather than against us.' Jack paused. 'But you lead me from my purpose.'

'Your purpose?' Emma tilted her head.

Jack was dressed in his overcoat and top hat. Emma's brow wrinkled. Surely he could not be planning on going out in this weather? He had said that work was suspended on the bridge.

'To ascertain how your father fares.'

'I have told you that he is recovering—recovering all too quickly,' she said with a wry smile. 'He will be complaining about resting within a few days. You may go in and see him if you like.'

'It won't be necessary.' Jack waved his hand, but his face had turned serious. 'I must bid you adieu.'

'Adieu? You are leaving?' Emma looked at him in dismay, and

her stomach dropped. The light appeared to go out of the day, and time stretched bleakly in front of her. 'But I thought you were staying until Christmas.'

'Urgent matters have arisen and I need to go to London. Stephenson needs to know about your father—about what we have decided.'

'Nothing is decided,' Emma said quickly.

'We agreed on the company, Miss Harrison.' Jack's face became stern. 'Stephenson and I have to discuss how best to proceed with the building of the bridge and its design. How to get the bridge built on time.'

'Until my father is well, I cannot say what he will do. I don't speak for my father.' Emma balled her fists. He had to understand. She had to give her father something to live for. 'He is alive. And he is going to recover fully. You said it was poisoning.'

'I hope and pray he does. In the meantime, someone needs to look after the bridge. It is too important a project to go unsupervised, and I do have other commitments, Miss Harrison. Places I need to be in the New Year. I accepted a contract in Italy. People are depending on me.'

Emma stared at Jack not quite taking in what he was saying. Other commitments. She had thought he would be staying. Another illusion. A great hollow place opened inside her. A huge Jack-shaped hole. She screwed her eyes shut, refused to think about that. She was overwrought about her father. That had to be it. It had no other cause.

'If it is arsenic poisoning, then my father will get well.' She forced the words from her throat.

'He should do, but it may take months.' He laid a hand on her shoulder briefly. 'You must face facts, Miss Emma. That bridge must have someone permanent in charge, whether your father retains ownership of his company or not. It needs a qualified and competent engineer.'

'The ground is frozen. Give my father time.' As she said the words she knew she was pleading for her own well-being.

Emma moved away from him. She had to think, to ignore the trembling that was developing in her stomach. Jack was making plans to go away—to go away and not come back.

'As you wish, but I need to speak with Stephenson in person.' He gave a careless shrug. 'There is little good I can do here. The ground is frozen. But the trains are running.'

'And your experiments?'

'Davy Newcomb knows what to do. I have sent him a list of instructions. He is trustworthy.'

Emma forced her lips to turn upwards. 'You appear to have thought of everything.'

'I like to have the details correct.' His eyes darkened. 'They need me in London.'

Emma wanted to whisper that she needed him to stay here. But the words refused to come. What was between them was too new and fragile. Perhaps it was only her own longing and not his. He had been quite clear about things that first day.

She adjusted the shawl tighter around her shoulders. 'I shall wish you Godspeed on your journey, then.'

'I will return…before the thaw, Emma.' A half-smile touched his lips. He took a step closer. 'Wish me luck.'

'I thought I had already.' Her breath seemed to stick in her throat. She knew if she took one step closer her body would brush his.

'So cold, so formal,' he murmured.

He leant forward, and his fingertips delicately traced the outline of her eyebrows, the line of her nose and the curve of her jaw. Soft touches, as if he were memorising her face. Intimate touches, creating little ripples of warmth that flooded through her body. Her lips ached, and she wanted to taste his mouth again. What mattered was the feel of him against her.

Her hand reached up to drag his face down. But the clock chimed and he stepped away.

'Next time, remember to say goodbye properly without being asked.' He touched his hat.

And he was gone before her mind could think up a suitable scathing retort. She heard his steady footsteps go down the stairs and the sound of the door closing.

She ran to the front of the house and rested her cheek against the windowpane, watching the black carriage disappear into the swirling white snow. She watched for a long time, until the tracks from the carriage became white and the world was covered with white down, refusing to think about trains becoming stuck or derailing.

The sound of the servants moving about the house roused her. She gave herself a shake. There was more to her life than mooning about like some schoolgirl. She had responsibilities, a life. But her mouth ached with the memory of what might have been.

Chapter Thirteen

'He will come back,' Lucy said, pressing her hand against Emma's as they sat in the little hut beside the frozen pond three days later. Her father had insisted she join the Charltons' skating party. He was tired of her fussing and fretting. 'There is no need to act the moon-calf about it either. He will be back before you know it.'

Emma froze. She thought she had been so careful. She had barely mentioned Jack Stanton. Only that he had gone just before the winter storm had set in. Newcastle and the rest of the North East slumbered under a blanket of snow and ice.

'What are you talking about, Lucy? Why this sudden penchant for riddles?' Emma bent her head and concentrated on fastening the strap of her ice skate.

'*Your* Mr Stanton.'

Emma pulled too hard and the leather strap broke.

'Now see what you made me do!' Emma held up the broken

strap with a rueful smile. 'You should not tease me like that. I had not realised the leather was rotten.'

'Is that what caused it?' Lucy's eyes danced. 'And I thought you were remembering the way Mr Stanton could not take his eyes off you at the pantomime. I assure you the other ladies were quite jealous. Lottie fumed about it. Even Henry remarked on it to Dr Milburn. I am certain he will make an offer. I can see wedding bells in your future!'

'Must you always indulge in such fairytales?' A wave of burning stained her cheeks. Wedding bells? The idea was laughable. Jack Stanton had no intention of marrying anyone, least of all her. His sole concern and purpose was ensuring Harrison and Lowe became part of his empire. He had made that quite clear.

'You are being deliberately blind.'

'You are seeing romance where there is none. Jack Stanton is a family friend.' Emma held out her skate. 'Anyway, whatever the cause, it looks like I shan't be skating today.'

'I will get you another strap. I won't have you getting out of skating this easily, Emma Harrison.'

'How can I skate on one skate? Be reasonable, Lucy.' Emma gave a small laugh, and privately heaved a sigh of relief. The subject had veered away from Jack.

'Let me solve your problem.' Lucy signalled towards a footman, who brought another piece of leather. Emma waited while he threaded the strap through and then handed the skate back. 'You see—no excuse.'

'I do like to skate, Lucy.'

'It is good that your father has improved enough for you to leave him. I had worried you would not make Lottie's party.'

'My father was determined I would. Unlike Mama, he wants peace and quiet. He says I fuss.' Emma nodded to where Lottie stood, pretty and poised on the ice. 'She looks like a fairy child.'

'Ah, but she knows it, and that is the problem. She is rapidly turning into a flirt, and just think what that will do for her prospects.'

'Thus far she has been careful.'

'But she gets bolder and bolder. I am worried. One slip, one misjudgement, and her reputation could be beyond repair. But neither Henry nor Mother Charlton is interested.'

'Thankfully I listened to Mama about the pitfalls and avoided most of them.' A shiver ran down Emma's spine. She hated to think how close she had been to scandal with Jack. She did not regret it.

'Ah, Stanton, you have returned. In good time as well.'

'My meetings took less time than I anticipated. It is good to see you looking so hardy, Harrison.' Jack handed his top hat to Fackler. 'Where is Miss Emma? I thought she might like to try out my new sleigh.'

'She has gone to that Charlton chit's skating party. She was getting on my nerves, always fussing.'

Jack was dismayed at the wave of disappointment that coursed through his body. All the way up on the train he had pictured Emma's face, her eyes lighting up, her cupid's bow mouth softening when she saw the sleigh. And now she had gone out and the surprise would have to wait.

'I see. There will be other occasions, no doubt.'

Harrison tapped his fingers together. 'But this might prove fortuitous.'

'How so?'

'I have been thinking. I can not go on running the project much longer. I want to spend time doing other things.'

'My offer stands. Your recent illness makes no difference.'

'Ah, but I have my daughter to think of. She loves that bridge, and cares about the employees.' Harrison raised his eyebrows.

I am going to give her the company as a dowry. It will be her problem then. I have enough from my various land investments. The railways have been driving the price of land, and for a man with an eye on how the land lies there have been opportunities.'

Jack stared at him as cold seeped through his body. Harrison was giving the company to his daughter as a dowry. Exactly who was she marrying? What had happened while he had been gone?

'What are you saying?' He forced a laugh from between his teeth. 'Which man should I be congratulating?'

'Now, now, I am not blind and deaf, Stanton. I know a thing or two about these matters.' Harrison tapped his finger against his nose. 'I know which way the wind is blowing.'

'I made an offer to you in good faith.' Jack stared at Harrison, unable to believe his ears. Harrison was offering *him* the company as Emma's dowry. 'Does Emma know of this proposition?'

'No…I hadn't thought to say anything to her. I wanted to speak to you first. It was only right and proper.'

Jack resisted the urge to curse long and loud.

'If you know what is good for you, don't.'

A smile beamed across Harrison's face. 'I thought I could pick 'em. But Margaret had her heart set on her daughter being able to wear a coronet. She wouldn't settle for anything less than a title. It was a mistake, and Emma paid for it.'

'What was between Emma and I was over a long time ago.'

'I have eyes and ears, Stanton. You don't fool me.' Harrison cleared his throat. 'Anyway, I have taken the liberty of obtaining a licence—an ordinary one, to save money.'

'A licence?' Jack stared at Harrison. Had the fit caused him to become touched in the head? 'You have organised a marriage licence?'

'Between you and Emma. It took some doing, but I am not without friends.'

'Why?'

'As I said, I knew the way in which the wind was blowing and after my brush with death it came to me. Harrison and Lowe must be protected, and what better way to keep it all in the family, eh? And no point in shelling out for a Special Licence if one doesn't have to.'

'Harrison, I do my own courting.' Jack bit out the words. 'When I marry, and I have no plans to marry at present, I will marry for a far better reason than acquiring a company.'

Harrison's face fell. 'What are you saying?'

'I fear you have wasted your money. I have no plans to marry your daughter.' Jack crossed his arms and stared at Harrison. No man ran his life.

'No plans...but I thought—'

'You mistook my intentions. We are friends, Miss Harrison and I,' Jack said through gritted teeth. He had spent the better part of the time he had been gone trying to get her from his mind and now he came back to this. It was not going to happen. Not in the manner Harrison prescribed.

'I can see I was a bit precipitous.' Harrison ran a finger around the rim of his collar. 'I had thought... Forget I said anything about it. Emma knows nothing about this.'

'You may call it what you like, but I never mix business with pleasure,' Jack said in a cold voice.

'Ah, but which is the business and which is the pleasure?' Harrison tapped his nose. 'It has been disputed before.'

'And if you are wise you will not say anything about it to Emma.' Jack clung onto the last vestiges of his control as anger surged through him. Harrison was prepared to sell his daughter in this way, to stoop to blatant manipulation. Emma deserved better than that. A marriage was more than a business arrangement. His parents' marriage had been. 'I bid you good day.'

'I do hope Emma is enjoying her skating expedition.' Harrison's voice trailed after him, causing Jack to pause in the doorway. 'I understand Dr Milburn is going. Her dear mama had high hopes for them once. In her final days she often used to speak of how well suited they were.'

Jack pulled on his gloves as he tried to refrain from shaking the man. Harrison's matchmaking attempts were pitiful. Emma had no interest in Milburn.

But… He paused, cold washing over him. What was Charles Milburn's interest? He could see the doctor's greedy eyes again, hear his voice proclaiming that he would soon marry Emma. An idle boast?

What if there was something more sinister afoot? The man had had no scruples as a boy. Jack clearly remembered the time Milburn had taken the opportunity to discover examination questions, and then blamed it on his hapless sidekick. Then there had been the time Milburn had lost the money from the charity box but had sported a new waistcoat. Nothing had ever been proved. It bothered Jack. Had Milburn really changed?

He quickly dismissed the notion as fanciful. But Emma could be in danger if she decided to quiz Milburn about the tonic. Jack's blood ran cold. Knowing Emma, she was quite capable of it. He cursed himself for being a thousand times a fool. Who knew what the doctor would do if he thought he was cornered?

Jack's heart skipped a beat. He had to make sure Emma was safe.

'You will forgive me, Harrison.'

'Where are you going?'

'To try out the sleigh.' Jack touched the rim of his hat. 'Good day to you, Harrison.'

'Give my regards to my daughter. You will find her on

Gosforth Common. Her dowry remains the same, whichever man she chooses.'

Jack slammed the door to the echoing sound of Harrison's laughter.

All around Emma the shrieks of laughter rose. The Charltons' skating party was in full flow. The ice teemed with the Charltons, a number of Lottie's soldiers and a variety of friends. Mrs Charlton had set up a warming area, complete with a portable stove and a steaming bowl of her famous wassailing punch. Emma finished fastening her skates and stood. After years of not skating her ankles felt wobbly and threatened not to hold her. She looked longingly back at the warm hut.

'Are you coming out on the ice, Emma? I promise not to tease you any more.'

'Give me a moment.' Emma practised a few steps, felt her legs going and flailed her arms, but she didn't fall. She took a cautious step forward, and then another. The ice began to glide under her feet. 'I think my feet remember more than I give them credit for.'

'Do you need some assistance? I may not be Jack Stanton, but I reckon I can help hold you up.'

'Very amusing, Lucy.'

Lucy started to skate back towards Emma, stopped, and then gestured towards the centre, where Lottie stood surrounded by her admirers. She had a particularly mischievous look on her face. 'Oh, dear, Lottie has not given up the idea, despite Henry's warning. She is insistent on this pairing-off game.'

'Come and join us, Emma.' Lottie skated over. 'I am searching for another *single* lady, and I am sure one of the officers wouldn't mind being paired with you. It is quite harmless fun. Lieutenant Ludlow assures me that he is willing to be your gallant.'

'I shall pass. Not steady enough on my feet.'

'There is that. I shall just have to have two gallants, then.' Lottie gave a toss of her head and skated away.

'She skates very close to the edge, does my sister-in-law,' Lucy said with a pained expression, as Lottie laughingly grabbed onto the lieutenant's arm. 'She'll bring down scandal on us all if she continues in this manner. And then what will happen to her marriage prospects?'

'There are worse things than remaining single.'

'Sometimes, Emma Harrison,' Lucy said, shaking her head, 'I think you quite like playing at being the old spinster. And…'

'And what?'

'And at other times I am sure of it,' Lucy called as she skated away with firm strokes. Her blue eyes danced. 'Catch me if you dare.'

Emma laughed. Out here on the ice the years melted away. It was as if they were young girls again, with few responsibilities, instead of being in their mid-twenties.

'You will regret those words, Lucy Charlton!'

'Make me!' Lucy put her hands on her hips. 'You have not the stamina you once had, old maid Emma Harrison.'

'Neither your teasing nor Lottie's attempts to organise games will ruin the day for me.' Emma gestured out towards where the snow sparkled 'I plan to skate, skate, skate, until the sun goes behind the clouds or I become too cold. But on my own terms. It is how I live my life.'

'That's the Emma I know and love.' Lucy looked over her shoulder towards where a great deal of shrieking was coming from. 'I see one of my boys is getting into problems with his nurse. I did tell him no snowball fights. Sometimes I think he takes after his father, and at other times I am sure he does.'

'Go on. I will be here when you come back.' Emma waved

Lucy away and watched her confidently skate over to where he little boy was looking mutinous. Emma watched for a little while, and then turned her attention to skating. She tentatively took a few more steps, found her rhythm and began to skate faster, her feet barely skimming the ice. The cold bit her cheek as she remembered the soaring feeling. It had been far too many years. She circled around and decided to try to skate backwards as she had been able to do once.

'Be careful, Miss Harrison.' Iron arms caught her and an imperious voice resounded in her ear. 'I would not want to be responsible for you receiving an injury.'

Emma froze, pulled firmly away from the restraining hands and turned to face Dr Milburn. She fought to contain her revulsion at his arrogant expression.

Nothing had been proved. Jack's friend had not yet given his report. There was still a chance that Jack was mistaken and her father was truly ill.

'Dr Milburn, how pleasant it is to see you.' Emma forced her voice to be polite as she tried to peer over his shoulder to where Lucy ministered to her son.

'You are looking sprightly, if I might say so, Miss Harrison. And your father…is he here?'

'My father finds the cold difficult.' Emma took a deep breath. 'I was sorry that the servants over-reacted the other night. Thankfully, it proved a false alarm. My father is fully recovered now.'

'I am pleased to hear it. I feared the worst when Stanton barred my entry.' Dr Milburn's face assumed a sanctimonious expression. 'It does my heart good to know your father's health improves. In these sorts of cases there is no telling how long such patients will last. It is in God's hands.'

'He has recovered.' Emma swallowed. She had to fight against

eing too cynical. Nothing had been proved. It could all be coincidence. She had to believe that somehow this had been a
mistake. She gave a light laugh. 'But I am surprised to see you
ere in this party.'

'Do you think me too old and staid for such doings?' His smile
did not reach his dead eyes. 'I am but a few years older than Jack
Stanton. We knew each other as young men. Did he ever say?'

Emma fought to keep her face pleasant. 'Not too old. I had
merely wondered about your patients. I thought they would
ave first call on your time.'

'Thankfully they, like your father, are being healthy at the
moment. I must take my pleasures while I can, Miss Harrison.
My bag is in my carriage in case I am required.' He touched his
and to his hat. 'I do like to think ahead. When I was a boy, I
used to skate on the rivers all day. It appears such a perfect day
or this type of innocent pleasure.'

'Yes, I agree.' Emma bit her lip. She had no wish to spend any
more time than absolutely necessary in this man's company.

'Perhaps you will do me the honour of skating with me for a
hort while?'

Emma saw with relief that Lucy had finished with her son. 'I
m sorry, but I promised Mrs Charlton…'

'Maybe later, then?'

'If it does not turn too cold.'

His eyes narrowed, and Emma's breath caught in her throat.
A cold wind blew around her. She willed him to go.

'I hear your overseer has left Newcastle, Miss Harrison.' He
leared his throat. 'Do you know when he plans to return?'

'Mr Stanton did not tell me. Was there any particular reason?'
he tilted her head to one side.

'There was a business opportunity I wanted to discuss with him,
at is all. Henry Charlton was saying that he might be amenable.'

'I will be sure to tell him you were enquiring after him.'

'You do that. And, Miss Harrison, pray do be careful. I have no wish to see any harm come to you.'

'I always am.' Emma skated away with forceful strokes, trying to ignore the sudden chill that went down her spine.

'Once more around the pond and I am finished,' Emma remarked. 'My legs are positively shattered.'

'You have kept going far longer than I thought,' Lucy replied. 'It is pleasant to have a skating companion who is older than five. Henry used to skate when we were courting, but these days he is far too busy.'

'My nose is getting very cold, and I lost feeling in the tips of my toes aeons ago.'

'Come and have a cup of Mother Charlton's lamb's wool punch. She reckons it is more potent than the insipid drink they served at the St Nicholas ball.'

Emma began to move forward, towards where the Charltons had set up their punch bowl.

'Watch out! Watch your back! Man out of control!'

Emma felt a bump from behind, and then she fell onto the cold ice. Lay there with a heavy weight on her back. She struggled to breathe, to move.

'Terribly sorry. I didn't see the good doctor, and I appear to have careened off in the wrong direction. High spirits and all that,' Lieutenant Ludlow said, holding out his hand. 'No harm done, what?'

'Nothing worse than a bruised elbow.' Emma started to level herself off the ice and sat back down again. 'My ankle is slightly twisted. The new strap did not give as much as I thought it would.'

'You are as pale as a ghost.' Ludlow's face creased. 'I will get

Michelle Styles 509

le sawbones for you. Put you to rights. I can't have a pretty
ning like you blaming me for a sprain.'

'No, no, I am fine.' Emma attempted to smile but knew it was
robably more of a wince. 'It is my injured pride, nothing more.'

'I must insist, Miss Harrison.' The Lieutenant helped her to
tand. 'Dr Milburn! Dr Milburn! I need your assistance and some
f your marvellous tonic for this woman. In avoiding you I ended
p colliding with this good lady instead. She is rather shaken.'

'Not the tonic,' Emma protested, scrambling to her feet. 'I
ave no need of the tonic.'

'Shouldn't we let the doctor be the judge of that?' Lieutenant
udlow replied. 'He's the one qualified in medicine.'

'Yes, Emma, you must be cautious,' Lucy said. 'Here is Dr
Milburn.'

Emma bit her lip and forced her head up. She would refuse
o take the tonic, but what if Jack was wrong? She did not want
o be responsible for ruining Dr Milburn's reputation.

'What appears to be the trouble?'

'Miss Harrison and I were involved in a collision. I believe
he needs some of your excellent tonic. She looks a bit piqued.'

'Not the tonic,' Emma said hastily, and then stopped, glancing
rom Dr Milburn to the Lieutenant and back again. 'I don't
vant to…I am not ill.'

'She does indeed look pale.' Dr Milburn's eyes glittered like
snake's. Emma wondered if he had noticed her hesitation. 'But
don't think she requires my tonic…yet.'

'What does she need?' Ludlow asked. 'I certainly did not
ntend any harm. It felt as if I was pushed from behind just after
passed you, Doctor. What can I do to make amends?'

'Besides skating with more care?' Milburn said. 'You nearly
nocked me down as well.'

'But what does she require?' Ludlow persisted.

'She needs a cup of Mrs Charlton's excellent hot punch. It i
guaranteed to put the roses back in her cheeks.'

Emma released her breath, felt her lungs fill with cold ai
Silently she offered up a prayer. Punch, and not tonic. 'A cu
of punch would be lovely.'

'I will get it for you, Miss Harrison.' Dr Milburn gave a lov
bow and skated off.

Emma allowed Lucy and Lieutenant Ludlow to help her ove
to the side. She sat on a long bench and shivered slightly.

'Are you positive that you suffered no injury, Miss Harrison?'
Lieutenant Ludlow asked again. He hovered over her in a pos
sessive manner. A lock of fair hair fell over his forehead, makin
him look barely out of his teens. 'I do not know what came ove
me. High spirits.'

'I think it is merely because I have stopped skating.' Sh
shivered as a bitter wind swept across the pond. 'After I hav
had my cup of punch no doubt I will feel better.'

'I have arrived just in time.' Dr Milburn pressed a steamin
cup into Emma's hand. 'As requested, my dear Miss Harrison
your punch. I trust it will be as the doctor ordered.'

His laughter sounded hollow to Emma's ears, and did nothin
to dispel her unease, but the soldier appeared amused by th
quip. She was seeing shadows where there were none. Had t
be. She had known Dr Milburn for years, and he had been mos
attentive to her mama in her last days.

She lifted the cup and took a tentative sip, choked, and resiste
the temptation to spit it out.

'Thank you, Doctor. You have been most kind,' Lucy said
'Now, drink it all up, Emma.'

'It will do you good, Miss Harrison.'

'I will in a little while. Just sitting is quite pleasant. I had no
realised quite how tired I was.' Emma eyed the cup. She planne

on pouring away the liquid once everyone had left her alone. It tasted foul. She had no idea what Mrs Charlton used in the celebrated punch, but she seriously wondered about people's tastebuds.

'I must insist, Miss Harrison. You need warming up. Drink it. I shall stand here watching until you do.' He gave a laugh, but she noticed his eyes had an intent look about them, much like a cat watching a mouse hole.

'It is a little warm for my tongue. I shall leave it to cool—' she began.

'Emma, do be sensible and do as Dr Milburn says,' Lucy implored. 'I want my partner back on the ice. You are wasting the daylight. I have never known you to be missish.'

Emma gritted her teeth. She wanted to be rid of the doctor and his stare. She made a face and forced the liquid down her throat, nearly gagging as she did so. She wiped her hand across her mouth. 'There—are you both satisfied?'

'Hugely satisfied,' Dr Milburn replied. His face assumed a very smug expression.

'I shall just take a turn around the ice,' Emma said. She wanted to get away from the doctor, and the prickly feeling that she had at the back of her neck. Something was not right. But it was probably an over-active imagination.

She set out with fast strokes, feeling the wind against her cheeks. It had turned much colder during the time she had been in the hut. Fewer skaters were on the ice. Emma started to go faster, turned a corner, and a wave of dizziness hit her. She shook her head to clear it.

In the distance, a broad-shouldered figure appeared, watching the skaters. His hands were behind his back, and his face shadowed, but Emma's blood gave a sudden leap. Jack! She started towards him. He wavered slightly. But she dug in, head held high. Every stroke of the blade seemed harder. Emma swallowed and redoubled her efforts, but when she got there he had vanished.

'Miss Harrison.' Dr Milburn's voice echoed in her brain. Emma squinted, managed to see straight. She put a hand to her face. As suddenly as the strange sensation had started, it ended, leaving her clear-headed, if a bit giddy. 'Are you sure you are all right?'

'I thought… That is…' Emma tried to explain the strange sensation that had filled her, filled her and then vanished. She readjusted her hood. 'It was nothing.'

'Perhaps the fall you took was greater than you imagined.' Dr Milburn gave a small bow. 'Allow me to escort you home.'

Every nerve screamed a warning. Dr Milburn's features swam in front of her, fading in and out. Emma attempted to concentrate. 'I don't think I want that. I really don't want that.'

She knew she sounded like a petulant child, but it made no difference.

'Nonsense,' Dr Milburn said. 'You need to return home before anything else happens to you. Look at you. You hardly know what you are saying. I must insist.'

Emma shook her head and refused to give in to the urge to sit down on the ice. She forced her back to remain straight, looked Dr Milburn in his fish eyes. 'I will find my own way home. I came with Mrs Charlton. There is room in her carriage.'

'You don't know what you are saying. The fall has addled your wits.'

'I don't think so.' Emma stood straight and stared determinedly straight ahead.

'You will be coming with me,' Dr Milburn said.

His fingers closed around her wrist like a vice. Emma tried twisting, first one way and then the other, but his fingers held firm.

'Unhand me. Now,' she said, in a low furious voice. 'Unhand me and we will say no more of this ungentlemanly behaviour.'

'I am afraid that would be impossible, Miss Harrison. I have your health to think of.'

Chapter Fourteen

'I believe the lady has spoken, Milburn.' Jack's voice resounded across the icy pond. Clear. Crisp. Firm.

Emma turned her head to see if she was simply hearing things. Relief flooded through her as she spied the tall man on the edge of the pond, muffled against the cold, but his outline clearly discernible. Jack had returned. *Returned!*

Suddenly, as if it were nothing, she could think again. She was not going anywhere with Dr Milburn—not if she could help it.

Dr Milburn turned his head slightly. Taking advantage of his distraction, Emma brought her arm down sharply, and Dr Milburn let go. Taking a step backwards, she caught her aching wrist with her other hand and tried to rub some warmth back into it.

'It is very kind of you to offer, Dr Milburn, but Mr Stanton will see me home.' She nodded towards where Jack was striding towards them. 'No doubt he has come from my father.'

'No doubt.'

Dr Milburn's eyes narrowed. Emma caught a look of intense hatred that was masked so quickly she wondered if she had imagined it. She pressed her hand against her forehead and tried to get her head to clear. The cold revived her a little, and focus returned to her world.

'I will see the lady home.' Jack's gloved hand caught her elbow. A very different sort of grasp from Dr Milburn's. His shoulder touched hers. Emma looked at him through her eye-lashes, trying to see if he had changed in the few short days that he had been gone. If anything, his features seemed finer than before. She had not realised quite how much she had missed him until he was standing there. Solid and real. 'I positively insist.'

'I leave it for the lady to decide,' Dr Milburn said, his face taking on a plump, sleek look.

Emma took a deep breath, forced air into her lungs. She no longer knew if her head was spinning because she was cold and tired or if it was due to Jack's nearness. 'Mr Stanton is here, and as he is lodging with my father and me it is not out of his way. I would hate to think I have deprived any of your patients of your attention.'

'If that is your choice, Miss Harrison, I must abide by it.' Dr Milburn made a stiff bow and stalked off.

Emma was relieved to see Lucy skating towards them.

'I shall leave you in Mr Stanton's capable hands,' she said with a beatific smile. 'My children are anxious to be off home. Look after her well, Mr Stanton. She is very precious to me.'

'I intend to.'

Before Emma could protest at such blatant matchmaking, Lucy had skated away, leaving her standing facing Jack. He lifted one eyebrow. Her heart sank. He knew what Lucy was doing.

'She worries…about her children,' Emma said, to explain away Lucy's behaviour. He had to believe her.

'Did I say anything?' Jack regarded Emma. The tip of her nose was bright pink and matched the colour in her cheeks. Her woollen hood emphasised the oval of her face. Her eyes sparkled. The dull ache inside his being vanished.

He had missed her. It had not occurred to him until he saw her exactly how much he had missed her. And what did he do about it? Harrison had made life more complicated, not less.

'No, it is just that…well, I thought you might wonder.' She wrapped the ribbon of her hood about her hand.

'Mrs Charlton appears to be an admirable mother. Her devotion to her children's welfare is to be commended.'

'She lives for her children. Until she married I don't think she ever thought much about being a mother. I am not sure if she even knew which end was up. But now she does. She is a very good mother.'

'Is that something you aspire to?' Jack watched for her reaction. How much did she know of her father's plan? Had she been party to it? He wondered if he should broach the subject and explain that he never mixed business with his private life, that he would never marry for the sake of a dowry.

'I have told you that I am on the shelf.' She gave an uneasy laugh.

'I had forgotten.' Jack touched his hand to his hat, satisfied. Emma had no notion of her father's plans, and he intended to keep it that way.

'Pray don't forget again.' She raised her chin and met his gaze full-on. 'I value my independence highly. It has allowed me to develop my mind, to realise there are things beyond balls, routs and dances.'

'But they do have their place.' Jack watched her mouth, remembered the feel of it against his, and her soft sigh. 'Waltzing can be a pleasurable pastime. Don't you agree?'

Waltzing with him? Emma forgot to breathe. The dizziness in her head increased. All too clearly she remembered what had happened when they'd waltzed—the pressure of his hand against her back. She gulped a mouthful of air, tried to focus somewhere other than his hands, his shoulders, his face, his mouth.

'How did you know where I was?' Emma asked, striving for a normal voice. She forced her body to ignore the dizzy feeling. If she didn't think about it, it would go away. Had to.

'I arrived back from London and your father sent me to fetch you.' His eyes were shadowed.

'He did?' Emma tried to control the sudden lurch in her stomach. The fizz in her veins had disappeared as though it had never been, leaving her empty and flat.

Jack had not come looking for her. He was here at her father's request. Here probably because he wanted to buy the company, and humouring her father was the best way to go about it. And her father was playing at matchmaker. He had to be. Everyone appeared to be. She pressed her hands together and strove for a normal tone.

'How is he? I mean, he was in good spirits when I left with Lucy earlier. Has he taken a sudden turn?'

'He is fine, but he feared you might be overdoing it. We decided it was for the best if I came out here and offered to take you back in my sleigh.'

The lines around his eyes crinkled, and Emma's heart turned over. It was as if she wanted to capture each moment and remember it for ever. She was certain his hair had grown slightly in the time he had been away, and the cut of his coat was different.

'My father worries too much. I was fine until one of Lottie's admirers collided with me.'

'Are you hurt?' Jack's hands reached out, stopped. 'How did you fall? Have you hurt your head?'

'Nothing but my pride.' Emma gave a small shiver. There was no point in telling Jack about her trepidations. Dr Milburn's sinister behaviour had melted away like snow in the sun now that Jack was here. 'I told Dr Milburn that. He appeared to believe me.'

'What Milburn believes is of little interest to me.'

'He gave me a cup of Mrs Charlton's punch. I assume that is safe.'

'I have no reason to doubt it. Is it any good?'

'It is a secret recipe for lamb's wool, perfected over the years.' Emma thought it best not to mention the awful taste of the punch. It seemed improbable that it had caused her problems. Other people, including Lucy, had drunk cups of it, and they seemed to be behaving perfectly normally. 'Lottie's young lieutenant thought some of Dr Milburn's famous tonic would set me right, but Dr Milburn said that I didn't need that.'

'Intriguing. Did you say anything about the tonic?'

'I am no fool, Mr Stanton.'

'I never said you were, Miss Harrison. And I make no judgement until the results come back.'

'But you distrust Dr Milburn.'

'Milburn and I have never been friends. I see no reason to start now.'

Emma examined her hands. This was not going the way she had planned over the last few days. She had thought of many things to say to Jack, and how she would say them. And now, when she did meet him again, she was entirely at a disadvantage.

'Which shall it be? Home, or a longer sleigh ride?'

Emma realised with a start that Jack had lifted an eyebrow and was staring at her with a quizzical expression. He had obviously been saying something. She had been paying attention to the way his mouth formed the words, rather than to what he was saying. 'You choose.'

'Then we shall try out my new sleigh and see how the blades rip the snow. The Town Moor should provide a good clear run. only thought about it on the way out here.'

A sort of reckless happiness infused her. He wanted her pinion, her help. He had not been simply doing his duty owards her father. She swallowed hard, and tried to banish the vooziness from her brain. He had come back to Newcastle to o a job, not to see her. She had to keep that in the forefront of er mind.

'Is there something special about the sleigh?'

'I have modified the runners. It is based on a Russian troika hat I saw when I had business there last winter. Mine is pulled y two horses, not three. This is the first opportunity that I have ad to conduct experiments with it. See if my theories actually vork.'

'And I presume they do?' Emma hoped her words were nough.

He smiled and his face was transformed. 'I can see from the vay your eyes shine that you do want to go.'

The past suddenly no longer mattered. Jack was right. It was nly the here and now. She clasped her hands together. The slightly voolly feeling her brain had would vanish once she sat down. She vas certain of that. 'Yes—yes, I would like that very much.'

Emma noticed how smoothly the modified troika ran over the now. It was black, with red leather seats that matched the lap obe, and the grey horses wore a double set of sleighbells. She vould not have thought the snow quite deep enough, yet it lided. Most of the others had used carriages to arrive at the ond.

The crisp air was filled with sounds—each separate and istinct—the falling of snow from the bare trees, the swish of

the runners and the peal of the sleighbells as the pair of grey
stretched out their necks. A piece of ice plopped onto the re
plaid blanket. Emma leant forward, tilted it out, and replace
the blanket more firmly about her legs.

'Cold?' He reached into his pocket and withdrew a silve
flask. 'Here—this will help keep you warm. Only a little as th
brandy is quite potent.'

'Happy,' Emma replied, after she had taken a small sip an
felt the fiery liquid trickle down her throat. Somehow it seeme
very daring to be drinking from Jack's hip flask. She carefull
wiped the top, replaced the stopper and handed it back to him
He returned it to his coat pocket. The pain at the back of her hea
had ceased, and a wild exhilaration had replaced it—as if sh
had been reborn and lived now only for this. 'This must be wha
flying feels like.'

'Some day man will fly. I don't mean simply float in the sk
in a gigantic balloon, but actually soar like a bird.'

'You sound confident.' Emma glanced at his profile. His eye
lashes were spiked with little crystals of ice. Each individuall
picked out. She wanted to think of a word to describe it, but he
head felt heavy, didn't want to work properly. She would think c
the exact word—the word to describe how his lashes looked—late

'As I told you, we live in an age when someone says I wis
to do something and it is done.'

'I will not quarrel with you today. I will agree with yo
instead. Some day men will fly, but how or why I have no idea

'Nor will I quarrel with you. It is far too lovely a day.'

She concentrated on the way his hands held the lines. Stron
hands encased in kid gloves, holding the leather lines with eas
and confidence. It was hard to believe that when they'd first me
Jack had never ridden a horse, let alone driven a spirited tea
like this pair obviously were.

'Do you want to drive?' he asked.

'Me?' Emma asked in surprise.

'I seem to recall you used to be quite handy with the whip and lines. And you are looking at the lines with such an intent expression.'

Emma inclined her head. 'Again, it is something I have left behind me. There isn't time to drive out any more. And a lady never drives in town.'

'Is there anything you didn't leave behind?'

Devotion to my parents and to duty. An attachment to a young civil engineer I thought had left without a word. A lump rose in Emma's throat. She should say something about the letter she'd found. But not now. Not when they were getting on so well. Perhaps he was correct, and the past no longer counted for anything. It was the future that was important.

She gave a brief laugh. 'Many things. I have no wish to tell you all my vices.'

'Vices? I didn't know spinsters were allowed vices.'

'They are allowed more than young ladies who are active in the marriage market. Spinsters are positively encouraged to be eccentric.'

'If they have money.' Jack's face sobered. 'I have seen many who become pale shadowy companions to even older ladies, living a sort of half-life, dependent on the good nature of their relations.'

'It will never happen to me.' Emma put her hand on the bar. On a day like today she refused to consider a bleak future. Her mind did not want to consider much of anything. It was a strange but not unwelcome sensation—rather like when she had had too many cups of punch, only this time the blood in her veins appeared to be moving more quickly. 'Can these horses go faster?'

'They can, but they need a steady hand.'

Jack clicked his tongue. The larger grey pricked up his ear and gave a low whinny. The pair then surged forward. The wind caught Emma's hood, sending it backwards. She reached up and set it more firmly on her head as the sleigh skimmed over the white snow. The horses shook their heads, seemingly simply for the pleasure of hearing the double set of sleighbells ring.

'They are wonderful animals…' She paused, carefully considering the lines, and the sleigh. She had never driven a sleigh before. The last thing she had driven was the governess cart this summer, but she knew her hands remembered. She watched as the lines stretched and pulled. Did she dare take a risk? 'Yes—yes, I would like to have a try at driving.'

'That's my Emma.'

His Emma. A warmth grew inside her, reached down to her toes. More fiery than the sip of brandy or even the hot punch. She had no desire to analyse the words and read more into them yet. They were carelessly spoken and meant nothing. Later, she knew she would turn them over and over in her mind, trying to remember the exact nuance of his words. Right now she was content with the slight thrill.

He pulled back on the lines and the horses instantly slowed their gait, first to a steady trot and then to a sedate walk. The bells slowed and then quietened. The whole world became wrapped in a hush, as if it were waiting for something to happen, something wonderful.

Emma drew in a deep breath, and focused on a point beyond the horses' ear tips. The dizziness that had threatened a moment before faded and the world became beautifully clear. She could do this. She took the leather lines, flicked them, felt the horses surge forward.

'It is almost as if the lines are alive. Are they strong enough t would be dreadful to become stranded out here. No one is round to help.'

'They will hold. I had the leather waxed and the joints reinorced. I did not want anything to happen.' He touched his hat. Attention to detail saves time in the long term.'

'Are the horses liable to run away, then?' Emma swallowed ard, and tried to keep the horses at a steady gait.

'They are from Tattersall's, and are well trained but lively. I ike to drive horses with a bit of spirit.'

And how do you like your women? Emma bit back the words nd wondered where the thought had come from. Something nside her insisted on being reckless, grabbing life with both hands.

'You like to live dangerously, then?' she said carefully.

'Dangerously? No, I like to take calculated risks.'

Emma glanced at him out of the corner of her eye. A calcuated risk? Was that what she was taking? She turned her attenion firmly to the horses, and watched the power of their stride s they moved over the unbroken snow of the Town Moor.

She pulled back slightly, and the horses responded much more harply than she'd thought they would. The sleigh turned, rising lightly on one runner. She slid into Jack, her thigh touching his hrough their clothes. She forgot her lungs needed air.

'Everything will be fine. Keep calm.' Jack's voice rumbled in er ear. He put his hands over hers. 'Like this. Steady, with a irm but gentle touch.'

She gave a brief nod. 'They respond quickly.'

'As I said—they are lively. A bit dangerous.'

Like their master. Emma held back the words, only allowing erself to nod. She screwed up her eyes, feeling a dizzy exciteent rise within her. Emma did not know which unnerved her nore—the horses' abrupt turn or the pressure of Jack's thigh gainst hers and the warmth of his hands. She had to remain in control. Keeping her attention focused on driving this team would help her do that.

'I believe I can handle them.'

'As you wish.'

Jack withdrew and settled himself against the backboard. He laid an arm across it, not exactly hugging her, but it was there, tempting her to lean back. Emma forced her back upright, reached forward, and gave the lines a flick.

The horses responded, and this time she was able to complete a turn without rocking the sleigh.

'It is amazing how things come back to you. Things you never forget.'

'Your confidence is returning.'

'Something like that.'

Jack glanced over and saw the brightness of her cheeks had increased. They were unnaturally pink, almost as if she had drunk far too much. There was something unusual about her, but he could not put his finger on it. A missing detail.

'Your horses are wonderful.' Her laugh rang out, tinkling like the sleighbells, and Jack decided to concentrate on that instead.

'I am pleased that my sleigh meets with your approval.'

'More than my approval. My admiration. It is very impressive. It is like something from a storybook—a dream.' His warm laughter resounded in the frosty air, warming her insides as surely as the lamb's wool punch had warmed her before, but somehow more potent—much more potent. The world appeared to spin slightly, as it had just after Dr Milburn had given her the drink. She glanced at Jack from under her eyelashes. 'Are you sure I am not dreaming? In many ways I think I must be.'

'If you are, we are experiencing the same dream. And that is an impossibility.'

She pulled the lines, slightly more jerkily this time, and the eigh slid once more. Her body hit his, her soft breast meeting is chest. Her hands slackened, and the lines fell between them. he sleigh rocked violently.

Jack took the reins from her slack grasp, concentrating on re-aining control of the horses, of his body.

'Be careful. You nearly turned us over.'

'I am trying my best,' Emma whispered. How could she explain oout her increased dizziness? He would insist on returning to her ither's, and she did not want the sleigh ride ever to end. She anted to be out here, with him. The chance might never come gain. Tomorrow she would return to reality, and he would go away gain. The thought sobered her. 'I lost concentration, that is all.'

'Losing concentration is when accidents happen.'

'I know.' Emma looked at her hands. 'It won't happen again. et's stay out a bit longer…please.'

Jack pulled the lines and brought the horses to a stop under ie shelter of some trees at the edge of the common.

'Do you want to explain what happened?' he asked. 'It was iore than a momentary lapse. You are an expert driver. How adly did you hit your head?'

'It has been a long time since I have driven. That is all. Jothing more. My head feels perfectly fine.'

Jack noticed the red ripeness of her mouth—a ripeness that emanded tasting. Her mouth was inches from his. And there vas no sound but the soft plop of snow as it fell from the trees. : was as if they were cocooned in their own little world.

He lifted a hand and touched her cheek. 'I share some of the lame, Emma. These horses are high-spirited, and the sleigh esponds instantly.'

'That is kind of you.' Her voice was small, her eyes big.

Jack fought to keep from taking her in his arms. Once he egan kissing her he knew that he'd be unable to stop.

Things were too complicated. Business before pleasure. Once ownership of the company was settled, then he could pursue Emma Harrison properly. She had to know that she meant more to him than a means to an end. This sleigh·ride showed he had been mistaken. He wanted her in his life. But on his terms, not Harrison's.

'We will go back.'

Go back? The fizzy bubbles in Emma's veins burst. She slumped against the backboard and braced her feet. She had been sure Jack was going to kiss her. Her whole body ached for the touch of his mouth against hers. Nobody was around. They were safe. No one would ever know.

Suddenly she knew she had to know how he felt about her. Once again the strange reckless feeling filled her. Acting on pure instinct, she leant towards him, lifted her mouth.

'Kiss me.' She caught his face between her fingers. 'Kiss me like you mean it, Jack.'

He swore, and pulled her into his arms, their bodies colliding once again.

Then his mouth descended on hers, devoured, feasted, and she knew she had never been kissed before. Everything that had gone before was tame. This was the essence of danger.

His tongue traced the edge of her lips, demanding entrance. She parted them, and plunged into a whole other world. Dark. Dangerous. Carnal. Her tongue touched his, retreated then advanced. A sigh was torn from her throat.

Her body arched forward and his arms tightened around her, holding her tight against his chest. The reckless feeling changed to something warmer, and her breasts began to ache, new feelings flooded through her. Everything in the world had stopped, had come down to one thing—him, his touch, his scent his everything.

His lips moved from her mouth to her eyelids and face. Hot against the cold, creating a heat that was burning inside her.

A tiny voice in the back of her mind warned her to stop, to protest. But her body seemed to have a will of its own. A hot fire was coursing through her body.

She reached up, sank her hands into Jack's hair and pulled his face closer, recapturing his mouth. This time their tongues touched, played, entwined. A wild dark thrill that somehow did not lessen her desire but increased it.

She wanted more than this. A deep burning sensation was growing within her. His body seemed impossibly hard against hers and yet she wanted to feel that hardness, feel his skin touching hers. She wanted… Her hands went to his shoulders.

'We must go back,' he growled in her ear as his tongue licked her earlobe. The briefest of touches, but it sent pulses of warmth through her body.

'Back? Why?'

He lifted a hand and brushed the hair off her face. His lips skimmed her forehead. 'Because.'

His eyes were dark pools fringed by even darker lashes. She wanted to stay here, in this little world they had created. She wanted this fiery ache to continue and grow.

She pressed her lips against his ear. Her breath fanned his hair just above the earlobe. 'That is no answer. You enjoyed the kiss as much as I did.'

He gave a groan and slid his arms around her. Iron bands holding her fast to him. His hand slipped downward, cupping her bottom, pulling her more fully on top of him. Emma allowed herself to fall, encountered the full hardness of his body. She allowed her mouth to echo his, to trail down his throat. Her hands pulled at his stock, releasing a small patch of skin—skin that begged to be touched, to be tasted, feasted on.

'What is going on? Why is this sleigh here?' The voice wa
sharp, insistent, and horribly familiar in its piercing tone, pene
trating her mind.

Emma froze, looked at Jack in horror. They were discovered
Her hair was about her shoulders in waves. His stock wa
mussed. He put his finger to his lips and gave a slight shake o
his head. She nodded her understanding. The people migh
move on. If she remained quiet there was a whisper of a chance

'Has there been a crash?' another female voice asked. 'Wh
has it stopped here under the trees?'

'The horses seem perfectly content. The sleigh is upright.'

'We should leave them,' a masculine voice said. 'It would b
folly to pry.'

'Nonsense. They might be hurt. I am going to see. It will b
fun. A mystery to be solved.'

'I really shouldn't do that if I were you…'

Emma's eyes widened. They were about to be discovered
Jack's hands released her, pushed her away. Emma hastily sa
up, trying to straighten her clothes. She offered up a prayer tha
no one had noticed, and that she had been mistaken in the voices
They could be from anywhere. The Town Moor was popula
with all sorts of people. It could be anyone. Total strangers. Sh
had to be mistaken.

The golden light of a lantern blinded her. She raised a hand
and saw several black silhouettes.

'Oh, my, oh, my, oh, my—Miss Emma Harrison. Who would
ever have guessed?' Emma winced at Lottie Charlton's smug
lip-smacking tones. 'I thought you were far too proper to indulge
in such games, but obviously I was wrong.'

'You may lower the lantern, Miss Charlton,' Jack said, and
his tone held ice.

'Mr Stanton—such an unexpected pleasure,' Lottie purred.

'We had some difficulties with the horses, but they are now olved.'

Emma's heart pounded in her ears. She knew what was happening. Her head began to spin as the enormity of what she had done hit her. She should protest, or at least make a pretence of being overwhelmed. Something to save her reputation. She should feel ashamed of what she had done. But huge great waves of tiredness hit her. Where there had been giddy excitement now there was only numbness and weary recognition. She was ruined. She was ruined, and furthermore she didn't care.

Shock, horror and general revulsion should be her emotion, he knew, but all she felt was regret and disappointment that the kisses had stopped.

Her eyelids felt heavy. Darkness pressed against her eyeballs. And the cotton wool feeling in her brain returned with a vengeance, swooped down and claimed her. She closed her eyes, intending to rest for a moment before she explained. There had to be a rational explanation for what she had done, what she longed to do again. Something she could say.

Perhaps it was all a dream? Perhaps she had hit her head in the collision with Lieutenant Ludlow and everything since drinking the punch was a dream? If she rested a moment, then she'd wake and discover what was real and what was fantasy.

'Jack,' she breathed, before the darkness claimed her.

Jack swore under his breath. He should have expected this. It had been far too easy. The woman far too willing. And now she had decided to faint. A soft snore came from her lips. No, not to faint, but to fall asleep. Almost as if she was drunk.

He gazed up at the treetops and tried to control his temper. What had she had to drink? Milburn had given her something to drink. There had been something in the way she'd said that. And why hadn't he realised the difference in her behaviour? He

gritted his teeth. The truth was that he hadn't wanted to. He ha‹
taken because he'd wanted to.

'You saw nothing,' he said, looking at the redness of a major'
coat. 'We stopped for a moment when the lines became entan
gled. We were in the process of untangling the lines.'

'That is not what I saw!' Lottie Charlton's voice held a ton‹
of amused outrage. 'You and Miss Harrison were in an em
brace—an intimate embrace.'

'It would be wise to keep your views to yourself, Mis
Charlton. You are out here without a chaperon.' Jack glared a‹
her.

'I know what I saw.' Lottie made a little moue with her mouth
'It is quite shocking. And you the confirmed spinster, Mis
Harrison. Tsk, tsk, tsk.'

Jack gritted his teeth. He should have erred on the side o‹
caution. Emma's head lolled against his shoulder.

He tried another approach. 'Miss Harrison is unwell. She
needs to get home to her bed.'

'She appeared well when she left the skating,' Lottie
answered. 'Otherwise my sister-in-law would not have let he‹
go, and Dr Milburn would have insisted on looking after her. He
fetched her some lamb's wool punch. I heard him ask most par
ticularly for it. He wouldn't let my mother take it to her either.

'Are you sure?' Jack looked at the blonde woman. Could i‹
be possible? Jack frowned and dismissed the thought. He ha‹
to stop thinking the worst about Milburn. He might be obnox
ious, but it would be an incredible risk to take. The doctor di‹
not even know about his tests for arsenic.

'I think she is shamming.' Lottie Charlton reached into the
sleigh. 'Emma—Emma, say something.'

Emma gave a quiet sigh, and snuggled closer to Jack. Her ful‹
lips parted as if she had fallen asleep. Asleep, or something

orse? Jack frowned. She had avoided saying how badly she
ad hit her head. Or was she feigning, hoping that everyone and
verything would go away? And yet Milburn had been less than
leased to see him. He had had Emma by the wrist. What had
e intended? Jack felt a deep anger grow through him.

'I do hope you intend to do the decent thing, sir,' the other
emale voice said. 'There is only one honourable way to rectify
is situation.'

'Yes—you have ruined Miss Harrison.' Lottie Charlton
macked her lips. 'Think of the scandal. Poor, poor Emma. My
eart positively bleeds for her. What will Mama say when she
ears? And Lucy won't be able to look down her nose at me
uite so much now that Emma has behaved like this.'

Jack ignored the pair of harpies. He stared hard at the Major,
ho was shuffling his feet. 'What was your purpose in coming
ere, and who sent you?'

'I saw the sleigh skimming across the moor,' the Major
nswered. 'Lottie thought it would be good fun if we could
atch it. We lost sight of it, but Lottie's sharp eyes spied it here
the trees and we decided to investigate.'

'You saw nothing untoward.' He looked hard at the Major,
ho gave a slight nod.

'Are you going to deny your responsibility?' Lottie gave a
aint gasp of horror. 'I know they have always said that you are
ot quite a gentleman…'

Jack stared at the group in astonishment. He curled his lip. 'I
m in the process of taking Miss Harrison home. The sooner she
ets there the better, for all concerned. Gossip and idle chit-chat
ill not reflect well on anyone.'

'But…but…' There came a little squeak of protest from Lottie
harlton, and Jack knew that gossip would spread and grow. The
lly woman would be unable to resist.

'I would think a modicum of tact might be worthwhile.' Jack regarded the man. 'I would take it amiss if gossip was spread about her. I would take it as a very great personal favour if it was not.'

'I can see no reason for any of us to say anything, provided the decent thing is done,' the Major pronounced. 'Miss Harrison enjoys a sterling reputation.'

'I always do the decent thing.'

Jack gritted his teeth. He was trapped. Emma was trapped. This was to have been a very different sort of sleigh ride, building their friendship. But he had been unable to resist.

He glanced at her oval face, now quiet in sleep. What would she say when she woke? Who would she blame? Neither of them had a choice.

'But he *is* going to make it right?' the silly blonde asked. 'Poor poor Emma. Ruined. It would be the gentlemanly thing to do.'

'You do not know very much about me, Miss Charlton, if you call me a gentleman. That is a title I have never claimed.'

'Of all the nerve!'

He heard the shocked gasps with satisfaction as Emma snuggled down against his chest, warm and delightful.

The Emma he knew would never have behaved in such a manner. But did he really know her? She had kissed him with an expert passion.

He clicked his tongue and the sleigh began to move.

'Where are we going, Jack?' she asked in a slurred voice heavy with sleep. 'I have had the strangest dream. You kissed me, full on the lips. It was lovely.'

Jack gave the lines a tremendous shake, gave the horses their heads, and braced his feet against the dashboard.

'Off home. We go home, Emma,' he said, forcing the words out one at a time. 'And then we see about making this right.'

Chapter Fifteen

⟢⟤⟢⟤⟢

'Do you wake, or do I carry you into the house?'

Rough hands shook Emma's shoulder. Her body protested at the sudden rush of air, and sought warmth again, but nothing was there. Her neck ached from being in the wrong position, and her nose was numb from the cold.

She sat up and tried to figure out where she was. The shape of her house loomed above her. She frowned and rubbed her hand against the back of her neck. How had she got here? The last thing she remembered was the sleigh ride and the lines slipping.

'I must have fallen asleep. I had the strangest dream.'

'You are back home. Do you feel capable of walking?' Jack's voice was hard and uncompromising.

The inside of her mouth felt woolly and her lips bruised. She ran her tongue along them and tried to rid herself of a sense of impending disaster.

'What is happening?'

'I am going to see your father.'

'Why?' Emma clambered down from the sleigh and put one foo in front of the other, slipping slightly. Instantly Jack's hand wa there, catching her. There was nothing lover-like in his hard fingers.

'We were seen. Your reputation is in tatters. That Charlton chit's mouth flows as freely as the Tyne.' Jack's face was hard and intent—nothing of the lover, everything of the irate business man.

'But nothing happened.' Emma drew herself up with dignity and tried to remember the lovely dream she had had, with Jack kissing her. His lips had been soft and his voice caressing bearing little resemblance to this. 'It was just a dream, and dreams don't count.'

'The devil you say.' The words were low and furious.

Emma rubbed a hand over her eyes, saw two doors. If she closed her eyes again all this would go away. It had to.

Emma stretched, pointing her toes and lifting her arms above her head. The linen sheets felt cool against her cheek. She regarded the bright light that shone through a crack in the bed curtains.

She tried to sit up, and rapidly put her head down on the feather pillows again. Pain shot through the front of her head. All her limbs were weak, and the ceiling showed distinct signs of moving. She closed her eyes, opened them again, and tried to focus.

'Annie,' she called. 'What time is it? I have had the strangest dreams. Dreams so vivid and real I could swear they happened but they were sheer fantastical nonsense.'

'At last you are awake, miss.' Annie twitched back the curtains and daylight flooded into the bed.

Emma put up a hand to shield her eyes and squinted towards

the mantelpiece clock. She scrubbed her eyes, focused, and then gaped. Her first glance had not lied. She doubted if she had ever slept so late in her life—not even when she was ill.

'You appear worried, Annie.'

'Your father wishes to see you directly. He has asked several times over the past few hours.'

'Why didn't you wake me?' Emma swung her legs over the end of the bed. 'I feel as weak as a newborn kitten today. Mrs Charlton's hot punch is notorious, but I only had the one cup. Is my father well?'

'Your father has been up since daybreak, miss, bustling about, sending letters here and there, barking orders.' Annie twisted her apron between her hands. 'And I would have woken you, but Mr Jack insisted I was to let you sleep.'

Emma grabbed onto the bedpost and sank back down on the bed. So Jack Stanton *had* arrived. She had thought it a dream. She wrinkled her nose. No, most of it had to be a dream. It had a dreamlike quality to it. More than likely she had hit her head, come home with Lucy and simply then heard Jack's voice as she lay dreaming. She closed her eyes with relief. That was what had to have happened. The alternative was too terrible to contemplate.

'Since when do you obey Mr Stanton?' she asked, keeping her voice calm.

'Since he became your fiancé, miss.' The maid gave a swift curtsey. 'I thought it best. He does appear concerned about you.'

All notion of sleep and beautiful dreams vanished, to be replaced by the ice-cold feeling of dread. Emma put a hand to her head and tried to think. Exactly how much had been a dream?

The sleigh with its bells and runners gliding over the snow? The feel of Jack's leg against hers? His warm lips seeking hers as his hands pulled her close? All of it? None of it?

Her lips ached faintly in remembrance. Had she acted in that brazen manner? Pressing her body against his? She could not imagine doing such a thing. Her entire being became numb. She blinked twice, going back over the events. It had to have been a dream. Was she dreaming still?

She pinched her wrist and discovered that she was definitely awake, and Annie was looking at her with an increasingly puzzled expression on her face.

'I don't believe I am anyone's fiancée, let alone Mr Stanton's.'

'Mr Stanton did say that you had bumped your head, miss. Are you sure you are fit?'

'My head hurts.' Emma explored the base of her scalp and found an egg-sized lump. 'But not in the manner I would expect. I think Mrs Charlton's punch must have been stronger than I first thought.'

'Bound to have been, miss,' said Annie, bustling about the room. 'It is an old wassailing recipe I had from Jeannine, Mrs Charlton's lady's maid. But you are definitely Mr Stanton's fiancée. There can be no doubt about that.'

Emma pressed her lips into a firm line. An old wassailing recipe? But that begged as many questions as it answered. No one else appeared to have suffered the difficulties that she had.

'Exactly when am I to be married? My memory is a bit vague on the precise details.'

'As soon as possible, or so the servants say.' Annie put her hands on her hips. 'And it is hardly surprising your memory ain't good. You were bundled up to bed the moment your foot touched the hall. On Mr Jack's orders. Right angry he was about everything, too.'

'Christmas is only three days away, and there are still preparations for the Goose Feast to settle. It will have to be in the New Year.' Emma tapped her finger against her mouth.

'It would not be for me to say.' Annie stood with her eyes downcast. 'But there was talk of a Special Licence. Servants' gossip only, mind. Rose the under-housemaid had it from Fackler, who heard it from Mr Stanton's valet.'

'Servants' gossip?' Emma gave her maid a stern look. 'You should know better than to go repeating tales.'

'Very good, miss, but I know what I heard.'

Emma pressed her fingers into the bridge of her nose. There was a slim chance that this was simply gossip—misheard rumours and innuendo. She had not agreed to marry anyone! She would know if she had. It was not something one easily forgot. 'It has to be just rumours, Annie. I would remember if Jack Stanton had asked me to marry him. I know I would.'

'I thought you would like to know, miss, just in case.' Annie bobbed a curtsey. 'I must say the thought of a Special Licence sent a little tremor through me.'

Emma drew in a breath, the woolliness vanishing as sweet relief flooded in. She *knew* she had not agreed to anything. She would not forget a detail like that.

A Special Licence…

Despite everything, a small thrill went through Emma as well. When her hair had been in plaits and she had dreamt of dancing all night, and of tall, broad-shouldered dukes who would sweep her off her feet, she'd also had a wish to be married by Special Licence. It had a certain ring to it, and was certainly more attractive than eloping to Gretna Green. Her mother had been furious when Claire had married simply by ordinary licence.

She forced her mind away from girlish thoughts. What sort of licence did not matter. What mattered was that everyone was under the impression that she was going to marry Jack Stanton. And he had never even asked her!

'I am certain you have heard wrong, in any case.' Emma started to dress, tying the tapes of her petticoats with practised fingers. 'When I go down I shall prove what nonsense this conversation has been.'

'As you wish, miss, but what shall I do about your trousseau?'

'My trousseau?'

'I can't have my lady being married without a proper one. I know your under-things are serviceable, but a married lady requires more. And there simply is not time to send a Marriage and Outfitting order out to the linen warehouse at Bainbridges. Even with the best will in the world it will take a few weeks. Christmas is nearly upon us.'

'I can always acquire the things later, if it is necessary.' Emma gave a smile and wished the pain in her head would cease. She would clear up the mystery and life would go on as before. This talk of trousseaux was premature. Things were rapidly spinning out of control—like a trickle of water that had become a stream and then a torrent, carrying all before it. She drew a deep breath and refused to panic. 'I am positive we shall have time. Bainbridges are very efficient.'

'But, miss, your wedding dress… You should send to London for that. I wouldn't trust any in Newcastle for such a thing as that.'

'My wedding dress will be dealt with when the time comes,' Emma said firmly.

She regarded her dresses. The one thing she absolutely refused to think about was a wedding dress. But Annie was correct. None of them would do. She raised a hand and stroked the rose silk. Jack's eyes had shone when he saw her in this. And when they had danced in the drawing room— She drew her hand back as if the dress had bitten her.

Enough of this foolishness.

She refused even to allow herself to build castles in clouds.

Her life had to be real and solid. Her future was not married bliss with Jack Stanton, despite the longings of her heart. She had to be sensible. She had spent seven years being sensible and mature. Now was not the time to revert back to the girl she had been. Dreams were for other people.

'I think my grey poplin would be best for today. It is serviceable, and I have much to do about the feast today. After I have spoken with my father and laid this bit of gossip to rest I have the twelfth cakes to inspect. Can you imagine how Mrs Mudge will click her tongue if the royal icing is not just so?'

Annie did not give an answering laugh. Her brown eyes sobered and she tucked her hands under her starched white apron.

'It is your choice, miss, but I think the blue brings out your eyes more. And grey always robs the colour from your face, if you don't mind me saying. Mr Stanton's face lights up when he sees you in the blue dress.'

Emma gritted her teeth as a pulsating warmth flooded through her. 'You are becoming very bold, Annie.'

'Someone has to take you in hand, miss. Don't you want Mr Stanton's eyes to light up?'

She wanted that, and more. Her treacherous body wanted the feel of his hands and his lips again. She wanted to taste his mouth. Emma put her hand to her head, tried to clear it of the image of Jack's expression just before his lips touched hers, of his hands entangled in her hair, the tiny beat of his pulse at the base of his throat.

'You are being ridiculous, Annie! Please get me a tisane for my head, and kindly refrain from comments about Jack Stanton.'

'Sometimes I think there are those that don't know what is good for them, like.'

'I do know. And concentrating on the upcoming Goose Feast is what I need to do. It means a great deal to the employees and their families.'

'Very good, miss.'

The worst part was that a large chunk of her hoped the servants' gossip was true—all of it.

She did want to marry Jack Stanton. She wanted his eyes to light up each and every time they saw her. She wanted to feel his mouth against hers again. But more than that she wanted to be with him. To spend hours discussing bridges and other engineering projects. To travel to unknown places and see the sights he had described. Just to be with him. But she wanted him to marry her because he wanted to. Not because he had to, because society dictated it.

It did not matter if the whole of her dream was true—including the nasty bit with Lottie at the end. Emma caught her lip between her teeth, considering the implications if the worst should happen.

Lottie would make much of it. She'd be unable to help herself from giggling and gossiping. The story would fly from lip to lip become embroidered. Some women might even pull their skirts away from her as she walked in Grainger Town near the Theatre Royal, or refuse to return her calls. The penalties for such scandals were severe, and strictly enforced for some time. But she would recover from the scandal…eventually. Such talk would die down and disappear over Christmas. Scandals were always nine-day wonders.

She was on the shelf. It was not as if she anticipated a brilliant alliance such as her mama had dreamt about. She'd rise above it. Hold her head high. Show it did not matter. What more could they do to her?

And Jack Stanton was not the marrying kind. He had made that quite clear that first day at the bridge. And after what had happened between them, would he risk humiliation by asking her?

No, she could not be engaged to Jack.

Emma forced down the tisane. The infusion of herbs and barley helped restore a measure of confidence. She was not stupid. She would know if that were the case. However much her heart whispered that she wanted it to be true.

Emma discovered both Jack and her father in the study. They were sitting in front of a blazing fire with cups of coffee at their sides, discussing bridges. Jack's legs, encased in tight-fitting cream trousers, were stretched out in front of him, and Emma glimpsed the tops of his black leather shoes.

Emma listened, half hidden by the door. Jack's voice flowed over her, making her heart pound. It had been just a dream last night. It had to have been. She forced her breath to come naturally.

Jack's long-fingered hand held his cup, and Emma was forcibly reminded of how his fingers had intertwined in her hair. How they had felt skimming her jawline. A warm fluttering sensation grew in her belly as she felt her jaw. It had to have been more than a dream. Surely she could not remember such a thing so vividly if it had never occurred? And yet she could not imagine what had caused her to so forget all notions of propriety.

She was glad that she had listened to Annie and chosen the blue wool in the end, rather than the much more practical grey.

The two men paused in their conversation when she rapped on the door. Only Jack rose, and as Annie had predicted his eyes did light for an instant, before becoming veiled.

Her father lifted a lazy hand but remained seated. 'You took your time, daughter.'

'My eyes have just opened. I have come down with a pounding head and little memory of yesterday afternoon.' Emma gave a smile, but there was no answering one on either man's face. Events appear to be a little hazy. The only thing I know for certain is that I left this house to go skating and Mr Stanton arrived to take me home in his sleigh. My eyes must have closed the moment I sat down.'

The explanation would have to suffice. To reveal her dream was unthinkable.

'Hazy?' Her father's face turned the colour of the Turkey pattern carpet. 'How much punch did you have to drink yesterday, daughter?'

'I had the one cup of lamb's wool that Dr Milburn brought me, and a sip of brandy from Mr Stanton's flask.' Emma kept her head high, but two spots of heat formed on her cheeks. 'I had thought my mind was clear, but it appears not.'

'Shamming serves no useful purpose.' Her father's voice was deceptively quiet. Emma shifted in her slippers. She could have dealt with him if he'd shouted, but when he was quiet like this she knew worse was to come. 'This is a scandal of immense proportions.'

She looked from his face to Jack's, found comfort in neither.

'I went for a sleigh ride. Nothing happened.' Emma wrapped her arms about her waist. 'Anyone who tries to say differently is mischief-making.'

Her father harrumphed. 'It all depends on what you call nothing. I never thought you a flirt, my girl. I thought your mother and I had brought you up better than that.'

'My head is so woolly this morning, Father, please try to understand.' Emma bit her lip. The last faint hope she'd had faded. Everything that she'd been certain had been a dream had in fact happened—her insistence on a kiss, and then the aftermath. Her cheeks flamed. She had behaved in such a brazen fashion, pressing her body against Jack's, demanding more. Her father was quite right. She was ruined. Her future lay at her feet, broken and shattered.

'I believe we have already discussed this, Harrison.' Jack moved between her father and herself. 'We have already determined the fault was mine.'

'You have behaved admirably without question, Stanton.' Her father harrumphed again.

Jack held up a hand, silencing him. Her father covered his mouth and nodded. 'We have reached an acceptable arrangement, with good will on both sides.'

'Your fault? An arrangement?' she whispered. Jack made it sound like a formal business deal. Good will on both sides, indeed.

'In light of what has happened I have offered to do the decent thing.' His eyes became hard black lumps of granite, his mouth uncompromising. 'We will marry with all speed.'

'And I have no choice in the matter?' Emma hated the way her voice squeaked.

'Neither of us has any choice.' Jack's voice was cold, his stare hard.

'There is always a choice.' Emma raised her head and glared back at Jack. 'No one has asked me to marry.'

'The asking was unnecessary,' her father blustered. 'It is all settled. You will marry and marry quickly, daughter.'

'Is it necessary for us to marry quickly?' Emma stared at Jack. His words from that first day clearly reverberated in her head. He had no wish to marry her. It was only the circumstances. How could she marry a man like that?

'I consider it a necessity,' her father said.

'Would we not be better to wait until the scandal has died down? See what happens then? This whole sorry episode will be forgotten by New Year.'

'No.' Jack's dark eyes pierced her and his lips became a thin white line. 'We marry tomorrow.'

Emma's heart pounded in her ears. She stared uncompre
hending at Jack, hoping for the slightest sign of softening
There was none.

'Tomorrow? But that will create a bigger scandal.' Emma
stared him. Tomorrow was tomorrow. Even for Jack Stanton and
his money it was surely an impossibility. There were convention
to be followed. Rules. Regulations. She had to concentrate
There had to be a way. She refused to be married in such a
fashion.

'I don't think so.' His mouth took on a cynical twist. 'We shall
explain that you and I were close seven years ago, but parted
Now that we have become reacquainted we have discovered ou
hearts remained true. In light of your father's recent illness we
wish to marry quietly but quickly, so that your father can see
you as a blushing bride.'

Emma walked over to the fireplace and looked at the embers
Our hearts remained true. She rejected the idea. It had no
happened. On either part. A cynical tale served up for public
consumption. She spun round on her heels.

'But the banns will have to be posted. Those take three weeks.

His lip curled upwards. 'Not with a Special Licence. You
know that as well as I do.'

'A Special—?'

'No need for such a thing. A common licence has already
been obtained,' her father said.

This was going altogether too fast. Emma clasped her hand
to her head. 'Stop—stop.'

'Is there something wrong, Emma?' Jack asked, in an infuri
atingly calm voice. He raised an eyebrow and his fingers beat a
slow tattoo against his thigh.

Emma struggled to contain her temper. 'I have not said yes
I have not agreed to marry Jack Stanton or any man.'

She heard the sharp intake of breath, saw Jack's eyes glitter, and she took a step backwards.

Her father pounded his fist against the table. 'You will cease this nonsense and do as I say.'

'Are you ordering me?' Emma put her hands on her hips. 'I am a grown woman, Father. I should have the right to decide my own life.'

'This discussion has little merit.' Jack's words cut through the room. 'Your father and I have reached an agreement.'

'I shall leave you, Jack, to explain the situation to my daughter. Perhaps you can make her see sense where I cannot. You are a man who can make things happen. Here and at the bridge.' Her father turned on his heel and stalked out of the room.

Make things happen. Here and at the bridge. A slight chill went down the back of Emma's spine. Jack and her father had intended on this happening. No one could get a common licence that speedily. It was a physical impossibility.

This marriage had already been decided. Signed and sealed. She had fallen into the trap. Jack's offer to buy the company at a decent price had been a ruse. All the while he had intended to acquire it in a different fashion.

The room started to spin slowly, and Emma sank down into the chair that her father had vacated. She put her head in her hands, willed it to stop.

The deal must have been done the night of the St Nicholas Ball. It must be why her father had allowed her so much freedom. She had been naïve. She had tumbled headlong into a manipulation—a merger between companies. She had been used as a pawn. What exactly *was* the agreement between her father and Jack? She did not doubt Jack had used it to his advantage. Her father must have bought her respectability with his company. It had to be her dowry. There could be no other.

Jack had cynically kissed her. Pretended to be her frien
Damning thought piled on damning thought. And all the whil
her mind was crying no, somehow she was mistaken, overreact
ing. He was interested in her. It was not all pretence.

'You appear less than pleased, Emma,' Jack said. 'I woul
have thought avoiding a scandal would be something you'
desire. You always set such great store by what society thought

Emma raised her face from her hands and looked directly int
his uncompromising face. She refused to let him twist things
This wedding was happening because it suited Jack's pur
poses—his business purposes.

'You are marrying me for my father's company. It is the pric
you have exacted for marrying me. You made my father promis
it as my dowry.'

A muscle jumped in his cheek but he stayed stubbornly silen

'I need to know,' she begged. Her insides were jelly. Sh
wanted him to say that it did not matter, that he was marryin
her because he could not imagine a future without her.

His eyes raked her up and down. Emma's heart beat so loudl
she thought he must hear it. He had to say something. Her throa
closed and she struggled for breath.

'I am a businessman,' he said, breaking the stretching silence
'I have made no secret of wishing to acquire your father'
company. That is the truth.'

'I see.' She kept her head high, ignored the sudden prickle o
tears behind her eyelids. Whatever happened she refused to cry
She gazed up at the ceiling, blinked rapidly, regained contro
Then she looked him directly in the eye and smiled. 'It make
perfect sense now. Thank you for being honest.'

'But perhaps you want soft meaningless words?' His mout
twisted into a hard smile. 'Should I say that I am suffering fron
an undiminished passion for you? That I have carried a torc

or you these past seven years? That not a day has gone I did not think of you and wonder how you fared? What words do you wish me to say? Tell me, and I will say them.'

Emma held up a hand. 'Stop, please. Such cynical sentiments do not become you. You must not think that because I am a woman I spend my day reading Minerva Press novels where the hero declares undying passion for the innocent maiden. Such things do not happen in real life.'

However much we might like them to, she added silently.

'Very well.' Jack gave a slight shrug. 'I won't say it.'

'It is not good to pretend things that one doesn't feel.' Emma strove for a normal voice, but it sounded high and strained to her ears. The knots in her stomach ached and her feet were rooted to the spot. She longed for him to draw her into his arms and whisper that he wanted to marry her, and only her. She wanted to believe his kisses had been real, that he hadn't simply been pursuing her for the sake of acquiring another company.

'Honesty is always best.' He checked his pocket watch, the gold gleaming in the sunlight, and closed it with a snap.

Emma wanted to scream. To do something to end this terrible formality. He had to see that marriage between them would be disaster. 'You caused this situation.'

He raised an eyebrow and a half-smile crossed his lips. 'Me? Miss Harrison, your recollections about yesterday's events may be hazy, but mine are crystal-clear.'

'What do you mean by that?' Emma put her hand to her throat and attempted to look anywhere but at his mouth. Yet every time she attempted to look away something dragged her gaze back, fastened it to that spot, the fullest part of the curve.

'It was you who asked me to kiss you. Begged me.' Jack's gaze never wavered. 'How could I refuse such a request when it was so prettily offered?'

'You should have known the impropriety.' Emma swallowed hard. She was being unfair. She knew it. But this situation was not of her making.

His eyes hardened. 'Perhaps it is I who should be complaining of manipulation?'

'How do you mean?' Emma's jaw dropped, and then she closed her mouth with a snap. She had not trapped him into anything. She hadn't… She stopped as the memory of her voice echoed in her brain. She had asked him to kiss her, begged him. She wanted to die. Emma fought against the tide of heat that was washing over her. 'What are you accusing me of?'

'Not accusing, merely pointing out the details.' He settled himself on the chair-arm, his right foot swinging slightly. 'It is vital to get the details correct. It makes for a firm foundation.'

'In what way?' Emma crossed her arms and glared at him and his maddening complacency. 'What are you accusing me of doing? I am the injured party here.'

'It was *your* friends who discovered us,' he said, ticking the points off on his fingers. 'And it was *you* who initiated the kiss. You demanded it. Let us be clear on that.'

His dark eyes flared with something, and Emma took a step backwards. Surely he could not think that she would be so underhanded as to try to get a husband in such a fashion?

'It was a series of unfortunate coincidences,' Emma said through gritted teeth. Lottie was not her friend. Never had been. Never would be. How that witch must be enjoying this, crowing to any who'd listen. 'That is all.'

'Tell me, Miss Harrison, do you often behave like that with men?' he asked softly 'Not being raised a gentleman, I sometimes lack the finer details.'

'You should know that it is unlike me,' she said to the fire. 'I ave never said that sort of thing to a man before. I have never issed a man like that before.'

'I am relieved to hear it. I should dislike it intensely if my wife ehaved in such a manner with any other man.' He paused and is voice dropped an octave, his eyes flaring with sudden intensity. 'I should welcome it if she decided to act that way with me.'

A tide of heat washed up Emma's face, and she hoped that e would think it was from the fire rather than from the memory f their impassioned kiss. Her hand plucked at her skirt, twisting t, and she tried not to see entangled bodies in the flames.

'Ah, you *do* remember more than you pretended earlier.' here was a definite note of derisive laughter in his voice now. I find it best, when one has taken too much alcohol, not to feign gnorance. You were a willing partner last night.'

'I have never denied it. My recollections of the actual event re hazy.'

'And how should I make you remember?' He tapped a finger gainst his mouth. 'Do you have any suggestions? A repeat performance?'

'You are teasing me now.' Emma's mouth twitched upwards. She knew she was on firm ground. The sinking sensation had vanished. He had not really meant it. He would not kiss her in her father's study. She looked again at his intent expression. Would he? Her pulse jumped slightly.

'What else would I be doing?' He gave a small shrug and trode over to where the silver coffee pot stood. 'The offer and he warning are both there. I expect my wife to cleave only to me.'

Emma wrapped her hands about her waist. This conversation was all wrong. She wanted Jack, she desired his kisses, but not ike this, with this hard, mocking expression on his face.

'You said that you had a licence—a common licence. You vere expecting this.'

'Expecting you to demand my kisses? No, that was an added bonus.' His eyes blazed and then became cold. 'I like to be prepared for all eventualities, Miss Harrison. I spoke to your father. My time is limited here. There are other projects that clamour for my attention. We must make the best of the situation.'

'And when did you know of my dowry?' She forced her voice to sound calm and not to break. 'When did it become certain that to get your hands on my father's company you would have to marry me?'

'Your father has ensured that you are adequately taken care of.' He examined his cuffs.

Emma gritted her teeth. The worst thing was that a man like Jack Stanton did not need a dowry. He could afford to marry whom he pleased. Why had he done it? She peered at him, but his face offered no clues.

'You are not going to tell me.'

'It is a matter between your father and me. He should tell you, not I.' His eyes burnt with a sudden intensity. 'You will not want for anything.'

Emma's jaw hurt. She wanted to reach out and shake some of the complacency out of him. 'It would have been better if you had spoken to me before getting the licence.'

'I prefer things to be done correctly as well.' His eyes were hooded.

'Then it would have been better if you had asked me to marry you rather than simply announcing it.' Emma crossed her legs and tapped her foot. 'It is insupportable. It makes me seem as if I am a puppet, a doll without any mind.'

'After what happened in the sleigh there was no choice for either of us, Miss Harrison, much as we might wish otherwise.'

'We do have a choice. There has to be another way.' Emma

heard the desperation in her voice. Didn't he understand? She wanted him, but not like this.

'I will not risk my business and all the employees who depend on me by being outside of society. Are you prepared to risk your father's?'

A lump rose in Emma's throat. She wanted to go to him and lay her head against his chest. She wanted to feel his hands on her back. Wanted the reassurance that she meant more to him than simply keeping society at bay. That she meant more to him than a means of securing the company. A company that would have been nothing without her intervention earlier this year. She had worked tirelessly to save it…for what? For him. Her heart bled at the thought of the employees and their families. What would it be like for them with a new master?

If she did not marry him, would they lose their jobs as the work ebbed away? She knew the power of whispers, how they could ruin a man.

'But—'

'No buts, Emma. A quiet yes will do.'

Emma attempted to hang onto some sort of reason. There had to be a way out.

'As neither of us desires this marriage, I expect it to be in name only.' She tilted her chin and gazed directly into his eyes, and was unprepared for the sudden blaze of fire.

'You are in no position to dictate terms.' He stepped closer. 'Shall I demonstrate?'

He reached and grabbed her shoulders, pulling her towards him, making her body collide with his. His mouth swooped down and took her breath. Plundered until her legs became jelly. Her hands lifted and clung to his shoulders. A soft sigh was drawn from her throat.

He let her go and she stumbled back.

'Point proved. Next time try telling the truth.'

Emma put her hand to her mouth. Tender, bruised, and aching for more. 'That proves nothing. You have not asked me to marry you.'

He looked at her. A half-smile curled on his lips. He made an oh-so-correct bow. 'Very well. Miss Harrison, will you do me the honour of becoming my wife?'

'I have not considered the matter fully.' Emma kept her eyes downcast. There had to be a way. She could not marry Jack like this. There had to be another way.

'You have one hour to decide. There will be no repeat of the offer.' His smile became crueller, more mocking. 'Remember that more than just your own personal happiness rests on your answer.'

Chapter Sixteen

Emma sat watching the clock tick past the quarter hour on the mantel. She'd give Jack fifty-five more minutes and then she'd give her decision. He deserved to sweat for his high-handed attitude, but he was correct. She could not think of a way out of the situation. They had to marry—or else be outside society.

She might be able to exist—just—but what about her father's business? She knew how many times her mother had said that a man's reputation stood or fell on his wife's. How she and her sister had to behave properly or their father might not win contracts. What if contracts were withdrawn? And the employees—why should they suffer simply because she'd been foolish enough to be compromised? And yet how could she marry simply for business reasons? How could she have a marriage with Jack on that footing…when she wanted more?

Emma willed the clock to stop, but the minute hand slowly headed for twelve.

'My dear Miss Harrison,' Dr Milburn said, barging into the room. 'Your butler said that you were in seclusion, but I insisted I may have a solution.'

'A solution?' Emma stared at the doctor. What was he going to offer her—more tonic?

'To the dreadful thing you are going through right now.' His smile was a little broad, a little too many teeth.

'How can I help you, Dr Milburn?' Emma forced herself to remain seated, to stay calm. She folded her hands in her lap and kept her back straight.

'My dear child, I cannot help but feel responsible for your current predicament.'

'I doubt you have anything to do with it.'

The doctor started to pace the small room, his coat-tails billowing out behind him. Emma sneaked another look at the clock, willed him to hurry.

'I have thought and thought and I am almost positive I made you drink the punch from Mrs Charlton's special cup.'

'What was in her cup?' Emma's hand trembled. Had this whole thing been a dreadful mistake? If she had been less worried about the tonic would she have drunk the punch? She should have said something.

'I do not wish to betray confidences, Miss Harrison.' He assumed a pious look. 'I have my professional oath to think of.'

'I cannot see how you will be able to remain silent, Dr Milburn. You must tell me all.' Emma leant forward. 'What was in that particular cup? Why should my drinking from it have any bearing on my situation?'

'The senior Mrs Charlton is overly fond of laudanum.' Dr Milburn raked his hand through his hair, but did not meet her eyes. 'I fear she poured a portion into her cup and I took it by mistake. I have turned it over and over in my mind. I am now certain of it.'

Emma stared at the doctor. Her stomach dropped. She had old Jack and her father that something was amiss, but they had not believed her. And now Dr Milburn was admitting to giving her the wrong cup of punch. It made no sense. Was this the miracle she had been praying for? And, if so, why did she feel so curiously deflated? 'What are you saying?'

'I have heard about the terrible scandal this morning, and want you to know that I do not hold you to blame.' He puffed out his chest. 'You did not know what you were doing.'

'It is kind of you, sir.' Emma pressed her fingertips together. 'But I do not believe there will be much of a scandal, or that it will be very long-lasting.'

'You are sadly mistaken there.'

Dr Milburn shook his head and his eyes grew troubled. The 'concerned doctor' look if ever she had seen one. Emma tried to control a sudden stab of anger. If what he was saying were true, then he was to blame…for everything.

'It is only a minor scandal. Nothing happened.' Emma aimed for an unconcerned laugh.

'This is not a minor scandal that will be forgotten by New Year.'

'Why not?'

'They are saying dreadful things—truly dreadful things about you and Mr Stanton. I have heard from three of my old ladies already. By nightfall all of Newcastle will know, and after that all of England.'

Emma forced herself not to flinch. 'Exactly what are they saying?'

'That you were caught in the embrace of that man Stanton, behaving as if you were the worst flirt imaginable.' His face took on a pious expression. 'I know you are not like that, Miss Harrison. I have never known you to behave without decorum. I want to do what I can to help.'

Dr Milburn stood upright, his feet slightly apart, certain that his words must be of great comfort.

'Thank you, sir, for supporting me.' Emma inclined her head and blinked back sudden tears. It seemed impossible that the odious Dr Milburn should be the only person to think well of her. Everyone, even her own father, was so quick to condemn. 'I am glad you think the best of me.'

'And to silence the whispers I wish to offer you my hand.'

'Your hand?' Emma stared at the pallid fingers, then back up at Dr Milburn's bulging eyes. 'My mind appears to be working slowly this morning. Why would you wish to do that?'

'I wish to marry you and save you and your father from this dreadful scandal. It will circle round and round you.' Dr Milburn placed his palm on his chest. 'I am sensible that Mr Stanton is no gentleman, and cannot realise the harm this little escapade will do to your reputation.'

Emma nearly opened her mouth to inform him that Mr Stanton was indeed determined to put matters right, but closed it. Obviously Dr Milburn had not heard the latest rumour. Nor did she quite believe his story about Mrs Charlton and laudanum. It was far too easy. He had some other motive—one that she could not discern.

'Pray enlighten me.' She leant forward. 'Why did you take the wrong cup?'

Dr Milburn blinked and shifted from foot to foot.

'I was in a hurry. Mrs Charlton had placed it down. I picked it up, and then I forced you to drink. I should have seen by your face that you found it distasteful.'

Emma stilled, remembering. He had known what was in that cup. He had made her drink it. He had wanted her like that. A cold shiver ran down her back. No, that was impossible. This was Dr Milburn, the man who had devotedly tended her mother in er last days. She had to give him the benefit of the doubt…for er mother's sake. 'Dr Milburn, neither of us can change the past.'

'I have thought it over, and it is the only thing to do. You must allow me to repair the damage to your reputation. You must marry me.' His mouth pursed, as if the very idea was distasteful. He captured her hand and held it between his clammy ones. 'You would do me the greatest honour.'

Emma drew on her inner resources and kept her face blank. 'You need not fear, Dr Milburn. I have already taken steps, and regret that I must decline your offer.'

'Decline my offer?' Dr Milburn opened and closed his mouth several times. 'Are you mad?'

'I know what I am doing.' Emma withdrew her hand. 'I have accepted a prior offer.'

'Whose?'

'Mr Stanton's.'

'It is good to know that you have finally seen sense, Miss Harrison,' came Jack's cold voice from the doorway.

Emma turned and saw him lounging against the doorframe. 'How long have you been there?'

'Long enough.'

'It is not the done thing to listen at doorways.' Emma silently cursed her wayward tongue.

'That is one of the reasons I am very glad not to be well bred, Miss Harrison.' He inclined his head. 'And now I believe I must ask you to depart, Milburn.'

Dr Milburn's face turned red, and then white. 'I was only doing my duty as I saw it.'

'As you can see, there is no need.'

'Ah, yes…well, that is to say…' Dr Milburn placed his hat on his head. 'Should you change your mind, Miss Harrison—'

'She won't.'

Emma heard the door close with a decisive click, but did no
turn from where she faced the fire.

'I thought you were going to give me an hour.'

'Shall I call Dr Milburn back?' His voice, silken-smooth, slid
over her. 'But then I forget—you have already given him you
answer. You are engaged to me.'

'I wanted him to leave with the minimum of fuss.' Emma
closed her eyes. Trapped, and she had no one to blame but
herself. She slowly opened her eyes and discovered Jack regard
ing her with an amused expression. 'I thought you were going
to give me an hour. You weren't meant to hear.'

'One can learn such interesting things, and your voice
were raised.'

'It is a bad habit.'

'Forgive me, Miss Harrison, but circumstances dictated.' Jack
held out a piece of paper. 'This arrived by messenger. I though
it best to inform you at once.'

'What is it?'

'The results from the laboratory. My friend was most thorough.'

'What does it say? You mustn't keep me in suspense.' Emma
looked over the spidery writing, and the notations. She could
follow most of it, but some of it made little sense.

'It is as I suspected. Your father has been ingesting arsenic
You are lucky that he has a strong constitution. The amount in
his body would have killed a lesser man.'

'It does explain why he was getting ill. But was it the
tonic?' Emma started towards the door. 'Why did you no
confront Dr Milburn?'

'I am having them check other bottles of tonic.' Jack hooked
his thumbs in his waistcoat. 'I need to be certain if I am to go
to the authorities.'

'But my father has high levels of arsenic in his body?'

'Yes.' His expression offered her no comfort.

'That means someone was trying to poison him. Who would do such a thing?' Emma clasped her hand over her mouth. 'I cannot think of anyone in the house. They are loyal servants. And I would never, ever hurt my father.'

'I never suspected you.'

'Thank you.' Emma closed her eyes briefly. Someone had tried to poison her father. His fits had definitely been caused by someone rather than something. He was not dying. She put her hand to her mouth and looked towards the door. 'You don't think it was Dr Milburn?'

'I may not like the man, but he is well respected in the community. He has a following, a reputation.' Jack shook his head. 'I cannot fathom a reason why he should want to poison your father.'

'Or why he might give me the wrong cup of punch,' Emma said quietly.

'I am sorry? I don't follow your line of thought.' Jack looked at her intently, his eyes suddenly flaring with emotion. 'The wrong cup of punch? How could that have bearing on anything?'

'That is why Dr Milburn offered me his hand, as distasteful as it was to him.' Emma bit her lip. 'He believes that he took Mrs Charlton's cup by mistake and says Mrs Charlton is a secret laudanum user. Therefore his sense of duty compelled him to offer for my hand as I am now a fallen woman.'

'Have you heard this of Mrs Charlton before?'

Emma paused. Her brow wrinkled. 'I have heard Mrs Charlton called many things. She and my mother were great rivals once. But never that. She is highly respectable, a pillar of the church. Though the punch did taste foul…'

'And…?'

Emma thought back to her encounter with Dr Milburn. The

cold, inexplicable fear washed over her again. 'What if D
Milburn had planned on kidnapping me?'

'For what purpose?' Jack crossed his arms and his mout
turned down in a frown. 'Why would Dr Milburn wish to kidna
you? Did you tell him of your suspicions about the tonic?'

'No, I never did.' She put her hand to her head. 'It makes n
sense. Nothing makes much sense. Why would he offer me hi
hand in marriage?'

'People need motivation to act, not some melodramati
reason.' He gave a sudden heart-stopping smile. 'And if hi
purpose was to marry you, I believe the situation has bee
remedied.'

'How so?'

'You have agreed to marry me…tomorrow…and there is ver
little Dr Milburn can do about it.'

'But what will we do about the tonic? Someone has tried t
poison my father.'

'There is very little we can do without proof. I will find tha
proof. Then act. Never fear.' Jack's fingers caught her elbow. 'D
Milburn will have no escape if he is to blame.'

The expression on Jack's face made her shiver. He was no
marrying her for love, but out of duty. And now it was duty tha
compelled him to protect her. To protect her, or the company
She longed to know which.

Grey light filtered through stained glass, providing the only
light in the church. Staff from the house occupied a few of th
pews but the rest remained empty. Even Emma's sister had bee
unable to attend. The journey from Carlisle was too long for he
and her children at this time of year.

Emma risked a look at Jack, perfectly correct, with not a hai
out of place, the very image of the successful gentleman. Hi

xpression bore no signs of welcome, but was black and furious,
eaving her little doubt that he was not pleased with the state of
ffairs. Any doubts she'd had about her father's hand in the
natter were dispelled by the radiance of his smile as he gave
er to Jack and the vicar began speaking.

Emma concentrated on looking at the altar and the vicar. She
ecited her vows in a mechanical voice and barely heard Jack's
eep ones. She kept feeling that this was somehow not right.
They were marrying for the wrong reasons. And yet she was not
nhappy to be married to Jack.

'And now I pronounce you man and wife.'

The vicar's words resounded in the nearly empty church. To
Emma, it seemed like the closing of a door. It had happened.
She was married. There was no going back. She could only face
he future and hope.

'You may kiss the bride,' the vicar intoned.

Emma could not control the slight surge in her pulse. Would
e kiss her like yesterday? Or the day before? Something to
demonstrate his power over her?

His cool lips brushed hers. A quick, impersonal kiss. Emma
it her lip.

'Shall we go, Mrs Stanton?' He held out his arm.

'We have no cause to linger. We are married. The wedding is
over.' Emma kept her voice brisk. This was not what her
wedding was supposed to be like. She had always envisaged
white silk and roses, but there hadn't been time. Instead it was
er best blue dress and a nosegay of white narcissi and green
vy. Emma forced her head to be held high as they exited from
he cold dark church, blinking into the sunlight. A loud cheer
ang out.

Emma's feet skittered into each other and she looked about
er in amazement. The churchyard was full of people. She rec-

ognised a number from the company. She glanced up at Jack, who shrugged but did not appear displeased. Had he known?

'Best foot forward, Emma,' he said in a low undertone. 'They have come to see the blushing bride.'

'What is going on here?' she asked. 'Who told them?'

'That is not for me to say.'

'We wanted to wish you and the gaffer well, like,' Davy Newcomb said, plucking at her sleeve.

'You mustn't greet the bride yet, lad,' Davy's mother said, pulling him back. 'I am begging your pardon, miss…I mean Mrs Stanton, ma'am. It wouldn't be right and proper until the sweep has been.'

A very blackened and sooty man came up and grabbed Emma's hand, shaking it heartily. 'May much good luck come to you and your marriage.'

A ragged cheer rose from the crowd. 'Three cheers for the gaffer and his missus.'

'Exactly what is going on here?' Emma asked again.

'Harrison and Lowe belongs to me now. The employees and their families have come to wish us well.' He touched his hat. 'As I plan to marry only once, it seemed like the right thing to do. I do not plan to have our marriage spoken of as a hole-and-corner affair. Appearances matter.'

'Me mam went and suggested it to him once she heard, like,' Davy remarked.

Jack laughed. 'Yes, I am afraid young Davy here has been my partner in crime. Are you upset by the attention?'

'Upset?' Emma shook her head. 'More surprised.'

'And we shall celebrate well at the Goose Feast tomorrow. Eh Davy?'

Jack ruffled Davy's hair.

'Yes, Mr Stanton. That there pine tree has been delivered to the hall, just as you asked. It's huge, like!'

'Good lad.'

'The feast is going on as planned?'

'I told you before, Emma, I keep Christmas as well as any man. A change in ownership means nothing.' He glanced up at the heavy skies. 'I hope for a thaw soon.'

Emma nodded. She knew what he meant. He would keep the employees on as long as possible, but if the present weather continued he would have to start letting them go. At least he was waiting until after Christmas, she thought.

'Emma—Emma, you bad, miserable excuse for a friend.' Lucy came hurrying up. Her little girl held out a sprig of holly for Emma. 'You might have confided in me. This has apparently been planned for ages.'

'We wished to keep the ceremony quiet as my father has not been well.'

'And to think how you must have laughed when I told your Mr Stanton to take care of you on your sleigh ride.' Lucy pressed her hand against Emma's. 'I nearly died of shame for you when I first heard Lottie's lurid account.'

'I am sure Lottie spared no details.' Emma cringed when she thought of Lottie's superior tone.

'Henry was furious with her when he heard. I thought he was going to shake her. He told her to stop spreading lies and rumours. He fairly thundered it, slapping his fist on the table. Mother Charlton was very taken aback as well. I was proud of him.' Lucy lowered her voice. 'Lottie has been sent to live with Mother Charlton's sister in Haydon Bridge in strict seclusion until Henry decides what to do with his sister. She won't be able to spread the tale any further. Her tricks have finally caught up with her.'

Emma reached over and squeezed Lucy's hand. 'Henry did not have to do that.'

'Henry cares about you, and about what happens to you. He was most distressed.' Lucy gave a smile. 'But sometimes he is forgetful. He told me that he'd thought Dr Milburn would marry you. That he would make it all right. But I knew Jack Stanton would prove his worth.'

'Dr Milburn?' The back of Emma's neck pricked. Henry had made a pairing of her and Dr Milburn? How curious, as she had never said anything to Lucy about Dr Milburn. 'I have never wanted to marry him.'

'And I know it is a real love-match, despite what everyone is saying.' Lucy pressed her gloved hand to Emma's cheek. 'You may try to hide it from everyone else, Emma, but I saw the way you two looked at each other by the pond.'

Emma shifted uneasily. She glanced to where Jack stood speaking to a few of the employees. The black material of his jacket was pulled tight across his broad shoulders. And she saw the spot where his hair curled as it met his neck. A lump grew in her throat. A love-match. Lucy was correct. It *was* a love-match. A one-sided love-match. She wrapped her fingers tighter around her bouquet. She had done the unthinkable.

She had fallen in love with Jack Stanton.

She watched Jack move down the line, chatting and laughing. Jack would never know. She refused to give him that sort of power over her. He was only interested in the company, in business. He was marrying her for the company and for social respectability.

It was impossible to discern a time or a place, but it had just happened, and now she knew. The full evidence of the emotion hit her between the eyes. She had fallen hopelessly in love with him, despite everything that he'd done.

'Are you all right, daughter?' her father asked. 'You are frowning. All is well that ends well.'

'Perfectly well, Father.' Emma leant forward and gave his cheek a quick peck.

'I thought just then you looked unhappy. I am doing what is best for you. It seemed the most sensible solution to the problem.' He gave her hand a squeeze. 'After my illness I knew I wouldn't live for ever. The company needs to be in safe hands. I needed to know that you would be looked after properly, just as I saw your sister looked after properly. I have a duty towards you. You are ideally matched, if I do say so myself—you share the same interest in civil engineering. I wish your dear mama had.'

Emma nodded. When the time came she would have to let Jack go. She remembered his words from the first day—he had too many projects, a wife and children would tie him down. 'I am sure it will be fine, Papa.'

'Emma, there are a few people here who would like to meet you,' Jack called.

Emma hurried forward and was swept into congratulations from the crowd. Jack and her father had been right, she thought. No one was questioning the suddenness of their marriage. As far as scandals went, it would be forgotten easily.

'You have married Stanton,' Dr Milburn said, coming up to her when Jack had turned to greet some well-wishers. 'Do you know what your dowry was? What your father had to pay?'

'I do not believe it is any of your business, Dr Milburn.' Emma's smile became more fixed. Now was not the time or place for accusations.

'What are you doing here, Milburn?'

'I came to wish you and your bride Godspeed, Stanton. You cannot object to that.' He raised Emma's hand to his mouth. Her flesh crawled, and it was all she could do to endure his touch.

Why had Dr Milburn wanted to marry her? And why had Henry

Charlton considered the match already made? The only person who could have told him that was Dr Milburn himself. But why?

'You are wearing a pensive face,' Jack said. His warm fingers guided her through the crowd and he settled her in the carriage, solicitously tucking the robe about her. But Emma knew it had to be for show, to dispel the rumours. 'Are you preparing yourself?'

'Preparing for what?' She pushed away all thoughts of Dr Milburn. She was safe. She had to concentrate on the man beside her—her new husband. 'What should I be ready for?'

'For the wedding breakfast your father has kindly laid on.'

'And after that?' Emma asked, finding breathing difficult.

'We stay here for a few days. I have things to do in Newcastle.'

Emma played with the button of her glove. She knew she should not feel disappointed, but somehow she did. Once when she had thought of her wedding she had thought of white lace and wedding trips to Europe, not a quick trip to the local church and then continuing on as if nothing had happened.

'Of course. I want to stay here in case my father has a relapse.' She kept her head high and stared out of the carriage window.

Jack's hand turned her head to face him. 'We shall stay the night in a hotel. I do not want my wedding night interrupted for any reason.'

Her cheeks prickled with sudden heat. To hide the telltale flush, she bent her head and pretended to smooth the folds of her gown. 'I had not really thought.'

'Has anyone told you what to expect?'

'I know the theory,' Emma said, with what she hoped was dignity. 'Lucy Charlton told me years ago, just after her mother spoke to her.'

'There is a world of difference between theory and practice.'

A warm tingle of anticipation rippled down Emma's spine. 'I doubt it,' she said.

He reached and enveloped her hand in his.

'It is all right, Emma Stanton, you are safe with me.'

Safe? Emma felt anything but safe as she waited in the hotel suite. The room was beautifully appointed and a fire burnt cheerily in the fireplace.

Emma paced the room. She should have found a solid reason to stay at her father's house. Then she would not have had to wonder what tonight would entail. She would have had an excuse to be elsewhere.

There were no flutters of anticipation. Nothing but a numbness. Everything had happened so fast. The only thing she felt was a great lump of fear. She wished she had taken more time, asked more questions of Lucy today. What if what she remembered was wrong? What if she did something wrong? The doubts crowded around her head like crows.

Emma fingered her white lawn nightdress as she looked at the large double bed, piled high with quilts and white pillows. She should get in the bed—or would that seem too forward? So many things she knew she ought to know but was in ignorance of.

It was probably her one chance to bind him to her.

'Shall we begin where we left off?'

Emma jumped at the sound of Jack's rich voice, a voice that flowed over her and teased her senses, promising much but revealing little.

She turned, and her breath caught in her throat. Jack had discarded his coat, waistcoat and stock. His fine white linen shirt was open at the neck. Pure male.

A shiver went down Emma's back. She drew a deep breath and attempted to remain calm, outwardly cool, when her insides appeared to have become molten.

'Whatever you want.'

He came to her. His hand caught hers, held it lightly in his grasp. 'Exactly how much do you know about what is going to happen here…tonight?'

'Enough.'

Emma gave a little shrug of her shoulders to show she was unconcerned. How could she admit that she knew next to nothing, just quick whispered gossip and the memory of Jack's lips against hers? No doubt he'd expected her to be in bed already. A mistake? She moved her hand and his fingers let her go.

'Women do talk,' she said brightly, and the double bed appeared to grow larger with each breath she took. 'Shall I get into bed first?'

'If you wish…'

Emma took a step towards the bed. If she lay there without moving a muscle it might be over quickly, and then she could get on with the rest of her life. Jack had married her for the company, not for her companionship.

'No, wait. I have a better idea.'

Emma paused and half turned round. He held out his hands, his eyes twinkling. 'May I have the pleasure of this dance, Mrs Stanton?'

'Dance?' Emma hesitated. All too clearly she remembered their waltz in front of the fire. Then things had ended in a heart-stopping kiss. Where would they end this time? But anything to delay that inevitable moment when he discovered she knew next to nothing. She tucked a strand of hair behind her ear. 'What sort of dance do you want? A polka may be a bit lively for here.'

'A waltz will suit my purpose.'

His hand caught hers, lifted it to his lips. She had expected a soft brush, but his tongue made a lazy circle on the inside of her wrist. He repeated the movement on her other wrist and a deep molten warmth rose within her.

'I believe I can manage a waltz.' She tried for a smile, tried to forget the warmth building inside her. She had to concentrate. 'Who will hum? Dancing is impossible without music.'

'Allow me.'

He put his hands on her shoulder and waist, and drew her in close. Their bodies touched. Emma realised with a start that, rather than being constrained in a ball gown and lots of petticoats, it was only fine lawn between them.

The warmth of his body radiated through and enveloped her. She could feel the strength of his thigh muscles, the hardness of his chest. She looked up and was submerged in his inexorable gaze. She should move, but had lost all power to do so.

'My feet are like blocks of lead,' she whispered. 'I am not sure if I can do this.'

'You will get the idea,' he murmured against her hair. 'Trust in me. Follow my lead.'

He started to hum a waltz—a Strauss waltz—in her ear. They moved about the room, but with each turn their bodies moved closer together, until it was as if they were one being.

She half stumbled and his hands came to catch her, pulling her firmly against his body. She glanced up and saw his dark gaze, tumbled into it and could not look away.

A sudden trembling filled her body. A sort of nervousness combined with something else.

His lips touched hers, drew back. A butterfly's kiss, but one that sent ripples of aching tension throughout her body.

She ran her tongue over her lips, tasting them. They seemed to have become fuller in an instant.

'There is no mistletoe here,' she said, with a smile and an attempt at a laugh. Her voice sounded husky and unnatural to her ears.

'How remiss of me.'

His hands cupped her face so she was looking up at him, and she could see every lash, and the fact that his eyes were not black at all, but filled with a myriad of dark colours, eyes to lose herself in.

His mouth swooped down and claimed hers. This time they were firm and lingered long. A heady warmth washed over her and she forgot to be nervous, forgot everything but the feel of his lips against hers.

She gave a sigh and curled her arms about his neck. She wanted, needed more.

He deepened the kiss, demanding entrance to her mouth. Her body responded with an aching need. He moved his legs so her body was positioned between them, the hardness of muscle pressed in on her.

Her lips parted and allowed him entrance. For a long time they stood there, mouth against mouth, tongues exploring, sampling, feasting. Everything had come down to this sensation.

A dark, raging sensation.

The fire grew within, and with each passing breath seemed to grow until it threatened to engulf her whole being.

'We take this slow…very slow,' he murmured against her mouth. His hands undid the ribbons that held her nightcap, let it fall to the ground, and then he ran his hands through her hair. 'I have dreamed of doing this. Pure silk.'

Emma shivered.

Her hands reached and entangled themselves in his hair, pulling his mouth closer. Then she felt herself falling as her knees gave way. Jack scooped her up and carried her to the bed.

He set her down and she sank into the soft cushions. In the firelight, she watched him divest himself of his shirt, and his chest was broader than she'd thought possible. She reached out a hand and touched the warm sculpted flesh while his fingers worked on the tiny buttons that fastened around her neck.

He trailed kisses down her neck, and she knew what she had felt that night in the sleigh was nothing compared to this burning ache inside her.

She started to speak, but he put a finger to her lips.

'Hush, we have all the time in the world. It is time to show you how imagination and creativity can add to the experience.'

He bent his head, and Emma knew everything before had been pure theory.

Chapter Seventeen

Jack propped himself up on one elbow and looked at his wife. Her dark hair was spread out like a carpet on the pillow. Her limbs were entwined with his and her skin still bore a rosy hue from their lovemaking.

She belonged to him now, and it was up to him to keep her safe.

Jack's lips thinned. He did not believe Milburn's story, nor did he think Emma melodramatic. Something had happened to her at the pond. Something had happened, she had not been herself, and he had taken advantage of it. He gave a wry smile. And would continue to take advantage of it for the rest of their lives.

He lifted a strand of hair from her cheek, let it slide between his fingers. Would she have married him otherwise?

Now it was his duty to make sure she was safe. And, until he had confronted Milburn with solid evidence, that meant keeping her away from things.

She gave a murmur that might have been his name and
uggled closer.

He had no wish to worry her. He would deal with the feast,
d then take her away for a protracted wedding trip. Edward
rrison could take care of the bridge for a while, and the rest
his investments were running smoothly. It would give them
hance to get to know each other better, to build on their foun-
tion. But first he had to keep her safe.

'One more day, that's all and then we leave,' he whispered,
d then stood up. If he stayed, he'd take her in his arms again
d, as delightful as that would be, he would be no further
rward. 'Sleep well. Dream of me…please.'

She moved into the warm spot he had vacated.

His heart clenched. Until he knew for certain, he did not want
worry her.

Emma woke to sunlight streaming into the room. She blinked
r eyes, intending to call for Annie, and then stopped. The
mories of last night came flooding back.

Her body ached in places she had never dreamt possible. She
ched out a hand and encountered empty space.

She propped herself up and looked. There was an indentation
the pillow, but the bed was cold. Jack had left. He had gone
thout saying a word.

She flopped back down on the pillows and stared up at the
ling. Without a word! She had meant that little to him.

No doubt he was out working…somewhere.

She sat up. But she had work to do as well. The Goose Feast
uld not run itself. She had planned it all, but there were
ways last-minute problems. A thousand things could go
ong, and then good will would be lost for ever.

She had to be there.

She wanted to be there.

Emma did not bother ringing for the maid, but started dress, quickly and with practised fingers.

Within moments she was ready. She gave one more glance the pier glass. Serviceable. Her eyes were perhaps a little larg and her mouth fuller, but outwardly nothing had change Nothing inwardly as well.

Emma placed her hand over her stomach. She had no reas to think that last night would bring forth a baby, but her arm longed to hold one. A child of her own to love and take care Unlike her mother, she would not try to relive her life throu the baby. If she ever had a child, she vowed, that child wou grow up to do what he or she wanted to do.

She put her hands on her face. *If* was a big word. One she w not going to think about. Later, her attraction to Jack mig fade, become something manageable instead of this great achin need. She was pleased that she had not given in to temptatio had not whispered her love.

How he would have laughed and felt pity for her. The on thing she did not want. She could abide many things, but n pity.

She grabbed her cloak and bonnet, opened the door and ga a small cry. Davy jumped backwards, banging his crut against the wall.

'Davy, you startled me. I wasn't expecting you. I wasn't e pecting anyone.'

'Begging your pardon, miss…Mrs Stanton ma'am, but I w told to be here, like. It's my duty, see.' He took off his cap a twisted it.

'Why are you here?' Emma glanced up and down the corrid but there was no one else. Jack had really gone, left witho saying a word.

'The gaffer told me that I was to make sure no one went into our room. And I have been doing that, like. Right boring it is so.'

'No one has gone into my room.' Emma gave a smile and started forward. She would go to the hall and see how the preparations were progressing. It would keep her mind from Jack and wondering why he had left.

Davy nodded, but did not move from where he stood, blocking her path.

'Are you going to let me pass?'

'Begging your pardon again, like. The gaffer did not mean for you to come out. Not now anyhow.'

'Where is Mr Stanton?'

'The gaffer? He has gone to help out. It's the Goose Feast day, like.'

Emma pressed her lips together. She could readily imagine Jack wanted to use the Goose Feast as an occasion to consolidate his power, to show to the employees of Harrison and Lowe that he now owned the company. She crossed her arms. He had forgotten one small detail.

'I believe you are mistaken, Davy.'

'You reckon?' The boy tilted his head to one side. 'Where exactly do you think I have gone wrong?'

'Did he actually say that I was to be held here? A prisoner?'

The boy's eyes widened, and his brow furrowed. Then he shook his head. Emma resisted laughing in triumph. She had no doubt that Jack wanted her to stay put, but she had other plans.

'You say that Jack—Mr Stanton—has gone to see about the preparations?'

Emma drew in a deep breath. She had guessed right. He was going to use the occasion to consolidate his power, but he had forgotten one thing—this company was her dowry, and she still retained some vestige of control over it. She was not about become some milksop miss. She wiped her hands against th skirt of her gown. 'Can you take me to him? We can ask hi then.'

'That wouldn't be wise, ma'am.' Davy readjusted the ang of his crutch. 'Really, you are better off staying here, like, un Mr Jack comes back. If you want to go back in quiet, like, it w be the best for the both of us.'

Emma knelt down so her face was level with Davy's. 'Wou you like to see the German Christmas tree? I understand the is going to be a gigantic one—one that reaches up to the ceilin There are going to be candles, white candy canes and present Old Christmas is going to come and give each person at the fea a present. Won't that be splendid?''

Davy slowly nodded his head. 'I never seen one 'for Decorated, you see. I have seen lots of pine trees before. It's monster tree, like. Do you think they will have a present for me

'I am sure they will. Mr Stanton and I think you have been very good lad…all year.' Emma resisted the temptation to p. Davy on the head. She would go and see what was happenin She would not be stuck here in this lifeless room with nothin to do but sit and watch the clock, going quietly mad. 'Mr Stanto is there now, getting things ready.'

'That's right, ma'am. He wants to make sure every detail correct. I don't know if we ought to. He's in a right fearful temper

Emma pressed her lips together. *He* was! What about her? N word of goodbye or anything. He had to learn that he was n going to have everything his own way. There was no way she wa going to sit around placing pins into cushions to make swe mottos. She had had a taste of life and she intended to keep it.

'And once we have found Jack Stanton we shall ask him if can come out of my room or not.'

'If you say so, ma'am.' Davy gave a shrug and adjusted the
utch under his left arm. 'But seeing how's you are going to
yway, what is the point, like?'

The hall bustled with activity. Everything appeared to be hap-
ning at once. Wreaths of holly and garlands of ivy hung from
e bare walls, transforming the hall into a Christmas wonder-
nd. The scent of pine and spices filled the air. Along one beam
e geese and one large turkey hung, each with a number
ightly displayed. The twelfth cakes and mince pies were piled
derneath along with brown nuts, winter pears, and all sorts
 apples, all hues and sizes, from the brown russet to the rose-
eeked pippin. Bunches of purple hothouse grapes vied with
d pomegranates.

Christmas bounty waiting for the employees to arrive. Every-
ing ready, everything going on without her.

A lump formed in her throat. She had worked hard to get this
ast organised, had thought herself vital. She'd believed the de-
ption. The reality was far harsher—she was not indispensable,
t missed, not needed. Was this the way it was going to be in
e future? She wanted to be needed, to make a difference.

'Will you look at that?' Davy gave a low whistle. 'You were
ght, ma'am, to say I should come. That tree is a monster—a
al monster. Can you see what is hanging from it?'

'Yes, it is.' Emma regarded the tree. Pen-wipes, needle cases
d smelling bottles vied with less practical items, such as
mming tops and little china dolls. White candle tapers stood
 the ends of branches, waiting to be lit. It would in time be
ansformed into a magical paradise for children. She had to
mit Jack's idea of a large German Christmas tree with presents
as inspired. She could easily imagine the tree being talked over
d marvelled at again and again throughout the coming year.

Emma scanned the room and discovered her husband—up a ladder, putting the final touches to a holly wreath. He clambered back down and gave Mudge a slap on his back. The sound of laughter echoed in the hall. Emma's throat closed. She was not required. She had no place here.

'Are you all right, ma'am?'

'Yes, of course,' Emma said quickly. She gave Davy a small push against his shoulder. 'Why don't you go and see the tree? See if any present has your name on it?'

She watched Davy go over to the tree. Jack stopped him, asked him a question. Davy pointed back towards her. His eyes searched the hall and came to rest on her. Emma shifted as they grew dark. She had thought that maybe they would light up, but if anything the light died.

She squared her shoulders and started forward. Her stomach appeared to be in knots, and the distance from the back of the hall to where Jack stood seemed to grow with each step she took.

Then suddenly he had crossed the distance and his finger closed about her arm. 'Emma, you should be at the hotel, resting.'

'I am here now.' She kept her chin held high and met his gaze directly. 'I did not know where you had gone.'

'I planned on returning in time to bring you here for the start of the feast.' A flash of a smile showed on his face. 'I wanted you well rested. You did not have much sleep last night.'

Emma's heart began to melt. Her body clearly remembered what it was like to be held against him, to have him murmur soft words in her ear. It would be very easy to forgive him. To forgive and forget. But that way led down a slippery slope. She had every right to be here.

'You did not leave a note.' She gave a small shrug and played with the ribbons of her bonnet. 'How was I expected to know?

He raked his hand through his hair. 'Shall we speak of this somewhere more private?'

'If you wish.' Dimly Emma was aware that everyone in the hall was staring at them. Emma allowed him to lead her away from the others. She kept her head held high. She was in the right.

'Why shouldn't I be here?' she asked when they were alone in the corridor.

'There's no need for you to be here. Everything is in hand.'

'I have worked long and hard for this feast. I have as much right to be here as you. More, even. Now, let go of me.'

His hand fell away from her arm as if it had burnt him.

'Everything is under control. You should be resting, or whatever it is that ladies do on the morning after their marriage. I thought you would sleep longer.'

Emma cast her eyes heavenwards. His reaction was not the one she had expected. She was not so naïve that she'd thought he would scoop her in his arms, but she had expected some sort of civility.

'I *am* doing what ladies do. I have come to supervise the decorating of the hall, to make sure everything is done properly. I have duties and responsibilities, regardless of our marriage. The feast must be right. The memory of my mother demands it.'

'It is all under control.'

'Are you asking me to leave?'

'Yes.' The single word fell from his lips and hung between them, as uncompromising in its tone as his face.

'I see.' She spoke around the huge lump in her throat. 'You have what you want. You have made sure the marriage cannot be annulled, and therefore I am to fade away.'

'You are putting words into my mouth!'

'It is what you think,' Emma countered.

'I am not going to have a silly argument with you, Emma.'

He turned to go. The gentle lover of last night had vanished as if he had never been. Here was only the hard businessman. Emma swallowed hard. All the doubts and fears of yesterday came crowding back in. 'Tell me this—why did you marry me? Was it to get your hands on my father's company?'

His eyes widened. 'Who has been talking to you?'

'I want to know. I deserve to know.' Emma crossed her arms and stared at him. Her life was about to become devoid of everything—with only a husband who did not love her and no place for her in the company. She had become meaningless, redundant. And he was about to dismiss it all as if it were nerves or an attack of the vapours. 'Was your price—the company?'

'You will have to ask your father.' His eyes burned with rage.

Emma took another step backwards, stumbled. His hand went out but she brushed it away. She straightened her spine. 'I intend to.'

She turned on her heel and marched out of the corridor, forcing her eyes to stay focused ahead and not glance behind her. She had thought he would come running after her. She reached the door, stumbled through it. Outside a fine mist was beginning to fall, making the grey snow become pock-marked.

Hot tears went down her cheeks. She scrubbed them away with the back of her hand. Her marriage was over before it had ever began.

'Emma, why have you returned home?' Her father put down his copy of *Punch* and stood up. Emma was struck by how much brighter his eye was. He was improving. He would get well.

She pressed her hands against her skirt, straightening the folds. She had to ask. Now, before her nerve failed.

'Papa, did you offer Harrison and Lowe as my dowry?'

Her father bit his lip and turned his face away. The pit i

Emma's stomach grew bigger. She wanted to bury her hands and cry.

'Papa, tell me. Is that why he married me?'

'It is not something a man likes to speak of.' He held out a hand. 'You are married now, and all your wants will be taken care of. Jack Stanton assured me. Why all this talk about your dowry?'

'I want to know.' Emma clasped her hands under her chin, forced her tone to be measured. 'I believe I deserve to know. I am not a child to be kept in ignorance about such matters.'

Her father shifted from one foot to the other. 'Some things are better left unsaid. Your dear mama was not interested in such things at all.'

'How can you say such things? I want to know. I *am* interested in the company, and its future. You cannot have sacrificed all the employees for my sake. They have worked for us for a long time.'

'What did Jack tell you?' Her father's gaze pierced her and his voice became stern. 'You have had a fight with him, haven't you? That is why you are spouting this nonsense about wrecking people's lives. I have done no such thing, and neither will Jack Stanton. You are attempting to find excuses, daughter.'

'Papa!'

'You love him very much.'

Emma put her hand to her face and started to pace the room. Was her face that transparent? How had everyone guessed when she had only fully known yesterday?

'My feelings don't come into it,' she said with dignity. 'It is what society demanded. I simply want to know the price you paid for my folly.'

'Oh, but your feelings do come into it. They have to. I told that to your dear mama when she wanted to marry you off to some jumped-up title-holder with no chin. We have to do what Emma wants, and never mind the social consequences.'

'Papa, what are you saying?'

'Daughter, do you love Jack Stanton? Would you have married him if this mess had not come about?'

Emma straightened her shoulders and looked her father in his eye. She knew she could not lie. 'Yes, I would have married him. But I wanted to marry him because of who I am now, and not because of my dowry.'

'I think I may have done more harm than good.' Her father dropped his head to his chest. 'I acted out of the best of motives. But, daughter, your quarrel is with Jack Stanton. You need to go back. You cannot stay here, hiding from the world.'

'I don't want to hide from the world. I want to be there, experiencing life.'

'But you have been. You gave up so many things to look after your mother, and then to look after me.'

'I thought that was what you wanted.'

'True love comes but once in a lifetime. Your mama thought she was doing what was best. She told me that if you and Jack Stanton were meant to be together, somehow you would be.'

'She did what she thought was right.' Emma gave a tiny shrug. 'And she did it out of love. I know that. But she should have given me the choice.'

Her father walked over to his desk. 'I took this letter from her. It explains everything. She would have wanted you to have it. Perhaps it will explain why I offered Jack the company. Why I felt the need to atone.'

Emma looked at the bold writing and knew it was Jack's. The letter he had sent years ago. Her father had it, had kept it. She shook her head. 'That letter is many years too late.'

'Are you sure, daughter?'

The pieces of paper were tantalisingly close. She scanned the first few lines. The words described another person—an angel lighting the darkness, a brilliant dancer, a paragon of virtue. Someone she never had been, could never hope to be. Was this who Jack thought he'd married? She could never be that person. Surely he had to understand that she had changed? She quickly read through to the end. His undying devotion. This proved nothing. He had changed in the past seven years, just as she had.

But what if he wanted the girl from the past? Had thought he was marrying that girl? A person she could never be? She wanted to know. She needed to know.

Emma folded the yellowing pages up small, stuffed them into her reticule. 'I have to go back. I have to go to the feast. There is little point in living the past, Father.'

The hall that had been empty before now teemed with people. Emma filled her lungs with air. She would go in now and brave them, brave Jack. It would have been easy to stay where she was, but she was determined to fight. Emma felt her father's hand on her shoulder. 'You will be fine, daughter.'

'I have every expectation of being so.' Emma kept her head up. She was pleased that she had decided to wear the rose silk. Her beaded reticule went well with it.

'Emma, I see you have returned.' Jack came up, perfection in his evening clothes. His eyes glittered dangerously.

'As I said before, I planned this feast. I could hardly let the people down.' She tightened her grip on the reticule's handle.

He raked his hand through his hair. 'Emma, we need to speak. But not here, not now. There are too many people.'

'I agree.' Her voice was tight. Emma concentrated on a point over his left shoulder. 'My father and I will be having Christmas lunch. Perhaps you will consider joining us? Unless your business takes you elsewhere.'

There was no change to Jack's face. If anything it became

colder. A wall of ice. Emma knew in that instant she had lost him—if she had ever had him.

'I regret that I will be leaving tomorrow. The train leaves for London quite early.'

Emma smiled, but inside her she knew a large piece of her was bleeding. He was leaving. Without her. 'How good of you to inform me of your movements. I shall look forward to your return.'

'Emma, I have said this badly.' He held out his hands. 'There has been no time to talk. I didn't think about your Christmas dinner.'

'It is fine.' Emma ignored the tightness in her throat. Her father was wrong. Jack didn't care for her. He was going to leave. 'If you will excuse me, there are people I need to greet. It would not do to let the company down.'

'We need to speak, Emma, but here is not the time or place.'

'Later, Jack. When you can fit me into your schedule. I understand completely about the demands of business.' Emma turned her shoulder and concentrated on greeting the employees and accepting their good wishes, keeping her head high and her smile bright, drawing on all her social skills. When she glanced back, Jack's eyes had become stone. He moved away from her, leaving a wide, cold chasm between them.

She scanned the crowd and stopped.

'Why is Dr Milburn here?' she asked her father, who had come to stand beside her.

'Dr Milburn?' Her father looked towards where she was pointing. 'He is the company doctor. He always gets an invitation.'

'But I thought…'

'You thought what?'

Emma shook her head. 'It is not important.'

Her father obviously did not know about Dr Milburn's treachry. As Jack still had the piece of paper, there was little she could do. She had to concentrate on what was happening.

'If you say so, Emma.' Her father gave a bemused smile. 'I have lost months with being sick. There are people I need to see—get everything set up for when work begins again in the New Year.'

'The New Year? But I thought Jack ran the company now.'

'He has other things he wants to do. Places he needs to be.'

Emma gave an unhappy nod. He was leaving. He simply had not found a way to tell her yet. It was what she had feared. They had married, and now she was going to be abandoned. Hadn't he said that he moved around too much for a wife?

'Be happy, daughter. Tonight is Christmas Eve.' Her father laid a hand on her shoulder. 'Come, your quarrel will be soon forgotten. Join in with the carolling and the feasting.'

Emma tried to smile. The carols all sounded hollow to her ears. There was no merriment here for her. She could see Jack up by the tree, surrounded by people.

'You had better get ready. The children are expecting Old Christmas to give them their presents.'

'I had forgotten that. Where are the robes?'

'They are out in the back room, I believe. Shall I fetch them for you?' Anything to get away from Jack. She couldn't bear another scene. Not now.

'Very well daughter, if you insist.' Her father held out his cup. 'Wassail, daughter, wassail.'

'Ah, Miss Emma.' Mrs Mudge came up, blocking her path. 'I wanted to say how pleased Mudge is with his bonus. Your father has been generous—very generous indeed this Christmastime.'

'It will be my husband who has been,' Emma said with a polite smile as her insides twisted. 'He owns the company now.'

'That's right.' A frown appeared in Mrs Mudge's face. 'He

bought it from your father—cash. That is why your father has given all the employees a bonus. A pretty penny he paid for it too, I heard. Your father stays on to oversee the project along with Mudge, as Mr Stanton is required elsewhere, and once it is done there are many more projects for Mudge to work on— branch lines to be built, stations. All the jobs are safe. Better than anyone could hope for. Mudge tells me everything, he does.'

'But I thought… I thought…' Emma looked up at where Jack stood, surrounded by men. He had done far more for the employees' security than she could ever have hoped for. And he had allowed her father his dignity. She swallowed. Hard. But he was going away…without her. Where to this time? Back to Brazil? Or somewhere else exotic? She didn't know. All she knew was that he had no desire to take her with him.

'If you will forgive me, I see Mrs Newcomb,' said Mrs Mudge. 'Yoo-hoo, Mary! You will never guess what has just happened.'

Cash. Money. Jack had purchased the company. Harrison and Lowe was not her dowry. All the things she had said, all her accusations. All false. A thousand questions sprang to her mind. Jack's broad back was towards her and he appeared in deep conversation with some of the men. She would not give in to impulse and demand an answer. She would have to wait. Patience.

Later she would find out the truth. She'd use the time it took to get the Old Christmas green robes and crown to regain control of her emotions.

All the way to the small room her heart pounded. She had been wrong, but she could do something about it. She could apologise, work to put things right. Ask to begin again.

The corridor was empty, and Emma's shoes sounded loudly against the tiled floor. She opened the door to the small room and her heart sank. The robes and the holly crown had obviously been moved from the wardrobe. A single holly leaf remained in he bottom. Her journey had been in vain. She needed to get back o the others. It was too quiet here, too remote. She wanted to ind Jack and apologise. She had to do that.

'Well, well, well, who do I find here? Mrs Stanton, you should ot be on your own. You never know what sort of folk might be bout, particularly on Christmas Eve.'

Dr Milburn's cold voice made shivers run down her spine.

'I was looking for the Old Christmas robes for my father.' Emma esisted the urge to barge past the doctor and run. She was safe ow. She had married Jack. She forced herself to gaze at the pale yes and smile brightly. 'Do you know where they have gone?'

'Me? Why should I know where such things are?' The doctor gave an elaborate shrug.

'Well, then, I had best be going. I dare say someone has noved them.' Her laugh sounded brittle to her ears, and she tried o ignore the growing pit of nerves in her stomach. She willed he doctor to move.

'I dare say.' Dr Milburn remained where he stood, blocking er path.

Emma clung onto her temper. She had no desire to fight with Dr Milburn, no desire for a scene. 'Please let me pass. I am xpected.'

'I am sorry, I can't let you do that.' Dr Milburn advanced owards her and put a cloth over her face. 'One way and another, Miss Harrison, you have been a terrible burden to me.'

Emma struggled against the sickly sweet smell that invaded er senses, but the doctor's grip was too strong and she found he world going black. She tore at his jacket and her fingers closed around a button, ripping it off. She dropped it and her eticule, sent them flying under the wardrobe.

The last sound she heard was a great cheer as Old Christmas appeared.

Chapter Eighteen

꧁꧂

'Where is Emma?' Jack asked Edward Harrison.

Harrison took another sip of punch. 'She was around here a few moments ago. I saw her before I started to give out the gifts. She was supposed to find my robes, but in the end, Mrs Newcomb found them for me. I have no idea what she is up to. Emma used to be so reliable.'

A cold fist closed around Jack's insides. Something had happened to her, despite all his precautions. He turned to his young employee. 'Davy, have you seen Mrs Stanton lately? Have you noticed anything amiss?'

'Not since before you sent me to check the experiments, sir,' came the answer. Davy fingered his pile of books. 'The thaw's progressing right fine. There was a light bobbing about in the keep, but that was all.'

'Did you investigate?'

'No, I was too busy thinking about the monster German Christmas tree.' Davy hung his head.

'But that was earlier,' Harrison said. 'The light will have nothing to do with Emma.'

'I am sure you are right.' Jack felt the small box in his breast pocket. He had wanted to give it to Emma when the others were around, so there could be no refusal. And now Emma had disappeared.

The crowd merged and parted, laughing and happy, showing off the various geese, twelfth cakes and presents they had received. A merry, pleasant scene—but something was wrong. His instinct told him just as surely as he had known the design for the bridge was off. Emma would never have left on her own.

'Where is Milburn?' Jack asked, looking around at the thinning crowd. 'I saw his oily face before.'

'Dr Milburn was called out on an urgent call ages ago. He gave his regrets to me,' Harrison said. 'He always enjoys the Goose Feast, you know.'

'Before or after Emma went for the robes?'

'Before, I think. That's right. He left just before, because Emma remarked on how strange it was for him to be here. Is it important?'

'It might be.'

'I trust Dr Milburn implicitly.' Harrison rose up on the balls of his feet. 'He has never done anything to harm me.'

Jack pressed his lips together. He should have denounced Milburn when he'd had the chance, but he had wanted to give the doctor an opportunity to reveal himself. He had wanted the doctor to explain why.

'Where were those robes kept?' he asked, focusing on the details. If he got the details right, where Emma was would become clear. He should have done things differently. He should never have let this quarrel go on.

'Mrs Newcomb can show you,' Harrison said, gesturing to the overly plump woman. 'She was the one who found them for me. She knows where they were stored.'

'Take me there now.'

Emma's eyelids were like lead. She forced them open. The ground against her cheek was hard, cold stone. Her mouth tasted as if it had been stuffed with cotton rags. She moaned slightly and moved her head, trying to get a better idea of where she was.

'Ah, good, you are awake,' Dr Milburn said, holding up a single lantern. 'I had worried that I might have given you too much.'

'Too much?' Emma struggled to sit up. Her hands were securely fastened behind her back.

'Too much chloroform. I doubted if you would come with me willingly. But sometimes, if the patient has had too much, the patient does not recover, and I rather thought that would be regrettable with you.'

Emma squinted in the light. Dr Milburn's features swam in front of her, barely discernible in the faint light. She wondered that she had ever thought him a kindly man. He looked pinched, and his face bore the certain sign of madness.

'Where am I?' she asked.

'That would be telling. But you are in no danger, Miss Emma.' The doctor rocked back and forth.

'Are you planning on killing me?' She forced the words from her mouth.

'Killing you? You mistake me, my dear.' The doctor leant in, so close that she could see the beads of sweat forming on his brow. 'You are still useful to my plans. You have a while to live yet.'

Emma turned her face away, unable to suppress a shudder. A while longer to live. There were so many things she needed to do, things she needed to explain.

'Where am I?'

'That is for me to know and for those searching for you to discover.' Dr Milburn put his fingertips together. 'And there is no use struggling, my dear. I made sure the knots were good and tight. You'd need a knife to cut them. And, alas for you, this room is bare.'

'You are insane!' Emma stared at him in astonishment. His lips were drawn back, baring his teeth.

'No. Determined. I am going to get what is rightfully mine.'

The distant pealing of bells sounded. St Nicholas's. It was at least eleven o'clock at night. She cocked her head. If she concentrated, she could hear the river. The walls of her prison were grey stone. She had to be in the keep, near the building site, but she doubted anyone would look for her here.

'There's no sign of her,' Mudge reported back, shaking his head. 'We have searched and searched, but Miss Harrison...Mrs Stanton...has vanished completely.'

Jack paced the small room. She had to be somewhere. People did not just go. And Emma would not have left without a word. She was far too responsible.

'Search again.'

'Begging your pardon, but where? It is getting late, like.'

'I've found something.' Mrs Mudge knelt down and pulled out a beaded reticule and a brass button. 'The button looks like one from the doctor's jacket. I remarked on them brass buttons to Mudge, I did.'

'Emma was definitely here, in this room. That's my daughter's reticule.' Harrison put his face in his hands and wept. 'She would never voluntarily leave it anywhere.'

Jack opened the clasp with a click. Several sheets of yellowed letter paper greeted him. He instantly recognised his own youthful writing. When had these come into her possession? He took them out and put them into his breast pocket. She always seemed to want to preserve the past—first the castle, and now these letters. His hand stilled. He picked up the brass button, sent it spinning into the air. Dr Milburn had to have seen her drop these. He wanted to be found. Why? If he had harmed one hair on her head, Jack would not be held responsible.

'Where can Mrs Stanton be?' Mrs Newcomb's face creased. 'It is so unlike her.'

'Your Davy said he saw a light earlier in the keep,' Mrs Mudge said.

A surge of excitement went through Jack. He had him. 'Has anyone checked there?'

'No, it's haunted, like,' Mudge answered. 'No one goes there. Unsafe, like.'

'That's where he will have taken her. He wants us to find her.'

'Who?'

'Milburn. Milburn has kidnapped Emma for some reason,' Jack said through clenched teeth. 'She will be alive.'

'I am confused,' Harrison said. 'Dr Milburn is a trusted member of this community. He has been my doctor for years.'

'There is no time to explain.' Jack ran his hand through his hair. Everything could wait until he had found Emma. Without her, life was meaningless. 'You need to go and rouse the authorities. Milburn must be brought to justice.'

'What are you going to do?'

'Save my wife.'

'What exactly do you intend doing with me?' Emma brought her knees up to her chest as she tried to ease the pain in her wrists. 'Exactly how long do I have left to live?'

'My dear Emma, you do like a touch of the melodrama, don't

you?' Dr Milburn's smile did not reassure her. He reached out a hand and lifted her hair away from her shoulder. 'I have no intention of harming you. I have every intention of marrying you. I told you that several days ago. Unfortunately you chose to ignore me.'

'I am already married,' Emma said carefully. She eyed the distance between where she was and the door. There was an outside possibility that she could run. The rose silk with its many petticoats would hamper her, but she might make it. Anything was better than being here, locked away with a madman. 'Married in a church before witnesses. There is no possibility of the marriage being set aside.'

'You were.' He reached over and lit his pipe from the lantern, pausing to take a long draw. 'It is such a shame that your first marriage was short and you will now have to wear widow's weeds.'

Short? Widow's weeds? Emma's mouth went dry. She fought against the ropes binding her wrists, twisting first one way and then the other. 'What have you done to Jack?'

'Such devotion is touching.' Dr Milburn's face became stern. 'I thought your marriage would be the end to my plans, but now I see it was divinely inspired. I am meant to have more—more of everything.'

Emma swallowed hard. She had to keep him talking. She had to find out.

'What plans?'

'It came to me after your dear mother died. I needed finance for my projects. Henry Charlton had refused me more money and threatened to pull out. Your father was ill and not getting any better. I heard about the plans for the bridge and purchased the land near the castle. Once the bridge's line was chosen it would become valuable, as they would need the station there.

No one thought that they would tear down the keep, but I made sure your father saw otherwise.'

'How?' The cold seemed to creep into the very fibre of Emma's being. Dr Milburn had planned this. He had somehow changed the calculations.

'You father is very suggestible after he has had a fit. It was a simple matter. I knew no one would ever discover the errors. But the money from the sale of the land was not enough. Costs had gone up. The tonic was not selling as well as I had anticipated. I needed more money.'

'And…?' Emma breathed the word. The full horror was starting to creep over her.

'I came upon a way to truly finance my needs. You. You would marry me after your father met his end. I explained the delicate situation to Henry, and he was content to wait and see if I managed to find someone wealthier. He knew there was no other suitor for your hand.'

'I had no plans to marry you.'

'You would have done. That or faced imprisonment for your father's murder.' Dr Milburn shook his head in mock sorrow. 'Nasty, nasty business when one finds poison in medicine. Particularly when it is more than in the other bottles.'

Emma gasped for air. She could see the future Milburn had mapped out

'You knew he had arsenic in his tonic. You were deliberately feeding him poison. First to control him and then to finish him off.' Emma bit her lip. 'But his bouts of recovery came when you were chasing that wealthy widow from Harrogate. Then she married a peer, and your attention once again fell on me.'

'Very clever of you to guess.' The light in Milburn's eyes burnt. He wiped his hand across his mouth. 'Who told you it was arsenic?'

'Jack had the bottle checked after my father's last fit.' Emma raised her chin and stared defiantly at Milburn. 'It had too much arsenic in it. He will ensure the truth comes out.'

'Stanton pays attention to too many details. It will be the death of him.'

'My father is going to get well again. His mind will be as clear as ever.'

'Your father is going to have an unfortunate relapse.' Dr Milburn's face became solemn. 'I shall weep.'

Emma stilled. Her ears strained. She was certain she had heard a noise. Whatever happened she had to keep Milburn talking, distracted. There was a slight chance that he hadn't heard.

'You are insane.'

'I assure you that I am quite sane, my dear.' He smiled. 'Once Stanton reappeared, I had to make sure my investment was safe. Otherwise Henry Charlton would have called in his loan. As it is, I don't have much time. I have thought through my plan long and hard. It suits my needs.'

'But it doesn't suit mine.'

'Your needs are of no concern to me.' He put his hand under her chin. 'Yes, you will serve me well, until I don't need you or your money any longer. Just think—the very wealthy young widow, grief stricken at the loss of her husband and father, consoled by her doctor.'

She wrenched her face away. 'That is something I would never do.'

'But you will.' His leer increased. 'My knowledge of drugs is extensive—a pastime, you might say. That is how I was able to spirit you away from the party. There is a lovely new compound called chloroform, and what people will do after they have tried opium—well, you really don't want to know.'

Emma heard the thump of something falling. She swallowed

and tried not to let her emotions run away with her. Was it someone trying to rescue her? How would they know she was here unless…unless Milburn meant her to be found. At a time of his choosing, with the way prepared for Jack. She closed her eyes and prayed it was not the case.

'How…how are you going to get rid of my husband?'

'You insisted on marrying him. If anything, his demise will be at your hands, not mine.' He gave a laugh that echoed eerily off the stone walls. 'He is just a jumped-up charity boy. A person of no importance.'

'You are wrong. Wrong, I tell you. He has done more for this country than anyone. And I for one am proud of him.'

'Such devotion is touching, but misguided. He cares for no one but his business.'

Emma closed her eyes and acknowledged the truth.

'You are wasting your time,' she said at last, watching Milburn move about the room. 'He won't come after me. Jack Stanton only married me for Harrison and Lowe. He is sure to stay away from here!'

'You underestimate the man's attraction to your charms,' the doctor said with a sneer. 'Such as they are.'

The door crashed inward with a splintering sound. Milburn was up, pulling her away from the door. His arm encircled her neck, squeezed, and then released her. She gasped for breath.

'That is one of her worst faults.' Jack's voice resounded in the room. 'Believe you me, Milburn, you would not enjoy being married to Emma. She is far too independent. Never stays where you think she will. Always follows her own path.'

Emma's heart gave a leap. Jack was here! He had come after her. But he had to realise that it was he who was in danger.

'Ah, Stanton.' Milburn lit a cigar from the lantern. 'You are a bit early. I was not expecting you until tomorrow.'

'Sorry to disappoint, but I happen to want to spend time with my wife at Christmas.' Jack shrugged. 'A little quirk of mine, shall we say? Paying attention to little details, particularly where my *wife* is concerned.'

'Jack, be careful. He's dangerous,' Emma called. She felt her body fly backwards as Milburn shoved her against the wall.

'You are right,' he sneered. 'The witch does speak too much.'

'You ought not to have done that, Milburn.' Jack's eyes were cold black lumps of stone. 'Nobody touches my wife like that and lives.'

'Jack, this is no joking matter.' Emma tasted the trickle of blood that was running down her mouth.

'Did I give the impression that it was?' Jack lifted an eyebrow. 'How very remiss of me.'

'Jack, he means to kill you,' Emma said urgently as she watched Milburn move about the room.

'I am certain that he means to try,' Jack remarked in a calm voice. 'Whether he succeeds or not is a moot point. Don't you agree, Milburn?'

'Exactly what do you intend, Stanton?'

'I intend to take my wife away from here unharmed, and to celebrate Christmas with her properly.' Jack permitted a smile to cross his face. Later he would think about punishing Milburn, but right now Emma had to be rescued. Milburn would not escape this time. Jack struggled to hang onto his temper. This was not like the time before, when they'd fought. Milburn then had held the advantage. This time, *he* did. He was certain of it.

'I am afraid I can't allow that.' Milburn tossed the cigar onto the floor and ground it in with his foot.

'Then I shall have to fight for her. It will give me great pleasure to tear you limb from limb.'

'I had rather thought you would say that.' Milburn gave a

yawn. 'In many ways, Stanton, you are predictable. Breeding will out. You will lose, as you have always done. Who was i that won the house cup? And the school prize? Not you, but me There is a certain order to this country. Tradition. It will give me great pleasure to re-administer the lesson.'

Jack crouched, tensed his muscles and charged. His shoulde: connected with Milburn's stomach. 'Fighting is what charity boys do well.'

Milburn reacted, landed a punch to Jack's jaw and sent hin flying backwards.

'I forgot to warn you, Milburn,' Jack said, fingering his jaw 'I don't intend to fight like a gentleman.'

He threw a knife over to Emma. The knife landed inche: from her feet. Emma scooped it up, understanding what Jack meant. She was to cut herself loose and leave.

She worked feverishly and felt the rope begin to give, but he feet were rooted to the ground as the men sparred with each other, neither one gaining the advantage. How could she leave when Jack was in trouble? She had to stay. She rubbed he wrists, and tried to look for an opening.

'Emma! Be sensible!' he cried as she hesitated. 'Go now. Ge help. Get to safety.'

She shook her head. 'Not without you. We go together.'

'How touching.' Milburn drew out a handkerchief and a tin: glass vial from his pocket. 'But you need to be ruthless to survive, Stanton, and you have gone soft.'

'Jack, be careful. He has chloroform.'

'Chloro—what?' Jack yelled over his shoulder as he side stepped Milburn's charge.

'It made me go to sleep.' Emma watched as Jack and Milbur lined up again. Each circling the other. The sickly sweet sme filled the room. 'Be on your guard.'

Jack beckoned Milburn closer. Milburn advanced with the handkerchief, a broad grin on his face. Jack reached out and put Milburn's head into a lock.

'Get the handkerchief,' he said as Milburn tried unsuccessfully to put it in front of Jack's face.

Emma darted forward, snatched the handkerchief, and held it firmly in front of Milburn's face. He tried to move his head, but Jack increased the pressure. Emma watched as Milburn's eyes rolled back and he ceased to struggle.

'You can drop him now,' she said. 'He has gone to sleep.'

'Powerful stuff that,' Jack remarked.

'Aren't you going to tie him up? I have no idea how long it lasts.'

'It will last a while yet, but what you say makes sense.' Jack used the remains of the rope that had bound Emma to tie Milburn up. 'He won't be bothering anyone for a very long time.'

'I only wish I had seen through him earlier. Did you know that he convinced my father to change his calculations? He had bought the land around the keep and thought to sell it at a high price. Later he hit on the idea of marrying me.'

'It explains much.'

Jack reached and held up the lantern, signalling out of the arrow window.

'Why are you doing that?'

'Mudge had instructions to storm the keep if I hadn't emerged by midnight. I'm telling him to come up now.'

'How did you guess where I was?'

'Davy saw a light earlier. I decided that it was worth a shot.' Jack's face became grim. 'Luckily I was in time.'

'It was you he wanted to destroy.' Emma started to shake.

Jack reached out and gathered her into his arms. 'You are safe now, my love. Your poor wrists. I can never forgive myself.'

His love? Emma wanted to sigh and rest her head against his

shoulder, but there was still too much between them. Did he
want her, or the girl she had been? How could she ask? The room
was suddenly full of men, shouting. Mudge arrived with a rope
and took charge.

'We are not wanted here, Emma,' Jack said. 'Mudge is highly
capable once he is given the right sort of direction. I want to get
you away from here.'

They left the keep. The cloud had lifted and the starlight cast
a soft glow over the snow-clad world. The bells of St Nicholas's
Church began to toll, and a quiet hush filled the air.

'It's Christmas,' Emma whispered as Jack drew her into his
arms again.

'So it is,' Jack said, against her hair. 'If you reach into my
pocket, I have a gift for you.'

'Why can't you?'

'Because I am holding you, and I never intend letting you go
again.'

Emma reached in and fished out a small box. She squinted.
The box was emblazoned with the name of one of the best jew-
ellers in London. With trembling fingers, she opened it. Inside
was a diamond surrounded by two pearls. On the gold band two
hands were clasped.

'Let me put it on.' Jack slipped the ring onto her third finger
over her wedding band. 'I bought it in London.'

'But…but…' Emma looked down at the ring.

'I intended asking you to marry me at the Goose Feast, but
events overtook me.'

'You let me think that you had married me for the company.'
Emma looked up into his face.

'I never mix business with pleasure. How many times do I
have to tell you that? I wanted my business concluded with
your father before I asked for your hand.'

Emma stared at him in wonderment. He had intended asking er to marry him. The proof was on her finger. It had nothing to o with Harrison and Lowe and everything to do with her. She aused. What if he expected her to be the same as she had been even years ago? She took the ring off her finger and held it in her alm.

'My mother hid the letter you sent seven years ago,' Emma aid. 'My father gave it to me today. It speaks of you holding ny image in your heart, a bright flame lighting the darkness of our life, an angel come down to earth.'

'A young man's nonsense. Easily forgotten,' he said lightly.

Emma leant back against his arms and he let her go. She moothed her skirt and stared out at the silent building site. She ad to say everything. She had to make sure there were no hadows between them. Tonight had taught her that, if no other esson.

'I am about as far from a bright flame as I could be. We did ot know each other very well then. Had I received that letter I vould have refused you. My first duty was to my mother, and could not have asked you to wait.'

'I understand.' His voice was tight and stiff.

Emma knew she was in danger of losing him, but she plunged on. 'Are you in love with the girl you thought I was even years ago?'

His fingers closed around the ring. 'Does it matter?'

'Yes, it does.' She raised her chin and stared at his deep black eyes. 'It matters very much. I grew up. I changed. I found things out about myself that I never dreamt possible. I do not want to be a social butterfly. I want to be me, with all my faults, including taking an interest in building bridges and the like.'

'I don't consider that a fault.' Jack reached out and pulled her into his arms again, held her tightly. 'Emma Stanton, the boy that I was will always admire the girl Emma Harrison. When you refused me and did not answer my letter, I used it as a spur to make my fortune. No one would ever again have the opportunity to dismiss me.'

Emma gulped, but said nothing.

'When I came back here and found you unmarried, my first thought was of revenge. But you piqued my interest. You would not stay in the box I had made for you. I tried to tell myself that I was only doing it to teach you a lesson in humility.'

'But you didn't.'

'It is you who have taught me. I knew at the ball that I did not want to administer a lesson. I wanted to protect you.'

'That night in the drawing room?'

'I took unfair advantage. I kissed you because I wanted to. I wanted to kiss the woman who was before me—who stands before me now.' His hand lifted her chin. 'It is you I want. It is you I made love to last night. I married you because I want you in my life.'

'But you are going away.'

'*We* are going away. We are taking my private railway car down to London, and then going on our wedding trip. Your father has agreed to look after the bridge with Mudge's help, to build it so the keep is saved. Stephenson will come up and help if needed. The bridge will be built to our design—yours and mine. And it will last. Mrs Newcomb will act as housekeeper and it will give your father a chance to tutor young Davy.'

'You have thought of everything.'

'I told you, I like to get the details correct.' He dropped a kiss on her nose. 'It is part of my charm.'

'I have no gift for you except my love,' she said in a small voice. He loved her—her, and not some idealised dream. He had married her because he wanted to spend the rest of his life with er. 'I had no idea you felt this way. I wanted to hate you, to espise you. You threatened my whole world. But the more I ried, the more I grew to love you. I want to go with you, to be vith you wherever you are.'

'Then accept the ring.' He slipped it on her finger. 'With this ing, I thee wed, Emma Stanton.'

'And with all my heart, I thee wed.' Somehow the vows they xchanged felt far more real and permanent than the ones they ad uttered in front of the vicar.

'Happy Christmas, Mrs Stanton,' he murmured against her ips as the bells of St Nicholas finished tolling the start of Christmas Day. 'You have shown me what Christmas is truly bout.'

'No, it is you who have shown me, Jack Stanton.'

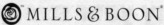

LOOK OUT...

...for this month's special product offer.
It can be found in the envelope containing
your invoice.

**Special offers are exclusively for
Reader Service™ members.**

You will benefit from:

- Free books & discounts
- Free gifts
- Free delivery to your door
- No purchase obligation – 14 day trial
- Free prize draws

THE LIST IS ENDLESS!!

*So what are you waiting for —
take a look* **NOW!**

DM/OFFER